DOING TIME

JODI TAYLOR

DOING TIME

HEADLINE

First published in Great Britain in 2019 by
HEADLINE PUBLISHING GROUP

1

Cataloguing in Publication Data is available from the British Library

Hardback ISBN 978 1 4722 6747 4
Trade paperback ISBN 978 1 4722 6748 1

Typeset in Times New Roman by CC Book Production

Printed and bound in Great Britain by Clays Ltd, Elcograf S.p.A.

Headline's policy is to use papers that are natural, renewable and recyclable
products and made from wood grown in well-managed forests and other
controlled sources. The logging and manufacturing processes are expected
to conform to the environmental regulations of the country of origin.

HEADLINE PUBLISHING GROUP
An Hachette UK Company
Carmelite House
50 Victoria Embankment
London EC4Y 0DZ

www.headline.co.uk
www.hachette.co.uk

For my Dad

Ut aliquando futurum praesidio.

Roll Call

TIME POLICE PERSONNEL

Commander Marietta Hay	Commander of the Time Police. Attempting to modernise. A bit of an uphill struggle.
Captain Charlie Farenden	Her adjutant. An astute young man.
Major Callen	Head of Recruitment and Training. A bit of an enigma.
Major Matthew Ellis	Recently promoted. Tipped for the top. If he lives long enough.
Lt Gordon Grint	Recently promoted. Leading his first team. A very conventional Time Police officer.
Officer Celia North	Formerly from St Mary's. Fancied a change of career.
Officer Sarah Smith	A bit of a bitch. Actually, quite a lot of a bitch.

TEAM 236 – TEAM WEIRD

Trainee Matthew Farrell	Life's a little more complicated these days. Still reluctant to have his hair cut.
Trainee Jane Lockland	Brighter than everyone thinks. Definitely brighter than she herself thinks.
Trainee Luke Parrish	Unwillingly trafficked into the Time Police. Not giving it his best shot.

TEAM 235 – ALL SHAPING UP TO BE NICE, CONVENTIONAL TIME POLICE OFFICERS

Trainee Alek Anders
Trainee Alan Hansen
Trainee Stefan Kohl
Trainee Marco Rossi

SECURITY

Officer Songül Varma	Prisoner's Friend, but not really.

ST MARY'S PERSONNEL – GRAINS OF SAND IN THE TIME POLICE SANDWICHES OF LIFE

Deputy Director Tim Peterson	Reprising his Roman patriarch role. Even less successfully this time around.

Dr Lucy Maxwell	Historian. Enough said.
Miss Greta Van Owen	Historian. As above.
Mr Markham	Security. Got his hands full. Again.
Chief Technical Officer Leon Farrell	Very pleased to see his son.
Professor Andrew Rapson	Unchanged over the years.
Dr Octavius Dowson	As above.
Mr Tom Bashford	Drowning – but only very slowly.
Miss Felix Lingoss	Hair expert.

A Brief History
of the Time Wars

A long time ago in the future, the secret of time travel became available to all. Naturally, everyone wanted it and because the implications were imperfectly understood, the world nearly ended.

Old wars were fought and refought as world leaders continually pressed 'Reset' hoping for a more favourable outcome this time around.

New nations emerged, flickered briefly and then disappeared. The Confederate States of America, for example, arose from the wreckage of North America, was defeated, emerged again and refused all attempts to dismantle it. The subsequent long, bitter and bloody struggle so distorted the timeline that, for a dangerously long time, the Confederacy and the Union existed side by side, playing out their own histories simultaneously.

All over the world, people lived, died, then lived again.

Events happened. Then didn't happen. Had never happened. Then happened again but differently. Some moments vital to the development of the human race never happened at all. Some happened more than once.

Everyone wanted to change the past for the better, but what

was better for A was not necessarily better for B. Not surprisingly, whole new wars broke out.

Many, whose minds could not encompass the many versions of the same events, went mad. History was written and rewritten so many times that the fabric of reality began to wear thin. The world began to spiral downwards to destruction.

At the last moment, when it was almost too late, the Time Police were formed. It was an international effort. Personnel were drawn from the military, from the police, and even a few from a tiny organisation known as the Institute of Historical Research at St Mary's Priory, situated outside Rushford in England, where they would explain, at enormous length, that they definitely didn't do time travel – they investigated major historical events in contemporary time, and they'd been doing this for some time without anyone being any the wiser and that all of this was nothing to do with them.

A series of international laws were passed to deal with the situation. The punishment for time travel was death. Anyone caught indulging in time travel faced summary execution – together with everyone else involved. Or even those unfortunate enough to be standing nearby. No one ever bothered with a trial.

Every citizen was required to cooperate fully and completely with the Time Police. Failure to do so was death.

Armed with these powers, the Time Police set about their task of saving the world from its own stupidity.

Thus began what were known as the Time Wars. The Time Police's remit was simple: to shut down time travel everywhere. No matter what it took – shut it down. With extreme prejudice if necessary. Just shut it down and get the situation back under control. They answered to no one. No one nation had overall control. Their reputation was fearful. Word soon got around. If the Time Police turned up, then things were not going to end well. Not for anyone within a five-mile radius, anyway.

It was bloody and brutal for a long time. A lot of people died. And not just the illegals, as they were known. The Time Police themselves paid an astronomically high price. After the first year, nearly all the original members were dead. Casualties were massive. It is doubtful whether they could have sustained these losses for very much longer but they never faltered, relentlessly pursuing their targets up and down the timeline. At one point they numbered less than thirteen officers in the whole world. No one ever knew how close the Time Police came to extinction.

Fortunately, by then, people were beginning to realise that possessing time travel is like holding a snake in your hand. If you don't know what you're doing, sooner or later, it will twist in your hand and bite you.

One by one, nations were induced to give it up. Many were secretly glad to see it go. They simply hadn't wanted to be the first to surrender it. And by then, big business had discovered the past was not theirs to plunder. Their massive investment had led to no returns at all. They too lost interest.

In the shell-shocked aftermath, it was the Time Police, politically neutral, who brokered agreements, treaties and accords or, if that failed, knocked a few heads together. When done at street level, that sort of thing is known as a brawl. Do it at international level and it's called diplomacy.

After a long while, things settled back down again but, as is always the way, those who had been the first to extol the virtues of the Time Police now began to perceive that the existence of an organisation with such wide-ranging powers might not be such a good thing after all.

Time travel, however, was not completely eradicated. There was Temporal Tourism – illegal but lucrative. Attempting to hide in another time to escape the consequences of an illegal act in this one was always popular. And every now and then, someone would put something up on the Dark Web, and armed with not even moderately accurate information, a hundred enthusiastic amateurs – for whom death by radiation was something that happened to other people – would beaver away in lock-ups, garages, spare bedrooms and science classes, apparently oblivious to the Time Police heading their way, determined to resolve the situation – whatever it took.

Whatever it took.

Jane

I'm where I am today because of a stuffed seagull. It stood in a glass case under a skylight at the top of the stairs in my grandmother's house and it frightened me nearly as much as she did. Which is to say – a lot.

My grandmother was thin and brown-leathery and for years I thought she was a witch. Her room was right at the top of her tall, narrow house and she rarely left it, but somehow, she always knew when I'd dropped a cup or if I'd dawdled on the way back from the shops or stopped to buy myself a rare bar of chocolate.

Her voice, with that imperious rasp, would drift down the stairs.

'Jane, come here at once,' followed by the tinkle of her bell, demanding my instant presence.

I hated that bell. Nearly as much as I hated the seagull. But not as much as I hated her.

She was only one woman but I might as well have been toiling away in a large hotel, the amount of work she caused. Clean sheets every day. Whole herds of ghastly china animals to wash several times a month. Furniture to be polished – and with the old-style wax polish too, not the permanent spray-shine you can get these days. The windows were to be done every month – because she wouldn't have stay-clean SmartGlass – and despite most of the rooms being shut up and never used, they still needed cleaning from top to bottom every month. Every now and then I would try missing one but she always knew. I never found out how.

I thought things would be easier after I left school because there would be more time for her insatiable demands, but that turned out not to be the case. There were just more of them. Her insatiable demands expanded to fit the time allocated. She could have had an army of servants and every single one of them would be as overworked and tired as I was.

My grandmother still left the house occasionally. She went to church on Sundays where, presumably, she harangued the Almighty for failing to wipe everyone not white, middle-class or English from the planet. With extreme prejudice. You always felt she was disappointed that God had confined himself to smiting only the firstborn of Egypt when he could, with just a little more effort, have wiped out the entire country. That would have taught them a lesson, wouldn't it?

On the third Tuesday of every month, she was collected by someone who almost certainly was unable to get out of it and taken to the Social Centre a couple of miles away, where she found fault with everyone and everything, consumed every mouthful of a lunch that was hardly worth eating and was returned home, refreshed, invigorated and complaining every inch of the way.

And then there was the shopping. I visited the shops every day because everything had to be fresh. In vain did I murmur of refrigeration and its benefits. Every day at ten o'clock in the morning I left the house, squeezed tomatoes, inspected fish, sniffed at melons and then lugged the whole lot back home again. Every single day. I actually expected to be doing this for the rest of my life.

Which brings me back to the seagull. Almost every moment of every day was overlooked by that awful bird with its predatory beak and evil eyes. One of them wasn't set quite right, giving it an evil leer which followed me wherever I went. Apparently, her husband, my grandad, had stuffed it for her as a personal gift – I'm not sure what that says about either of them – and then died shortly afterwards. The two events were probably unconnected, but it was enough for her to enshrine the thing in pride of place at the top of the stairs, where it was an eternal reminder of her dead husband.

And then I dropped the stupid thing.

I don't know how it happened. Probably I was away with the fairies, which was how my grandmother usually described me. According to her I was a feckless daydreamer – a useless wimp – who would have starved to death on the streets if she hadn't taken me in. Or perhaps I was more tired than I thought. I only know that as I picked up the glass case to dust underneath – because she'd know if I hadn't – it was heavier than I remembered and the whole thing slipped out of my hands and crashed on to the floor.

The glass case shattered and the long-time inhabitant just fell apart. Heaven knows how old it was or how long it had been there, but it didn't take kindly to being bounced off the gleaming parquet (forty-five minutes hard polish every other Thursday). The body hit the floor with a soft explosion of what looked like sawdust and the head skidded off underneath the

7

highly polished walnut chest of drawers (fifteen minutes hard polish every other Thursday – before doing the floor but after cleaning the windows) and out of sight.

I stared, appalled. I had no idea what to do. When I thought of the way she carried on if I so much as dropped a cup, I could hardly begin to imagine what this disaster would earn me. My agitation even caused me to run in small circles as I tried to work out whether I should try to reassemble things – no chance. Or try to hide the evidence – no chance. Or even try to deny there had ever been anything there in the first place. 'What seagull, Granny?'

Or – and I don't know where this thought came from – I could simply . . . go. It wasn't as if I'd never thought about it. I'd done it a thousand times in my dreams. I could grab a few things and leave. And never come back. I remember standing stock-still, suffering all the paralysis of someone whose dream could suddenly come true.

It was Tuesday. She would be gone for hours. I could be miles away before she got back. And then what would she do? What *could* she do? And she was perfectly capable of looking after herself if I wasn't there to do it for her.

'Don't be so silly,' said the voice within. 'Where would you go?'

A good point, I had to concede – Gran always said I was about as much use as boil-in-the-bag ice cream – the venom in her voice robbing the comment of any humour – but compared with staying here with a shattered seagull, starving to death seemed a very viable option. If I remained, my life would hardly be worth living. And besides, I was old enough to go. In fact, I was too old to stay. Whoever heard of anyone my age living with their granny? And she could manage on her own. It wasn't as if she needed me. She didn't even like me. Thoughts I never knew were inside me came suddenly bubbling to the surface.

Wimpy Jane was horrified. 'But I have no money.'

'There's the housekeeping. She keeps it tucked in her pillowcase.'

Wimpy Jane nearly fainted. 'You mean . . . steal it? She'll go ballistic.'

'More or less ballistic than when she sees what you've done to her seagull?'

Wimpy Jane folded without a fight. 'Good point. I should go. Now.'

'What?'

Wimpy Jane cast aside the shackles of years. 'I'm going.'

There's nothing like suddenly giving yourself permission to do something you haven't dared to do nearly all your life to catapult you into a vortex of panic and indecision.

I ran to my room. Halfway there I thought I'd better clear up the mess and veered off towards the stairs for a dustpan and brush. Halfway there I suddenly thought, what are you doing? Leave it. She'll see what's happened and at least then you won't have to bother with an explanatory note along the lines of:

Dear Granny,
I broke your bird and by the way I've hated every moment here, and you claiming my carer allowance for yourself for my board and lodging was a really mean trick so I'm running away. I've taken the housekeeping in lieu of

9

*non-existent wages and I can promise you'll never see
me again.*

Jane.

*PS The seagull head is under the chest of drawers. Don't
think you'll be able to reach it. Hope it doesn't start to
smell. Goodbye.*

On second thoughts . . . why not? Why not leave a note just
like that?

I left it lying on her pillow. Right next to where the housekeeping used to be.

My heart was thudding fit to burst. I think I was terrified
she'd come home early and catch me. She never had – she
paid what she always classed as 'an enormous sum' of money
to the Centre to take her and feed her and entertain her and
she'd never leave until she felt she'd had her money's worth.
I had plenty of time.

I made myself slow down, select stout shoes, something
waterproof, warm clothes and some underwear. I stuffed the
money – I hadn't had time to stop and count it – into my toilet
bag and shoved the whole lot into a carrier bag, because I never
went anywhere, so why would I have a suitcase?

I threw on my coat, flung open the front door and ran down
the path. I heard the door slam behind me and realised I'd left
my key behind.

Now I couldn't go back even if I wanted to.

I see I've begun in the middle but the seagull thing was a truly
major event for me. It changed everything. Fear, coupled with

shame and anger at being so afraid, propelled me from the house and out into the street and then deserted me completely. I found my way to the High Street and stood on the pavement watching the world go past. Where to go?

I couldn't stay here. Everyone knew my grandmother, therefore, everyone knew me. I turned left for the airbus station. I would buy a ticket to . . . somewhere. In the meantime, I needed to survey my resources.

Actually, I was astonished at the really rather large sum of money I'd grabbed. Given the way she doled it out in pitifully small amounts whenever I went shopping and snarled at me if she thought there was insufficient change, there was a lot of money here. I could go almost anywhere.

I stuffed it all back into my bag before anyone saw it, bought myself a coffee and sat down on a bench to think. There was one of those holographic news and advertising boards on the wall. I sipped my coffee and watched the adverts slide by. Cheap airship travel, the latest blockbuster holos, Parrish Industries, cheap loans, national news, international news – image after image flickered by while the words slid past at the bottom of the screen. It was all on a continuous loop and I think I watched it twice before it registered.

The Time Police were recruiting. And they especially wanted women.

I don't know at what point it occurred to me that this could be just what I was looking for – a job with living accommodation provided. I watched it go by a couple more times – I was worried in case they changed their minds suddenly and took it down, but they didn't so I caught the airbus to London and enlisted.

Luke

The bleeping woke me. I had a message coming through. I blinked and tried to focus. Blinked again, tried again, blinked again and gave it up, hoping the whole thing would go away.

It didn't.

When I couldn't stand it any longer, I sat up and waited vainly for the pounding behind my eyes to go away, until I was finally able to focus on the read-out.

Hey, what do you know? A message from dear old Dad. Had he remembered my birthday? A bit of a first for him. And it's not as if he had any excuse – he had armies of people to remind him about things like this. There it was, though. His name flashing on the screen.

I hadn't heard from him for quite some time, and actually I'd rather been expecting to be on the receiving end of massive parental displeasure over the Tannhauser business, but there had been complete silence and since that had been some time ago now, he'd obviously missed it.

Like an idiot, I was pleased to hear from him. I thought he was messaging me because today was my birthday. Celebrations had begun last night – hence the pounding head this morning – and were due to continue for quite some time. And then I read the message and thought – shit.

It was a bit of a bugger getting the girl out of bed and I couldn't remember her name. Dianna? Dinah? Yes, Ruth – that was it. Actually, it turned out her name was Deidre so I wasn't that far out. But calling her Ruth would account for her snippy exit.

Heroically and despite the hangover, I made a real effort to clean up my apartment. Well, technically, I just shoved everything into a black bag and hurled it into the incineration chute. I can't think why people find housework so difficult. It wasn't wonderful, but thirty minutes later things did look considerably tidier. He'd never been here before so I wanted to make a good impression. It would be nice if he liked the place.

I'd just selected Scottish Heather for the air conditioner when the doorbell rang. He was here.

No, he wasn't. He'd sent his PA, Ms Steel, instead.

I don't like Ms Steel. Steel by name and steel by nature. She is extremely good-looking in a severe sort of way. It really gets my goat that it's OK for Dad to surround himself with shit-hot women but not me. Anyway, there I was, staring gormlessly at the severe but sexy Ms Steel. I really wouldn't have minded easing her between my sheets – freshly changed after Ruth, before anyone gets the wrong idea – but so far that opportunity hadn't been granted me.

There was no opening preamble. No 'Hello, Luke, how are you? Do you fancy a spot of afternoon delight?'

'A message from your father,' she announced, laying a whole rainforest of documents on the table.

A bit environmentally irresponsible, as I pointed out and she

13

ignored me. I did try a quick squint at them, but my head was still pounding and quite honestly, my eyes weren't focusing that well, either.

Ms Steel sighed, conveying an entire continent of impatience and judgement. 'Can you even *see* the papers, Mr Parrish?'

'I'm actually having difficulty seeing the table. Can't you just tell me?'

'Very well. These are enlistment papers for the Time Police.'

I was shocked. Seriously shocked. 'What? Why the hell is the old man joining the Time Police?'

She didn't bother to laugh. 'Your father feels that after the Tannhauser incident last year, your life would benefit from more structure. Hence, you will serve two years in the Time Police.'

I had the feeling I was fighting a losing battle but I had a go anyway. 'He can't do that.'

'He has already done it.'

I said with confidence, 'They're not going to take someone like me.'

'With the right inducements, they would take even someone like you.'

I thought the 'even' was a little bit offensive and said so.

She shrugged, giving an excellent impersonation of a woman who really couldn't give a fu . . . give a damn.

Time to turn on the old Parrish charm. Never lets me down.

I inched my chair closer. 'I feel sure there's been a mistake somewhere along the line, Ms Steel. He didn't actually mean me to join. It's just to scare me. And it's worked. Obviously, I'll be a good boy from now on. Please pass on my congratulations regarding his tactics. Is he coming to my birthday party tonight?'

'No. And neither are you. These papers order you to report immediately. Later today, in fact.'

I blinked furiously. As if that would make any difference. He can't do this.'

She didn't bother with a response this time.

I stirred the papers with my finger. They all looked horribly genuine. Not that I'd know any differently but they did all the same. My headache redoubled its thumping. I couldn't join the Time Police. What was the old man thinking?

'I can't join the Time Police,' I said. 'I have . . . responsibilities. Commitments I must honour.' The old man was very big on honouring commitments. Now was obviously a good time to make a start. 'I've got Glastonbury. And Wimbledon. A fortnight at a mate's house in the Caribbean. There's the test match next month. I can't let people down.'

'Mr Parrish has instructed me to say that letting people down is second nature to you. And that you have never shown the slightest inclination to shoulder any of your responsibilities. The Tannhauser affair was the last straw, I'm afraid. Responsibilities are about to be imposed upon you.'

'I know the Time Police,' I lied. 'You can't just waltz in and sign on the dotted line. There are tests and interviews and . . . things.'

'All of which have been completed on your behalf.'

I scoffed. 'They wouldn't take me sight unseen.'

'They know you by reputation. Everyone knows you by reputation.'

Ten minutes ago I might have thought that was a compliment.

'I am sure your vanity will be happy to hear it took a very

15

great deal of persuasion and an extremely large sum of money to induce the Time Police even to contemplate the idea. You are not cheap, Mr Parrish.'

Time to switch on even more Parrish charm and get myself out of this. I pulled my chair closer still, smiled into her flint-hard eyes and said, 'I've never been cheap, Ms Steel, but I can assure you I am extremely good value.'

Not a flicker. Not a bloody flicker. I was obviously a lot more hungover than I thought. Or she was a lesbian. Yes, that was far more likely. Typical Dad to send a lesbian.

'Officially, your father has made a very generous contribution to their Widows and Orphans Fund. They were extraordinarily grateful.'

The net was closing. 'I'll bet they were.'

'To the extent they would take even you.'

I noticed we were back to the 'even' again. Lesbian, for sure.

'So,' she said, indicating the dead trees strewn across the table. 'It's all here. Travel documents. Joining instructions.' She paused for the kicker. 'Contract of employment.'

I leaped at a perceived opportunity. 'I haven't signed a contract.'

'Haven't you?' She pushed a document across the table and I peered at it. The throbbing behind my eyes now quite bad and getting worse by the second, because there was my signature. Quite definitely mine. The clouds of alcohol grudgingly parted to make room for the airbus of memory. I had vague memories of signing an enormous number of bar bills. This must have been among them and I hadn't noticed.

I pushed it back. 'Signed under the influence of alcohol. And a couple of other things as well. Probably not legal.'

16

She pushed it back again. 'Substance abuse these days is punishable by considerably more than a two-year gaol term, and is invariably served in institutions far less benevolent than the Time Police. The end result will be the same, however – you out of harm's way for at least two years. Your father is graciously offering you a choice. I'll tell him you've declined the Time Police and chosen the other option, shall I?'

She began to gather up the papers.

It started to dawn on me with a very nasty thud that there was no way out of this other than to do as my father . . . well, I was going to say 'wished', but 'commanded' would probably be more accurate.

I held out my hand for the documents. Could be worse, I suppose. The uniform was pretty cool and you got to shoot people. And thcy were based in London, so apart from showing up for work occasionally, I could just carry on as before. My dad's not as clever as he thinks he is.

'One other thing,' she said. 'During your period of service, you will receive no money other than that which you earn.'

I must have gaped like an idiot.

'Your allowance is rescinded. Your social engagements are cancelled. All your accounts except one have been closed and that one is now empty. Your property – all your property – is confiscated. You may take with you one small suitcase. I advise you to choose wisely – the contents will have to last you two years. And now I must take my leave, Mr Parrish.'

Honour demanded I have one last try.

'Oh, don't go yet, Ms Steel. I thought we could spend a little time discussing things and . . .'

'I'm a very busy woman,' she said, clicking her case closed.

'You are simply number three on my list of Things To Do Today, Mr Parrish. Good luck with your new career.'

And she was gone. Just like that. I know I was well hungover but surely I hadn't lost that much of my touch.

I made a giant pot of coffee and sat down to read. There were more words there than I'd read in the last five years put together. It made my eyes ache but at the end of it there was no doubt. Like it or not, I was now a member of the Time Police.

Matthew

I always knew I'd join the Time Police. I hadn't said anything because I knew my parents wouldn't like it. They work for the Institute of Historical Research at St Mary's Priory and the two organisations tend to hate each other on sight. St Mary's does work with the Time Police occasionally – although not *for* them, as my mother is always very keen to point out. Sometimes it ends well, although usually it doesn't, so I was expecting all sorts of fuss when I told them.

There was a long silence and then Dad said, 'For how long?'

'Two years,' I said, and they both looked so relieved that I felt compelled to add, 'to begin with.'

'And then?'

'I don't know. Depends how it goes, I suppose.'

'But why?' said Mum.

'The initial contract is always for two years. After that there's a variety of options, ranging from . . .'

'No, I mean why on earth would you want to join the Time Police? They have the combined intelligence of a pencil sharpener.'

I nearly said, 'It's my home,' but although this was true to some extent – the Time Police had once housed and educated

19

me – it wasn't what Mum and Dad wanted to hear at that moment, so I told them the work interested me.

'They shoot people,' said my mother, waving her arms about. 'They race up and down the timeline wearing stupid black cloaks and buggering up everything they touch. They're a bunch of lying toerags with no principles or honour. They don't keep their word. You can't trust them an inch. They . . .'

Dad pulled her back down again and she subsided. 'We agreed,' he said mildly, 'that Matthew should choose his own way and that whatever he decided to do with his life, we would support and encourage him.'

'I am supporting and encouraging him,' she said, crossly. 'I'm just making sure he understands what a terrible mistake he's making and that he's aware of the true nature of the imbeciles with whom he intends to spend every moment of the next two years. Always supposing they don't manage to kill him on his first day. Which could happen. Especially the way they go about things. Seriously, Matthew, if you want to join a bunch of mindless thugs who can't get anything right and ruin people's lives, why don't you become a politician?'

'It's no different to the way things have been up till now,' I said, keeping calm because one of us had to. 'I've been in and out of the TPHQ for a couple of years now and you've been all right with that.'

'Yes, but that was different. You could come home any time you liked. You were a sort of guest there. This is something else completely. You'll be one of them. You'll belong to them and they could have you doing anything. Do you honestly think you could kill someone?'

'I don't know,' I said, because I didn't. 'I suppose there's

20

training for that sort of thing. I might not get through. In which case . . .'

'Are they making you do this?' demanded my mother. 'Have they been putting pressure on you to join them? Because if so, then just tell me and I'll shoot off and have a quick word with Commander Hay.'

'No, no,' I said, meaning no, they weren't putting any pressure on me and no, for God's sake, don't shoot off and have a word with Commander Hay. Mum and Commander Hay frequently had far too many words together and the results were never happy for anyone. 'Look, you said yourselves, you'd support any career choice I made and this is it.'

She seized at another straw. 'But you're too young, surely?'

'Well, that's just it, isn't it? No one knows how old I am. The Time Police have chosen to believe I've reached the minimum age.'

'But . . .' she said, because she never goes down without a fight. Dad put his hand on hers. 'Max . . .'

'I know,' she said, 'but even so . . .'

'I was never going to come and work here,' I said as gently as I could, because she really was upset and I felt a little guilty. They're my parents and I love them.

'I know you weren't,' said Mum. 'And I wouldn't have encouraged that, anyway, but I thought . . . Oh, I don't know. It's as if they've been . . . grooming you. That's it, isn't it? They're like a cult and you've fallen under their influence.'

I shook my head. 'Of course they're not and I haven't.'

'But that's just it,' said Mum. 'You wouldn't know, would you? But don't panic – there are people out there who can de-cult you and . . .'

21

'They're not a cult,' I said. 'And if it makes you feel any better, I approached Captain ... no, he's a major now ... Major Ellis some time ago and said I'd like to join and he said because I was so young, I had to think about it for at least six months before he'd put my name forwards and I have. Waited six months, I mean, and I still want to do it. Now it's time.'

'Will they accept you?' said Dad.

Mum rounded on him at once. 'Why wouldn't they?'

'No reason,' he said calmly. 'No reason at all.' But I knew exactly what he meant. He wasn't referring to the Time Police as an organisation as a whole, but rather the many individuals who made up that whole. Individuals who had not been selected for their good-natured ability to embrace diversity and live and let live.

Major Ellis, to give him credit, had touched on this.

'You might find, Matthew, that there's a big difference between a little boy trotting up and down the corridors clutching his schoolbooks under his arm, and a young man with a defiantly non-regulation haircut and an attitude problem. They still remember that incident when you broke the Time Map.' And now it would seem that Dad was thinking along the same lines.

'I've thought about that,' I said to him, because I had. 'And I still want to do it.'

'Well, in that case,' he said, sitting back, 'good luck, son. Your mother and I wish you well.'

'So what does all this entail?' asked Mum, suspiciously. I think she was convinced the Time Police ran special courses for racing up and down the timeline, endangering history and generally getting in her way.

'Six weeks' basic training, then six months of what they

call "gruntwork". Dealing with minor problems, sorting out naughty people, probably *not* shooting anyone, that sort of thing. Then I can select my speciality. IT, or admin, or one of the active squads – whatever.'

'Have you thought about yours?' enquired Mum.

'I want to work with the Time Map,' I said, and could see their relief immediately. I must remember to tell Major Ellis his plan had worked. To get them believing and expecting the worst, and then tell them I wanted to do something benign with the Time Map.

'Your parents will be so relieved,' he'd said, grinning at the thought of putting one over on Mum, 'they'll agree to anything.'

And it looked as if he'd been right.

Marietta Hay, commander of the Time Police, settled herself at her desk, fired up her scratchpad and gazed at her adjutant.

'Well, Charlie, what do you have for me today?'

Captain Farenden opened his first file.

'Not a lot, ma'am. The finance section has the budget figures you requested.' He passed them across. 'Visitor figures are slightly down on last month but not by enough to cause concern; maintenance on the North Chimney has been completed and we lost four officers last month.'

'Did they run away?'

'One invalided out and three resignations. They think they can earn more money in the private sector.'

'That's the official reason,' she said. 'What they mean is they don't like the direction in which I'm leading this organisation.'

Captain Farenden had not achieved his position without mastering the use of massive tact.

'It's a difficult time, ma'am. People don't like change. They're bound to feel a little . . . unsettled.'

She sighed. 'If we don't get a grip – if I don't get a grip – if I can't turn them around and get them facing the threats of today rather than those of yesterday . . .'

'But you are making progress, ma'am.'

'Not quickly enough. We're an organisation of two halves, Charlie.'

'Yes, ma'am. The old and the new.'

'There's nothing wrong with the old, Charlie. Just as long as they'll let me lead them into the realms of the new. Sadly, there are those who just won't be led.'

'Albayans, ma'am.'

'After the late and very unlamented Colonel Albay, yes. Getting rid of him is about the only useful thing St Mary's has ever done.'

'Yes, ma'am.'

She sighed. 'Well, if these . . . Albayans won't come around, then they'll have to be induced to leave. Somehow.'

'Or you could just shoot them, ma'am.'

She brightened. 'Very true. Before they shoot me.' She paused. 'You're supposed to say, "It will never come to that." Seriously, Charlie, I sometimes wonder if you've quite grasped the full extent of your role as my adjutant.'

'I beg your pardon, ma'am. I was giving you a moment before diverting you with the next piece of bad news.'

'Thoughtful of you.'

'Simply part of my role as your adjutant, ma'am.'

'Go on then. Divert me.'

'Sadly, it's only a very small piece of bad news.'

'Well, never mind. I'm sure we'll manage to turn it into a crisis by the end of the day.'

Captain Farenden sighed. 'Our trainees.'

'What about them?'

'It's their last day of basic training today. Graduation ceremony on Friday.' He looked pointedly at her scratchpad. 'It's in your diary, ma'am.'

'Can't you shunt it on to Major Callen?'

'Er . . .'

'He shunted it on to me, didn't he?'

'Er . . .'

'Recruitment and Training is part of his remit. Why isn't he addressing the proud parents and relatives?'

'Recruitment drive, ma'am.'

'In Outer Mongolia, no doubt. Some place so remote and with such primitive travel links that he can't possibly get back here in time.'

'Glasgow, ma'am.'

'Oh, yes – that would do it. So, what's the bad news you think you've successfully distracted me from?'

'The trainees, ma'am.'

'Yes?'

'We've lost one.'

'Dead or mislaid?'

'Dropped out.'

Commander Hay picked up her paper knife. Never a good sign.

'Well,' said Captain Farenden mildly, 'we do tell them they can leave at any point before they formally complete their training.'

'That doesn't mean they should. Or that I have to be happy about it.' She had a sudden thought. 'Which one? Please tell me it was Parrish.'

'Larsson, ma'am.'

'Bugger. He was . . .' She pulled herself up.

'The normal one?'

'They're none of them normal, but he was . . .'

'The closest, ma'am.'

'Exactly. And the point you're dancing around is . . . ?'

'We no longer have enough people to form two teams, ma'am. We have one team and . . .'

'And three left over. And we both know which three, don't we?'

'Well, I do, ma'am.'

'Matthew Farrell, Jane Lockland and Luke Parrish.'

'And so do you.'

She sighed. The Time Police traditionally work in teams of four. There had been eight trainees – now there were seven. One complete team and three . . . misfits.

'It would be those three, wouldn't it?'

'I'm afraid so, ma'am. And they're a weak team. Farrell is very young, Lockland is very wet and Luke Parrish is – despite intensive efforts by his instructors – still Luke Parrish.'

She nodded. Notwithstanding their reputation as an organisation that firmly believed in strict control and discipline, the Time Police had realised quite early on that recruits are best left to form their own teams. Attempts to impose their own preferences never ended well. The best and strongest teams were those who selected each other. One team had already sorted itself out – which left three remaining.

A thought struck her. 'Did Larsson leave because he saw himself being landed with these three?'

'Not an impossibility, ma'am. They do have a certain reputation. Parrish the playboy, Lockland the mouse, and Matthew Farrell . . .' He paused.

27

'The weird one from St Mary's.'

'If you say so, ma'am.'

'Has anyone yet induced him to have his hair cut?'

Her answer was in the silence that followed.

Captain Farenden shifted his weight, stretched out his bad leg and said delicately, 'I have to ask, ma'am . . . why have we taken on Parrish, of all people?'

She sighed again. 'After his son's latest headline-grabbing escapade, Parrish senior came to see me with a proposition. He would see to it that the Amendment Bill curtailing our powers would never make it through the next reading *if* I accepted his son for the minimum term. Two years.'

Captain Farenden was shocked. 'And obviously you said no, ma'am.'

'Well, of course I did. I told him straight – not without a considerable donation to our Widows and Orphans Fund to sweeten the deal. Just a tip, Charlie – if you're going to accept a bribe, always make it a big one. People despise you if you settle for a piddling little sum. Ask any senior cabinet minister.'

'I shall do so at the first opportunity, ma'am. So we can look forward to having Mr Parrish for at least two years.'

'Yes. I probably shouldn't have accepted him. He's all wrong for us. He's intelligent enough – too intelligent, probably – but there's no sense of responsibility there. Or loyalty.'

'Great,' said Captain Farenden. 'Rich, handsome, entitled and a babe magnet.' He paused. 'A babe magnet, ma'am, is . . .'

'I know what a babe magnet is, Charlie. How old do you think I am?'

He stared straight into her damaged face. 'Difficult question to answer, ma'am.'

'Sorry, didn't mean to put you on the spot. Anyway, we're stuck with him. He's signed a contract for two years. We're supposed to instil discipline, responsibility and some sort of work ethic. Frankly, I'm not optimistic. He'll do the compulsory six months' gruntwork like all the others and then I'll transfer him downstairs. He can finish his time on the front desk, meeting and greeting the public. He's handsome and charming – there'll be a stampede of young women – and probably some young men – all clamouring to join up as quickly as possible.'

'Speaking of girls, ma'am . . .'

'Oh yes, Jane Lockland. Well, we were supposed to take on more women.'

'But Lockland, ma'am . . .'

'She was the only one who applied.'

He sighed. 'Why is it that most women seem to avoid the Time Police like the plague?'

'More sense than men,' Hay said shortly. 'Anyway, she might not be all bad. Her theory results were excellent so she's obviously quite bright . . .' She trailed away.

'Ma'am, she's so terrified of doing something wrong she writes everything down. Everything. In a notebook. The general consensus is that she's wetter than a wet weekend. She'll probably burst into tears if she ever has to arrest someone, and worst of all, word on the street says she's not the sort of person you want watching your back. You know as well as I do, ma'am – they'll ditch her at the first opportunity. They'll fling her into some God-awful situation and leave her to cope. Make or break.'

She said doubtfully, 'Don't be too sure she'll break, Charlie. But she has to do her six months like everyone else. Then, if

29

she hasn't already left, I'll transfer her to admin where she'll be perfectly happy moving files around, and it will free up . . .' She stopped.

'Free up a proper officer to get back in the game.'

'Such a politically incorrect thought never entered my mind.'

'She's a gesture towards the quota, isn't she?'

Commander Hay closed her eyes and with the air of one quoting the Oracle at Delphi, intoned, 'The make-up of the Time Police must at all times reflect the diversity of those whom they protect and serve.'

Captain Farenden made a rude noise.

'You do our leaders an injustice, Charlie. I'm simply following their shining example. At least thirty per cent of seats at the next general election will have female-only candidates.'

'What? Regardless of ability?'

'I don't believe ability is high on the selection list when it comes to any MP, male or female.'

'Diversity is good, ma'am.'

'So it would seem. So far it's got us Miss Lockland and Mr Parrish.'

They fell silent.

'Which brings us to Matthew Farrell, ma'am.'

'His abilities with the Time Map are well beyond his years.'

'Sadly, that hasn't made him any friends. And then there was that incident when he was younger. When he brought the Map crashing down.'

She sighed. 'No one wants to work with him, do they?'

'They find him . . . disconcerting. And his background is against him. He's tainted by association with St Mary's.'

She said firmly, 'That will not be a problem. He's destined for

IT and the Time Map and I'll happily sacrifice the other two –
indeed, the entire intake – to keep him here. So again, he does his
gruntwork and then straight to the Map Master for our Mr Farrell.'

Captain Farenden said nothing.

She sighed. 'It's only six months, Charlie. In six months,
Farrell can be transferred to the Time Map where he can really
do some good. Jane Lockland will either have succumbed to
terminal anxiety or grown a set, and Parrish . . .'

'Yes?'

'I suspect we'll have discharged him long before six months
are up, let alone his two years. Whatever his father says.'

He began to put his papers away. 'As you say, ma'am, only six
months. We just have to get them through their gruntwork. Which
brings us back to the original problem. The missing fourth man.'

'Yes,' she said thoughtfully. 'Could you ask Major Ellis to
step in, please.'

Five minutes later he was ushered into her office.

'Good morning, Major.'

'Ma'am.'

'Congratulations on your promotion.'

'Thank you, ma'am.' He raised an eyebrow. 'Would I be
correct in assuming I'm about to pay the price?'

She smiled. Only half her face moved. As a young officer,
Commander Hay had fought in the Time Wars and there had
been an accident. During an emergency extraction, their pod
had lost its door in mid-jump. Commander Hay had survived
but by the time they could get to her, one half of her face was
older than the other. She was the lucky one. Everyone else had
died. It had not been pretty.

'Your promotion was on merit, Major, and well deserved.

31

However, before you take up your new duties, I have an assignment for you. One which you may refuse if you wish. There is no obligation.'

'You want me to take on Matthew Farrell and the others, don't you?'

'For the six months of their basic training, yes. I can't waste three potential officers and they have to do their gruntwork like everyone else – but that's all. After that, I'll break up the team. They can all go their separate ways and you can return to normal duties.'

'I was Matthew Farrell's mentor for some years, ma'am, and I'd have no problem overseeing his gruntwork, but surely it would be better for him to have someone new.'

It was very obvious from the silence that no other officer would take on Matthew Farrell. Or any of his fellow trainees.

'To be honest, Major, we should probably never have taken two of them in the first place, but we did. We've expended a great deal of money and effort on their basic training and now we need to see some return.'

Major Ellis frowned thoughtfully and for some reason, Commander Hay's earlier comments on making sure the size of the bribe was commensurate with the inconvenience sprang to Captain Farenden's mind.

Ellis said slowly, 'Obviously, I'm always happy to oblige, ma'am, but it won't be easy. As I'm sure you will have noticed, they're not a strong team and will require a great deal of supervision. Furthermore, given the potential value of Farrell to this organisation . . .'

He paused to let the rest of the sentence hang in the air.

'Gratifying to see you've acquired the Machiavellian skills

of senior management already, Major. What do you want? What price must I pay?'

'Officer North, ma'am, to assist me.'

'And what compensation will *she* require for being pulled from her normal duties?'

'Expedited route to the Hunter Division, ma'am.'

Commander Ellis didn't even blink. 'Agreed.'

He sighed. 'I can't say I'm looking forward to resuming the struggle to get Farrell to cut his hair, ma'am.'

She smiled. 'I have every confidence, Major.'

Ellis stood up. 'Then with your permission, ma'am, I'll go and advise Officer North of her good fortune and assemble my new team.'

'Thank you, Major.'

'Just as a matter of interest, ma'am, who has the other team?'

'I've given them to Lt Grint. His first assignment as a team leader.'

'Interesting.'

The door closed behind him.

He met Officer North outside one of the briefing rooms and broke the glad tidings.

She remained quiet for some time.

'It's your choice,' he said, sensing reluctance. 'You don't have to do it.'

'But why me, sir?'

'I felt this particular squad would respond well to a gentler touch.'

Celia North stared at him in complete incomprehension.

Ellis sighed. 'So that will be up to me, then.'

2

Their official designation was Team 236. Parrish was disgusted.

'How pathetic is that? What sort of a name is that for a team? We should be Team Terror. Or Team Timeshredder or something. What's the point of wearing a really cool uniform,' he glanced complacently at his black-clad self in the mirror, 'if you don't have a cool name to go with it?'

Typically, neither of his teammates made any response. One because silence was his habitual state – Parrish wasn't even sure he *could* speak – and the other because in the unlikely event she was bright enough to have opinions of her own, he was pretty sure she would never express them in case they upset someone.

He rotated slowly in front of the mirror, apparently unable to drag his eyes away from his own image, saying absently, 'How long before our first assignment, do you think?'

Again, no response. He sighed and turned around. 'I knew being in the Time Police was going to be tough, but I never thought it would be this bad. Let me try again. Our fellow trainees – Team Two-Three-Five – went out yesterday. Everyone else is out. Surely it must be our turn soon.'

He pulled an imaginary gun from his hip and fired at his reflection.

'Missed,' said Farrell, sardonically.

Parrish ignored him. 'What do you think we'll get? Illegal assassination attempt? Treasure hunters? Someone building a dimension-warping device in their spare bedroom?'

He fired again. From the hip, this time. 'And as soon as we're qualified, we can go armed all the time. Pretty cool, eh?'

Farrell rolled his eyes. Parrish sighed. 'Have you exceeded today's word quota? Or is it me?'

Farrell shook his head. If addressed, he would respond briefly but he rarely initiated conversation or made small talk. His attitude was very clearly that talking just wasn't something he did if he could help it. It wasn't just Parrish who thought him odd. The consensus around the Time Police was that there was something seriously wrong with him. Well, his parents were from St Mary's so there was certainly something seriously wrong with him.

Time Police officers are not noted for their sensitivity or tact and so the bulk of them usually stayed well clear of Matthew. Something which suited him well enough. Being small and wiry he had, on occasions, found himself pushed into a quiet corner and given some grief. The more intelligent of his tormentors found his lack of response worrying, and within a few minutes would pull their less enlightened colleagues away with the time-honoured phrase, 'Leave it, mate – he's not worth it,' thus displaying an intelligence and acumen entirely wasted on the Time Police.

The door opened and while two members of Team 236 immediately rose to their feet, Trainee Parrish appeared to be experiencing his usual difficulty adjusting himself to the correct method of addressing senior officers.

Accustomed as he was to Time Police standardisation, Major Ellis regarded his new team with resignation. Two of them, Farrell and Lockland, only just cleared the minimum height requirement and Parrish, though tall, was slight. The traditional Time Police officer bulked himself out with long hours in the gym but these three showed no signs of even knowing where the gym was. Ellis sighed. The weirdo, the mouse and the playboy. However, as Commander Hay had said, only six months, and then they could all go their separate ways and Matthew Farrell would be safely ensconced in the Map Room, which was everyone's goal. Including Farrell himself. All he, Ellis, had to do, was get them there.

He cleared his throat. 'Right, Team Two-Three-Six. We've got one. Briefing Room 3 in ten minutes.'

Despite six weeks of basic training, and seemingly still unaware that the correct response to any order given by a senior officer was, 'Yes, sir,' Parrish demanded to know what they had got. 'Where are we going? How long will we be gone?'

'Full briefing in ten minutes. Get your gear and be there, Parrish.'

'I only ask because I have quite an important appointment this evening and . . .'

'Be there, Parrish, or be on the end of my boot. Your choice.'

Ten minutes later in Briefing Room 3, Major Ellis called them to order. 'Right. Pay attention. Something harmless for your first assignment. This . . . is Henry Plimpton.'

Activating the screen, he brought up a blurred picture of a plump, balding man in his early- to mid-fifties, peering amiably from behind thick spectacles.

'He doesn't look like a criminal mastermind,' said Parrish, doubtfully.

Farrell stared fixedly at the wallscreen, giving it his full attention and saying nothing.

Lockland was busy scribbling in her notebook, a deep frown furrowing her brows.

'I mean,' continued Parrish, oblivious to Ellis's impatience, 'you expect a giant bald head, don't you? And scars. And a signet ring with skull and crossbones. And an evil leer. And possibly a white cat. I'm not sure this one's read the *Handbook for Megalomaniacs*. What's he done?'

'Well, if I can get a word in edgeways, I'll tell you,' said Ellis, and let the silence hang for a few seconds.

When he was sure he had their attention and that Lockland had stopped writing and looked up, he said, 'Lottery ticket.'

Parrish raised his hand. 'What's a . . . ?'

'Similar to a giant raffle.'

Parrish raised his hand again.

'Shut up, Parrish.'

Parrish lowered his hand.

'It was a stealth tax in the late 20th and early 21st centuries,' said Ellis. 'You bought a ticket – as many tickets as you liked, actually – and there was a weekly draw. A small part was set aside as prizes and most of the rest went to the government.'

Up went Parrish's hand again. 'So what was the first prize?'

'Several million pounds.'

Even Parrish was rocked. 'Wow. Why don't we do that now?'

'Well, money wasn't worth as much then as it is now, plus the odds of winning were astronomical. You had more chance of being eaten by a dinosaur than of winning the big prize. And

eventually people realised that a smaller and smaller propor-
tion of the ticket money was being allocated to something that
would benefit them and the whole thing fizzled out.'

'But people still did it?'

'It was a time of great economic hardship. Millions of people
bought tickets in the hope of changing their lives.'

Parrish raised his hand. 'But . . .'

'Shut up, Parrish.'

'I thought we were supposed to ask questions.'

'You're also supposed to be a Time Police officer – intelligent, loyal, dedicated and hard-working. How's that working
out for you so far?'

Aware that he was, once again, on a disciplinary charge for
reporting in late, Parrish sighed heavily.

'Problem, Parrish?'

'Well, I was hoping for something a little more exciting. You
know – tomb robbers, or someone trying to kidnap Genghis
Khan or, you know . . .'

'No, I don't know. Enlighten me.'

'. . . Illegal time travel. You know – a chance to kick some
arse. I mean, a lottery ticket is hardly world-ending, is it?'

More silence indicated that it wasn't just some hapless time
traveller who was about to get his arse kicked.

'If I might continue . . .'

Parrish indicated he might do so with his goodwill.

Taking a deep breath, Ellis soldiered on.

'It would appear our Mr Plimpton has built something
naughty, either in his spare bedroom or in his garden shed,
and now he's working the lottery ticket scam.'

'Um . . .' said Lockland, scarlet-faced, and hesitantly raised her hand.

'You don't need to do that, Lockland – just ask your question.'

'Um . . . how do we know this, sir?'

'Radiation signature. Homemade machines always have a radiation problem. Those unfortunates who manage to avoid our attention invariably die horribly sooner or later. Which shouldn't be a problem – in a perfect world we could just leave them to glow in the dark and then expire – but the subsequent pod explosion could possibly level a small town. And, of course, their inevitably messy end rarely occurs before they've bounced around the timeline leaving chaos and disaster in their wake. Hence the need to get them out of circulation as quickly as possible. Our plan is to apprehend Mr Plimpton, locate his machine, identify the coordinates and send in a clean-up crew.'

Lockland's head snapped up. 'A clean-up crew? What for?'

Clean-up crews are bad news. They do exactly what it says on the tin.

'To destroy the pod. To ensure no trace remains. Nothing that can be ever used again. Total destruction.'

'And Plimpton?' enquired Parrish.

'We bring him back here and hand him over.'

'And then?'

There was a pause. 'Not our concern.'

There was silence in the room.

'Did you not cover this in training?'

They nodded.

'Then you already know. Time travel is against the law. It is our job to uphold the law. We arrest the perpetrators and bring them back here so the law can take its course. What will happen to Plimpton afterwards is not our concern any more than what happens to criminals after their trial concerns the civilian police. If he's found guilty, then he will be punished according to the law. If he's not, then he'll be returned whence he came.' He stared at them thoughtfully. 'Should I be anticipating any difficulties?'

'Not from me,' said Parrish.

Farrell silently shook his head.

After a moment, Lockland shook hers.

'Right, I don't think any of you have yet jumped to the 20th century?'

They shook their heads.

'Well, it's before the civil uprisings, so governments were weak and generally ineffective. There's a great deal of crime, a lot of it opportunistic and up close and personal, so although you look the biggest bunch of shambolic incompetents I've ever clapped eyes on, I'm sure anyone from the 20th century would think twice before taking you on, so you should be safe. Air and water quality will be poor, so don't drink anything that hasn't been boiled. It's the age of the automobile and they drive on the left. On the *left*, people, so watch how you cross the road. Times are hard – although not as hard as they're going to be – so keep your hands on your holiday money.'

His team eyed each other sideways in bafflement at the reference.

He sighed. 'Any questions?'

'Um . . .' said Jane.

'Yes, Lockland.'

'Do they know about us? I mean, the Time Police?'

40

'No. Too early. Which is why you won't be carrying blasters. Only sonics.'

Luke blinked. 'So how are we supposed to quell these savages?'

'You are Time Police officers with all the authority that entails.'

'But . . .'

'Two minutes ago, you were commenting adversely on Henry Plimpton and his lack of criminal characteristics. Make up your mind, Parrish.'

Luke subsided, scowling.

'Right, draw your weapons from the Armoury and meet me in the Pod Bay asap.'

The Pod Bay was underground – in case of accidents – and a good part of it was under the Thames itself. 'To help contain the spread of radiation' had been the cheerful explanation during their induction tour. It was a very large, sound-deadening space, well lit and spotlessly clean. On the far wall, swing doors led directly to the MedCen. Another door in another wall led to Stores, Logistics and the workshops. At the moment, however, the Pod Bay was comparatively empty.

Pods are the centre of Time Police operations. Unlike St Mary's, whose function required their pods to be unobtrusive in any time period, the Time Police favoured big, bad, trouser-soiling pods, designed to put the fear of God into anyone unfortunate enough to be present at the time, and most of their pods were just a plain black box, accessed either by a door or a ramp.

Two of the four hospital pods were already out, as were most of the all-purpose pods. As Parrish had said, they were the last to be allocated an assignment.

'Team Bottom of the Barrel,' murmured Farrell as they entered their designated pod.

None of them were unfamiliar with the pod layout. There had been plenty of simulation exercises during their training and they had accompanied and observed other teams. This, however, was their first proper assignment and as Ellis was aware, no one can predict how a team will react to their first taste of action.

To the right of the door stood the console, an array of flashing lights and read-outs. Basic metal seats were bolted around two of the walls and the fourth wall contained the weapons safe, equipment lockers and first-aid kit. The space wasn't large, but it was well lit. The fixtures and fittings were all Time Police beige – the Time Police not being an organisation that embraced vibrant colour – and the floor covering was Time Police grey. The whole pod smelled pleasantly of Mountain Pine.

Somewhat apprehensively, they filed in and waited, standing around, unsure what to do next. And, as if the day wasn't going to be bad enough, the dreaded Officer North was waiting for them.

Perfect was a word frequently used to describe Celia North. She was tall enough to be elegant but not so tall as to be gangly. Her hair was blonde and well managed, adapting itself quite happily to whichever style was currently required of it. Her carefully planned academic career had been exceptional. Head girl at the same exclusive public school attended by her mother and her mother before her, she'd gone on to graduate from Durham with a first-class degree and a CV filled with memberships of all the right societies and committees likely to prove useful in her future career – which, since her family owned extensive land and properties all across northern England, she hardly needed.

Recruited to St Mary's, she was understood to be efficient, effective and capable. She was admired without being much liked. Held in respect, not affection.

On arrival at St Mary's, she had, as usual, identified her goals and set up two-, five- and ten-year plans for achieving them. These included – but were not necessarily limited to – becoming Head of the History Department. She would, naturally, go on to become Director of St Mary's, after which the place would be run on very different lines to its current shambolic system of administration.

A chance encounter with the Time Police had led to her spending some time with them while St Mary's extricated itself from one of its many crises. There was always some sort of crisis at St Mary's – something she had planned to rectify at the earliest opportunity – but to the surprise of everyone – including Officer North herself – there had been a mutual attraction between herself and the Time Police.

The Time Police themselves were not unaware of the value of the historical perspective Officer North could provide and Officer North, scenting accelerated promotion, promptly revised her game plan.

Events, as they always did, played out to her advantage. Several discreet conversations with Commander Hay had left them both pleased with each other, and even the problem of leaving St Mary's short-staffed had been overcome by the fortuitous wish of a former St Mary's colleague, Officer Van

Owen, to return to her own time and place at St Mary's. Dr Bairstow had raised no difficulties and she and Miss Van Owen had simply exchanged places.

The results of her transfer had been beneficial to all. St Mary's, released from her steady stream of constructive criticism, had heaved a massive sigh of relief – 'Rather similar to taking your corsets off,' Miss Sykes had remarked – and the Time Police had acquired a new member who was destined to be valued as she had always felt she should be.

Whether being among so many kindred spirits had softened her edges a little or whether it was relief of at last being part of an organisation that *did things properly,* both Officer North and the Time Police had benefitted from the arrangements. Frequent and well-deserved promotions had settled her. She no longer had the feeling of not only being a square peg in a round hole, but also of facing the daunting task of converting all the other pegs, too. Here, everyone was a square peg. She relaxed into her job and, slightly to her surprise, found she was enjoying herself.

She stood at the console, arms folded, disapproval radiating from every pore and turned a frosty glare on them as they entered. Nothing personal – an ancestor of Officer North's had once resigned from the court of Queen Victoria citing its frivolity and reckless informality – frosty disapproval was her family's default state.

'Right, first thing on entering a pod – always check your weapons are in safe mode. You can shoot yourselves and each other outside the pod, but I don't want any accidents in here.'

'We don't have any real weapons,' said Parrish, resentfully.

'You have sonics, I presume?'

Awkwardly, they drew and checked their sonic guns.

'Safe,' said Parrish.

'Safe,' said Farrell.

'Um . . . yes, safe.'

'Try to sound more confident, Lockland.'

'Um . . . yes, all right.'

'Um, yes, all right, what?'

'All right, ma'am.'

'Better. All of you go and stand over there. Do not touch anything.'

Since Lockland appeared to be paralysed with anxiety, Farrell took her arm and the three of them shuffled into a corner out of the way.

Major Ellis entered the pod and nodded at North. 'All set?'

'All systems green, sir.'

'Coordinates?'

'Not yet, sir.'

'Right – who wants to lay in the coordinates? Don't all rush at once.' He eyed the trainees. Lockland closed her eyes. Don't let it be me. Don't let it be me.

'Lockland, what about you?'

Some people enjoy being the centre of attention. Parrish, for example, had no problems in that area. For Jane Lockland, this sort of thing was her very worst nightmare. Everyone was looking at her. Automatically her hand reached for the safety of her notebook. North cleared her throat in a manner that could halt armies in their tracks and so, taking a deep breath, and telling herself she could do this, Jane stepped up to the console. North moved aside to make room. 'Here. Sit down.'

Lockland seated herself and ran her eyes over the con-

45

sole. This pod was different to the training simulator she was most accustomed to. Nothing appeared to be in the right place. Nothing was as she remembered. And everyone was watching. Panic was making her blind.

She took a deep, controlling breath. I can do this. I can do this. I've done this in training. Many times. I've watched other teams do this. I can do it. Just stop. Slow down. Stop and think. There must be something I can recognise. There's the chronometer. Those are the camera controls. Which means this must be the . . . The silence dragged on as she worked her way around the console, conscious of the seconds remorselessly ticking by.

Parrish sighed loudly and shifted his weight impatiently.

'Take your time, Lockland,' said Ellis, quietly. 'There's no rush. I think I speak for us all when I say we'd rather you were slow and correct than fast and flashy.'

For some reason his eye fell on Parrish, who scowled.

Hands shaking, she laid in the coordinates. She could imagine Parrish behind her, fidgeting impatiently as she went through the final checks, all ready to shoulder her aside and do it himself in a fraction of the time. Her heart felt as if it were about to leap from her chest. She knew her face was bright red – it always was when she became anxious – but there was nothing she could do about that. In fact, she realised with a sudden revelation, the only thing she could control was herself as she performed this small test. All right, she was slow and fumbling, but how much worse would it be to be slow, fumbling and *wrong*?

Eventually, when she was certain everything was correct, she sat back and said, not without a tremor, 'Coordinates laid in, sir.'

'All right,' said North, quite gently for her. 'Let's have a look.'

She ran an experienced eye over the console.

'Everything correct, sir.'

'Well done, Lockland.'

Lockland, whose face was just beginning to return to something of its normal colour, flushed again but this time with pleasure.

'All right. Positions, everyone. When you're ready, Lockland.'

Oh my God . . . what?

A tiny, trembly voice she vaguely recognised as her own said, 'Pod – commence jump procedures.'

The pod's AI responded. 'Jump procedures commenced.'

The world flickered like a broken film and they were gone.

3

They landed with just the tiniest bump.

Matthew Farrell, accustomed to the St Mary's scramble to the cameras to ascertain their landing time and place and then allocate blame accordingly, was rather surprised when nothing happened. In fact, Ellis sat back and stretched. 'Well, it's all rather up to you three now, isn't it? Don't just sit there looking gormless.'

There was a moment's frozen silence and then, predictably, Lockland fumbled for her notebook.

'Put it away,' said North, without even bothering to look round.

The three of them clustered around the screens.

'Where are we?' demanded Parrish, staring in disbelief. 'Where the hell have you dropped us, Lockland?'

She flushed again, feeling the familiar panic. Had she got it wrong after all? No. No, she hadn't. The coordinates were all correct. She said, as firmly as she could manage, 'Exactly where and when we should be. 1996. The small town of Lower Spurting in the county of Rushfordshire. Pod – please provide brief details of Lower Spurting.'

Parrish sighed impatiently. 'You don't have to say "please", Lockland. It's a machine.'

The pod responded in a pleasant, female voice. 'Lower Spurting. Created in the early 19th century as an overspill town for industrial Whittington. While Whittington prospered, Lower Spurting did not.

'There are no buildings of historical or architectural interest.

'Population approximately seventeen thousand five hundred.

'For every one hundred females there are eighty-seven point four males.

'Thirty-eight per cent of the population are over sixty-five.

'Thirty-three per cent of the population are under sixteen. Of those aged between sixteen and twenty-five, thirty-six point three per cent have no academic qualifications and twenty-seven per cent are unemployed.

'Overall unemployment is seven per cent higher than the national average at this time.

'A small light-engineering park to the north-west provides minimal employment. The public cinema closed two years ago. The public leisure centre closed one year ago. There are no rail links. There are . . .'

'Stop,' said Parrish in an attempt to end this doleful litany.

'I hold more information on behavioural patterns and population clusters.'

'I said, enough.'

'I can provide details of air quality, pollution, water purity . . .'

'FOR GOD'S SAKE, SHUT UP.'

'. . . religious groups, census statistics . . .'

'No,' said Lockland, quickly. 'That's enough. Thank you.'

There was a short pause and then the pod responded, 'You're welcome.'

Parrish stared at her. 'Why would it say that?'

'Because I said thank you. It's a polite AI.'

'Not to me.'

'You shout at it.'

'Lockland, it's a bloody machine.'

North cleared her throat and made a gesture indicating that if Parrish knew what was good for him, he would direct his attention towards the screen where Lower Spurting sprawled in all its late 20th-century glory.

'Dear God,' he said, staring at the screen.

'I suspect Lower Spurting will be equally unimpressed with you,' said Ellis, drily. 'Right – the three of you – check you have everything you need – although if you don't it's too late now – and get out there and apprehend Henry Plimpton before he does any serious damage. The clean-up crew will be one hour behind you. Make sure you have everything ready for them.'

Lockland's head swivelled. 'You're not coming with us, sir?'

He shook his head. 'Perfectly straightforward assignment. North and I will monitor your progress from here.'

'Where are the clean-up crew?'

'Discreetly waiting until called for.'

'So which of us is team leader?' demanded Parrish. The tone of his voice said there could be only one possible choice.

Ellis surveyed them silently. The obvious choice was Parrish. Lockland had done well but needed to be brought on gradually. Let her have her small success today and build on it again tomorrow. And if he selected Farrell, did he lay himself open to charges of favouritism because he'd once been his mentor? Which only left Parrish.

He surveyed his team. 'Do we have a volunteer?'

50

As he suspected, only one person was willing.

'Very well, Mr Parrish. Let's see what you make of this one.' He raised his voice a little. 'Mr Parrish is in charge until I say otherwise.' He held Parrish's eyes for a moment, saw nothing but overconfidence and self-assurance there, and sighed.

Parrish turned to his team, full of importance. 'OK, people – safety check. Vests?'

'Yes,' said Jane.

Farrell nodded.

Parrish scowled at him. 'I can't hear you.'

Farrell nodded more firmly.

Both Ellis and North were very careful not to catch each other's eye.

'Weapons?'

More nods.

'Cuffs? Batons? Liquid string?'

They nodded, patting their utility belts from which their equipment hung. Once, long ago, someone had referred to this useful piece of equipment as Batman's utility belt and the name had stuck.

'Coms check.'

'Check,' said Lockland, obediently.

Farrell nodded.

Parrish gritted his teeth. 'Don't make it a personal challenge to get you to speak.'

They regarded each other for a moment and then Farrell said, 'Check.'

Both Farrell and Lockland tightened their chinstraps. Parrish had declined a helmet. Too uncool for words, apparently. Ellis had let it go. Parrish would change his mind soon enough when

51

he got the first brick round his ear, and if he survived that, then he wouldn't make the same mistake again.

Ellis surveyed his team. Lockland tightly buttoned up, Farrell solidly silent. And Parrish, bright-eyed and cocky. Doing things his way. The next few hours were going to be interesting.

'Remember, this is not your first jump. You've done this before. You've accompanied and observed other teams. You've practised simulations. The only difference between those jumps and this one is that today you're in charge of yourselves. As you will be in the future. However, Officer North and I will be monitoring your progress should you find yourself in any difficulties.' He paused, but there was no reaction. 'Very well, Mr Parrish. You may proceed.'

The ramp came down and they marched out. At the bottom, Lockland looked back over her shoulder. Ellis and North were sitting at the console, drinking coffee. North made a shooing motion then the ramp came up behind them and Lockland suddenly felt very alone.

Looking around, they appeared to be in some kind of public area. A large open concrete space was before them, surrounded on three sides by garages with heavily graffitied up-and-over doors. Old pieces of shredded plastic, caught for eternity in the branches of a dying tree, fluttered in a light breeze. In one corner, a rusted old wreck of a car perched precariously on crumbling bricks. Weeds grew between the cracks in the oil-stained concrete – the only green things in sight. Litter had blown into small heaps. A faint smell of burning rubber permeated the area and an air of weary defeat hung over everything.

Above them, the small drone which had silently followed them down the ramp hovered unseen.

'Well,' said Parrish, stirring something unidentifiable with his boot, 'I'm betting this is the sort of place where the appearance of armoured police officers isn't going to cause any sort of stir at all.'

There was no response from his teammates.

'He needs to get them moving,' said North, adjusting the pod's cameras to tracking mode. 'They can't stand there all day.'

The same thought had obviously occurred to Parrish. 'Right,' he said, crisply, suddenly realising he should have done this before they left the pod. 'Who's got the address?'

Lockland pulled out her notebook. 'Seventeen Beaver Avenue.'

'Any idea where that is?'

She shook her head.

'Why not? You should have checked that before you left the pod.'

'Leave her alone,' said Farrell.

'Oh, great. Now you decide to talk.'

He shrugged. 'It's hard to get a word in when you're around.'

'It's over there,' said Lockland, quickly, before the quarrel could develop.

'How do you know?' demanded Parrish.

'Um . . . because it's the only exit from this space?'

Parrish sighed. 'Great. I'm with a dummy and a smart arse.'

'And we're with a dickhead,' said Farrell.

Parrish rounded on him. 'Is that why you don't talk? Because you never have anything useful to say?'

'Dear God,' said North, back in the pod. 'Permission to nip out and bang their stupid heads together?'

'They have to sort these things out,' said Ellis, calmly. 'It's all perfectly normal.'

'There is nothing normal about this team, sir.'

The not-normal team emerged from the garage area into a street stretching away to left and right. The sign opposite said, 'Beaver Avenue.'

'Don't forget to tell him you told him so,' said Farrell to Lockland.

Parrish gritted his teeth. 'Can you just shut up, please.'

Farrell nodded in satisfaction. 'They all say that sooner or later.'

'Look at all these cars,' said Lockland, staring around. 'They're everywhere.'

There were indeed cars everywhere. Parked at the side of the road. Parked on the pavement. Parked higgledy-piggledy in what had once been people's front gardens. Cars roared up and down the road, music thumping from the open windows, hooting at each other or the occasional small child running out into the road.

Jane peered. 'What are those hump things in the road?'

'Sleeping policemen,' said Farrell.

'They bury policemen under the road? What for?'

'To slow down the traffic, I think.'

'Can we get on?' said Parrish impatiently. 'I have a date tonight with that blonde in Logistics.'

Farrell stared. 'What, the big one with the scar?'

'No – that's a bloke.'

'Turned you down, did he?'

'Just because the two of you never have any sort of sex life that's no reason for me to fall to your level.'

'Number Seventeen's this way,' said Lockland pointing. 'Bit of a rough area,' she said, as they picked their way along the cracked pavement.

'Well, yeah,' said Parrish. 'They bury policemen under the road. Watch your backs, people.'

'All these cars,' said Lockland, as they squeezed between two parked on the pavement. 'I've never seen a car up close.'

'You've never seen a car?'

She flushed at his patronising tone. 'Well, there aren't many of them around these days. You have to have money to own a car.'

'And no social conscience,' said Farrell.

'I had two. Cars, I mean.'

'Why?' enquired Farrell with great interest.

'Why, what?'

'Why did you have two cars? Did you drive them simultaneously? Did you straddle the roofs like a Roman rider?'

'What? Of course not. I had a sports car and a 4x4.'

Farrell grinned. 'I suspect you didn't have them for very long.'

Parrish scowled and made no response.

'There were no cars where we lived,' said Lockland, still looking around. 'They were really scarce.'

'With Parrish here making them scarcer by the moment.'

They continued down the street.

'It's quite noisy, isn't it?' said Lockland, and it was. People shouted to each other over the noise of passing traffic. Their children shouted over the noise of their parents shouting over passing traffic. Dogs barked just to make themselves heard. Thumping music dopplered past them.

Lockland bent over something on the pavement. 'Oh my goodness, is that a piece of poo?'

Parrish and Farrell leaned over to inspect it. 'It's a turd, yes,' said Parrish. 'Have you never seen one of those up close, either?'

She was horrified. 'But . . . *it's on the pavement.*'

'It's the late 20th century, Lockland. Society was breaking down. People probably crapped on the pavements all the time.'

'It's only a dog turd,' said Farrell, taking pity on her. 'No one's squatting in the street.'

Luke sighed and shifted his weight. 'Can we just get this over with, please. Blonde. Sure thing. Tonight.'

'It's all very pungent,' said Lockland, walking wide around the alleged dog poo and sniffing the cocktail of exhaust fumes, wet pavements and burning rubber.

They stopped outside Number Seventeen and peered up at the sad house. The curtains drooped. The paintwork was peeling. At one point, someone had tried to tame the small front garden by hurling a ton of gravel on it. Weeds and coarse grass had found the strength to overcome this attack and flourished triumphantly. The front gate hung from only one hinge. The hedge was old and straggly. More unrecognisable loud music pounded from the open bedroom window.

Lockland suddenly felt a twinge of sympathy for Henry Plimpton. Who wouldn't want to escape this?

'Number Seventeen,' she said, bringing up the information on her scratchpad. 'The pod says this is the residence of Henry Plimpton. One wife. One son. One daughter. All resident.'

'Listen up, everyone,' said Parrish, as they negotiated the wonky gate. 'I'll do the talking.'

'No,' said Farrell, in disbelief. 'Will you?' Jane stepped smartly between them.

Luke led them up the path. 'Stay behind me, team, and be ready for anything.' He rapped sharply on the front door.

They might have thought themselves ready for anything, but all three were completely unprepared for the great blast of noise as the front door opened.

The enormous woman in front of them appeared to be singing. '. . . *But don't look back in anger . . .* '

'What?' said Parrish in disbelief, but whether he hadn't heard or simply did not comprehend was not clear.

Two ratty mongrels raced down the stairs, hell-bent on defending their property to the death. In the way of small, irritating dogs everywhere, they bounced into the air, yapping furiously. In the way of small, irritating dogs everywhere, they also wagged their stumpy tails, presumably in case the visitors had biscuits in their pockets and were feeling generous.

The AI hadn't mentioned dogs. Parrish took a deep breath. 'Madam, we are the police.' A phrase he thought successfully juggled truth with enough impact to install the fear of God chez Plimpton.

Sadly, he failed on both counts. The woman simply stared at him and then shouted, 'What? I can't hear you. Shut up, dogs. What?'

No one noticed the small drone high above them. Back in the pod, Ellis and North were staring at the screen, coffee forgotten.

Wisely, Luke abandoned the introductions, shouting, 'We're looking for Henry Plimpton.'

'I can't hear you.'

Since Matthew was grinning quietly behind his leader,

Jane leaned forwards and said very quietly, 'Hello. Is Henry Plimpton here, please?'

The effect was magical.

'Hang on, love, I can't hear you.'

She shrieked something over her shoulder, the song ceased abruptly and near silence fell, along with the dogs who paused their vertical perambulations and watched, bright-eyed and tongues lolling.

'Thank you,' said Jane, and Matthew smiled brightly, just to annoy his team leader.

Parrish pulled himself together. 'Madam, good morning. We are with the police.' He fumbled for his ID.

North sighed. 'Should have had it ready.'

Ellis sighed. 'Should have sent someone around the back.'

'We're looking for Mr Henry Plimpton.'

At the back of the house, a door slammed.

'Shit,' said Parrish, trying to peer over her shoulder.

'Language,' said the woman.

North sighed again. 'All wrong. They're going to have to chase him down now.'

'Well, they won't make that mistake again,' observed Ellis, topping up his forgotten coffee.

'He's bolted,' shouted Parrish. 'You two – go around the back and get after him.' He struggled to elbow his way past the enormous woman and made for the back door. The dogs ceased to regard him as a friend.

'Ow. Bugger. Get off, will you? Madam, get your dogs under control.'

'What's going on?' enquired a youth, appearing from the

kitchen where, judging from the size and shape of him, he must spend a lot of time.

Upstairs, the music started again.

'Who are you?' shouted the boy over the Gallagher brothers at their best. 'What are you doing in our house?'

The dogs were, by now, almost apoplectic.

'Get out of my house,' shrieked the woman. 'Dwayne, call the police.'

'Madam, I am the police,' panted Parrish, endeavouring to squeeze himself between the wall and the youth and failing. 'Get out of my way, will you?'

Something nipped him on the back of his leg. 'And get these bloody dogs under control before I shoot them.'

The woman shrieked, 'Monster.'

Another face appeared on the stairs. 'What's going on? I can't hear my music.'

Parrish was privately of the opinion you'd have to be dead not to hear the music and possibly not even then. He redoubled his efforts to get to the back door, unsure whether the family was actively attempting to prevent his pursuit or just not quite right in the head due to too much brain-rattling music or inhaling too many dog turds.

'Everyone get out of my way before I arrest you all.'

Someone was beating at his head and shoulders. Resolving never to be without a helmet again, he somehow forced a passage between two hysterical dogs, the enraged housewife, the monolithic son and the whiney teenage daughter, none of whom were happy. The noise levels were ear-bleeding.

Emerging into the back garden, he was just in time to see a plump rump disappear over the back wall.

Cursing horribly, he opened his com and shouted, 'He's getting away. Over the back wall. Where are you?'

'I can see him,' said Farrell. 'There's an alleyway. He's not very fast. We'll get him easily. Lockland?'

'I'm just . . .' Lockland appeared at the other end of the alleyway. 'We've got him trapped between us.'

'On my way,' said Parrish and sprinted for the back wall himself, confident that the Plimpton family – if that was who they were, because he suddenly realised he hadn't checked – would be too elderly, too young, too unfit, too fat, or too stupid to follow him. Heaving himself over the wall, he dropped heavily on to two large black plastic containers which appeared to have been placed there for the sole purpose of interfering with the Time Police in the execution of their duties, had anyone in the late 20th century actually been intelligent enough to think of such a thing.

He hit the bins with a crash, bounced and hit the ground with another crash. Both bins tipped over with him, their lids came free and he found himself rolling among the remains of every meal the Plimptons had enjoyed over the last seven days, together with some dubious-looking material of a very personal nature.

Fighting free, he rolled over and stood up to assess the damage.

'What the fu . . . ? What am I covered in?'

'Household rubbish,' panted Farrell, joining him. He pointed down the alley. 'He went that way. Is that smell actually you?'

Parrish had lost interest. 'Why don't these people have household incinerators? Are they living in the Dark Ages? Why are they not all dead of plague or worse? There must be rats everywhere. I tell you, we're all going to die of something unspeakable. None of us are likely to survive this assignment.'

There was a shout from further up the alleyway. Lockland was using the plastic bins with which the alleyway was generously endowed to climb over another wall.

Back in the pod, North and Ellis were barely able to stop laughing long enough to refill their mugs.

Farrell and Parrish pounded down the alleyway and followed Lockland over the wall, only to find themselves in an open space covered in coarse grass and with a broken goalpost at one end.

'There,' said Farrell, pointing at the plump figure racing away from them, albeit very slowly. Lockland was not far behind. A handful of small children, who should almost certainly have been in school and weren't, watched them go, shouting derisive comments.

'I swear I will never set foot in the 20th century again,' muttered Parrish. 'It's full of dirt and disease and disgusting people. Do you think those kids are feral? What's the betting that when – if – we ever get back to the pod, the little buggers've got it up on bricks and had it away with the wheels.'

'Come on,' said Farrell urgently. 'We can't leave her on her own.' He set off at a run and after taking a moment to gaze down at his soiled self in disgust, Parrish followed him.

At the end of the park, a pair of wrought-iron gates led out on to another, busier street, where they could see traffic zipping by.

'They've got to get him before he gets out into the street,' said North, not moving. 'If they lose him, we'll have to bring in another team to assist and that'll be embarrassing for everyone.'

'They will.'

61

'You're very confident.'

'They're doing fine.'

'It's hardly a textbook retrieval, sir.'

'Their methods are just a little unorthodox, that's all. I bet you they get him.'

North regarded him for a moment and then said, 'I bet you Lockland gets him.'

'No. It'll be Farrell.'

'Not Parrish?'

'He's all mouth and trousers, that one. No, it'll be Farrell.' She grinned.

'No, I'm not saying that because I was his mentor. It's not favouritism. I just think it'll be him.'

'You're wrong, sir. It'll be Lockland. Bet you anything.'

He looked sideways at her. 'A drink in the bar afterwards. Loser pays.'

'Done. Don't forget your wallet, sir.'

'They're closing on him,' he said, swivelling the drone controls. 'Hello, who's this?'

Panting along in the rear, the Plimpton family were lumbering across the grass. Complete with dogs.

'You're not telling me they climbed over that wall? Look at the size of them.'

'There was a gate,' said North, straight-faced. 'Which, in the excitement of the moment, everyone seems to have missed. Look at those dogs go. Legs like little pistons.'

Glancing over his shoulder, Henry Plimpton veered off in a different direction.

Ellis sat up straighter. 'Hang on. Is he running from us or from them?'

North shrugged.

Parrish was breathless. 'Lockland – can you hear me?'

Her response was even more breathless. 'Yes.'

'He's coming your way.'

'No, he's not. He's gone into someone's garden.'

'Whose?'

'Well, how the . . . how should I know?' she snapped back, hot, breathless and just for once, entirely forgetting always to be polite and considerate to others.

'I bet you,' said Ellis thoughtfully, 'that she swears before this assignment is out. Properly, I mean.'

'Not a chance,' said North confidently. 'She doesn't have the vocabulary.'

'We'll see. She's still with him.'

Lockland was panicking. 'Where are you? There are hundreds of people here, hanging out of the windows and shouting at me.'

'Just grab him, will you, before the whole thing becomes a circus.'

'I'm not the one who let him get away. Hang on.'

She crashed through another gate. What might once have been a garden was now someone's scrapyard. Pieces of car, old washing machines, a glassless greenhouse, even more of the ubiquitous plastic bins . . .

She dodged round a breeding group. 'What are these things?'

'People put their rubbish in them, I think,' said Matthew.

Jane was baffled. 'Whatever for?'

'No idea. Presumably they like the smell of garbage. Or perhaps it's a form of currency. Where are you?'

'Closing.'

'Well . . . close faster,' shouted Parrish, obviously feeling it was time to impose his authority.

There was a pause and then, for the first time in her life, Jane said, 'Why don't you just shut up.'

Ellis turned to North. 'Did she just tell him to shut up?'

North nodded. 'Well, someone should.'

Time Police officers were scheduled regular periods of physical activity. Attendance was compulsory. There was running, self-defence, weapons training and such. No sessions ever included dodging small dogs, screaming women, feral children and large plastic wheelie bins.

Henry Plimpton climbed on top of a ferret cage and scrambled over another wall.

'Oh . . . f . . .' Hot and dirty, Lockland threw herself after him.

'Nearly,' said Ellis. 'Get your money ready.'

North made a derisive noise, but, mindful of his rank, ended it respectfully with, 'Sir.'

They were back in the alleyway again. Not a hundred yards from Henry Plimpton's back gate.

Lockland stopped, chest heaving. 'We've run in a circle. He's nearly back home again.'

Parrish was galvanised. 'We've really screwed this up. He's heading for his pod. He's going to make a run for it. The only way to avoid lifelong ridicule is to get the bastard before he gets there. Farrell – you go that way. Cut him off.'

'Ah,' said Ellis with satisfaction. 'He's learning.'

'Indeed, sir. On-the-job training. You can't beat it.'

'Look at the state of him. Is that a sanitary item hanging off his shoulder?'

'A tea bag, I think, sir.'

'Thank God. I wouldn't have let him back in the pod, otherwise.'

Lockland, gaining with every step, was breathless but determined. 'Henry Plimpton, I arrest you in the name of . . .' She heaved a breath. 'I just arrest you. Stop. Stand still. Before you collapse, sir. Please.'

Indeed, Henry Plimpton's condition was alarming. Red-faced, he was dripping with sweat. His chest heaved as his lungs struggled to cope. Summoning a last effort from somewhere, he made to run.

'He's resisting arrest,' yelled Parrish. 'String him. String the bastard. What are you waiting for?'

Fumbling at her belt, Lockland pulled out an aerosol. Bright yellow liquid string enveloped Henry Plimpton's trembling legs and he fell heavily to the ground.

Farrell and Parrish arrived in not much better condition and some time was spent bent double, hands on knees, trying to get their breath back. Parrish had added a colourful mix of household rubbish to his general ensemble.

As soon as she could speak, Lockland peered at Mr Plimpton. 'Oh God, I hope we haven't given him a heart attack.'

Parrish ceased to try and brush off the remains of the last seven days chez Plimpton. 'Given what's going to happen to him, that might be a bit of a blessing.'

There was a sudden silence as the implications hit all three of them.

'And this,' said Ellis, sitting up, 'is where we find out whether the training section has done a good job or not.'

4

Lockland glanced around. The family was still some distance away. They were obviously not people who had embraced long-distance running as a regular activity. Or any activity more strenuous than picking up the biscuit tin. Even the dogs had lost interest and were running in circles, noses to the ground.

'What do we do now?' she enquired.

'I'm all for cuffing and stuffing,' said Parrish, reaching for his handcuffs.

'You would be,' muttered Farrell.

'What's that supposed to mean?'

'Exactly what you think it does. He's not going anywhere. Give him a moment to get his breath back and clear the string off his legs.'

'And escape.'

Lockland leaned over Henry Plimpton. 'Do you promise not to try to escape?

Still gasping for breath, he nodded.

'Oh, for God's sake,' said Parrish, disgusted.

Ellis frowned. 'Not often I find myself in agreement with Parrish.'

Parrish leaned over the unfortunate Mr Plimpton in a rather

more threatening manner. 'Where is it? And don't say "Where's what?" because I'm on a promise this evening and if you mess me about, I'll shoot you where you stand.' He surveyed the prostrate, chest-heaving Henry Plimpton and added, more accurately, 'Lie.'

Ellis opened his com. 'Never mind your bloody sex life, Parrish, find his pod.'

'Yes, yes, all right.' He knelt beside Henry Plimpton. 'I'll ask one last time. Where is it?'

Levering himself up on one arm, Henry Plimpton cast a desperate glance at his family, now almost upon them, and whispered in his ear.

Parrish heaved himself to his feet, nodded to his prisoner and then said, 'Farrell, go and check out the garden shed. If it's not there, then try those garages round the back. Find Mr Plimpton's device, note the coordinates and relay to Major Ellis for him to direct the clean-up crew.'

'Nice work,' said Ellis to North. 'See, he can do it when he tries.'

'He's just worried he's going to miss his blonde.'

'I don't really care what his motives are as long as he performs.'

'Hmm,' said North.

With a thunder of hooves, the Plimpton family arrived heavily on the scene. Recriminations reverberated off nearby buildings, distributed indiscriminately between Henry Plimpton and the Time Police. Lockland lowered her visor, thus cutting out the main part, but Parrish had no such luxury. Spittle flying, a red-faced and thoroughly agitated Mrs Plimpton screamed in his unprotected face. She was an enormous woman, with equally large offspring. They congregated around the tiny, tubby Henry Plimpton like cathedrals around a rabbit hutch.

'Too public,' said North, disapprovingly. 'He should get them all out of there. If the neighbours turn up as well, we could have the makings of a riot.'

The same thought had apparently occurred to Parrish. The unfortunate Mr Plimpton, although still with the look of someone whose day wasn't going well, was now a much better colour. Lockland couldn't help wondering if he knew just how much worse his day was going to get.

'Give me a hand,' said Parrish and together they pulled off the last of the liquid string and hauled him to his feet.

'Where's your house from here?'

Henry Plimpton pointed a trembling hand.

Parrish regarded the still-shouting Plimpton family with dislike. 'Is there any way of shutting them up?'

He shook his head. 'Not that I have ever discovered.'

They set off down the alley, preceded by two yapping dogs and followed by baying Plimptons. Jeering neighbours hung from bedroom windows. It was only a matter of time before someone threw something. A gang of youths congregated threateningly.

'Oh good,' said Parrish. He drew his sonic. 'I'm just in the mood.'

Lockland was less happy. 'Suppose they call the police.'

'Lockland, where have you been for the last six weeks? We *are* the police.'

'I mean the real police.'

'Then we shoot them, too. I'm really not in the mood to pander to 20th-century sensibilities. In fact, given the choice,

I'm never setting foot in this century again. Pack of bloody barbarians.'

The pack of youths advanced. The average age was probably around thirteen. Most of them were smoking. Some of them clutched cans of alcohol. Because they couldn't drink the water, Parrish assumed.

'Here. That's our Henery. Wossee done?'

Luke tried to brush them aside. 'Nothing you need concern yourself with.'

'You with the social?'

Jane turned to Parrish. 'Social what? What's he talking about?'

'Jane, don't engage with these people. You'll catch something.'

A chorus of voices joined in.

'Bastard cheek. Who are you, anyway?'

'He says he's a policeman. Don't look like any policemen I know.'

'SWAT – they're SWAT.'

'Like I said – what's he done?'

'He hasn't done nothing,' shouted a tearful Mrs Plimpton.

'Heard he's won the lottery.'

''Kin hell. You won the lottery, Henery?'

They had, by now, reached the back of the Plimpton house with its disturbed bins and scattered rubbish. The dogs immediately lost interest in the human element and began to rummage through old takeaway cartons and soggy tea bags. Mrs Plimpton shouted and waved her arms. The dogs ignored her. Parrish could only conclude they must be deaf.

Farrell was waiting for them just inside the gate. He nodded back over his shoulder at a dilapidated wooden structure decorated with an ancient tin bath. Luke's already rock-bottom opinion of the 20th century plummeted even further.

'It's in the shed.'

'What's it like?'

'Pretty much as you'd expect. Primitive. Dangerous. And dead. Completely blown out. Single-use, I reckon. Not a long-term project, anyway. I've notified the major,' he glanced at his watch, 'and the clean-up crew will be here any minute.'

Parrish nodded.

Farrell looked over his shoulder and innocently enquired, 'Why have you brought along all these people?'

Parrish gritted his teeth. 'They brought themselves.'

'Who are they?'

'I have no idea. Let's get him inside.'

They hustled Henry Plimpton through the gate, closing it firmly in the faces of everyone not a Plimpton or a Time Police Officer. Once inside the house, things were a little quieter. Without a by-your-leave to anyone, Farrell shut the dogs in the garden and Mrs Plimpton in the kitchen, and the teenagers gravitated to their rooms of their own accord, much in the way of all teenagers across the universe. Thirty seconds later the music started again.

No one noticed the tiny drone zipping in through the door and taking up position near the light fitting.

Looking around their sitting room, Lockland reckoned she'd never seen such a dispiriting space. There was no art on the walls, which were still painted in builders' magnolia, even after all these years. There were no family photos, no proud certificates. The curtains at the windows hung in loops. Two scruffy and stained sofas and an armchair were arranged around the walls like furniture in a doctor's waiting room. A small electric fire stood in an empty fireplace. The clock on the mantle had long since stopped functioning and was now serving as a paper-weight for a variety of papers, bills and money-off coupons.

The most important item in the room appeared to be an enormous TV set with an astonishingly small screen. There were no books or magazines of any kind, not even a TV guide. The TV was on. Garish colour flickered and two figures screamed raucous insults at each other across a table. Some sort of soap opera, she concluded, although given the world around them, possibly two prominent public figures discussing issues of national importance on a current affairs programme.

Parrish picked up the remote and muted the TV. That rare commodity – peace – descended upon the Plimpton household.

'Sit down, please, Mr Plimpton.'

The little man collapsed into his armchair and put his face in his hands.

Farrell stationed himself in front of the door, arms folded across his chest. Lockland inspected the sofa and then perched on the very edge, saying quietly, 'Why did you do it, Mr Plimpton?'

He lifted his head and made an obviously huge effort at pulling himself together. 'What will happen to me?'

'Well, we're with the Time Police, Mr Plimpton, and you've broken the law a little bit. We have to ask you some questions.'

She couldn't bring herself to mention where and what form this questioning would take.

He blinked behind his shiny spectacles. 'I don't understand. Time Police? What Time Police?'

'A select organisation of hand-picked officers,' said Parrish. Ellis snorted.

'Time travel is forbidden in every place and every time. I'm afraid you are now an illegal, Mr Plimpton, and subject to our jurisdiction.'

Mr Plimpton panicked. 'Oh, no, no, no. I didn't mean any harm. I didn't know. What will happen to me?'

'Not just you, I'm afraid, Mr Plimpton. The Time Laws give us the power to remove your family as well.'

The unfortunate Mr Plimpton covered his face and rocked to and fro. Jane's heart went out to him.

'Perhaps,' said Luke, sternly, 'if you cooperate fully then your family might be spared.'

Jane was certain this magnanimous attitude was only because he didn't want a pod full of Plimptons, but it appeared to be effective.

Henry Plimpton lowered his hands. 'Oh, yes, yes. Anything I can do to assist.'

Jane nodded. 'So again, why did you do it?'

'Never mind that,' said Luke. '*How* could he do it? It's only the 20th century. Where did he get the technology from? People here barely have fire. They've only just stopped living in caves and eating raw mammoth.'

'Unkind but accurate,' observed North.

'It was sent to me.'

Back in the pod, Ellis and North looked at each other.

Parrish scoffed. 'What? By post, I assume?'

'I don't know. I just came home from work one day and there was a crate on the doorstep.'

Lockland frowned at Parrish and continued. 'Addressed to you?'

'Yes.'

'By name?'

'Yes.'

'Bit of a miracle it wasn't pinched,' said Parrish.

'That's what I thought. Anyway, electronics have always been my hobby and I put it all together in the shed.' He smiled tremulously at Lockland. 'There were full instructions and I'm quite skilled with my hands.'

'She's good at this,' said North. 'Extracting information, I mean. Quiet and unthreatening but persistent.'

Luke, rummaging among the papers on the mantelpiece, said, 'And then you jumped forwards one week to get the winning lottery numbers.'

He nodded. 'And then, afterwards . . . when I got back . . . it . . . well, it just shorted out. Bang. Just like that. I'd only just got clear. It nearly took me with it.' He shook his head. 'It was a nasty shock, I can tell you. I panicked and locked the shed door and haven't been near it since.'

Luke turned to Matthew. 'Residual radiation?'

He shook his head. 'A little. Nothing to cause any alarm.'

He turned back to Henry Plimpton. 'Did you keep the crate? Or the instructions?'

Henry Plimpton shook his head.

'Did you notice anything unusual about the crate?'

'Other than it containing the parts for a time machine? Not really.'

Jane peeled her elbow off the chair, examined the shiny spot with distaste and said again, 'Why did you do it, Mr Plimpton?'

Luke gestured around. 'Isn't it obvious?'

'He's such a sweetheart,' said North to Ellis.

Henry Plimpton flushed. 'It may not be much to you but this is our home.'

'Which you endangered by building an illegal time machine in it. Which subsequently blew up.'

'I didn't know it was illegal. I certainly didn't know it was going to blow up.'

Luke ignored this. 'Weren't you suspicious at all?'

'Well, I didn't really think it would work. I was quite surprised when it did.'

'And then you indulged in a spot of illegal time travel. For the purpose of cheating the lottery. What were you going to do with the money, Mr Plimpton?'

Henry said nothing.

Jane said gently, 'Mr Plimpton ... Henry ... you're due a long prison sentence at the very least. Why would you take such a risk?'

There would have been a long silence except for the bass thudding through the ceiling. Finally, his voice little more than a whisper, he said, 'For them. For my family. So I could leave.'

Luke sneered. 'You wanted the money so you could run away?'

'No. I wanted the money to give to them so I could leave. So I would know they were provided for. Without me.'

'You've got a girlfriend?' said Luke in disbelief.

'Of course not,' he said, indignantly. 'I'm a married man.'

Matthew could hear Mrs Plimpton crashing around in the kitchen behind him and wondered if any member of this family was capable of doing anything quietly. Or even if any of them actually knew the meaning of the world silence.

74

'And then what? After you'd left them. What were you going to do?'

Mr Plimpton twisted his small, plump hands. 'Live alone. In a little flat somewhere. In the country. By myself. Before I go insane. Somewhere quiet. Where I could enjoy some peace. Hear the birds sing. So they would stop talking at me. All the time. So I could eat what I want. When I want. Sleep when I want. Read. I can't remember the last time they left me alone long enough even to read a newspaper, let alone a book. I wanted to listen to a little music. Real music. Not something shaking the plaster from the ceiling.'

Instinctively they all looked up to the ceiling.

'You had a time machine, Henry. Why not just push off and leave them?'

He sat upright in his chair, pathetic but oddly dignified. 'Oh no – they're my family. It is my job to provide for them.' He buried his face in his hands again. 'What will happen to me?'

Silence – or as close to it as could ever be got in the Plimpton household – descended upon the room. Because that was a very good question. And one to which they all knew the answer.

5

'Time to check in on them,' said Ellis, putting down his mug and standing up. 'Are you coming?'

'If it's all the same to you, sir, I'll stay and pilot the drone safely home.'

Checking his weapon, he exited the pod and entered the 20th century. Having confirmed his destination and the route before he left the pod, it took him no more than a few minutes to find Seventeen Beaver Avenue.

The clean-up crew were waiting silently in the alleyway behind the house. The inhabitants of Beaver Avenue, knowing trouble when they saw it, were nowhere to be seen.

'Through the gate,' he said. 'The pod is inside the wooden structure on your left. Be aware this is a residential area. Quick and clean, please. The illegal will be delivered to you in a few minutes. Collect and go.'

They nodded and opened the gate. The dogs took one look and backed off to the other end of the garden. Ellis proceeded up the path to the back door, where he was met by an outsized and outraged Mrs Plimpton.

Blocking the doorway completely, she demanded to know,

'What is it? Who are you? What's happening? What are you doing to my Henry?'

He could see she was upset. Tear tracks had run through her heavy make-up leaving her face looking like a ploughed field. Her startlingly auburn hair was falling down. She was only two steps from hysterics.

He made his voice calm and soothing. 'All in good time, madam. Perhaps you'd like to make us all a cup of . . .' He ran his mind back over 20th-century habits and preferences. 'Tea.'

The words appeared to act as some kind of magic talisman. Mrs Plimpton immediately turned back into the kitchen and began to fill the kettle. Ellis slipped past her into the next room.

A very unprofessional-looking tableau met his eyes. An unsecured Henry Plimpton was neither zip-tied nor face down on the floor babbling his confession as fast as he could go. In fact, Major Ellis was not convinced that leaving the prisoner to sit comfortably in his own armchair was official Time Police procedure. Nor should two of the arresting officers be murmuring gently and reassuringly to him. Of all of them, only Parrish, still rummaging through the mess of papers on the mantelpiece, appeared to be doing his job properly.

As Major Ellis said a long time afterwards, it was at this point that the . . . uniqueness . . . of this team began to make itself apparent.

Things were to get worse. The kitchen door opened to reveal Mrs Plimpton staggering slightly behind a large and heavily laden tray – because in the Plimpton household, tea was always accompanied by biscuits, cake and scones.

Mindful of his manners, Matthew stepped up and took the

heavy tray from her and Lockland pulled out the coffee table for him to set it down. Ellis rolled his eyes and sighed.

Parrish picked up a steaming mug and said, conversationally, 'So – this is tea, is it? It looks absolutely bloody awful. You know, I'm sure the 20th century would be a much more cheerful place if you all stopped slowly poisoning yourselves with . . .' He caught Ellis's eye. 'Mm . . . this looks delicious.'

They were joined by the Plimpton offspring who had had – by the process of osmosis, presumably – become aware of refreshments and left their natural habitats to help themselves.

In the flurry of the chase, Luke had caught only a very fleeting glance of the younger Plimptons, and that at some speed, and this was his first chance to see them properly. His proud boast had always been that not much rendered him speechless – he now realised this was no longer something of which he could claim.

Both *les enfants Plimptons* were so heavily tattooed as to suggest they were perhaps considering careers in the Merchant Navy. Or – and this seemed much more likely – they had been compulsorily tattooed by the authorities as a warning to others; he could see the sense of that.

The male Plimpton was encased from head to toe in camouflage gear, from which large, wobbling white areas were already spilling over in a way he, Luke, couldn't feel met even basic military requirements. On the other hand, his hairstyle would have won instant Time Police approval, being so short it was merely a dirty shadow on his head.

The daughter, while nowhere near as large as her brother, was an equally arresting sight. Long skeins of purple and blue false hair hung down around her face. Her make-up was astonishing, and for some reason, a small ring protruded from one nostril, purpose unknown. Luke wondered briefly if perhaps her mother clipped a dog lead to it and took her out for walkies.

She was gazing at Luke with an alarming expression – well, it was alarming him, anyway. Too late he remembered the AI statistics concerning the lack of young men in this area.

'Are you really a policeman? That must be so exciting.'

Her brother intervened. 'Kylie, don't talk to them.'

'Why – what's going on?'

'You don't talk to the pigs. Remember?'

'Dear God,' said Luke, staring around and visibly appalled. 'Do you actually keep livestock in the house?'

'I think,' said Ellis, drily, 'you'll find he's referring to us.'

Luke leaned insolently against the mantelpiece and took his time looking Plimpton junior up and down. 'They're calling *us* pigs? Have you seen the size of *them*? Have *they* seen the size of them?'

The younger Plimpton took a hasty step towards him. Luke straightened up. 'Bring it on, buster.'

'Enough, Parrish.'

'So we're allowed to shoot them but not insult them?'

'I said, *enough*.' He turned to the younger Plimptons. 'We'll call you if we need a statement.'

Magic words. Pausing only to heap his plate with a gravity-defying pile of food, Dwayne disappeared upstairs. His sister lingered in the doorway, peered at Luke through her hair, smiled in what she probably imagined was a beguiling manner and returned whence she had come. Ten seconds later, the music started up again. It would seem that if you wanted to kiss the sky, you'd better learn how to kneel. *On your knees, boy!*

79

Matthew, who never missed an opportunity to eat everything put in front of him – Jane had no idea how he stayed so skinny – finished everything on the plates and when it was all gone, Mrs Plimpton disappeared back into the kitchen with the tray.

The room seemed to draw a deep breath.

'Bearing in mind this is a training mission,' said Ellis, 'I invite you to submit your reasons for taking Mr Plimpton into custody.'

'He broke the law,' said Lockland, red-faced but determined.

'Illegal time machine,' said Farrell.

'His dogs bit me,' said Parrish.

'Are there any reasons for *not* taking him into custody?'

A thoughtful silence fell.

'Don't want a pod full of Plimptons,' said Parrish.

'He won't do it again,' said Jane, quietly.

Matthew looked at the cowed figure in the armchair. 'Actually . . .' He stopped.

'Yes, Farrell?'

'Actually, sir, I think perhaps we should leave him here.'

'Because . . . ?'

'So we can keep an eye on him. Whoever sent him the crate might try to contact him again.'

'Well done, Farrell. An interesting thought. A word outside, if you please, Parrish.'

Once outside in the garden, Ellis checked carefully in all directions and then, having ascertained they were completely out of sight and alone, suddenly and violently pushed Parrish back against the wall.

Parrish was outraged. 'Ow. What the hell? Are you allowed to do that to junior ranks?'

'Hand it over.'

Parrish was suddenly still. 'Sorry, sir, not with you.'

'Hand it over.'

'Hand what over?'

'The lottery ticket.'

There was a tiny, almost infinitesimal pause. 'Sorry, sir, not with you.'

'The lottery ticket. The one you took from underneath the clock. The one you were asking about when you said, "Where is it?" to Henry Plimpton and everyone else thought you were asking about the pod. Give it to me, now, and if you say "Sorry, sir, not with you" one more time, I will beat you to a bloody pulp and then remove the ticket from your possibly lifeless body. Choose life, Parrish. Give me the damned ticket.'

The pause was much longer this time and then, very slowly, Parrish unzipped a pocket and pulled out a crumpled slip of paper.

'Hand it over.'

He did so.

Holding his eye, Major Ellis stepped back, tore the ticket into tiny pieces, let them fall, and then ground them into the damp earth with his heel.

The two of them looked at each other.

'Why would you do that, Parrish? Your family is rich.'

'My father is rich. I'm not.'

'But you will be. One day. And how would you ever have cashed in the ticket?'

Parrish sighed and stared over Ellis's shoulder for a moment. Lowering his voice, he said, 'I'd have thought of something. Because that money . . .' he nodded down at the mangled remains of the ticket, '. . . would have enabled me to be my own man. I could have bought myself out of the Time Police – and don't tell me there wouldn't have been massive rejoicing on your part because I'm not stupid and I know very well how much no one wants me there. But with this money I could have met my father on equal terms. Well, not equal because he'd still have about a hundred times more money than me, but I wouldn't have been the dependent pauper he sees whenever he looks at me. That money would have bought me some respect.'

For the first time, Major Ellis, himself a much-loved son of beloved parents, put himself in the shoes of Luke Parrish, son of an indifferent and absent father, and now forced on to the Time Police, who didn't want him either. Was it possible that many of his exploits – especially the more spectacular ones – were nothing more than a young man shouting, 'Look at me, Dad. Please look at me'? It was at this moment that Major Ellis realised that leading this team might be more challenging than he had anticipated.

'No, it wouldn't,' he said quietly. 'Trust me, Luke, you can't buy respect. It has to be earned. You can't swagger up to your father, pockets stuffed with stolen money and expect him to regard you as an equal. Why are you trying to compete with him financially, anyway? You'll never be his equal in that area. He's one of the richest men on the planet. You need to find your own area in which to excel.'

'Well, I'm not going to do that trapped here in the bloody Time Police, am I?'

It was on the tip of Ellis's tongue to agree but he changed his mind slightly, saying, 'Possibly not, but if you open up your mind to the opportunities you will find during your time with us, we can help you lay a solid foundation on which to build. You're going to be in some tough situations, meet some unpleasant people and probably have to do some things you don't want to. How you handle yourself through all that is entirely up to you, but – and I'll only make this offer once – if you ever feel the need for guidance or advice, knock on my door. It's going to be a long hard road for you and it'll be even longer and harder if you try to take a shortcut.'

Staring down at the muddy grass, Parrish nodded. 'I'm on report again, aren't I?'

'Son, your report is so crowded I doubt there's even room. Now then – you led this mission. I asked for the team's opinions on what to do with Plimpton. You're the team leader today – what is your formal recommendation, Mr Parrish?'

Parrish drew a hasty breath to speak, then paused and took a moment to think properly.

Ellis waited patiently.

Finally, Parrish said, 'I recommend we follow Farrell's suggestion and leave him here. I think, in the heat of the moment, we had forgotten the most important part of his statement, which was that he didn't initiate this. He's just someone's pawn. Someone deliberately sent him the wherewithal to make a pod. I recommend we monitor Henry Plimpton and see what, if anything, happens next.'

'Except . . .'

'Except what?'

'Think, Parrish. You're supposed to be bright. Stop thinking about yourself for five minutes and concentrate.'

Luke stared at the ground, concentrating as instructed. 'Oh.'

'Say it aloud.'

'Well, Farrell's plan is a good one except that I personally don't think they – whoever they are – will ever come back – I know I wouldn't – but I suppose there's always a chance that whoever left the wherewithal to build the machine will contact Henry Plimpton again. It's just . . .'

He paused, trying to assemble his thoughts while still juggling guilt, shame, embarrassment and . . .

'Go on, son. You're nearly there.'

And then he had it. 'Sunday.'

'What about it?'

'He said he jumped to next Sunday. To check the winning numbers. Which means that when next Sunday arrives, Henry Plimpton will already be there. We can't leave him here, otherwise there'll be two of him here at the same time.'

'Well reasoned, Mr Parrish. Your recommended course of action?'

'We inform Henry Plimpton of our – your – decision to take him into custody. For seven days at least. For interrogation. After which we will return him to his loving family and monitor the situation.'

'Excellent plan, Parrish. And your next move?'

'I round up the team and we make our way back to the pod before the 20th century kills us all.'

'The clean-up crew is waiting outside the gate. You don't need me here. Carry on.'

'But what happens when we return him to his family?' said Lockland anxiously, as Parrish issued his instructions. 'They'll just go back to making his life a living hell.'

'It's not our job to fix his life, Lockland. He should count

84

himself lucky he's only getting seven days' incarceration. If it wasn't for the faint possibility he might be contacted again, he would have got life. Or worse.'

'But think what he'll be coming back to.'

'And lucky to have it.'

She said nothing.

'Stop that.'

'Stop what?'

'That.'

'I'm not doing anything.'

'Exactly.'

'Please, Luke.'

He said in exasperation, 'What the hell do you expect me to do?'

'Persuade him to be more assertive,' she said, and then blushed at the irony.

Henry Plimpton had been offered the opportunity to bid farewell to his family, who were taking the opportunity to make their views known to him. And to their neighbours through the party walls. And possibly even to those on the other side of the street. The air was full of raised Plimpton voices. Mrs Plimpton hung around his neck, wailing. Jane's attempts to reassure her he would almost certainly be returned to them in a week's time were just a light breeze in the wind tunnel of her lamentations. The unfortunate Henry Plimpton was barely visible behind his family. They broke off at Luke's re-entrance.

Luke placed himself in front of their hapless prisoner.

'Henry Norman Plimpton.' His voice rang around the room.

'Oh God.' Henry Plimpton closed his eyes.

'Henry Norman Plimpton, you will accompany us to Time

Police HQ to give a full statement. You will be required to answer all questions fully and completely. Failure to comply will lead to a period of incarceration, the length to be decided by a court convened for that purpose. The extent of your cooperation will be taken into account when determining the length of your detention.'

'Doesn't he go on?' whispered Farrell to Lockland.

Both Mrs and Miss Plimpton burst into tears again. A second later, Mr and Master Plimpton followed suit. Even the dogs began to howl.

'Do something,' said Lockland to Parrish over the cacophony.

'Why?'

'You're upsetting them.'

'Lockland – *we're the Time Police*. They should count themselves lucky they're not all in chains and their . . . home . . . a smoking hole in the ground.'

From across the room, Matthew looked over and raised an eyebrow.

'And you can pack it in as well,' said Luke. 'This *I don't talk to anyone* routine isn't cutting any ice with me, you know.'

Jane touched his arm. 'Luke, please. Look at them. They're terrified and there's no need. Can't you just . . . you know . . . be a bit . . . nicer? Calm things down a little. Before they all have hysterics. There's more of them than us.'

'Yeah,' said Farrell, 'and they're a lot bigger than us as well.'

'Oh, for heaven's sake.' Luke cleared his throat and began again. 'Henry Norman Plimpton.'

The family visibly braced themselves, clutching each other for support.

'On behalf of the Time Police and by the authority vested in

86

me by that organisation, it is my honour to thank you publicly for the unnamed but vital services you have performed for the Time Police today.'

'You'd better get back there,' said North to Ellis as he entered the pod. 'I rather think our Mr Parrish might be snatching defeat from the jaws of victory.'

'I can't be bothered,' said Ellis, sinking into his seat. 'We'll let him screw up and then shoot him as he comes up the ramp.'

Luke was well into his stride. 'Your devotion to duty, your selfless dedication and hard work have ensured that justice has been done today. Your name will ring forever in the halls of the Time Police.'

Farrell nudged him. 'Don't get carried away.' And indeed, the young, female Plimpton had dried her tears and was now regarding Luke with glowing admiration. And something else he found vaguely disquieting.

Plonking herself directly before him, she smiled. 'Hello. My name's Kylie. What's yours?'

He stared and then looked quickly away, realising for the first time that the poor girl had something metallic embedded in her belly button. Obviously at some time in her past, a surgical procedure had gone horribly wrong; she deserved his compassion, not his condemnation. He would be the first to admit there were many areas in which he wasn't particularly over-endowed – respect, punctuality, self-discipline, or any other Time Police virtue you cared to name, for example – but in one particular area, he was world-class.

Bowing slightly, he murmured, 'Madam, I am honoured, but to be allowed to address the daughter of the famous Henry Plimpton is a privilege to which I could not possibly aspire.'

'You could try,' she said, hopefully.

'And, sadly, fail. Please accept my compliments and best wishes for a long and prosperous life.'

He bowed again.

She blushed. Henry Plimpton blushed. Jane blushed in sympathy. It's possible the dogs blushed, too.

Back in the pod, Ellis was snorting with laughter and even North looked amused.

Ellis pulled himself together. 'Parrish, report.'

'Job done, sir. Henry Plimpton is ready for collection. His time machine has been safely destroyed. Sadly, no radiation cloud is wreaking improvements on Lower Spurting.'

'Get yourself back here, then.'

Once outside, they handed a visibly terrified Henry Plimpton to the clean-up crew and began to make their way back down the alleyway.

'Why are you limping?' demanded Farrell of Parrish. 'The dog barely broke the skin.'

'Well, firstly for sympathy and secondly, the dog is from the late 20th century. Have you any idea how dirty these people are? Dirt, decay and death everywhere. Disease is rife, you know. You wouldn't believe some of the things they go down with. And if you're really ill, they send you to a hospital so their special germs can finally finish you off.'

Farrell blinked at him. 'Where do you get all this rubbish from?'

'Old newspapers. It was a terrible time, you know. The infrastructure was failing. People were eating rats and selling their children.'

Lockland shook her head. 'None of that's true.'

'Well, there was a major civil war some years later so someone must be eating rats and selling their kids. Or possibly the other way around.'

'Luke, what have you been reading?'

'*Daily Mail.*'

'Isn't that banned?'

'That's why I'm reading it.'

Emerging from the alleyway they found, to their dismay, that the crowd had not dispersed. They were not, however, the same recruits they had been two hours ago.

'This is an illegal assembly,' said Luke, sternly. He drew himself up and said commandingly, 'Disperse. Be about your business.'

'I think it's all rather gone to his head, don't you?' murmured Ellis.

'Here,' said someone. 'You SWAT?'

'What is this SWAT?' whispered Parrish to Farrell. 'Do you know?'

He shrugged his ignorance. 'Is that Sealed With A Loving Kiss?'

'No,' whispered Jane. 'That's SWALK.'

Parrish stared at her. 'How do you know?'

'Dunno,' said Lockland, who all her life had dreamed of receiving a letter marked SWALK.

The crowd hadn't finished. 'So what's with old Henery?'

'Mr Plimpton is assisting us with our enquiries,' said Luke, haughtily. And rashly, as it turned out.

'Wrong thing to say,' muttered Ellis. He stood up. 'We may have to go and save the day after all.'

An unmistakeable air of hostility was surrounding Team 236.

'They're not going to let us through,' muttered Lockland.

Luke sighed. 'Oh, for God's sake. I just want to go home.'

Neither of his colleagues found anything about that to argue with.

He sighed again. 'Obviously, once again it's all up to me.' He struck a dramatic pose. 'Lower Spurting is safe. All thanks to Henry Plimpton.'

No one looked impressed. Or even grateful.

'What?' said someone. 'What does that mean?'

'It means you get to live a while longer, you pathetic little arse-wipe.'

'What?'

'Henry Plimpton – saviour of the universe.'

'What?'

Stamping to attention, he snapped off a magnificent salute. 'Hail Henry.'

'Um . . . hail Henry,' echoed Jane, loyally.

Farrell nodded, expressionless.

'He never bloody salutes me,' muttered Ellis. He opened his com. 'Parrish, get your arse back here *now*.'

6

Back at TPHQ, their first duty was to return their weapons. Parrish was reluctant to hand his in. Going armed was the mark of a qualified officer.

'What do you care?' said Farrell, carefully depositing his weapon in the lock box and signing the sheet. 'You're always saying you can't wait to get out of this place.' But Parrish had found something else to complain about.

Scanning the assignment list posted on the wall, he said, 'Team Two-Three-Five have had three assignments so far. We've only had one. Why have we only had one?'

Farrell shrugged. 'Well, it wasn't exactly a huge success, was it? The whole town knew we were there. And then you were bitten by a tiny dog.'

'It wasn't that tiny.'

'And you nearly had to marry the daughter.'

'Yes, but they gave us tea, which was nice,' said Jane. She turned to Luke. 'Will we be in trouble over that? What if Grint and the other team find out? Can they make trouble for us?'

'How could we possibly be even more disparaged than we are already?' said Luke, handing over his own sonic and string

91

and scribbling his signature. 'But they might make trouble for Ellis and North.'

'That's Major Ellis and Officer North to you,' said North, calmly, appearing in the doorway. 'And who might be making trouble for us?'

'That idiot Grint,' said Parrish.

'That's Lt Grint to you,' said Lt Grint, appearing behind North in the doorway. 'Report to me afterwards.'

Jane closed her eyes, wondering if the day could get any worse, but Parrish was made of sterner stuff. 'After what?'

North intervened, physically placing herself between Parrish and Grint. 'Can I help you, sir?'

'I've come to look at the idiots who couldn't even capture a civilian properly.'

'Plimpton wasn't doing any harm,' said Parrish hotly, completely forgetting his earlier enthusiasm for the complete annihilation of the Plimpton family, their bloody dogs *and* most of Lower Spurting.

'Who are you to judge? You haven't seen what we've seen.'

'Those times are gone,' said North, quietly.

'They'll be back soon enough if you don't get your idiot team in order.'

'Hey,' said Parrish, indignantly. 'I have it on good authority that I'm lazy, careless and lacking in respect, but I'm not an idiot.'

'You're more than an idiot, Parrish. You're a bloody liability. You and the rest of your idiot team. All you had to do was bring in one illegal . . .'

'Which we did.'

'. . . destroy his equipment . . .'

'Which we did. Really not seeing the problem here.'

'Your prisoner was neither restrained nor unconscious.'

'He's been brought back for questioning. A bit tricky if he's out cold – or, of course, the preferred Grint method – dead.'

'It's what we do, girlie.'

'Yeah? Like at Kiev? The great Victory of Kiev? Two days' vicious hand-to-hand fighting. Three survivors: two Kievans and one Time Police officer, who whips out his gun, kills the two Kievans and claims the victory. The great victory, my arse.'

'That's enough, Parrish,' said North quietly and he subsided.

Lt Grint was a big man who could loom with the best of them. He loomed now. 'What is your problem, Parrish?'

Seeing that Parrish was all set to explain exactly what his problem was – and probably with gestures – North interposed herself between them again. 'Thank you, Trainee Parrish. Dismissed.'

'But . . .'

'I said, *dismissed*.' This was North. There was no need for her to raise her voice. Lockland, watching carefully, could only sigh.

Parrish slammed the door behind him.

Despite being eight inches shorter, North had no difficulty looking Grint in the eye. Ten centuries of aristocratic ancestors, all accustomed to getting exactly what they wanted, exactly when they wanted it, and giving the peasants hell if they didn't deliver, lined up behind her. 'Major Ellis asked me to say Captain Farenden is looking for you, sir.'

Grint paused for a moment for everyone to benefit from his Time Police stare. 'Farrell – get your bloody hair cut.' And then slammed the door behind him.

Matthew watched him go. 'Tosser.'

North wheeled around. 'Farrell . . .'

He sighed. 'They want you to talk. You talk. They're still not happy. Yes, yes, I know. I'm on report as well.'

He slammed the door behind him. The room was suddenly testosterone-free.

North surveyed the remaining member of her team. 'Idiots.'

'Not all of them,' said Lockland, defensively.

North regarded her in a not-unsympathetic manner. 'You quite like him, don't you?'

Lockland stared at the floor. 'I wasn't sure it was allowed.'

'Well, I think as long as you don't actually have sex in front of senior officers, they're generally OK with it. Does he know?'

She shook her head again and the usual unwanted colour flooded her cheeks.

'Why don't you say something to him?'

'I don't want to be just another notch on his bedpost.'

'What's preventing you from making him another notch on your bedpost?'

Jane sighed again.

North was amused. 'What's the matter? Don't you have any notches?'

'I'm not even sure I have a bed post.'

Leaving the Armoury, North met Major Ellis in the corridor.

'Well, sir. Wasn't that an exciting afternoon? I feel the need for a team-leader-financed beverage coming on.'

'Why?'

'Lockland got her man, sir. Did you miss it?'

'Actually, there was so much going on . . .'

94

'Good, wasn't it?'

'Are you sure it was Lockland who actually arrested him?'

'She did, sir. Check the recording.'

'I think we should destroy that recording. In the interests of everyone's credibility.'

'Agreed, sir. So – this drink then . . .'

He sighed. 'Bollocks.'

'Ah. Do I detect a St Mary's expletive?'

He looked down at himself. 'I should get cleaned up.'

'I was hoping you would, sir. Shall we say in twenty minutes, in the bar?'

'What can I get you?'

She pondered. 'Something expensive. And with an umbrella, I think.'

There were three recreational facilities at TPHQ. The first, designated the 'Pig's Bar', was for those who, for whatever reason, couldn't be bothered to make the effort. For those returning from a mission covered in blood and mud and who lacked the strength or inclination to shower and change – this was the place. Or for those fresh (or otherwise) from the gym. The dress code was very informal. Only nightwear was discouraged – Commander Hay had made her displeasure known to those who drank in their pyjamas – but almost anything else was acceptable.

The second bar, located on the second floor, enjoyed a view out over the Thames and was for those who were neat, clean and not actually bleeding.

A third bar, on the top floor, although democratically open to all, was usually frequented only by very senior officers, it being felt the organisation as a whole benefitted from them being up there out of harm's way while everyone else got on with doing real things in the real world.

Major Ellis had tactfully chosen the second floor. There were fewer fights and the view was better.

They settled themselves and North sipped her drink. Ellis couldn't help noting she was one of the few people able to drink from a glass containing a paper umbrella without blinding herself.

'You've been with us for a couple of years now, Officer North. How are you finding it?'

'Good, thank you.'

'I'm still not completely sure what made you leave St Mary's in the first place.'

'Well, I wanted to run the place, but I could see that was never going to happen. Then when I came here to give evidence against those illegals who forced Max and me to jump to 1st-century Jerusalem, I rather liked what you were doing here.'

'So you thought you'd run this place instead?'

'Well, not immediately, of course. I estimate it will take between ten and twelve years.'

He blinked. 'I was joking.'

'I wasn't.'

In another part of the building, things weren't going as well. Parrish had disappeared, presumably in search of his blonde from Logistics. Lockland had been detained by North, so Farrell heaved his gear over his shoulder and set off for his cubicle.

He was diverted along the way.

In Matthew's experience, the Time Police and the Institute

of Historical Research at St Mary's Priory had very little in common. They had no joint purpose and no shared goals. St Mary's – as they will explain at tiresome length, do not do time travel – *so* sci-fi. They 'investigate major historical events in contemporary time', and tend to regard the Time Police as a bunch of illiterate, knuckle-dragging morons whose job could better be done by semi-trained gibbons coming in one morning a week.

The Time Police, on the other hand, *are* time travellers and generally regard anyone pretentious enough to be investigating major historical events in contemporary time as being dangerously far up their own arses. It was generally felt on Time Police turf that the St Mary's 'Who us? But we're only a bunch of harmless academics' attitude fooled no one. They were certainly going to bring the timeline crashing down around everyone's ears one day. And, in fact, had nearly done so on several occasions. And no one at Time Police HQ believed St Mary's attempts to persuade the authorities that something hadn't gone badly wrong with their infamous jump to Troy, because the evidence of the Time Map said otherwise, no matter how cleverly St Mary's thought they'd buried the evidence. And dodged the investigation afterwards. And there had been one or two other instances they'd been lucky to get away with, as well. The prevailing feeling was that one day, sooner or later, St Mary's famous luck would run out and those too-clever-by-far, dangerously over-educated imbeciles would do some serious damage. The upside being that it would at least give the Time Police a good reason to shoot them.

So – not a lot of common ground between them.

The difference between the organisations could possibly

best be illustrated by their corridors. St Mary's corridors are comprised of bare boards, and are littered with broken bicycles, pieces of sarcophagi, various bits of armour and spare welding equipment, together with the occasional dollop of chicken shit. The pockmarked walls are decorated with an eclectic range of official notices, graffiti, scribbled reminders, scorch marks, next week's lunch menu, dubious stains and directions to the nearest defibrillation point.

Time Police corridors are furnished with the latest sound-reducing materials and contain neat notice boards displaying official bulletins, mission statements, the new diversity policy, instructions to walk in single file and forbidding running in the corridors.

Fighting in the corridors, however, was another matter.

Matthew rounded a corner, heaving his kitbag over his shoulder. His plans for the evening were simple: shower, change, get something to eat and settle down with a technical manual. Maybe watch a holo later . . .

There were five or six of them and they were waiting for him.

He was aware he was disliked. Regarded with suspicion. He'd spent a large part of his life at Time Police HQ – possibly more than with his parents at St Mary's – and they still didn't trust him. On the other hand, he'd always known his life here wouldn't be easy so he couldn't complain. Well, he could, but he didn't.

This – or something like this – happened to him occasionally now he was a member of the Time Police and attitudes towards him had hardened. Notices inviting people to report instances of bullying were posted at regular intervals throughout the building, but never acted upon, because it was generally recognised that if you couldn't handle a bit of high-spirited mischief from your colleagues then you weren't going to be much use in a tight situation. And – the old favourite, of course – if you couldn't take a joke, then you shouldn't have joined.

The group of men spread out across the corridor. His heart sank. He didn't recognise any of them but he recognised the type. These were older officers. Grunts. Not high rankers. Officers who'd been in a long time and would never rise any higher. Officers with fondly held memories of the good old days. When things were done the way they should be and they had the authority to do it. When people did as they were told or else. When people respected the Time Police properly. When being a Time Police officer really meant something.

They came with built-in resentment. Their lack of promotion would always be someone else's fault – never theirs. They were dimly aware that the organisation was changing around them but lacked the flexibility or intelligence to adapt. They were the sort who caught all the dull and dirty jobs if there were no trainees to do them. Old-fashioned in their outlook, they were being left behind in Commander Hay's new Time Police and they were about to take their resentment out on him.

'Look,' said someone. 'It's the St Mary's runt.'

'Is it?' said another. ''Cos with all that hair it looks like a girl to me.'

His tone implied that not only was *girl* the lowest of the low, but that there were far too many of them in the world who didn't know their proper place in the scheme of things.

From experience, Matthew knew that the worst thing he could do was show any reaction, but this was not how things normally went. This was not the usual push him about a bit and tip the contents of his bag over the floor situation. He caught a whiff of alcohol. They'd clearly been drinking somewhere – the Pig's Bar, probably – given themselves artificial courage, egged each other on – and here they were. He was going to have to defend himself and he was going to have to do it alone. Luke Parrish would be well entangled with his blonde by now and Lockland had been delayed by North and was somewhere behind him.

He shut his face down. No expression at all. He dropped his bag in front of him for the scant protection that would offer and put his back against the wall.

Slowly, they fanned out until he was completely surrounded.

Matthew Farrell had learned a lot from his early life. How to climb a chimney. How not to get stuck. How to avoid the worst blows. He had also learned not to run away. Dreadful things happened to apprentices who ran away from their masters. So following his instincts and experience, he stood his ground.

Grinning, someone produced a pair of scissors. 'Grint said to get your hair cut.'

Shit. He had a choice: he could fight like a tiger and hope no one gashed his carotid by accident. Or blinded him. Or he could just let them get on with it and hope . . . No, he couldn't. Matthew Farrell was his mother's son. She never fought fair and neither did he.

He picked up his bag and threw it at the three nearest. At the same time, he danced sideways and kicked a shaven-headed grunt on the knee. There was a shout of pain.

Sadly, that was as far as his resistance went. Someone grabbed him from behind. The scissors flashed in front of his eyes.

'Hold him still.'

He struggled as much as he was able. He could hear the

scissors snipping away. Something light and tickly fell across his face. Hair.

It was at this point that Jane, entirely minding her own business, appeared around the corner and saw immediately what was happening.

Her first thought was that she wished she'd gone back to her room by another route. That she was there safely now. She liked her room. But she wasn't in her room. She was here. And so was Matthew.

And then she saw the dark hair on the ground and genuine shock took over.

'What? What are you doing? Leave him alone.'

One of the officers hanging around the back – one of the ones not quite brave enough to be actively involved, turned, saw who was standing there and sneered. 'Push off, girlie. Unless you want us to do you, too.'

Suddenly they weren't all looking at Matthew. Suddenly some of them were looking at her. She went cold with the knowledge that something bad was about to happen and it was about to happen to her. Fear twisted a knot in her stomach. Her blood turned to ice-water. She had shoulder-length hair pulled tightly back into a plait. How easy would it be to hack that off? She took a step backwards and banged her head painfully on something metallic. Someone laughed. Which turned out to be a mistake because the object she'd just banged her head on was a fire extinguisher.

She gave no thought to any possible consequences, ripping it off the wall. She'd done this in training. It was easy, they'd said. Just pull the ring and point. She pulled the ring and pointed.

The extinguisher was designed primarily for extinguishing

fires, but self-defence came a close second and it performed well, covering everything in a thick, fire-suppressing, dirty-grey foam, but not for anything like long enough, and as the stream lost pressure and died away, it dawned on Jane that she possibly might have made things considerably worse.

Five or six foam-covered figures were looking for a fight and now she'd given them a reason.

'Jane. Over here with me.'

Still clutching the extinguisher, partly for moral support and partly because it might come in useful, she edged along the wall to stand alongside Matthew.

Both sides drew breath . . .

Someone walked around the corner and stopped dead. 'What the hell is going on here?'

They had no idea who had spoken but that was unimportant. Jane dropped the fire extinguisher with a clang, Matthew grabbed his bag and the two of them fled.

A solitary Time Police corridor, just like St Mary's, is now distinguished by blobs of hardened grey foam making interesting patterns up the walls.

There were repercussions, of course.

Ellis was not amused. 'Farrell, what the hell have you done to your hair?'

'It was me,' said Jane, blushing. 'You're always telling him to get it cut so I tried to tidy it up. I'm not very good.'

And indeed, they had spent twenty minutes in Matthew's room trying to tidy up his semi-bald patches. The result was regrettable.

'I don't think I've helped,' she'd said eventually, staring at him in the mirror. 'You now look as if you have a dreadful scalp condition.'

'Well, thank you, anyway. I'm very grateful. Cool move with the extinguisher.'

'I'm going to be in trouble over that, aren't I?'

He regarded her steadily for a moment – his usual precursor to saying something important. 'Jane, you should speak up for yourself more. This is the Time Police. They're not deep thinkers and most of them are the sort of people who equate quietness with stupidity.'

'You don't say much yourself.'

'I don't have to. I know I'm not stupid.'

'But they don't.'

'I don't care what they think.'

'But they can . . . I mean . . . sometimes they're a bit . . . you know . . . I mean, look at what they did to you.'

He shook his head. 'It's only hair. I've known far worse than anything this lot can do to me.'

She opened her mouth to ask, but something held her back. She could go along with that. If she asked him about his past, then he might ask her about hers and there was no way she was telling him about that cold, silent house and her grandmother's rasping voice and that eternal bell and always being so tired. Besides, that was another world now.

'I mean it,' he said. 'They don't bother me – mostly . . .' he added, remembering the scene in the corridor, 'but you don't want them starting on you.'

'I can handle myself,' she said, stoutly.

He smiled slightly.

'Well, I can.'

He said nothing.

'That's a very irritating habit, you know. I'm not surprised you get thumped in the corridors.'

'What is?'

'The way you say things by not saying anything at all. I'm pretty sure Luke thinks so, too.'

He shook his head. 'Luke's so wrapped up in himself I'm surprised he's even noticed.'

She gathered her courage. 'Why are you here, Matthew?'

He shrugged. 'Long story.'

'Which you're obviously not going to tell me.'

'It's not very interesting.'

'Well,' she surveyed her foam-splattered self, 'I'd better change. I'm in enough trouble as it is.'

He shrugged. 'Self-defence. I wouldn't worry about it. Tell them it was me if you like.'

'That doesn't seem fair.'

'Least I can do. Thanks.'

She smiled shyly. 'You're welcome.'

And now they were standing in front of Major Ellis. Who was still not amused. 'Farrell, get your hair cut properly. By someone who knows what they're doing. Not you, Lockland. You're banned from holding scissors within a three feet radius of Farrell. Forever.'

'Yes, sir.'

'Yes, sir.'

'Anything either of you want to tell me?'

'No, sir.'

'No, sir.'

There was a short silence and then they were dismissed.

Curiously, no one ever said anything about the illegal discharge of a fire extinguisher.

Later that day, Farrell applied for permission to return to St Mary's.

'Do you want to come, Jane?'

'Why?'

'Well, I feel I owe you.'

'No, I mean, why do you want to go back to St Mary's?' A thought occurred to her. 'You're not leaving the Time Police, are you?'

'No, of course not. I go to visit my parents occasionally and get my hair cut. Do you want to come? See if it's as bad as everyone says?'

She stared in astonishment. 'You go to St Mary's to get your hair cut? I didn't know you could do that.'

'Well, I don't tell people. They call me Mummy's Boy as it is.'

'Are we allowed? Are *you* allowed?'

'You heard the major. He told me to get my hair cut.'

'I think he envisaged you popping down the corridor to the barber, not jumping back through time and space.'

'He knows where I get my hair cut.'

'Will they give us a pod?'

He shrugged. 'Let's find out. If they won't, you can threaten to give me another haircut. Bet you they let us go then.'

North tapped on Ellis's door. 'Sir, I have a request from Farrell and Lockland for an afternoon's home leave.' She regarded her scratchpad disdainfully. 'And to get his hair cut.'

'You disapprove?'

'I have mixed feelings, sir. I don't want to stand in the way of him beginning to look like a proper officer, but to run home just to get your hair cut . . .' She held Ellis's eye. 'On the other hand, I do think it might be a good idea to get the pair of them out of the building for a while after that incident. Let things cool down a little.'

Ellis signed the authorisation and they were allowed. The senior mech pointed to a small pod in the corner, spoke into his com and thirty seconds later a yawning and grumpy mech dropped them off with instructions to be on this spot in four hours' time and not to keep him waiting.

It was Jane's first glimpse of St Mary's and she wasn't sure quite what to make of it. At first glance, it was beautiful. To her left, a long drive led up to a golden-stoned building smothered in some sort of creeper just beginning to glow red in the autumn sunshine. A mass of chimneys rose from the flat roof and a set of shallow steps led to a pair of nail-studded front doors. Off to her right, a small lake glittered and swans glided serenely on the smooth surface. She turned to Matthew. 'They're blue. All the swans are blue.'

'No, they're not. That one over there is pink.'

'But . . .'

He nodded in the direction of the front door. 'This way. I'd better sign you in.'

She looked around again. They were in the depths of the countryside and all she could hear was birdsong and a dog barking in the distance. 'This is St Mary's? It's so old. Where are the pods?'

'Out of sight in a hangar round the back. Come on.'

An elderly man signed them in and from there they made their way through the vestibule into the Great Hall. Jane stopped dead. It was all so very different to the Time Police. She could smell old building smells – dust, damp stone, mushrooms – all overlaid by the smell of toast, socks, sulphur and cabbage. The Hall was stuffed full of precarious-looking trestle tables, all sagging under the weight of files, scratchpads and screens. Scribbled whiteboards stood around or leaned against the walls. Post-it notes and scruffy pieces of paper were plastered randomly over every surface. A group of people clad in blue jumpsuits were bending over a data stack. One of them looked up, ghostly words and figures illuminating her face.

'Hey, Matthew. Your mum's not here. Do you want the Chief?'

He nodded. She spoke into her com and a few minutes later a silver-haired man to whom Matthew bore a passing resemblance appeared in the Hall.

They seemed quietly pleased to see each other.

'Hey, Matthew. Nice surprise.'

'Dad.'

'Back for the weekend?'

'No – just this afternoon. For a haircut.'

'Well, that's a relief. You look like Markham with mange.' He turned to Jane. 'Hello. Welcome.'

'Dad, this is my stylist, Jane Lockland. Jane, this is my dad, Leon Farrell.'

'Ah.' He regarded Matthew's hair again and grinned at Jane. 'Well, I'm sure it's very fashionable. Somewhere.'

'Mum's not here?'

'Your mother's in 9th-century Iceland. She's gone to check out Ingólfr Arnarson and his high-seat pillars. She'll be sorry to have missed you.'

'If you say so, Dad, but I don't think I can compete with actual Vikings.'

'I don't think either of us can. And volcanoes, glaciers, geysers, lava flows, whales and the Northern Lights, of course.'

Matthew grinned. 'How ever will she manage to pass the time?'

'Mikey's not here, either.' He looked suddenly vague. 'She, Adrian and Dieter are out somewhere . . . field-testing a pod.'

Matthew nodded. 'Understood. Going to see Auntie Lingoss.'

'She's up in R&D as usual. Do you have time for a coffee before your much-needed haircut?'

They made their way into a large dining room with gracious proportions, floor-to-ceiling windows, ornate but battered plasterwork, and the air of a heavily used room drawing breath before the next onslaught. Matthew went off to get the coffee and Jane and Matthew's dad seated themselves at a quiet table by the window.

He smiled at her, his blue eyes crinkling at the corners. She felt the usual blush begin.

'I'm pleased to see he's making friends. It's not always easy for him.'

A memory of the scene with the fire extinguisher flashed through her mind. Something warned her to say nothing. That Matthew wouldn't like it.

'He's a very private person,' she said.

'So . . . the hair?'

'Glue,' said Jane quickly, resigning herself to never going to heaven. 'The tube burst. I tried to cut it out but it didn't help.'

He smiled at her and said nothing in a way that perfectly conveyed his understanding. He really was nice, she thought, and just for one flickering moment she wondered how different her life would have been if she'd had such a father. To have a comforting presence there when she needed him. And best of all – someone who would always know when she needed him.

'Are you a member of the Time Police too, Jane?'

'Not a full member yet, sir, but I hope to be. Soon.'

'You don't have to call me "sir".'

'Oh. Um. No. All right,' said Jane, confused as to how to address him and resolving never to call him anything at all.

'Have you yet decided what you'll do after you complete your training?'

'Um, well, I'm not sure yet. I'm not even sure I'm going to get through my gruntwork.'

He smiled kindly. 'I'm sure you will. And with flying colours, too.'

Jane smiled back. 'Thank you. I hope so.'

'What do your parents say?'

'Um . . . my parents were killed in the Time Wars. I lived with my grandmother.'

'I'm sorry to hear that. Is that why you joined the Time Police?'

Memories of the murdered seagull resurfaced. 'No, it was a kind of spur of the moment thing.' She trailed off.

'Are you regretting it?'

'No,' she said, with sudden certainty. 'No, I'm not.'

He smiled again. 'Good.'

Matthew reappeared. 'Three coffees.'

To give Matthew and his dad time to talk together, Jane got up and walked the length of the room, looking out of the windows. Some sort of football match appeared to be taking place outside. Even through the windows she could hear the occasional scream of pain, which she was able to ignore until an unconscious body was stretchered past the window. No one took any notice so Jane decided she wouldn't either. She returned her attention to the conversation between Matthew and his father.

'So, how's it going, Matthew?'

'Good,' said Matthew, nodding. Jane could only assume he had forgotten the whole enforced-haircut thing.

'That's all I've got to tell your mother, is it? There will be extensive questioning when I tell her you've been here and the best I'm going to be able to come up with is *good*.'

Matthew thought for a moment. 'Very good.'

Leon nodded. 'You do know that if I can't satisfy her penetrating interrogation then she'll be jumping to TPHQ to find out for herself and that never ends well.'

Matthew grinned. 'All right then – in the interests of world peace – we've finished our basic training. Now we're on our six months' gruntwork. Jane's on my team, as well.'

'Just the two of you?'

'No – there's another. Luke. He couldn't come today.'

'Special assignment?'

'Sort of. Blonde in Logistics.'

Leon laughed. 'Understood. You know it's your mother's birthday soon?'

'Hadn't forgotten.'

'Try and make it back. I know she's looking forward to seeing you.' He looked at Jane. 'We'd be delighted to see you, Jane, as well.'

Jane glowed, but in a good way, just for once. 'That's very kind. Thank you.'

Leon looked at his watch. 'I must go. You'll find Miss Lingoss in R&D. They're having an exciting day up there.' He smiled at Jane and she smiled back because he really did have a very nice smile. And he looked so much like Matthew. Except for the eyes. Matthew's were a golden brown while his were a brilliant blue.

'Congratulations, Jane. You've picked an afternoon that will showcase St Mary's at its most . . . typical. Nice to have met you. Come and say goodbye before you go back.'

He disappeared.

'This way,' said Matthew, ushering her through the Hall. People waved and smiled.

'You're very popular,' said Jane in surprise, and then blushed at such a personal remark.

He grinned. 'I was the first baby ever born here. My mum had to send round a memo telling people I wasn't a draught excluder.'

He led her towards a magnificent but scuffed wooden staircase with ten shallow steps leading up to a half-landing. From there, the staircase branched right and left. They chose the right-hand stair, aiming for the gallery that ran around the Hall. Halfway up, however, they were elbowed aside by a small, round, very angry man swathed in yellow oilskins and a sou'wester. Pushing past them, he pounded on a door.

'Open up. I know you're in there, Andrew, you old fool.

111

It's coming through the ceiling again. I told you this would happen. I warned you. I don't know why you have to do this sort of thing inside the building. In fact, I don't know why the rest of us have to share a building with you and your bunch of madmen at all. None of us do. Open this door.'

There was silence from within. He pounded again.

'Andrew, my library contains one hundred and twenty-seven books on siege warfare. It's going to take more than you pretending you're not in to keep me out. Open this door.'

There was the sound of bolts being drawn back. The heavy door creaked open.

'Occy, is that you? My dear fellow, I had no idea you were there. Have you been knocking for long? Whatever are you wearing?'

'Never mind what I'm wearing. What's going on in here? I've got water coming through the library ceiling again.'

'I've no idea what you're talking about, Occy, and I certainly don't have time to stand here talking all day. If you must know, we're all about armour at the moment. Oh, hello, Matthew. Didn't know you were here. Dear boy, whatever have you done to your hair? Come in, come in. Not you, Occy.'

Too late. With much the same determined expression as Alexander heading for India, the yellow-clad figure surged through the door. Matthew followed on behind and Jane, wondering what she'd got herself into, brought up the rear.

A very large and cluttered room lay before her. Tables and desks were covered in tools, bits of metal, springs, coils, string, pots of glue, weapons, breastplates, hammers, strips of something that looked like cork and several Roman helmets. A tin of something dark and wriggling stood at her elbow.

She drew her hand back. 'Ew – what's that?'

Matthew leaned over. 'Just a can of worms they've opened.'

A stuffed chicken sat atop a battered cupboard that looked as if it might have been involved in a small fire at some point in its life. In the middle of the floor, in pride of place, stood an enormous circular inflated swimming pool, dangerously full of water, a large amount of which was slopping around on the floor. Most of the people present wore waders, including the woman with the clipboard and vibrant scarlet hair who was writing rapidly.

'This is my friend, Jane,' announced Matthew to the room in general and Jane tried not to glow with pride. 'Jane, this is R&D at St Mary's. This is where Practical History happens.'

Everyone ceased glaring at each other and beamed at their visitors.

'This is Professor Rapson.' A tall, skinny man with Einstein hair nodded vaguely. 'And this is Dr Dowson.' The small, fat man nodded vaguely. 'And this is Miss Lingoss.'

Lingoss waved her clipboard in greeting. 'Matthew, please tell me you've come about your hair.'

He nodded.

'Be with you in a minute. Just a few adjustments to make here.'

Matthew frowningly surveyed the room. 'I think you'll be safer up here,' he whispered, pulling out a stool and helping Jane up on to the table. 'They're not always completely up to speed re the exciting combination of electrical cables and sloshing water.'

About to thank him, Jane was distracted by a sudden and vast underwater disturbance. A flailing figure wearing the uniform of a Roman soldier erupted from the centre of the swimming pool, gasping for breath.

Fighting its way to the side of the pool, it rolled over the side – displacing transatlantic-liner amounts of water in the process – and clanged to the floor, wheezing and fighting for breath.

'Didn't work, then,' said the professor, disappointed.

Wordlessly, the armour-clad figure pulled off his helmet and shook his head.

Jane plucked at Matthew's sleeve. 'Is he all right?'

'Uncle Bashford? Yeah, he's fine.'

Concern for the unfortunate Mr Bashford evaporated far more quickly than the puddles of water on the floor were likely to do.

'Andrew, what is going on here?' enquired the short, round man, staring around in horror.

The professor turned, eyes aglow with what a kindly person would describe as enthusiasm and definitely not mania. 'Oh, you'll like this, Occy – Pontius Cominus.'

Dr Dowson snapped to attention. 'Really? How interesting. And does it work?'

They regarded the still gasping Bashford.

'Not quite.'

'Where did you put it?'

'On the inside of his breastplate.'

'Obviously not enough buoyancy to cancel out the weight of the armour.'

'No.'

'Shame.'

They stood in silent thought.

114

Jane nudged Matthew. 'What's Pontius Cominus? What is happening here? Is he in trouble?'

She was the recipient of the professor's full R&D beam. 'No, of course not, my dear. This is Practical History. This is where we make things happen.'

She blinked. 'You mean you make things work?'

'Not quite as often as I could wish, but yes. So glad you're here, Matthew – you can lend a hand. On three.'

They heaved Mr Bashford to his feet.

'What *are* you doing?' Jane persevered.

'Floating armour, my dear.'

They propped Bashford against the side of the pool, which sagged again, releasing still more water across the floor. Matthew dragged up a chair and helped him sit down.

Bashford nodded his thanks and croaked, 'Angus?'

'Of course.'

Standing on another chair he carefully lifted down the stuffed chicken which turned out not to be stuffed at all. Chicken and man crooned happily to each other.

It was at this moment that Jane realised that not only was everything she had ever heard about St Mary's absolutely true, she hadn't known the half of it. 'What is that?'

Lingoss was busy with her clipboard again, ticking off boxes. 'That's Angus. She's getting on a bit now so we put her up there to minimise the possibility of her being swept away in a tidal wave.'

Bashford was shrugging off his breastplate. Eager heads bent to examine it more closely.

'Damn,' said the professor. 'I was really hoping that would do it this time.'

'It nearly did,' said Bashford. 'I *was* drowning but only very slowly. It just wasn't quite enough to achieve escape buoyancy.'

Jane craned her head to see.

'Strips of cork,' said Matthew to her. 'Sewn underneath his breastplate. See.'

'I think I speak for everyone not actually a member of St Mary's: why?'

'390BC,' said the professor.

'Or possibly 387BC,' countered Dr Dowson.

They beamed at her, obviously under the impression that all was now crystal clear.

'Um . . .' said Jane.

'Rome was under attack,' said Lingoss. 'The army had lost the Battle of the Allia and needed to get a message into Rome, which was besieged at the time, and so a soldier named Pontius Cominus floated himself down the Tiber. Roman mail shirts weighed around thirty-five pounds. Some say he made a cork float. Some say he fashioned a cork life jacket. Some say he sewed cork strips into his armour. That's what we're trying out now.' She grinned wickedly. 'You're lucky you didn't come tomorrow.'

'Why?'

'Some reports say he used an inflated sheep's stomach. We have half a dozen being delivered tomorrow.'

'Sheep?'

'Oh, good heavens, no. Just the stomachs. We're still working on methods of inflating them. They rupture very easily.'

R&D shook its collective head at this massive flaw in sheep design.

The professor was examining the armour. 'It would appear

the cork strips are not sufficient, Miss Lingoss. All they do is cause him to sink more slowly. I'm thinking of tying more cork to his boots. Roman sandals were quite substantial so this would keep his other end afloat as well.'

The obliging Bashford sat quietly while his feet were enveloped in cork. Not something on everyone's job description.

'Can someone pass me my pen,' said Lingoss, suddenly. She wrote busily on Bashford's feet for a minute then pushed the pen into her hair where two or three of its fellows already resided. 'Ready when you are, professor.'

'In your own time then, Mr Bashford. I'm very hopeful this will be successful.'

Bashford passed Angus to Matthew. 'Can you hold her for a bit? She likes to feel involved. I think she enjoys it,' he said, hobbling awkwardly in his new platform soles. 'She sleeps a lot now, of course.'

'She slept a lot before,' said Lingoss.

'Well, yes, but now we treat her gently and try not to give her any shocks.' He lowered himself into the pool. 'This water's freezing.'

'So was the Tiber. We need everything to be as accurate as possible. So – in your own time, please.'

'Right,' said Bashford, letting go. 'I'm floating down the Tiber now.'

Oh no, he wasn't.

Later, Jane would find it hard to describe what happened next. Slowly and gracefully, Bashford upended himself, his upper torso sinking beneath the surface but his feet slowly rising above it. As she said afterwards, it was quite balletic. Within ten seconds, the only part of Bashford still above the

117

Tiber was his feet. To be more accurate – the soles of his feet, bobbing authentically.

People stared. 'What's he doing?'

Lingoss gave a shout. 'His feet are more buoyant than his head. They're pushing his head down into the water.'

'Interesting,' said one of the team. 'Do you think there's some sort of buoyancy ratio? Feet to head?'

'Well, you don't see many flotation devices for feet,' said another, 'so you may have a point.'

'I wonder if we could draw up some sort of equation.'

'Um, excuse me,' said Jane.

Everyone looked around.

'I'm up here. Look.' She pointed to the pool.

Written on the soles of Bashford's innovative but unsuccessful footwear were the words:

Matthew grinned at Jane. 'Lovely people here. Very poor grasp of priorities.'

Jane was horrified. 'Shouldn't we pull him out?'

'Yes, probably.'

It took the entire R&D team to yank him out. There was now nearly as much water on the floor as in the tank itself and an indignant Angus was giving a visual demonstration of the phrase *madder than a wet hen.*

'Enough for today, I think,' said Lingoss. 'We're upsetting Angus. And this young man is in desperate need of a haircut.'

'True,' said the professor, despondent over his failure. He brightened. 'Still, it's sheep's stomach day tomorrow. Something to look forward to. And next week we have the origins of the Sacred Geese. Which reminds me . . .' He turned to Miss Lingoss.

'Already sorted, professor,' she said. 'Geese arriving Tuesday. If you'll excuse me, everyone.'

She and Matthew disappeared for the haircutting session.

Remembering their manners, someone put a steaming mug in front of Bashford and another in front of Jane.

'Oh, thank you. What is it?'

'Tea.'

'Oh.' She floundered in a welter of social embarrassment. She hadn't enjoyed the tea given her by the Plimptons – it had tasted like cabbage water. They were all beaming at her. She smiled uncertainly and took a sip. Yep – still cabbage water. She put it down carefully, hoping they'd think she was leaving it to cool.

Matthew returned some twenty minutes later, his shorter hair rendering his bald spots considerably less conspicuous. His hair still wasn't styled to the demanding requirements of the Time Police but, as he said, that was their problem; it was time to go.

'Well,' said Jane, as they trotted down the stairs, 'I never thought I'd be somewhere where I wasn't the wettest person in the room.'

He stared in astonishment. 'You're not wet. Who told you that?'

'My grandmother. All the time.' She felt her cheeks begin the familiar burn. 'If you hear something twenty times a day, every day, you do begin to believe it after a while.'

'Well, your grandmother was wrong.'

She wasn't quite sure how to respond to that so she changed the subject. 'We mustn't be late for the pod.'

Matthew's dad escorted them outside.

'Nice to have met you, Jane.'

'And you, um . . .' She tailed away.

'Leon,' he said, and smiled as if she were the most important person in the universe. Her blush became very nearly incandescent.

She walked away a few paces to give Matthew and his father some privacy, breathing in the fresh air. There could not, she reflected, be a greater contrast between St Mary's and the Time Police. TPHQ was in the centre of London; St Mary's was out in the countryside – where it could do the least damage was the perceived wisdom of the Time Police. The Time Police dealt with Time; St Mary's with History – and each of them regarded themselves as of prime importance and the other as being a menace to society in general. She knew there had been a big battle fought here once and the Time Police – to use an expression – had had their arses handed to them on a plate. Part of the reason for Matthew's unpopularity, she guessed, although she suspected his being a long-haired weirdo would also be at the top of the list.

The pod turned up. Exactly on time. Because they were the Time Police and it was always Time that was important. Time is the framework of the universe. The empty room. History is just the furniture therein. To be moved around, added to or discarded as fashion dictated.

Entering the pod, she smiled shyly at Matthew. 'Sorry I didn't get to meet your mum.'

He just grinned. 'First member of the Time Police ever to say that.'

On their return, Jane met North in the corridor, who raised an eyebrow. 'What did you think of them?'

'Well,' she said, recalling her afternoon. 'Someone called Bashford nearly drowned while they were arguing about the best way to save him and his chicken got very upset. Two old men kept shouting at each other. They tipped the pool over and the flood of water shorted out the electrics. There was a woman with scarlet hair but she was very nice. They made me drink tea. It was horrible. Matthew's dad was nice, though.'

'You didn't meet his mother?'

'No, why?'

'Oh – no reason. It always amuses me to think that one day some unfortunate woman is going to find herself with the mother-in-law from hell.'

7

Every team was ranked after each assignment and the ratings posted in the main briefing room. Luke was surprisingly furious to find Team 236 at the bottom.

'We're just a bloody joke, aren't we?'

Major Ellis considered him for a moment. 'In what way?'

'Well, look at the assignments we get.'

'You've only had one.'

'Exactly my point.'

'What was wrong with it?'

'Henry Plimpton?'

'Would you rather have shot him?'

'No, but we haven't actually shot anyone at all, have we?'

'Did you want to?'

'Well . . . no . . . not really, but . . . we are the Time Police, after all. It's what the Time Police do.'

Ellis tried not to sigh. 'It's not all we do.'

'But you're famous for it.'

'And because we are famous for shooting on sight, we don't have to. These days it's usually enough for us just to turn up and give someone a hard look.'

'But . . .'

'I'm telling you – those days are gone.'

Jane looked at him, remembering her experience with Matthew in the corridor. 'Are they really?'

Ellis perched on the edge of a desk. 'Well, that's up to you and people like you, isn't it? The young ones just beginning to climb the rungs. You are the ones who will help to shape the sort of organisation the Time Police will become. Consider how things would have turned out if, for example, Lt Grint's team had gone after Henry Plimpton.'

Luke frowned, opened his mouth to speak, frowned again and then said, 'This is . . .' He stopped.

'More complex than you thought. Not used to making your own decisions, are you?'

'Not really. The old man always told me what he wanted from me and I did the opposite.'

'Lockland?'

'People always told me what to do.'

'Farrell?'

'I make up my own mind.'

Ellis stood up. 'I have a meeting with Commander Hay in ten minutes. Do you wish me to make your views regarding the quality and quantity of your assignments known to her?'

They shook their heads.

Commander Hay put down her scratchpad and sat back in her chair.

'Well, Major, how are things going?'

'Their first mission was successfully accomplished. The time machine was destroyed. Henry Plimpton is enthusiastically

123

assisting us with our enquiries. A possible anomaly was avoided and peace has returned to 20th-century Lower Spurting.'

'Interesting. And Parrish was team leader, I see. How did he perform?'

Ellis paused. A memory of Parrish stealing the lottery ticket was overridden by a picture of his face when he spoke of his father. 'He led the team. Yes, he made some stupid mistakes, especially at the beginning, but nothing we haven't all done at some point or another. By the end of the mission I don't think he was quite the same person who had set out.'

'Again – interesting.'

'They're an interesting team, ma'am.'

'I am delighted to hear it. Now tell me how things are actually going.'

He sighed. 'Well, normally at this point in their training, I'd be looking for at least some level of cohesion and cooperation. With this team, it would be fair to say that half the time they're barely speaking to each other. They don't eat together. They don't drink together in the evenings. They barely even communicate except to have a go at each other. They're not popular with the other teams, either. There was . . . an incident . . . the other day and it was necessary to get Farrell and Lockland out of the building for a few hours. At this stage, ma'am, I really have no idea how this is going to turn out.'

'So,' she said brightly. 'It's all going excellently well, then.'

He sighed. 'If you say so, ma'am.'

8

Technically speaking, the Time Police are on duty 24/7. Perpetually poised to swing into action at a moment's notice. Though there aren't that many emergencies because, as one of their many instructors had patiently explained over and over again during training, 'It's time travel, people. It doesn't matter what time you set out – it's the time you arrive that's important.'

The alarm bell was designed to wake the dead. All over London the dead would rise from their graves shouting, 'Turn that bloody thing off, will you?'

That was Matthew Farrell's first thought this evening. That the dead had risen. He sat bolt upright in his bed wondering what the hell was happening. Even Luke Parrish – never at his best when first emerging from slumber – was standing outside his door mumbling, 'What the bloody hell . . .' or would have been had anyone actually been able to hear him.

Yet another layer of sound elbowed its way into the already deafening racket. 'All officers report to the main briefing room. All officers report to the main briefing room. All officers report to the main briefing room.'

All along the corridor, officers were tumbling from their cubicles, pulling on their clothing as they went.

Jane kicked her legs clear of the covers and grabbed for her uniform. Emerging from her cubicle she collided with Matthew, who was emerging from his. The last officers were disappearing through the door at the end of the corridor.

He shouted, 'Where's Parrish?' and she nodded her head towards his cubicle. Parrish had retreated back into his room, scratching his head and yawning and generally displaying the signs of one who intended to take all the time in the world.

Farrell thumped on his half-open door. 'Parrish – come on.'

'Yeah, yeah, yeah.' He looked vaguely around.

Farrell withdrew his head, shouting over the din, 'We'll have to go without him.'

'We can't.'

'We have to. He's going to be late; there's no reason he should make us late as well.' He pushed her down the passageway towards the lift.

'Matthew, any idea what's going on?'

'No idea, but by the time we get there it'll probably all be over with. Parrish probably has the right idea after all.'

Lockland's private thoughts were that whatever it was, no one was likely to want them to be involved anyway.

They followed the others down to the briefing room, slipping in through the door just as the alarms were shut off. Blessed silence fell. People arranged themselves in teams as their officers ranged up and down ticking off names.

'Where is everyone?' whispered Lockland, looking around.

Farrell shrugged. 'Not here, obviously. Maybe they've already gone on ahead.'

North was doing a head count. Turning to Lt Grint, she announced, 'Twelve, sir. Including trainees.'

'Should be thirteen, North.'

And here was that awkward moment. It always arrives sooner or later. Someone is missing. What do you do? Report him and cover yourself? Or count him in and cross your fingers he turns up in time? For lesser mortals this might be a dilemma. North had no such difficulties. For her there was only ever one way to do things and that was the right way.

'Parrish is missing, sir.'

'Get him.'

'Yes, sir.'

Sizing up those in front of her, she selected the biggest person present. 'Trainee Anders, please locate Parrish immediately and persuade him to join us. By whatever means necessary.'

An enormous and already armoured officer nodded and clumped out through the door. Several other people, possibly familiar with his seek and find tactics, winced.

Grint put away his scratchpad. 'Listen up, men.' His gaze fell on Lockland. 'And non-men. We have a call for assistance and it's a good one. You'll like this. 1320BC. Valley of the Kings. Tomb robbers.'

He was regarded with even less enthusiasm than is normally met with in the small hours of the morning. 'Oh shit,' muttered someone. 'History. I hate bloody history.'

Grint stepped back. 'Bring them up to speed, North.'

'Yes, sir. Location – the Valley of the Kings. Specifically, the tomb of Tutankhamun. KV62. Discovered almost intact in 1922 by Howard Carter and Lord Carnarvon.'

People were yawning and nodding. They knew this.

'The tomb had been robbed on at least two occasions before discovery. We think this is one of those times.'

Someone raised a hand. 'What has this to do with us?'

'It's not contemporaries robbing the tomb. It's illegals. From our own time.'

'How do we know this?'

'Some years ago, we – you – did a good job of bringing down Atticus Wolfe and his criminal empire. The Time Police ended his illegal temporal activities and the civilian police took care of the trafficking, drugs and art forgery side of his business. However, when you take down someone that big, you leave a vacuum. There have been a number of contenders waiting to pick up where he left off and we think that tonight another of them is making his move.

'Earlier today we received a tip-off that a large and well-equipped team was about to break into Tutankhamun's tomb in the Valley of the Kings. At the time we thought it was nothing more than a spot of temporal vandalism, but it seems we were wrong. Our estimate is that at least two or three pods are out there. The individual signatures are unclear because people are getting better at masking them, which is another sign this is a more professional operation than we first thought.

'Major Ellis has taken four teams and gone after them. He disturbed them before they'd finished. At this point, we're not sure whether they're still on site or whether they've jumped away. That's for the major to deal with. What we do know is that they've left the tomb open. Wide open. They've penetrated the outer door, tunnelled down the steps, breached the inner door and accessed the tomb. I've returned to obtain additional manpower. Your task will be to secure both the tomb and the surrounding area against their possible return, to prevent opportunistic looting by any passing locals and to render assistance to the major as required. This tomb must remain intact and ready for Carter's discovery three thousand years later.'

People nodded. This was no big deal – it happened occasionally. Tutankhamun's tomb was a known target. Over the years any number of hopeful fortune hunters had bundled themselves into their homemade, radiation-leaking contraptions for the sole purpose of helping themselves to a little treasure. Tomb robbing, however, is nowhere near as easy as most people think. Standard Time Police procedure was to let the miscreants expend an enormous amount of hot, sweaty, sandy effort and then swoop in and pick them up before they could do any real damage to the tomb or its contents.

If they were feeling benevolent, the Time Police would then bring them back to face trial. If not, then they would leave them to take their chances with the Medjay, for whom the answer to pretty much everything was a quick beating to the feet and then impalement upon any large sticks that happened to be handy. Jane shivered. According to the info on her scratchpad, the ancient Egyptian police were to be feared and avoided.

Someone, obviously not happy at missing his beauty sleep, raised a hand and said in exasperation, 'Why do they do this? They can't remove anything from its own time. Surely everyone knows this by now. We tell them often enough. Why are some people so shit-thick?'

Grint nodded.

'Good point. This bunch, however, are using their brains. They're pulling stuff out of the tomb with the intention of taking it off-site and reburying it at some secret location. They then return to their own time, cross their fingers that their loot will survive, undisturbed, over however many centuries, and then they dig it up again. If it's not there – because someone else got there first, or it's been destroyed in a natural disaster – well, it's just a case of better luck next time, guys, we'll nip off and have another go somewhere else. And if it *is* still there, then it's a case of drinks on me, everyone, because we're going to be rich.'

'The St Mary's method,' said someone, sourly. 'Burying treasure to be discovered centuries later.'

'Legitimate search and rescue to protect major artefacts,' said North quickly, because while you can take the girl out of St Mary's, you can't always take St Mary's out of the girl.

'Barely,' said someone. 'And now someone's worked it out and is copying them.'

For some reason, all eyes swivelled to Matthew, who stared back, impassive under his still very non-regulation haircut. Unconsciously, Lockland moved closer to him in silent support. Someone made a rude noise.

'All right, that's enough of that,' said Grint. 'We—'

The briefing room doors crashed open as Anders emerged, a semi-dressed Luke Parrish dangling from one massive paw.

'Ah, Trainee Parrish. So glad you could join us.'

Very wisely, Parrish said nothing, concentrating on pulling his clothing into some sort of order.

Grint continued. 'So that's the situation, people. This is not a couple of amateurs having a go. This is a large, well-funded, well-organised gang with two or three pods and major financial backing. They've breached the tomb and removed a ton of stuff. Major Ellis and the other teams will intercept them and retrieve the artefacts.'

He paused. 'This is what we do. We prevent people looting the past.' He raised his voice. 'What do we do?'

His team responded in well-practised unison. 'We prevent people looting the past. Sir.'

'Jesus,' muttered Parrish.

'Shh,' whispered Jane.

Grint was continuing. 'Our task is to apprehend anyone still remaining, guard the tomb until we can replace what's been taken and assist the other teams as required. The usual things to watch out for: snakes, scorpions, the Egyptian police, armed tomb robbers . . .'

'And the Curse of Tutankhamun,' muttered Parrish.

'Thank you for your contribution, Mr Parrish – we'll leave you to cover that particular aspect of the job, shall we?'

Several people laughed.

'Where's Ellis?' muttered Parrish from behind Farrell, still trying to tuck in his T-shirt.

'Already on site,' whispered Lockland. 'Gone after them.'

Someone raised a hand. 'So what can we expect to see?'

At a nod from Grint, North continued the briefing. 'It's night. It's cold. You will disembark at the very centre of the Valley of the Kings. The terrain is rocky and rough underfoot. There's a great deal of debris from the tomb – broken rocks, chippings, maybe tools and baskets left behind. Be aware the valley is dotted with guard posts, with four or five Egyptian guards to every post. It's a forbidden area, so they will assume anyone who isn't them is a tomb robber. And don't underestimate them. They're professional warriors and they make us look like a basket of kittens. Visuals of the valley and of the tomb itself have been flashed to your visors.'

She nodded at Grint, who drew himself up. 'Right, people. Usual teams. You all know what to do.' He appeared to remember Lockland, Parrish and Farrell, who very obviously did not know what to do. 'Your team leader is already on site so you three are on my team tonight. Get yourselves on board.'

'Weapons?' offered Parrish, optimistically.

'I'm not taking the chance of any of you shooting real officers in the dark.'

'We had weapons for Henry Plimpton.'

'You had sonics. The only thing you could damage was each other. Tonight is different. You've got your string – not that you'll need it – now get on board and stay there.'

'Bastard,' muttered Parrish.

'I heard that, Parrish. Consider yourself on report. Any questions, anyone?'

There were none.

'Assemble in the Pod Bay, everyone. ETD five minutes.'

Grint's team – Team 235 – were already on board. They stared in silence at the newcomers and no one moved up to make room.

It's only a few weeks since we did our basic training with these people, thought Jane, trying to avoid their hostile stares. We were all together once. And now we're just . . . nothing.

Depression settled on her even more heavily. The only thing keeping her here, she realised with a sudden flash of insight, was that she had nowhere else to go. Anyone who had a normal, happy home life to return to would surely be off like a shot. Her stupid dream of becoming someone to be reckoned with, respected and admired by her colleagues, had shrivelled under Time Police indifference. More than ever she was aware of her inadequacy. She looked around. Everyone stood in their place – ready, waiting, eager, confident. Part of their team. Part of a greater whole. Confident in the identity of themselves and the organisation they worked for. Why hadn't that happened to her? She'd done the same training as everyone else. She wore the same clothes as everyone else. Why wasn't she one of them? Why wouldn't they open their ranks and let her in?

She felt tears prick behind her eyes and knew, instinctively, that if she gave way now, she'd be outside the front door first thing tomorrow morning, discharge papers in one hand, carrier bag of possessions in the other. If you want something you fight for it. If you want it badly enough. So what did she want?

Not to be on the other side of the door with her discharge papers in one hand and a carrier bag in the other was the very firm answer to that question.

Jane sighed, lifted her chin and took up her traditional position at the back.

Grint's team were checking over their equipment. They moved quickly, professionally and with precision. They might all have started out together but the gap between the two teams widened every day.

They were the usual standard team of four. Stefan Kohl, with his very blond hair, who was very nearly as silent as Farrell and known, for never satisfactorily explained reasons, as Socko; Alan Hansen, laconic and slow-speaking, who hoped, on completion of his six months' gruntwork, to be assigned to the Pod Bay; Marco Rossi, dark and intense, with a smile as big as he was, whom she had rather liked during training; and the infamous Alek Anders, massive and very useful to hide behind in times of crisis.

North sat at the console. 'Awaiting the word, sir.'

'Consider it given.'

'Jump procedures commenced, sir.'

The world flickered and then settled again.

9

Everyone clustered around the screens.

'Remember,' said Grint, who, for all his many faults, was an experienced officer and knew what he was doing, 'no one and nothing here is on our side. The Medjay, the tomb robbers themselves, lions, snakes, scorpions and so on. The terrain is rough – watch your footing. Don't raise your voice and do not shine a light. Night visors if you need them. Our usual procedures. Quick and quiet. Stun anyone who isn't us. Try not to kill anyone. We don't want to upset St Mary's delicate sensibilities.'

All eyes went to Farrell again and someone sniggered. Again, he stared solidly at Grint, showing no reaction and saying nothing. Wise, thought Jane, beginning to appreciate his strategy. She turned her attention back to Grint, who hadn't finished.

'Hansen, you'll remain with the pod to coordinate. Keep your eyes peeled and inform me of any activity in the area. Switch internals to night mode. Night vision, lads.'

They pulled down their visors.

'Let's go.'

Kohl and Rossi exited the pod and vanished into the dark-

134

ness. The rest of them awaited the word: 'Proximities show all clear, sir. Clear to disembark.'

Grint gave the word and they disembarked.

Jane trotted down the ramp, behind Parrish and ahead of Matthew. She was very aware of her own thumping heart. This was their first real assignment – no one counted Henry Plimpton. Even they didn't count Henry Plimpton. Still, at least they hadn't been told to remain behind and 'guard the pod'. The traditional instruction for no-hopers. But given their lack of a leader, team cohesion and experience, exactly why were they here?

The thought occurred to her – was she to be frightened out of the Time Police? Was this their way of getting rid of her? She'd done well in the theory part of her training, but if she didn't measure up physically then they still had grounds for dismissing her. Or what if she performed so badly, they had no choice but to let her go? How shameful was that? The Time Police took just about anyone who could fire a gun. Rumour had it there were several clean-up crews who hadn't yet mastered speech. Jane squared her shoulders and trotted down the ramp.

They followed the standard exit procedures. Ahead of her, Parrish peeled off to the right so she went left, finding deep shadows in which to crouch. She heard the ramp go up and silence fell on the desert. She couldn't see much, but they appeared to be alone.

Grint's voice sounded in her ears. 'Area checked and secured. Let's move.'

She tucked herself in behind Anders as they made their way along the floor of the valley, ghosting from shadow to shadow, watching where she put her feet. Several hundred yards along, Grint called a halt. She melted into the dark and looked about her.

The famous Valley of the Kings.

It was nothing like she'd imagined. The whole area was just a jumble of rocks. There were no magnificent entrances. No statues. No decorated pillars. No banners. There weren't even any obvious signs of construction.

The ground beneath her feet was dark and treacherous with loose stones, making it hard to move quietly. She looked up. The sky above was crammed with stars, as if someone had spilled a pot of glitter across the heavens; providing more than enough light to see by. Around her, officers were lifting their visors. She followed suit.

The air was chilly, but not bitterly cold, and smelled of dust, rocks and a strange, almost spicy smell. She realised Grint was dividing up his team and leaned forwards to pay attention.

'OK – listen up men. This is our objective. KV62. There's no one here but us. Our job is to mop up any stragglers and secure the tomb, which is, at present, open to any passing looter. My team will split up. Kohl, take Rossi and go up. Check out the higher ground. Watch your step – lots of loose rocks hereabouts. I don't want either of you starting a landslide. Anders, you and I will take the lower ground and rendezvous with Ellis's teams. Keep your eyes open and remember to keep checking your proximities, people.'

'What about us?' enquired Parrish.

The embarrassing pause lengthened.

Grint turned and peered into the dark tunnel that was the entrance to what would, in three thousand years' time, be the most famous tomb in the world.

'Good point, Parrish. What do you see?'

Parrish lowered his visor and walked towards the entrance, peering down into the darkness. 'Sand. Everywhere. Half-buried steps leading downwards. Covered in spoil. Looks as if they've broken through the door at the bottom – there's a small hole.' He looked around. 'There are baskets everywhere. Full of broken stone and chippings.' He kicked one with his foot. 'They've just been dropped by the look of it. There's been no attempt to conceal their presence here.'

'What does that tell you?'

'That this could be a one-off job. They don't intend to come back so they don't care how much damage they do. And they're not local, otherwise they'd have been a lot more discreet, because they'd want to come back again in the future.'

'Correct. We need to check whether the whole tomb has been breached and then secure it. You and Lockland here will do that. You take the entrance, Parrish. Lockland, you're small enough to get yourself through that hole at the bottom and confirm there's no one hiding inside the tomb.'

Lockland's insides slid sideways.

As one, she and Parrish turned to face the entrance. Rough stone steps led down into darkness. Or, as Lockland's imagination tried to avoid thinking, led down into the gaping maw of the underworld. The black hole yawned at them.

Oblivious to her panic, Grint continued. 'Parrish – you wait up here. Keep an eye on the entrance. Don't get yourself caught. Stay here until someone comes back and tells you what to do next. Lockland, you don't have to do anything. Just get down there, secure the tomb and wait there until someone tells you otherwise.'

There was a tightness in her chest. Suddenly, laying in pod coordinates with all eyes upon her seemed nothing compared to this.

'I'll go down into the tomb,' offered Parrish.

Grint shook his head. 'I detailed Lockland. You stay here and cover her arse.'

'It should be me.'

'You're too big. You'll never get through.' His tone was dismissive.

'I'll go then,' said Matthew, stepping forwards. 'I'm small and everyone knows I have experience in confined spaces. I'm the obvious choice.'

'And I'd be happy to let you, but you'll be coming with me. Apparently you're too valuable to have anything happen to you.'

The unspoken inference being that Lockland was not. She felt the familiar hot flush of humiliation and suddenly she'd had enough. She'd complete this mission and then apply for her discharge. Yes, she was signed up for two years, but she was prepared to bet they'd cheerfully let her go. How humiliating was that?

Matthew stepped back. He and Jane exchanged glances. The little that could be seen of his face was expressionless, but knowing him as she did, she could see the shame there as well. Even Parrish looked angry. They stood together in a tight little group. On their own.

'We're useless,' she thought. 'All three of us. Luke's dad practically sold him to the Time Police. Matthew's being singled out just because his parents are from St Mary's, and no one wants me at all.'

She swallowed hard and tried to tell herself she'd been selected for a task of special importance.

'You're sending her in unarmed,' said Parrish, his stance hostile and still apparently unaware of the correct method of addressing his seniors.

'There's no one down there,' said Grint contemptuously. 'Unless it's Tut's ghost, of course. Go on, Lockland. Why are you still standing there?'

Because my legs won't move, thought Jane. She looked up to find Luke watching her closely. 'Here,' he said, quietly. 'Take my lightsticks.'

'And mine,' said Matthew, digging them out and passing them over. Like her he'd pushed up his visor and she could see the concern in his eyes. 'Look – I've done this loads of times. There's a knack. Move slowly. Stay calm. Breathe slowly. You're not alone.'

She nodded gratefully.

'Have you got water?'

She nodded.

'Parrish will watch this end. You'll be quite safe. And leave your com open.' He glanced at her white face and added, 'You'll be fine. Just think, you're going to see the tomb for free.'

She nodded again, not trusting her voice.

'We'll probably be gone less than thirty minutes,' said Grint, possibly yielding to a compassionate impulse in the face of her unspoken but massive panic. 'No longer.'

Jane switched on her night vision again, turning her world a creepy green. Because that's just what you need to see in the middle of the night when you're all alone in the Valley of the Kings, she thought. A creepy green world. Could things get any worse?

She stood at the top of the steps looking down. Parrish lined up behind her.

'Where do you think you're going?' said Grint, obviously having exceeded his compassion quota for the day. 'Even Lockland can't get lost on a flight of steps.'

'To boost her through the hole in the door,' said Parrish. 'It's too high for her to climb through on her own. I know it would be your team's idea of a good time to watch her struggle, but as you yourself would agree, we don't have all night.'

Lt Grint, accustomed to the more typically built Time Police officer, and who, to be fair to him, hadn't even considered that the slight stature which made her so ideal for this part of the job would also make it almost impossible for her to gain access through the tiny opening in the top left-hand corner of the outer door, contented himself with instructing them to sort themselves out and get on with it, and then disappeared into the darkness.

Jane threw Parrish a grateful look.

'Good luck,' said Matthew, preparing to follow the others. 'Look after yourselves. Both of you.'

The pause had a slightly surprised air to it.

'Look after yourself, too,' said Luke.

They nodded at each other and then Matthew joined the others.

Lockland could hear the teams moving off into the night. Suddenly, all was silence. There was only her and Luke and the sound of the wind sighing its way through the valley. And her thumping heart.

They made their way very cautiously down the sand-covered steps. Piles of limestone chippings lay everywhere and despite their best efforts, they couldn't help dislodging them. The sound of hundreds of tiny stones clattering down the steps was very loud in the still night air.

Jane stared at the door ahead of them. 'Now they know we're coming.'

'The robbers are long gone,' said Luke. 'The tomb's empty. Trust me.'

At the bottom of the steps, a rock and plaster barrier loomed ahead of them. A black hole had been hacked through the top left-hand corner.

Jane stared in dismay. Luke had been right. She would never have been able to access the tomb by herself. Without him she could have done nothing more than scrabble uselessly until exhausted, and then wait for Grint's return and her shameful confession.

Luke cupped his hands. 'Put your foot here. I'll boost you up and you can pull yourself through. Carefully. Don't fall through the hole and damage the tomb. It's a world-famous site. Or will be.'

She nodded, swallowed, placed her foot as instructed and reached up.

'Ready?'

She really, really didn't want to do this. 'Yes.'

He heaved her up. She scrabbled at the sides of the hole and pulled herself through slowly, as Luke had advised.

There was no nasty drop on the other side. In an attempt to prevent tomb robbing, the narrow passage beyond had been packed tightly with more limestone chippings. As a deterrent they hadn't been tremendously effective, because a small way through had been cleared between the wall and the low roof, along which a person could, with care, scrabble her way to the far end. Very painfully.

Jane stared, appalled, at the tiny, green-tinged, down-ward-sloping passageway. Ahead of her she could see another solid door with another corresponding hole at the top. All hopes the illegals hadn't made it into the actual tomb and she could return to the safety of the valley floor disappeared into the night.

'All right?' said Luke, behind her.

'You're still here?'

'Yeah – I'll stay until you get through. Once you're in the tomb, I'll push off back up the steps and keep guard.'

'You should be there now. Suppose they – the tomb robbers – come back. You're not even armed.'

'Then I'll glare at them as they come down the steps. I'm not leaving until you're through this tunnel.'

'Thank you,' she said, suddenly warming to him.

'So get on with it.'

The warm feeling faded. 'OK.' She snapped a lightstick.

She could only assume that the robbers had used either children or tiny adults for this part. The passage was very narrow. Sideways movement was impossible. She stretched her arms ahead of her and pushed herself along with her feet because scrabbling at the loose rock only resulted in broken fingernails. She could hear her helmet scraping the ceiling. Her left shoulder rubbed painfully along the wall.

They must have been well-padded children, too. Her vest protected her to some extent, but her legs, arms and especially her knees were being scraped raw on the sharp chippings. Occasionally a jagged pain would stab at her knees or forearms as she put her weight on something particularly sharp.

Panting with effort, she pulled herself along, telling herself the passage couldn't be more than twenty or thirty feet long. Not that she was particularly sure the tomb itself would offer any sort of reassurance when she did arrive. Now was not the moment to remember the Curse of Tutankhamun. The one that promised death to all who violated the tomb. And he had. Lord Carnarvon, the man who had led the expedition, had died. He'd actually died. She blamed Luke entirely for putting that thought in her head and then recalled his unexpected kindness. He had known she was terrified. Perhaps he too had a fear of enclosed spaces.

Sweat poured down her face and stung her eyes. Blinking rapidly did not help, and for a moment her vision blurred, the walls rushed in and the ceiling fell. Panic enveloped her.

'Are we there yet?' said Luke, chattily.

She took a deep breath and said shakily, 'No, we are not.'

'Well, get a move on.'

'Got another date lined up, have you?'

'Of course.'

'Which unfortunate drew the short straw this time?'

'Same one.'

'She's coming back for more?'

His reply was lost as, without warning, the stones shifted beneath her. For one moment she imagined herself disappearing under a sea of chippings, like a toddler in a ball pit, unable to fight her way to the surface; slowly suffocating as her lightstick failed and she died in the dark because they'd never be able to get her out. Apart from Farrell, there was no one else small enough. Unless they were prepared to enlarge the existing holes to the passage and they'd never do that. The noise, the danger of discovery ... They'd have no choice but to abandon her here. And then the Medjay would return, bringing workmen with them, and they'd tidy up the damage and reseal the tomb, leaving her buried here forever. Alone. In the dark. Apart from whatever else might be here. Visions of walking mummies and jackal-headed gods filled her thoughts to such an extent that when she banged her head on the far wall, both the noise and the impact made her scream.

Luke's voice was in her ear. 'Jane? You all right?'

'Yes. Yes. I banged my head but I'm OK. I'm here. I'm at the far door. There's a hole in this one, too.' She drew a breath. 'I'm going in.'

'Lucky devil.'

'What?'

'I've always wanted to say that.'

Despite herself, she couldn't help smiling. 'Beat you to it.'

'Watch your . . .'

She pulled herself through the hole, realised too late she was still about five feet off the ground, passed the point of no return, somehow twisted in mid-air and fell heavily on her shoulder.

'. . . head,' said Luke. 'Whoops. Too late.'

'I'm all right,' she said, lying to both of them. A considerable number of chippings had fallen through with her and had not provided a soft landing. She could feel warm blood running down one arm and wondered whether this would be enough to – in the popular phrase – wake the dead.

The next thing that hit her – after the cold, hard floor – was the smell. Damp plaster, mould and must. And underneath everything, a strange, charred aroma. As if something had been burning.

Sitting up, she groped in her vest for another lightstick, having left the first one in the passage, where its otherworldly glow was not helping to dispel her supernatural fears.

Snapping it, she looked around her. The tomb layout was superimposed on her visor. She was in the antechamber; the first and biggest room in the tomb.

Somehow, she had expected something larger. And more magnificent. Everyone was familiar with the three beautifully decorated but sadly empty tombs accidentally and unexpectedly uncovered in a joint Egyptian Department of Antiquities/ Thirsk University dig twenty years ago. News footage had shown chamber after chamber of wonderfully painted scenes from both life and death, underneath ceilings of royal blue and decked with stars. This was nothing like those. Here, the walls were not only unpainted, but still rough in places. She'd also expected something a little less chaotic. It was obvious that thieves had been in here. The shadows were dark and heavy, but the room had a just-ransacked air about it. Everything was either out of place, upside down or strewn across the floor.

She could see carved wooden boxes, their lids wrenched off and the contents spilled everywhere. Ornate chairs inlaid with gold – or gilt, anyway – lay on their sides. One was badly broken. Light glittered off a jewelled cat's eyes. Couches had been thrust aside, beds overturned. Chariot wheels which had once stood against the walls had been knocked over or thrown aside. The room was filled with a chaos of jars, chests and furniture. That the illegals had departed in a tearing hurry was obvious. A handful of golden rings lay scattered across the floor.

Nearby, a piece of torn linen dangled from a painted wooden leopard's ear. She propped her lightstick against the wall and

145

carefully, not wanting to dislodge anything in all this tangle and bring the whole lot down on top of herself, she twitched it free, bent down and picked up the rings. Knotting them in the linen to keep them safe, she laid them gently on top of a tiny, exquisitely carved chest that still smelled of cedarwood.

Luke's voice was in her ears. 'Jane, I'm back at the entrance now. Everything's quiet here. You still OK?'

'Yes.' Her voice sounded hollow in this stone chamber.

'You don't sound too sure.'

She looked around the chamber. Behind a crooked couch, another hole loomed in the wall directly in front of her, and over on the right-hand wall, a large, dark opening was very definitely not tempting her to stick her head through and investigate. 'I'm trying to decide whether to stay in here or venture into the rest of the tomb.'

'You need to check it out.'

She lowered her voice to a whisper. 'Suppose there's someone in here. Suppose someone got left behind when they heard us coming.'

'Then he's crouching in the dark pissing himself. Trust me – he'll be far more scared of you than you of him.'

Jane doubted this. Aloud.

'Look, Jane, he'll be an illegal. He'll know who we are and what we do. We're the Time Police, remember? We're utter bastards. Well, most of us are. He knows the best he can hope for is arrest and a little gentle roughing up on the way to the cells. If he's unlucky, we'll leave him here to take his chances with scorpions and cobras. And that's not counting the Medjay, ghosts, spirits of the dead . . .'

'Aren't ghosts and spirits the same thing?'

146

'Go and have a look. You'll feel much better when you know it's empty.'

If it *was* empty.

'OK.'

Reluctantly, being careful where she put her feet and trying not to stand on anything priceless, she inched her way towards the door directly ahead of her. The one leading into the annex. Every movement sounded impossibly loud in this tiny underground room. It did occur to her that poking her head through a hole into a dark and possibly robber- or ghost-filled chamber might not be such a good idea, so she snapped yet another lightstick, crouched as best she could, and peered cautiously through the hole. Light winked off even more golden objects.

The first thing she noticed was that the floor level was lower in this chamber. The second thing was that it was as disordered as the first. There was more furniture, more baskets – some still closed, others not – models of long, elegant structures she took to be boats, and everywhere, little wooden figures. She'd read about these at school. They were called shabtis. Servants whose purpose was to serve the pharaoh in the underworld. They lay everywhere, torn from their original positions and just dropped. Their reproachful eyes stared up at her. She could see wine jars, wooden chests and everywhere, the glint of gold.

Wonder competed with terror. She remembered that only a handful of people had seen what she was seeing now. The next person to lay eyes on these marvels would be Howard Carter, three thousand years in the future.

Words would not come. 'Wow. Luke. Oh . . . just . . . wow.'

'What can you see?' said Luke, sounding anxious.

'Wonderful things.'

147

'Very funny.'

Other than a mountain of priceless clutter, however, the room was empty. No robbers remained in the annex.

Taking a deep breath, she withdrew her head, wriggled back into the antechamber and consulted her visor. 'I'm going to try the burial chamber now.'

She left the lightstick propped up in the hole, wiped her clammy hands on her trousers and pulled out another. Again, she picked her way across the cluttered floor. Something crunched beneath her feet and she winced. 'Sorry, sorry, sorry.'

Quietly and cautiously, she approached the opening to the burial chamber. A carved wooden cat observed her every move. She said, 'Stop that,' quite severely, but it continued its unblinking stare, watching her cross the room.

The lightsticks were doing their job, giving off a steady glow, and she could only conclude that the way her black shadow appeared to be jumping around the chamber was due to her own nerves.

She was half-expecting Luke to say that if any illegals still remained then the burial chamber was where they would be, tearing the shrines apart and ripping off the golden death masks, but his next remark was surprisingly helpful.

'Remember, Jane, don't stick your head through until you're certain it's empty and then if anything moves – shoot it.'

'I'm unarmed – remember?'

'Look around you, Lockland, you numpty. Find something heavy – gold is good – and then fetch them a wallop if they try anything.'

'I suppose that will work for humans, but what if it isn't?'

'Isn't what?'

148

She swallowed. 'Human.'

'Not sure I can help you there. You could try reciting that psalm. You know. *You will not fear the terror of the night or the arrow that flies by day . . .*'

Well, that was surprising, coming from Luke Parrish, of all people.

'How do you know that?'

'Birgitte taught me.'

'Is Birgitte that blonde from Logistics?'

'Can we talk about this another time?'

'You really think that would help?'

'Would what help?'

'Quoting the psalm.'

'Not even a little bit.'

'Just like you, then,' she snapped. 'Not helping even a little bit.'

Nevertheless, she selected a stout piece of wood that might have belonged to the broken chair in the corner, edged her way towards the door and, heart racing, cracked another lightstick.

Nothing happened. No uncarthly screams . . . no supernatural entities . . .

'Just the long, dark silence of the tomb,' said Luke cheerily in her ear.

'Parrish, I promise you, if I survive this – you won't.'

But her heart was slowing. She was alone in the tomb. Apart from the owner/occupier, of course.

The burial chamber was some three feet lower than the room in which she currently stood. The smells of mushrooms and burning were stronger in here. In contrast to the rest of the tomb, this room had been decorated. The smooth walls glowed a soft golden yellow. Painted figures posed formally in a kind of frieze around the walls. The scenes denoted the passage of the pharaoh to the afterlife, she assumed. The fourth wall seemed to be divided into squares, each one containing what looked like a blue baboon. Which no doubt meant something to someone. Again, the thieves had been in here. A couple of broken necklaces lay on the floor.

'From the lack of screaming, I gather the chamber's empty,' said Luke in her ear.

'I don't scream,' she said with dignity.

'I wasn't talking about you.'

'Yes, you're right. It's completely empty.'

'God, I hope not . . .'

'Well, yes, apart from the dead pharaoh and his great golden shrine, of course. It's massive, Luke. I never before realised how big it is. It fills the room. I've no idea how they would have got it in here. It looks as if they had to knock part of the wall away. It's amazing. Absolutely amazing.'

'I know. I've seen it.'

'When?'

'Oh, either about six or seven years ago now – or about three and a half thousand years in the future – you choose.'

'I thought they'd closed all the tombs to the public after those terror attacks ten years ago.'

'Private viewing,' he said briefly.

The lightstick burned steadily, illuminating everything around her. She tried to relax, flexing her shoulders to ease the strain. She was conscious of her sweat-soaked T-shirt under her vest. But her job was done. The tomb was empty. She was alone. All she had to do now was sit and wait until everyone came back.

150

With one last look at the exquisite paintings, she moved back into the antechamber and found a clear space where she could rest comfortably against a wall. Somehow, the idea of using one of the many pieces of furniture didn't seem right – and from here she could keep all the other doors in sight.

'What about the treasury?' said Luke.

The old, cold sickness came back. She'd relaxed too soon. 'The what?'

'Really, Lockland, didn't you do this at school? You know – Carter and his discoveries?'

'Of course I did it at school, but it was a long time ago and I never thought I'd actually *be* here.'

'So what about the treasury?'

She looked around. There were no other doors. 'What treasury?'

'The last room.'

'There aren't any more doors.'

'No – you can only access the treasury through the burial chamber.'

'And you know that from your private visit, I suppose?'

'Well, yes, but it is common knowledge.'

She flashed up the display on her visor. He was right.

Her heart started up again. 'I'm going to have to go in there, aren't I? Into the burial chamber. With . . .'

''Fraid so.'

'Can't I just stay here and . . . ?' She tailed off as the implications sank in.

'Exactly. So when Grint asks if you've cleared the tomb, you'll say – in front of everyone – "Yes, I mostly cleared it." Then he'll say, "What do you mean, you mostly cleared it?" and you'll have to admit – in front of everyone – that you wimped out and left the last room – the room most likely to be occupied – unchecked. He won't say anything, but he won't have to, because that's the moment he – and everyone else – will decide you're not worth bothering with. I don't suppose you've yet done much in your young and blameless life to be ashamed of, but on those long, dark nights when you can't sleep, you'll remember and regret this moment. Trust me, Jane, this is the moment that will define you for the rest of your life.'

Something flared inside her. 'That's all very well for you to say. You're . . .' She stopped. Luke was out there all alone, facing whatever might come out of the night. He was as exposed as she was.

She sighed, moved aside a probably priceless wooden chest and scrambled through the entrance, down into the burial chamber itself.

His voice was sharp with alarm. 'I'm what? For God's sake, Lockland, don't break off like that. I thought the jackal god had got you.'

The burial chamber was filled with Tutankhamun's shrine. She left one lightstick behind her to light the way out and cautiously edged her way around the wall. It still felt damp to her touch. The smell of mould was very strong in here. She wiped her hand on her trousers and worked her way slowly around the shrine until she arrived at the dark entrance to the treasury.

Taking a deep breath, she snapped another stick and tremblingly thrust it through the opening. If there *was* anyone in here with her, then this was his or her last hiding place.

She held the stick high and found herself eye to eye with a black-faced jackal.

She drew a sharp breath. Her brain screamed at her to run but her legs weren't listening. She stared at the black-faced jackal and the black-faced jackal stared right back again. There was no sound except her heavy breathing. And then she took in the blank-faced stare. The unblinking eyes.

It was a statue.

Relief flooded through her. Her legs weakened for a moment. It was a statue of Anubis, carefully placed at the entrance to the treasury to watch over the king as he slept and guard his treasures.

She leaned against the wall, waiting for her heartbeat to return to something like normal and then lifted her lightstick. The chamber was empty. Well, no, not empty, it was full of yet more priceless treasures, but for her purposes it was empty. And now she could truthfully report she'd checked every single chamber in the tomb and every single one was clear. Luke had been right. She'd been given a job to do and she'd done it. She would be able to look Grint and all the others in the eye after all.

'Because,' she said to the black-faced Lord of the Underworld, and her voice hardly trembled at all, 'I'm the Time Police and I am an utter bastard and don't you forget it.'

'Lockland, who are you talking to?'

'Everyone,' she said, and meant it.

'Well, utter bastard, if everything's clear, then you might as well return to the antechamber and make yourself comfortable while we await the return of all the other utter bastards.'

His words reassured her and she withdrew her head, climbed up out of the burial chamber back into the antechamber, pulled out a probably priceless chest and made herself comfortable against the wall.

She'd done it. She'd checked and secured the tomb. She'd conquered her fears. She leaned back against the wall, closed her eyes and enjoyed the moment. Exhaling, she slowly began to relax. 'Do you think Matthew will be all right?'

'Oh, yeah. Grint will keep an eye on him. He'll be fine.'

Behind her – in the burial chamber – something flickered.

10

Matthew, however, was far from fine. He was crouched, glowering and resentful, behind Grint and Anders as they peered down the slope into a rock-strewn basin some twenty feet below them. It had been made very clear to him that he was more than superfluous to requirements.

From the little he could see, there were three largish pods – little more than basic cubes – and about fifteen people, five of them women, all half-heartedly disguised in linen rags of a vaguely Egyptian appearance, but with modern armour showing through. Just over half of them were scurrying around, busily packing objects into crates. The other half were facing outwards in a tight, defensive ring, weapons ready. None of them were working with lights but they were quick and quiet all the same. This was a professional gang, accustomed to working together and who had rehearsed for this. And they were nearly finished. He wondered where Ellis and his teams were. Nearby, concealed in the rocks and all ready to go, he hoped.

He shifted for a better view. Someone pulled him back down again, dislodging a few small pebbles which clattered against a rock.

'Quiet,' hissed Grint. 'Stay still and stay behind me.'

'But . . .'

'Don't argue with the officer,' whispered Anders. 'Sir, Major Ellis reports his teams are in position. We're good to go.'

'Night vision off, you two.'

Barely had he finished speaking than, without warning, dazzling white lights split the night. Shadows fled. With a huge roar, a score of black figures rose up from behind the boulders and began to pour down the hillside. Rocks and loose shale poured down with them.

'You stay here, Farrell,' said Grint, who had been shifting uncomfortably. 'You too, Anders. Take care of him.' And then he too was gone into the dark, ignoring both their protests.

Anders cast Matthew a look of utter disgust, conveying that not only was he very much unessential to things in general and this operation in particular, but also managing to tie up a good officer into the bargain. Intentionally or not, he pushed him hard against a rock and Matthew overbalanced and fell into the dust.

'Stay down. Stay quiet, kid.'

'But I can . . .'

'I said, "stay quiet".'

Matthew struggled up into a crouching position. Anders cast him a calculating look as if deciding whether to push him down again or leave him as he was.

Matthew tightened his grip on his baton. Why, he wasn't sure. It seemed unlikely he would be called upon to use it. His legs began to ache with the strain of squatting for so long.

Down below, those working on the crates wasted a whole second trying to work out what was happening and then, faced with an unknown number of giant black figures hurtling down the hillside out of the dark and heading directly towards them, and blinded by the brilliant lights, they scattered, seeking cover among the rocks. Around them, small landslides clattered noisily down the rocky hillside. Clouds of dust swirled wildly in the searchlights.

Anders cursed.

'What's happening?' said Matthew, again trying to stand up.

A giant hand thrust him back down again. 'The sonics are loosening the already loose rock. Setting off rockfalls. Shit. They're coming this way. Stay here.'

Anders began to edge away.

Matthew tried to see around him. 'Where are you going?'

'To intercept them. Stay down. Back in a minute.'

'Wait.'

Too late. Anders too had disappeared into the night. Matthew suddenly felt very much alone.

At least some of the illegals were armed with conventional weapons. Gunshots cracked in the night. With no one to tell him not to, Matthew wriggled around a rock for a better view and as he did so, two or three rag-clad figures emerged only yards away, scrabbling frantically for purchase among all the loose shale and heading in his direction.

He crouched even lower and fumbled for his liquid string – that little known and completely useless protection against armour-piercing bullets.

The leading figure reared up in front of him, climbing fast, dislodging rocks and shale as he came and panting hard in the dark. Not attacking, decided Matthew. Running away. He should do something. But what? Delay them. Delay them long enough for reinforcements to arrive. Taking a firm grip on his liquid string, he jumped out from behind his rock, pointed and squirted.

Thick yellow tendrils wrapped themselves around the figure's legs, bringing him down with a crash that dislodged half the mountain. An avalanche of loose shale cascaded down with him, causing Matthew to stagger, and half-burying the illegal. His two companions, following closely behind, lost their own footing and fell over the top of him. Unexpectedly, all three of them were on the ground. Right in front of him. He had a chance to delay them. To prevent their escape.

Heart racing, he clambered to his feet and pointed and squirted for dear life. There wouldn't be sufficient string to immobilise all three of them, but if he could just slow them down until Anders came back . . .

One of the illegals must somehow have got an arm free because Matthew suddenly found himself staring at a silver-grey handgun, glinting in the starlight and pointing directly at him. He froze.

The violence in his life had always been up close and personal. Fists. Boots. Sticks. This wasn't the first time someone had tried to hurt him, but this was his first gun.

His world stopped. He sat down with a bump. Yes, he was armoured, but at this close range . . . Disjointed thoughts rattled around his mind. Of Mikey, and the way her hair stood in a golden halo around her head. His hopes, his dreams, his plans . . . The ones he'd shared with no one. The ones that only lived inside his own head. The ones he always kept to himself because, even now, even after all this time, you didn't tell people the important stuff. You didn't show emotion. You didn't engage. You were never vulnerable . . . Not that it mattered, because they would all come to nothing now. Life would go on – Mikey would go on – the world would go on – but without him . . .

Away to his left, someone fired a sonic. He felt the painful rumble in his chest, but the blast wasn't pointed directly at him and the small, residual kick of the shock wave was enough to snap him out of his trance. With nothing to lose, he threw himself at the gun.

He'd once heard his mother say, 'Keep your friends close and your enemies closer still – the same applies with guns. You either want to be fifty miles away or the one who's safely behind it.' So he lunged for it. He remembered his training. Go for the weapon, not the man. If he could just hold on until someone else turned up. His momentum rolled the two of them down the rocky hillside. Sharp rocks dug painfully into his unprotected limbs.

Someone was panting hard in his ear. Hot, wet breath. He was dimly aware of blows to his head and back. Someone was kicking at him but that wasn't important now. The single most vital thing in his life was to keep that gun pointing away from him. He could hear footsteps clattering across the rocks and voices shouting all around him.

A single shot rang out – loud in the night air. For a moment he thought it was him. That the gun had gone off and he was dead – and then something heavy fell across his legs.

With half the mountain falling down around them, someone had obviously realised sonics might not be the best way to go. He could hear the hiss and smell the burned-rubber smell of more liquid string. Thick yellow tendrils enveloped the illegal's arms. And part of Matthew as well.

Someone – Anders – said, 'I've got him, lad. Out of the way, now.'

Matthew shoved the body off his legs, rolled away, yanked

at the strings before they could harden and, panting, struggled to sit up and see what was happening.

Anders had the three illegals face down in the dust and was cuffing and stuffing as per official Time Police procedures. And, at the same time, aiming the occasional kick at them, as per unofficial Time Police procedures.

The body on the ground turned out to be Major Ellis. His eyes were open and his lips moving. The language was not suitable for sensitive young recruits nor anyone of a nervous disposition.

Matthew stared down at his palm, black with blood in the harsh white lights. His mind struggled to keep up. The blood wasn't his. Someone had been shot but it wasn't him. The blood wasn't his. So whose was it? He crawled to Major Ellis and groped.

'Left leg,' gasped Ellis, his face paper-white, and now Matthew could see the dark blood soaking slowly into the darker dust.

For a moment he stared helplessly. His mind a blank. There was a procedure. He should . . . He should . . . This was Uncle Ellis . . . although it had been a long time since he had called him that. Uncle Ellis who had sheltered him, guided him . . . Uncle Ellis bleeding in the dust . . . He should . . .

'He's hurt,' he said, and his voice trembled. 'Do something.'

'Busy,' said Anders.

Matthew's mind snapped back into working order. Adrenalin coursed through his system like an express train. No time to search for a medkit. Anders was busy securing the illegals. Which was the right thing to do. It was up to him. He found the wound and, two-handed, applied as much pressure as he could manage.

Ellis grunted in pain.

Regardless of the need for stealth, Matthew lifted his head, shouting, 'Over here. Officer down. Officer down. Medic.'

A solid figure appeared beside him. He could see the field medic flash on his sleeve.

'Keep applying the pressure until I tell you,' he said, and Matthew nodded, staring down at the blood still seeping silently between his fingers despite his best efforts, while the medtec ripped his pack open.

'When I say ready, lad, let go and get out of my way. Not till I say, though.'

Matthew nodded again, suddenly aware of his aching and cramped legs. He might not be able to move when the time came.

The medtec looked up. 'Anders . . .'

'Yeah – OK.'

'Then – ready.'

Anders grabbed Matthew under the armpits and heaved him roughly out of the way. 'Good job you're so little.'

Matthew, who silently resented any comments on his size, scowled furiously at Anders who simply shrugged. The medic bent over Ellis then looked back over his shoulder and nodded at Matthew. 'Is he OK?'

'Dunno.' Anders looked down at him. 'You OK?'

Matthew nodded.

Anders was impatient. 'No. None of that. Need to hear you say it. You're not hurt?'

'No. I'm not hurt.' Aching, still scared, festooned with broken string, covered in Egyptian dust and Uncle Ellis's blood, but not hurt.

'Are you going to throw up?'

'No,' he said, inaccurately.

'Best to keep an eye on him,' said the medtec.

Anders sighed heavily and pulled a small flask from his utility belt. 'Here. Sit down and take a sip. Only one.'

One was enough. Matthew swallowed, coughed, coughed again and finally lifted his head to look about him. Around them, the Time Police were herding the illegals into groups. They knelt awkwardly on the rough ground, hands behind their heads.

'Anyone else hurt?' enquired Matthew.

Anders shook his head. 'Rossi twisted an ankle when he fell and there's a few scrapes and bruises, otherwise nothing serious. You?'

'I'm fine now,' he said, handing the flask back again. 'You should go and help somewhere. I'll wait here with the major.'

'No, they seem to have everything under control. Always stay out of the way if not needed. I'll wait with the major, too.' He paused and then said, not quite grudgingly, 'Good work with the string. Slowed them long enough for us to run them down.'

Matthew nodded. Only now was his heart rate beginning to slow to something acceptable. He leaned over to talk to the medic. 'How is he?'

'Through and through,' said the medtec, spraying the wound. 'Painful and messy but not serious.'

'I had a girlfriend like that once,' said Anders, stowing his flask.

North appeared, her visor raised. 'How is he?'

'I'm fine,' said Matthew, bravely.

'I *meant* the major.'

162

Matthew blushed in the dark.

'Flesh wound,' reported the medtec, getting stiffly to his feet. 'It's going to hurt like hell for quite a while. I've given him something for the pain. Safe to move him.'

They all bent over Ellis. Matthew moved further back, out of the way and into the shadow of a big rock. Now that everything was over with and he was safe, his legs had chosen this moment to turn to rubber. He leaned back against the rough surface. The residual warmth was comforting. His heart was still thumping like a hammer. He tried to relax.

He later described it to himself as a waking dream.

At the corner of his eye – where the dark things lurk – always just out of view but not out of reach – something moved. Something big and black. The rock was no longer warm. A cold feeling crept over him. Something watched them from the dark. He pulled his visor down, turning his head back and forth. Searching . . . because there was something . . . he knew there was something . . .

'What's that?' he said, straightening up and peering into the dark.

'Where?' said Anders, immediately alert. 'What can you see?'

They all stared. No one said anything. Anders pulled out his proximity meter. 'There's nothing there,' he said, eventually.

'There was,' said Matthew, defiantly. 'I saw something.'

'No, you didn't,' said Anders. 'You imagined something. Understandable. It's been a hectic twenty minutes.'

'No, it's not. I definitely saw . . .'

'And I'm telling you, there's nothing there. No one's seeing anything but you. I understand if you're shit-scared, but just sit down and stay quiet. There are officers here trying to do a job.'

'But there was something there. I . . .'

Anders and the medtec exchanged looks. Anders reached up to his temple and twirled his forefinger. The universal symbol for loony.

'You want me to take him back with me to the medpod?' asked the medtec, picking up his gear.

'No,' said Matthew swiftly. 'It was just a shadow. I know that now.'

Anders stared at him for a moment. The kid's eyes looked weird. Well, they always did. Weirder than normal, then. His mother's were the same, they said, and it was unsettling. But Anders's instinct was always to ignore anything he didn't understand and drag things back into the realms of the normal. 'Did you bang your head?'

Matthew pulled himself together and seized on the excuse. 'No. I banged my elbow, though,' he said, artistically rubbing his elbow.

'Can you move it?' asked the medtec, displaying a professional interest.

'Oh yes,' he said. Facing Anders, he clapped one hand on his bicep, clenched his fist and moved his lower arm up and down. Up and down. Up and down. 'As you can see, everything works just fine.

Anders glared suspiciously, but Matthew had turned his attention back to Ellis and the medtec, who winked at him and went off to organise a stretcher.

'Isn't this nice?' said Matthew to Anders, because he had inherited more from his mother than just her eyes. 'Now it's just you and me and all those lost souls denied access to the afterlife.' He dropped his voice an octave. 'Doomed to wander the

164

softly sighing desert sands forever. Wreaking bloody revenge on all who cross their path.'

Ellis regarded him from the ground. 'You do know everyone is much happier when you don't speak, don't you?'

'Mum says that.'

'Not often I find myself in agreement with your mother.'

'Dad says that.'

'Are you going to regale me with tales of your family all night or help me stand up?'

North appeared again, followed by Lt Grint. Matthew was unsurprised to note she was wearing considerably less desert dust than everyone else. She bent over Ellis. 'Sir, the clean-up crews are here.'

Ellis nodded, and closed his eyes. 'Casualties?'

'Minor on our side.'

'Did we get them all?'

'We did. Two are dead and those that are left aren't feeling very well at all.'

She gestured down at the broken crates and all the priceless objects lying among the rocks. 'We need to put these artefacts back in the tomb as quickly as possible.'

Ellis shook his head and grimaced. 'No time. The Medjay will be here any moment. Remove the illegals' crates and anything not contemporary to this time. Leave the rest here. They'll make sure it's all replaced and the tomb resealed. Lt Grint, where are Lockland and Parrish?'

'Securing the tomb.'

'Who with?'

'Just those two. I couldn't spare anyone else.'

'You left them there alone? Unarmed?'

'They're safer there than here.'

Ellis said nothing.

Matthew turned his head suddenly and looked over towards the east. 'We need to get back to the tomb. Now.'

'Why?'

He blinked. 'Why what?'

'Why did you say that?'

'Say what?'

Grint stirred impatiently. 'Stop arsing around, Farrell.'

'No,' said North slowly. 'With respect, Major, Parrish and Lockland are alone there. We should send someone.'

'Yes,' said Ellis, still wincing in pain. 'We don't need you, Lt Grint. Thank you for your assistance. Get yourselves back to the tomb, pick up your people and then head back to TPHQ. No need for you to hang around. We'll finish things off here.'

'Yes, sir. Anders, get the team together.' He looked around. 'The sun will be up soon.'

'And so will the Medjay,' said North. 'You'd have to be dead to have missed our little sound and light show. We all need to get a move on.'

'And we will,' said Grint. 'Come on, Farrell.'

11

Back at the tomb, Luke was crouching in the shadows, his back against the rock face, staring up at the stars, when Jane's voice sounded in his ear.

'Luke?'

'Still here,' he said, cheerily. 'Were you worried I'd gone for a burger?'

'Luke?' Her voice trembled.

'What's wrong?'

'Do lightsticks flicker? At all? Ever?'

He stood up slowly and took a few steps towards the tomb entrance.

'No, they don't. Or they shouldn't. Are you sure it's not just running out? You know . . . fading away.'

'No. It's quite strong. They all are. They're fine. I left one in the burial chamber and it's as if . . . something passed in front of it. Just for a moment the light went out. And then came back again.'

'OK. Jane, you need to check the tomb again. You need to be sure you didn't miss anything.'

'I've done that already. There's no one here but me.'

Her voice was beginning to rise in panic.

'All right. Try to stay calm. You've probably just got a faulty stick. Look, there's no need for you to stay in there if it's empty. Climb back up the tunnel and we'll wait here together.'

She sounded doubtful. 'Grint said to wait in the tomb.'

'If it's empty, it doesn't matter whether you're down there or up here.'

'But he said I was to stay here until someone told me otherwise.'

'I'm telling you otherwise.'

'I'm sorry, Luke, I don't think you count. It has to be someone more important.'

'Well, thank you.'

'I know, but I tried to say it nicely.'

'I can't get down to you. I'm probably too big to get through the tunnel. Even if I take my vest off.'

'Don't do that,' she said quickly. 'Grint told you to stay there. And if you do come down here, they could block up the entrance and then we'd both be trapped.'

'Who's they?'

'Anyone.' Her voice was beginning to rise again, and all things considered, he didn't blame her.

Striving to sound casual, so as not to alarm her, but at the same time concerned she would feel he was underplaying the fears of someone standing alone and abandoned in a possibly cursed tomb, he said, 'Well, if you're going to stay put, then my advice would be to check out the tomb again. The last thing you need is to be sitting there imagining all sorts of things in the dark. Or come out now. The choice is yours.'

There was a pause and then she said, 'I'm going to look.' Despite the brave words, her voice trembled.

'Do you want me to keep talking to you? Will that help?'

'No, I don't think so. I need to be able to hear as well as to see.'

'All right, if you say so, but keep your link open, just in case.'

'All right.' Luke heard the rustle of her clothing as she moved away.

He took a few paces to stretch his legs, stared for a while at the brilliant black and silver sky above him and then turned to survey the rest of the valley. Nothing moved. Other than the mournful wind there was silence. The immediate hills showed dark and jagged against the slightly lighter sky. The darkest things were the long, sharp, black shadows all pointing towards him. The landscape was still black and silver. The air was chilly. Dawn could not be far off. He wondered what was happening where Matthew was.

He turned back to face the tomb.

Luke Parrish was the son of a very rich man. His slightest wishes had been indulged since an early age. He had the means and the ability to engage in almost any pastime that had taken his fancy and dangerous sports had figured high on that list. He was a passable rock climber. He'd undertaken several parachute jumps, including free-fall. He drove fast cars. They hadn't been particularly fast before they encountered Luke Parrish, but they'd certainly been fast during their relationship. Some of them not for very long. He'd white-water rafted. He'd even bungee-jumped, although that might have been the result of a too-convivial evening rather than a genuine desire to risk life and limb. In other words, he'd experienced situations that had made his heart race and his adrenalin pump.

He was experiencing another one now.

An indeterminate shape squatted on the hillside above the tomb. The phrase 'as black as night' flashed through his mind because it *was* black. Thick, impenetrable black. Blacker than the night sky. Blacker than the rocks around it. Blacker than anything he had ever seen in his life.

For long moments – too long – he stood paralysed. His throat closed. His mouth dried. His heart kicked in his chest. He stared. And stared. And then, some fragment of his training kicked in. Identify the threat and then proceed accordingly. He flipped down his visor to engage night vision.

It made very little difference so he pushed it back up again. The shape was still there. He was unable to distinguish any features or make out any form. It was just a thick, dark, hunched, shapeless shape. If it hadn't been for the lack of noise and dust, he might have thought there had been a sudden rockfall.

Not daring to look away, he took a careful pace backwards. Then another. His shoulder brushed against a rock. Instinctively, he put out his hand to steady himself. His heart was pounding. Because this was more than fear. This was the deep, primeval instinct of our early ancestors. When the night was full of terrors.

I will not fear the terror in the dark . . .

He thought of Birgitte. Where was she now . . . ?

With a suddenness that made him jump, white lights slashed through the sky and lit up a part of the mountain off to his right. A second later, he could hear shouting. And then, a scattering of gunfire.

The thing on the tomb turned its head. Now, suddenly, there was a recognisable shape. A shape that sank his stomach and made every hair on his head stand up on end. A giant head was black against the black rock behind it. Two enormous pointed ears and a long, sharp snout. The head of a jackal. A monstrous jackal. A monstrous jackal was squatting over the tomb.

Luke had had the best education money could buy. And yes, all right, he'd squandered most of the opportunities that this had offered, but some of it had stuck. He would have done rather well if he had bothered to finish his degree. Even so, he knew exactly what he was looking at. He also knew this was no figment of his imagination. It was there. Right in front of him. A legend come to life. Anubis, Protector of Graves. Lord of the Sacred Land. Guardian of the Scales. He Who is Upon the Mountain. And he was. Anubis was right here. Right now. Upon the mountain. Crouching protectively over the open tomb. Even as Luke looked, it lowered its head at him, drawing back black lips to expose dog-like teeth.

He felt no surprise. No disbelief. This was Egypt, after all. Where the dead were as important as the living. Where the whole point of this life was to prepare for the next one. Egyptians had believed in the afterlife for thousands of years. They believed that the gods and goddesses they'd created had made them, the Egyptians, special. That the gods had bestowed perfection upon the land of Egypt. That the gods had sent the Nile to provide for them. That the Nile gave them fertile soil in which to grow their food. The food that would be offered back to the gods. And that only those who found favour with the gods – those whose hearts were weighed against a feather and found worthy – would enter the afterlife.

He suddenly wondered – how would his heart fare against a feather? Not well, was his honest but unwelcome suspicion.

Suddenly it was very easy to believe in all that belief. Had

171

the thoughts and prayers of all those people over all those millennia given tangible life to their gods? Or had the gods always existed? Were they here before the first man? Which came first – the gods or the belief? Had the gods created man to believe in them or had man created the gods in whom to believe? The gods of Egypt had lived for thousands and thousands of years. Whether they still existed in modern times was a matter of some debate among more learned minds than his, but he wasn't in modern times. He was here, now, in Egypt, land of magic, in the Valley of the Kings, standing before a desecrated tomb, and the Protector of Graves had turned up. To protect the grave, presumably. And Jane was inside.

Before he could even think about that, the figure raised itself slowly to its feet. In the darkness it was hard to see where mountain ended and figure began, but he was sure it was massive. Tall and slender, with the body of a man and the head of a jackal, its eyes glowed in the dark like a cat's eyes in headlights. Luke could see starlight glinting on a golden collar and kilt. And then, with its eyes fixed on the white lights in the sky, with one bound, it disappeared. Ordinary night rolled back into the valley and Luke found he could think and move again. He opened his com and steadied his voice.

'Hey, Jane, it's all kicked off out here. There's a huge sound and light show over to the west. Lights in the sky and gunfire. I reckon they've found them. Hope Matthew's OK, although I don't suppose they'll let him come to any harm, will they? And it's all happening here, as well.'

He opened his mouth to tell her about the jackal-headed figure on the mountain, and then realised, just in time, that possibly this was not information that would be enthusiastically welcomed by someone stuck in a tomb all on her own. And besides, what would he say? What could he say without earning himself a spell in psycho?

'Well, never mind that. The important thing is that they've caught them. A few minutes to mop up and get the stuff back into the tomb and then we can all call it a night. Good news, eh?'

Silence.

He persevered. 'And Matthew'll be fine, I guarantee it. They're not going to let anything happen to him. Grint's a shit but he'll keep an eye on him.'

Silence.

'Jane – are you there? Stop messing about.'

Silence from the tomb.

He swallowed hard and lowered his voice. 'Jane? Can you hear me? Jane?'

He thought of the larger-than-life figure. He Who is Upon the Mountain. Crouching over the tomb. The tomb that contained Jane.

Swallowing hard on rising panic, he said, 'Jane. Please. Answer me. There's some bad shit going on here. You've got to get out of there. Right now.'

At long last she answered, and her voice was ragged with fear. 'I can't.'

'What do you mean, you can't? You must.'

She was whispering. 'Luke, I can't. He's behind me.'

12

It was at that moment that Jane realised she'd never actually been frightened before. Yes, there had been moments of what had been, compared to this, mild anxiety over school performances, or minor apprehension over new places or meeting new people. She'd experienced a slight concern over destroying her grandmother's seagull – that was all. Because *this* was fear. This was all-enveloping, paralysing, overwhelming terror. This was the fear that all future fears would be measured against and found to be lesser.

She realised she'd stopped breathing. Stopped everything, actually. She couldn't think. She couldn't move. She could only stand, petrified. Frozen. Knowing – just knowing – that something was standing behind her. Something unknown. She waited to feel the weight of a cold, dead hand on her shoulder. To be dragged, living, into the realms of the dead. To be devoured by a trapped and vengeful spirit.

A second dragged by – as long as a week. And then another. For her, time had almost stopped. It was hard to believe that out there, seconds were flying by on their way to becoming minutes, while in here . . .

She remembered her teacher dwelling on the Curse of the

Pharaohs at school. The one that said anyone disturbing the tomb would die. And it was true. Lord Carnarvon had died of an infected mosquito bite. And at the very moment he died, all the lights went out in Cairo. Although, to be fair, that would have been far more impressive if the lights didn't go out in Cairo all the time.

And now here she was. In a cursed tomb. True, she hadn't been the one to desecrate the tomb, but, typically, she was the one stupid enough to be caught here, and she doubted very much whether whatever was here with her would take that into account. The tomb had been violated. And here she was. A sitting target.

The shadows flickered again. As if, for the briefest moment, something stood between her and the light. There was a strong scent of burning dust, incense and mould. A faint, greasy blue smoke wafted over her shoulder. At one and the same time she could feel great heat and great cold.

Disconnected thoughts flew around her head. The world had always been fascinated by Tutankhamun. Documentaries speculated endlessly on how he died. Had he been murdered? He died at eighteen so that was a definite possibility. Then there was the mystery of his underwhelming tomb. A tomb so small and inferior they had to knock down part of the wall to get his sarcophagus in. And as if that wasn't bad enough, they'd then had to cut his toes off to get him into the sarcophagus. Poor, young king, to be so mistreated in a culture that placed such value on the afterlife. To be buried with what were, compared to the magnificence of other tombs, very second-rate grave goods.

Now this tomb had been disturbed for at least the second or third time. How was she any different from the ghouls who had picked over the treasures so carefully placed here to ease his passing into the afterlife? Suppose that because of that – because the meticulous placing of each object had been disturbed – he hadn't made it. Or perhaps the goods themselves hadn't been rich enough to ensure his safe passage. Only one room in his tomb was decorated and the paintings on the walls were very hurried and very basic. Perhaps the instructions for his passage to the afterlife were incomplete. Perhaps he hadn't been able to complete the journey and was now forced to linger here forever, bitter and resentful, trapped in the cold and dark between the two worlds. Craving the unattainable warmth and light of the afterlife. Unable to return to the world he had left. Seeking revenge against the people who hadn't cared enough. A minor king who did not yet know he was destined to become the most famous pharaoh of them all. Greater even than mighty Ramses the Great. Or the female pharaohs, Hatshepsut and Cleopatra.

And even when he was discovered – would be discovered – the indignities would continue. Howard Carter would rip his mummy apart in an effort to pry him loose from his sarcophagus. His grave goods would be scooped up and taken away. He himself would be removed from his own tomb, to dwell in a museum. He would later be returned, but after the destruction of the wonderful Seti II tomb in that infamous terrorist attack, his mummy now resided permanently in a purpose-built exhibit in the Cairo Museum. How did he feel about that?

It actually hurt her to drag in a breath. There was a dizzying sense of standing on the brink of some yawning chasm. The world whirled around her. A dreadful cold began to seep up from the ground. Despite being underground, the air moved around her. Something said her name . . .

By the pricking of my thumbs

Something wicked this way comes.

'Jane? Talk to me. What's happening?'

Luke's voice recalled her. Hardly daring to move her lips, as if any movement she made would bring whatever it was down upon her, she managed to whisper, 'Luke. It's here.'

'What is?'

The words tumbled over each other. 'Something . . . I didn't see . . . something moved. It's behind me. Something's in here with me. Luke . . .'

Her voice trailed away. Pushing aside the still vivid picture of the darkness-shaped jackal squatting over the tomb, he said, as calmly as he could, 'What is, Jane? What's in there with you? Tell me.'

'It's him. He's here. He's awake.'

'Who's awake?'

'The king.' Her voice was barely a whisper, but Luke heard her clearly enough. Striving for calm, common sense, he said, 'No. No, he's not. Really, he's not.'

'He is.'

'Where?'

'Behind me.'

'He's really not.'

'He is.'

'How do you know?'

'Luke, I can see his shadow. On the floor. It's long and black and it's covering mine and I can't get out. I won't be able to get past him. What shall I do?' She was gasping for breath. She couldn't get enough air in this tiny room so far underground. Crushed by the weight of rock and sand above it, her chest heaved in panic.

177

'Jane, listen to me. Turn around and face it. You'll see there's nothing there. It's your imagination. I promise you.'

'It's not, Luke. It's not.'

'All right, all right, don't get upset. I'm coming down.'

'No. Stay away. I mean it.'

'Where are you?'

'In the antechamber. Facing the burial chamber. It's behind me. Between me and the door.'

'Snap all your lightsticks. You need lots of light to make the shadows disappear.'

'And when they run out, I'll be left in the dark.'

'No. When the shadows disappear, they'll take whatever it is with them. That's when you make a run for the tunnel. I'll be waiting up here. I'll get you out.'

'I can't. I'm trapped.'

'Jane, it's OK. Deep breaths. It's OK. I'm here. Now – turn around and tell me what you see.'

She fumbled for another lightstick and held it above her head. The room grew brighter. On three. One . . . two . . . Taking the recommended deep breaths, she turned, very, very slowly, expecting the worst at every moment.

There was nothing there.

Relief surged through her, to be swamped almost immediately by hot embarrassment at her own monumental stupidity in allowing her mind to play stupid tricks on her like this. Of course there was nothing there. How could there be? This wasn't one of those holos where screaming nightdress-clad women fled lurching, bandage-wrapped mummies. And now she'd told Parrish, of all people. Mocking, sophisticated Parrish. She'd never hear the last of it. And there was nothing here. The whole thing was simply ridiculous superstition. Obviously, there was no curse. How could there be? Howard Carter, the man responsible for finding the tomb and first to enter it, had lived for many years afterwards. Sometimes she was so stupid . . .

The air moved again. Something that was at one and the same time very close to her and yet a long way off emitted a long, tired exhalation. Her entire body went rigid. Because it was behind her. It was still there. Somehow, it was still behind her. She knew then. There was no escape. No matter where she stood . . . No matter how fast she ran . . . or how far she ran . . . it would always be just behind her. It would stand behind her for the rest of her life.

Because of all the clutter in this tiny space, sudden movements were impossible, but she carefully shifted her feet and tremblingly raised her lightstick high above her head. What seemed like a hundred eyes stared directly at her. Statues, shabtis, cats, leopards. Painted eyes. Wooden eyes. Jewelled eyes. The tomb was full of eyes and all of them were looking directly at her.

For one moment, she considered bolting for another chamber, but that would take her further from the way out. This was the only exit. If she moved into another chamber and it got between her and the door again . . . Panic crawled across her mind.

Right. No. Stop. Think.

As with Luke, it was her training that kicked in. This room was her exit and Time Police protocol said the first priority was always – *always* – to secure your exit. She heaved a heavy wooden chest across the floor until it was directly underneath the entrance hole. The one she had come in by. Standing on it, she peered up the tunnel. Back to the surface. . Back to another world. The real world.

She thrust away a picture of herself struggling back up through the limescale chippings as something seized her ankles and dragged her back again . . . kicking and clawing . . . breaking her fingernails on the rough, rock chippings . . .

She could see the green lightstick she'd left halfway down the tunnel still glowing. Almost the whole length of the tunnel was visible and the way was clear.

Stepping back down off the chest, she was a little concerned to find her boots had left dusty footprints on the fine carvings. Echoes of her grandmother's voice came down through the years.

She needed a weapon. Something with which to defend herself. She checked her string and then stooped and picked up the chair leg again. A small part of her mind told her she was an idiot and it wouldn't be of the slightest use against a long-dead king.

Hefting it in her hand, she stopped to think. Actually, no, he wasn't, was he? He hadn't been dead that long. Not long enough for the smell of wet plaster to dissipate. Nor the faint whiff of sweet perfume hanging in the air. Nor the smell of burning – whatever that was all about.

She would discover later that the chemicals used to embalm the mummy had caused it to smoulder within its own sarcophagus and actually, at some point, it had spontaneously combusted. She would be very grateful she hadn't known that at the time. A flame-enveloped mummy, rising out of his sarcophagus, roaring in rage and anguish and revenge was not something to think about at any time, let alone when he could be less than two feet away.

Again, the light flickered. Just fractionally. A split-second later it burned as brightly as before. Luke was right. The lightstick was faulty. It was nothing. Nothing to worry about. Everything was fine.

Holding the lightstick like a torch, she stared around the disorderly chamber. Again, a hundred eyes watched her.

And then, suddenly, something changed. She didn't know what, but they weren't looking at her any longer. Suddenly, all the eyes were looking past her. Looking over her shoulder. Looking at something that stood behind her.

In vain did she tell herself all this was impossible. They were inanimate objects. Their eyes could not follow her around the room. They were not all looking over her shoulder. Because there was nothing behind her. Nothing at all. She'd proved it to herself once and all she had to do to prove it again was turn around. Just turn around and see for herself that nothing stood behind her. There was nothing there.

The air moved again. Another soft sigh. Her teeth began to chatter. She was cold. In fact, she was freezing. The air down here was icy. Her breath puffed a small cloud in front of her face.

Something stood behind her. She could feel it. In the same way that some people always know when they are being observed, she knew, with a certainty as cold as the air around her, that something stood behind her.

The smell of burning was stronger, overcoming the faint aroma of incense and flowers. She dragged her eyes down to the floor. A long black shadow enveloped her own. Because something stood behind her.

The logical part of her brain told her to turn around. To face whatever it was. She'd done it before. She'd be quite safe, because there was nothing there. There hadn't been then and there couldn't be now. The famous curse was simply a fanciful tale that had grown down the centuries. Something over which to shiver deliciously in the warmth and safety of home. The dead do not walk.

'Tell that to whatever stands behind you at this moment,' said Wimpy Jane. 'See if they believe it.'

A warm tear trickled down her cold cheek. 'Oh great, Jane,' said her other voice. 'Crying again. That's always helpful.'

The air moved once more.

Her nerve snapped. 'Stop it. Please. Just stop it. We're trying to help you.'

Silence and stillness were the only response. And then . . .

She never knew where the idea came from, but what was the one thing these mighty pharaohs had wanted? What was the whole point of the tombs and the pyramids and the elaborate grave goods? That they would never be forgotten. That their names would be remembered and honoured for all time. She acted without thought.

She switched off her com and then, in a tiny, trembling voice, she said, 'I know you. You are Tutankhamun, Lord of the Two Lands. You died young, but do not despair. You do not know it yet, but you will be the most famous of all the pharaohs. Your face is the face of Egypt. You should not feel ashamed before the gods. Your name will last until the end of time. Have no fear. Rest now. Sleep. Be patient. Your time will come. I promise you.'

The shadows swelled. For one heart-stopping moment she thought she would be swallowed up forever. Her throat closed with terror. Her chest was tight.

And then it was gone. She could breathe. The lightsticks burned without a flicker. The air was still. Whatever it was had gone.

Outside the tomb, Luke could hear the sounds of people making their way back along the valley floor. From the clatter of sliding rocks and the occasional curse, he assumed Grint's team was on their way back.

Telling himself he was only doing his duty and following protocol, he slipped into a deep, vertical fissure, and waited until they were almost level with him. Then, in best Time Police fashion, he intoned, 'Halt. Who goes there? Identify yourselves or be shot.'

Grint halted. Matthew was right behind him, followed by Anders supporting a limping Rossi and Kohl bringing up the rear.

Grint appeared to have suffered a sense of humour failure. 'Stop pissing about, Parrish.'

'Not the correct response. I may have to shoot you now.'

'What did I just say about pissing about?'

'I don't know. Still waiting for you all to identify yourselves correctly and according to Time Police protocols.'

Anders lowered Rossi to a rock.

Grint stared around. 'Where's Lockland? She run away?'

Mentally crossing his fingers, Luke said, 'Still in the tomb. As you instructed.'

Everyone turned to look at the dark tunnel. There seemed to be a general reluctance to approach.

Grint held Luke's gaze for a long, disbelieving moment and then opened his com. 'Lockland. This is Grint. Report.'

Luke held his breath, half-braced for hysterical sobbing or worse – ominous silence – and then, there it was. Jane's voice. Miraculously normal.

'The tomb is empty, sir. I searched every chamber. Parrish stood at the outer door. No one got past us. In or out.'

He grunted. 'Right then, out you come,' which, Jane recognised, was about the only acknowledgement she was ever likely to get. Not that she cared. She was pulling herself back up the passage almost before he'd even stopped speaking.

Luke, waiting for her at the other end, helped her down, whispering, 'All right?'

'Yes. You?'

'Yes. Well done.'

'Matthew?'

'He's fine.'

Grint turned his attention back to his team. 'Right, men, we're out of here. Check you've got all the gear you came in with. The Medjay will be on their way. We'll leave them to replace the grave goods. Good job, everyone. Whoever thought he might be the next Atticus Wolfe is about to wake up to a very bad day.'

He was right about not being caught here. Jane could see faint lights in the distance and hear shouts echoing off the cliffs. The Medjay were coming to investigate.

Anders turned to Grint. 'Sir, Officer North reports the clean-up crews have dealt with the pods. The crates have been removed for evidence. They and all the prisoners are jumping back to TPHQ. It's just us still here.'

'Right, Parrish, you and Farrell take a quick look around. Make sure we haven't left anything behind.'

He turned to Lockland. 'And what about you, Lockland? You did clear the tomb before you came out? No lightsticks? No litter?'

Luke stiffened. Had she remembered to clear the site behind her? It would be understandable if she hadn't – although not by Grint.

Jane shook her head, answering with unusual confidence. 'No, sir. The tomb is clear. Everything accounted for.'

'No problems in there?'

'None at all, sir. It was all very quiet.'

Her legs were trembling, her clothes were glued to her body with cold sweat, and she was certain she'd never again be able to close her eyes without reliving the terror of knowing something stood behind her, but taking her cue from those around her and because something still seemed to be required of her, she enquired, 'Did we miss all the fun? Did you get them?'

Grint nodded. 'We did. It was a bit lively for a moment, but while you and Parrish were sitting on your backsides down here, yes, we got them all. And their pods.'

They took one final look around. 'All clear, sir,' said Kohl.

'Right. Do the headcount and let's get back. Alert Hansen we're on our way. Kohl, you go first. Anders, keep an eye on Rossi. Make sure we don't have to carry him. Let's go, everyone.'

Back at TPHQ, everyone slowly dispersed, either towards the showers or the bar, depending on their own personal tastes. Luke,

Matthew and Jane trailed slowly down the corridor towards the dormitories. For different reasons it had been an exciting night for all of them, with fear and exhilaration equally mixed.

Luke turned to Jane. 'Are you all right now?'

'Now?' asked Matthew, turning to look at her. 'What happened?'

She was reluctant to talk about it. 'When I was in the tomb on my own . . . my mind started to play all sorts of tricks on me. I thought I saw something.'

There was a long pause and then Matthew said quietly, 'Actually, so did I. Just for a moment. Something big. On the mountainside.'

Parrish sighed. 'Who am I to be left out? I thought I saw something, too. Big jackal-headed god thing. I tell you I am *never* going back to Ancient Egypt.'

'You said you were never going back to the 20th century, either,' reminded Jane. 'That's two for two, so far. You're certainly cutting down your options.'

Luke shrugged. 'Doesn't matter. I'm not going to be here that long.'

'Long enough to take a shower, I hope,' said Jane.

'Lockland, before you start making snarky remarks, take a look at yourself in a mirror.'

She ignored him. 'Matthew, is Ellis badly hurt?'

'I don't know. Why do you ask?'

'If he's off for any length of time, then we might have to become part of Grint's team.'

There was silence as they thought about that. Jane envisaged a lifetime spent crawling through enclosed spaces.

Parrish yawned. 'Oh, shit. I'm going back to bed.'

Back in her room, Jane examined herself in the mirror. There was no doubt about it, she wasn't looking good. Her uniform was torn, dusty and bloody. Her hands and arms were covered in scrapes and small cuts. Her knees and elbows were both swollen and skinned. The medics had told her to shower and keep them clean. There was no need for special treatment.

She still looked a mess the next morning – in fact, as is frequently the case, she looked slightly worse – but as she was to discover, these were badges of honour. Word had somehow got around – she wondered whether Parrish had had a hand in that – that she'd stayed in the tomb – all alone – right until the moment she was ordered out by Grint. There was a certain amount of grudging admiration. One or two people admitted they wouldn't have fancied it very much. Others stopped her in the corridor to congratulate her. She was encouraged to recount her experiences. What was it like in the tomb? Remembering how terrified she had been made her feel a fraud, so she deliberately downplayed the experience, making a joke of being alone with the Curse of the Pharaohs. This was apparently the right way to go. She was several times complimented on a job well done.

It was very hard not to feel a glow of satisfaction. Luke had been right. If she hadn't stuck it out, then they would have despised her. But not anything like as much as she would have despised herself.

'Well,' said Commander Hay, gazing down at the bedridden Major Ellis. 'No need to ask how that one went.'

Ellis struggled to sit up. 'It's not serious, ma'am. Just a day or so to ensure there's no infection.'

'That's not what the doctor says. You're going to be out of the game for a while.'

He shook his head. 'I don't think so, ma'am.' He paused, torn between embarrassment and good manners. 'Er . . . would you like to sit down?'

She plonked herself in the visitor's chair, pulled over his fruit bowl and began to rifle the contents. 'You'll be pleased to hear our guests are all singing like . . . what's that bird again? Begins with C.'

'Cassowary,' said Ellis, deriving comfort from being as high as a kite on painkillers and intending to blame it on the drugs afterwards.

'Really?'

He nodded.

'You're sure?'

'Absolutely.'

'Well, singing like cassowaries then. We're liaising with the civilian police and it looks as if we're about to take another clump of illegals out of circulation.' She frowned. 'One of your bananas appears to have mutated.'

'Carambola, ma'am.'

'Isn't that a cheese?'

'I believe not, ma'am.'

She sighed. 'Where's Charlie when I need him? He knows all about this sort of thing.'

'Very high in vitamin C,' he said.

'Who said?'

'Officer North, ma'am. It was she who brought it.'

If Commander Hay thought this an interesting fact, she did not say so. 'How does one eat it?'

188

'One doesn't intend to try, ma'am.'

'Very wise, I think.' She stared out of the window. The rainy season was upon them and visibility was poor. Tall buildings were outlined in flashing red lights for the benefit of low-flying airships. The Shard and the Cheesegrater were brightly lit – the Folded Napkin and the Startled Hamster were out of sight.

'I've been reviewing the mission reports.'

'So have I, ma'am.'

'Farrell did well.'

'All the members of my team performed well, ma'am.'

'They did, didn't they? I think they surprised us all. Farrell took on three illegals with nothing more than liquid string and blind optimism, and whether or not Lockland did see something in that tomb, she stood her ground.'

'Yes, I was impressed.'

'It's certainly made a difference to her. I passed her in the corridor this morning and she definitely had a bit of a strut on.'

'She surprised us all, ma'am. She certainly surprised herself.' He paused. 'And Parrish . . .'

'Yes . . .' she said thoughtfully. 'Parrish.'

'I think he held things together very well.'

'So do I. Another surprise.'

She got to her feet and replaced his much-fingered bowl of fruit. 'I see more visitors looming.'

Major Ellis looked up to see the mixed bunch of individuals generally referred to as his team slowly approaching and bearing the sort of gifts they each considered appropriate for the sick. Farrell carried a technical magazine obviously intended to provide him with a little light reading, Jane a bunch of flowers – always the first choice of any rufty-tufty Time Police officer – and Parrish – for reasons known only to himself, but which Ellis knew with certainty would not be good – clutched a large, stuffed giraffe.

He groaned. 'Oh God, what fresh hell is this?'

Amused, Commander Hay affected not to have heard him. 'I'll leave you to enjoy your visitors.'

'Please don't.'

She patted his shoulder. 'Get well soon, Major.'

14

Feeling oneself to be on the verge of acceptance was all very pleasant, but as Jane was very aware, she wasn't quite there yet. They were still regarded as Team Weird. If, she thought, we are indeed a team. Other teams ate together, socialised together, did all the things that teams did. Team Weird emerged from the shadows, came together for the mission and then went their separate ways again.

She was sitting at lunch one day. She always sat alone. No one ever wanted to join her or asked her to join them. Other teams crowded around tables together, telling tales, exaggerating exploits, shouting and laughing. Roaring testosterone was, as usual, bouncing off the walls. The room was loud with male voices. Jane sat in her usual corner. More accepted she might be, but she still ate alone. She usually brought something to read so she wouldn't have to watch them all talking, arguing, calling from group to group.

The dining room, like everything else to do with the Time Police, was bland and utilitarian. Tables and chairs were grey and easily wiped down. An attempt had been made to enliven the walls with a series of innocuous but somehow depressing landscapes. They weren't reduced to plastic plates or plastic cutlery, but it wasn't a cheery room. No one ever lingered. She sometimes wondered if that was deliberate. Get your food down and back to work as soon as possible.

She was finishing her sensible salad and piece of fruit and contemplating a rare free afternoon – Luke and Matthew had been scheduled a self-defence session from which she was, until all her scrapes and bumps healed, happily exempt – when a strange voice said, 'May we join you?'

She looked up in surprise.

She knew he was a senior officer by his insignia, which was puzzling. The dining room was democratically *sit where you like*, but senior officers traditionally clustered together in a quiet corner. Far from the madding crowd and herded together for mutual protection, as Luke had once remarked.

There were three of them. A major, a captain and a lieutenant – Lt Grint. Guilt kicked in. Was she sitting at their table? Should she leave? She was uncertain whether to stand up or not. The dining room was supposed to be an informal no-man's-land where rank need not be formally acknowledged.

They sat down. Without waiting for her permission, she noticed. Not that they needed it, but in that case, why ask? None of them had a plate with them, so they weren't here to eat. Two sat opposite her with Grint at the end of the table. Not exactly blocking her way out, but making it difficult to squeeze past.

The major spoke. His name badge read Callen. 'Nice job, Lockland.'

She assumed he was talking about the tomb and felt her face flood with the familiar hot colour. 'Thank you, sir. Sirs.'

Grint performed the introductions.

'Lockland, this is Major Callen. Overseeing new recruits is part of his remit.'

He smiled at her. 'Hello, Lockland. I'm sorry we haven't met before this – I usually get to speak to all the teams at the beginning of their gruntwork but everything has been a little hectic recently. How are you finding things?'

She was so surprised she barely managed to stammer, 'Very well, thank you, sir.' She realised her answer barely made sense and blushed harder than ever.

Grint stared out of the window and the so-far-unnamed captain folded his arms and stared at her unnervingly.

Callen continued. 'We've been watching you.'

The familiar panic started up again. Why would they have been watching her? Had they heard about her little meltdown in the tomb after all? Was she being eased out? Psychologically unstable.

She realised the major was still speaking and pulled herself together.

'So,' he was saying in a friendly tone. 'What are your plans, Lockland?'

She looked at him in surprise. Actually, he was rather nice. A little older than Ellis – considerably older than she was herself – with dark blond hair and crinkly blue eyes. He continued. 'Where do you see yourself going after you finish your gruntwork?'

She was so surprised they expected her even to complete her gruntwork that she was momentarily lost for words. It would have been nice to have a coherent career plan to place in front of him – the sort of thing North could probably produce in her sleep – but that was never going to happen, so she told the truth.

'Well, I haven't given it a lot of thought, sir. There's still a few months to go yet and I'm concentrating on trying to do a good job now.'

A nice, safe answer.

He nodded. 'Well, you might want to consider joining my crew. Always room for someone like you.'

She felt another wave of hot colour flood over her. Her face burned like a beacon. Like me? she thought. What am I like?

Major Callen pushed his chair back, nodded and walked away, followed by the captain.

Grint lingered. 'Bear it in mind, Lockland. Could be your big chance.'

Unable to stop herself, she babbled, 'Yes, indeed, sir. Thank you. Definitely something to think about.' She paused. She should let it go. Her face burned again. 'But why?'

'I don't follow.'

'Why me, sir?'

'You stuck to your post. You did the job. A few people have their eyes on you now, Lockland.'

He nodded and then he too disappeared, leaving her staring after them, hot, baffled and anxious. She had always been quiet, shy and not one to put herself forwards. But that didn't mean she was stupid. She had a fair assessment of her talents and capabilities. Yes, she knew she wasn't as stupid as she often thought she was. Yes, she knew she had confidence issues. But to be told she'd shone to such an extent that people actually wanted her on their team . . . before she'd even completed her gruntwork . . . She was willing to bet that anywhere in this building you could still get good odds on her not finishing her time here.

She finished her meal and lost no time seeking out Luke and Matthew, waiting for them outside the gym.

They seemed surprised to see her.

She nudged them into a quiet corner. 'Do you two have a minute?'

Parrish was towelling his still damp hair. He stopped and looked at her warily. 'Why?'

She told them what had happened, relating their words as closely as she could remember them and waited, somewhat nervously, for Parrish's disbelieving, 'You?'

'Yes,' she said defiantly. 'Me. They wanted me. I don't understand it.'

'Neither do I,' said Parrish.

'Oh thanks.'

'Well, seriously, Jane . . .'

'Oh f . . .' She bit off the word.

Parrish grinned. 'Oh . . . what? Come on, Lockland, you know the word. Begins with f and ends in uck.'

Her temper snapped. 'Oh, fire truck off, Parrish.'

She stormed off down the corridor.

Matthew watched her go, a worried frown on his face, and then turned back to Parrish. 'That's . . . odd.'

'What's odd? Jane's attempt at profanity or Callen's very unexpected interest?'

'Both. But mostly Callen.'

Parrish nodded. 'Unexpected enough to be troubling. She's right. Why would they want her? Is someone trying to break us up? Why? If they want to do that, then why don't they just say, "Farrell, you're too weird for words and Parrish, you're too good for this place. Both of you get out of here." Eh?'

'Dunno.'

'Well, no one can do anything until we've finished our gruntwork, surely?'

Matthew frowned. 'Suppose they don't wait for her to finish her gruntwork? She might just move to someone else's team if they asked her. She's desperate for someone to like her.'

Luke looked up, surprised. 'Why wouldn't they like her?'

'For the same reason they don't like us.'

'Their loss. I'm adorable,' said the tall, handsome, and above all, rich boy, who never had any problems getting people to like him. He slung his towel over his shoulder. 'Suppose she does?'

'Does what?'

'Leave our team.'

'Why do you care?'

Luke considered this. 'Not sure.'

15

The memo was flashed to all their scratchpads after the morning briefing.

'What's this?' said Luke. 'June 1st – Stop the Clock Day. What does that mean?'

'It means several things,' said North, gathering up her files and preparing to depart. 'Firstly, and quite importantly, that you weren't listening to the series of lectures entitled History of the Time Police, which, I think, will come as no surprise to anyone. And secondly, and more importantly, that your presence will be required on that day at 1100 hours in the atrium.'

'What for?'

'It's not my job to provide study notes for the memo, Parrish. Read the damn thing yourself.'

Jane looked up from her scratchpad. 'Are we able to attend this? It says full officers only.'

'You may observe but not participate.'

'Because we're not yet qualified.'

'Correct.'

'Do we have to go?' asked Parrish. 'I mean, if we're not yet qualified, then surely . . .'

'We're all aware you consider the Time Police to be a waste

of space, Parrish, but some of us think that what we do here is quite important and that the sacrifices made by those in the Time Wars should never be forgotten. The ceremony is to honour those who did their duty. Not something you'd know anything about. Go or don't go. I don't think anyone will care either way.'

The door slammed behind her.

'So I don't have to go then?' said Parrish, hopefully.

'Only if you don't mind becoming one of the fallen yourself,' said Matthew darkly, and followed Officer North out of the door.

It rather looked as if Luke Parrish had taken them at their word. The overhead walkway was lined with trainees and the few civilian support staff who worked at TPHQ and Jane couldn't see him anywhere.

Fully qualified officers formed neat ranks in the atrium below. Serving officers lined up on the left-hand side and former officers on the right. These were the heavily decorated veterans of the Time Wars. There weren't many of them. Jane guessed there would be fewer and fewer every year. One day, inevitably, there would be none at all, and the Time Wars would slip from memory into history, and then from history into legend, until, finally, they passed from knowledge into nothingness.

She knew the Time Police kept an Archive where veteran officers were encouraged to share their memories of the conflict for future generations to learn from.

That's me, she thought. I'm a future generation. I should learn from this.

There was a disturbance beside her. Luke Parrish had turned up. He elbowed his way between Jane and Matthew. Like them, he'd taken some trouble with his appearance. His uniform was wrinkle-free, his boots buffed and his hair combed.

Jane smiled at him. 'You made it, then?'

He shifted his feet. 'Yes . . . well . . .'

Below them, the big, old-fashioned clock began the preliminary chimes. It was almost eleven o'clock.

Silence fell.

There was another ceremony, Jane knew, a public affair when the Time Police joined members of the royal family, politicians, foreign dignitaries and so on in a formal show of remembrance, but this ceremony was theirs alone. Just for the Time Police themselves.

Because we're the people who understand, she thought, suddenly. They were us once. Before they made the ultimate sacrifice. When they went on and left us behind to count the cost.

Looking down at the survivors, the cost had been massive. There were far fewer complete people than there should have been.

Commander Hay stepped forwards. The sun shafted through the glass roof, glinting off medals and belt buckles. The chimes had ceased and the great bell was about to toll the hour. Her voice rang around the atrium.

'Stop the clock.'

In mid-chime – the clock stopped.

There was absolute silence. No one moved.

A lectern had been set up on which reposed a large book. Slowly, carefully, Commander Hay opened the cover. Jane could hear the stiff pages crackle.

In a clear, strong voice, she began to read, her voice carrying easily around the atrium. This was the annual reading of the names of those who had died in the Time Wars. Or had died later as a result of their injuries.

And every year, thought Jane, the number of those present would decrease and the list of names in the book would increase and then, one day, it would be all list and no people.

She looked down at the serving officers far beneath her. A lot of them were too young now to have fought in the Time Wars, but they carried their own memories and their own losses just the same.

Just like me, she thought, struggling, as she always did, to resolve the hazy memories of her parents into something more solid. Something she could hold on to . . .

She looked at Matthew, staring solidly into space and giving no clue as to what his thoughts were. Even Luke was standing quietly, looking down at his feet. What was he thinking at this moment?

The reading took a long time. At one point, a man in a wheelchair shifted and made a sound of distress. Or pain, perhaps. The officer nearest to him, a big man whose many combat flashes denoted an exciting career, crossed the aisle to bend over him and murmur something, placing a gentle hand on his shoulder. The two of them stayed together for the rest of the ceremony. Jane felt a sudden lump in her throat and looked away.

Eventually, Commander Hay read the last name, paused and then carefully closed the book.

Major Callen stepped forwards and called the room to attention. The crash of their feet echoed around the atrium. Overhead, on the walkway, the trainees did the same.

Next year, thought Jane. Next year I'll be down there with them.

There was the traditional minute's silence of remembrance and then:

'Start the clock.'

The clock began to strike the eleventh hour. There was more to this than ceremony, Jane knew. This was the Time Police demonstrating their defiance of Time. Stopping the clock to honour their dead.

Captain Farenden picked up the book. Someone else removed the lectern, and by the time the last chime had died away, the atrium was empty.

16

As the son of one of the richest men in the world, Luke Parrish had never really bothered whether people liked him or not. In his experience, most people did. With the exception of Ms Steel, of course. And the Time Police. Now, however, he was about to discover just how much the Time Police really did dislike him.

Because his plan had always been to get out at the earliest possible opportunity – even if it meant being thrown out – he'd never gone out of his way to be pleasant. He had a sharp tongue and never hesitated to use it. For someone who'd only been with the Time Police for a few months, he'd managed to annoy almost everyone who crossed his path. Instructors, senior officers, colleagues, teammates – his proud boast was that with the exception of the big blonde in Logistics, everyone hated him. And now he came to think of it, he wasn't that sure about the blonde – what was her name now?

Rounding a corner the next day, he found a small knot of officers – all male – grouped together in a quiet corridor. Something about the way they were standing told him they were waiting for him and at that moment he rather wished he'd gone with Matthew to the technical library. He wasn't looking for trouble and there were a lot of them. Too many.

Discretion is frequently the better part of valour. He wheeled about, intending to retrace his footsteps.

Too late. They were behind him as well and, in a moment, he was surrounded.

No one said a word. Their silence was ominous. His heart sank. This was serious. This wasn't going to be a case of insults exchanged – all sound but no fury. It was obvious a bit of a punch-up was brewing.

A sensible man would assume a placatory manner and endeavour to get his arse out of there with all speed. Luke Parrish didn't do sensible.

He patted his pockets artistically. 'Hang on – I've got some peanuts somewhere. Do you do tricks?'

Someone – he never discovered who – said, 'Orduroy Tannhauser's sister was a friend of mine.'

Shit. This wasn't, as he had first thought, the old having a go at the new again. This was personal.

The shock left him frozen for just that moment too long. And then they all moved at once.

He blocked the first blow but never saw the second one at all. He staggered backwards against the wall and came out swinging. Much good it did him. He was dimly aware that corridor brawls aren't in the least bit like the films. His assailants didn't wait politely so he could deal with them one at a time. They all piled on at once. There were more kicks and punches than he could possibly deal with. His main thought was to protect his head and stay on his feet. The moment he was on the ground this would become serious. Well – serious for him. He suspected being kicked to a pulp would be regarded as just typical Time Police high spirits by everyone else.

Blows rained down. He was just beginning to wonder if he'd be better off curled in a ball on the ground after all when a tremulous female voice called, 'Hey. Stop. Stop that. Leave him alone.'

Oh great – of all the potential rescuers in this building, he'd got the little wimpy one. Bloody Lockland. Who should get out of here. He didn't think they'd start on her but at least she could go for help.

The blows ceased. Everyone stepped back, panting slightly.

He couldn't see all that clearly, but he knew she'd pushed her way to his side. He felt some exasperation. They hadn't gone away. What did she think she was going to do? This was more than just a quick scuffle in the corridor. This was going to be ugly and he wanted her out of there.

His lips felt stiff and puffy. 'Lockland, what are you doing here? I know you mean well but you're not really a lot of help, are you? Even against a group of Neanders, some of whom are barely sentient.'

He was dimly aware of a surge towards him.

Lockland held up a finger. 'One moment, gentlemen, if you please. I believe I have a prior claim.'

Astonishingly, probably more surprised than obedient, they halted.

She turned to Luke. 'What do you mean – not a lot of help?'

He wiped a trail of blood off his chin and raised his arms in exasperation. 'Well, for God's sake, Lockland, look at you, you're about as much use as . . . Ooooof.'

He staggered sideways, briefly hung on to the wall for support, and then when that failed him, slowly sagged to the floor where he rested on forehead, nose and knees. Several of those present instinctively winced in sympathy.

A voice sounded at the back. 'What's going on here? Let me through,' and North was pushing her way through suddenly frozen Time Police officers like a Russian icebreaker determined to get back to port before the vodka ran out.

North-like, she summed up the situation at a glance and then turned to address a pale and trembling but resolutely determined Lockland.

'As a senior member of your team, Lockland, I cannot let this pass. This was wrong on so many levels. Firstly, you lifted your knee far too high. You were lucky you didn't lose your balance. Secondly, if you miss your target and your knee hits bone instead . . .'

Everyone flinched, apart from Parrish who had passed the flinching stage several minutes ago and was approaching blind agony.

North was assuming lecture mode, demonstrating on an officer who hadn't had the sense to get out of the way in time.

'Remember for the future – use your upper thigh.' She pointed to her upper thigh. 'Which gives you a wider area of impact.' She demonstrated the much wider area of impact on the cringing officer. '*And* there's more cushioning – for you, that is. And much less chance of losing your balance and falling over. Let's try it again, shall we?' She turned to the crowd. 'Do we have another volunteer?'

The front row scattered. The back row, suddenly finding itself the front row, followed suit.

Lockland sighed enviously and wiped the sweat off her face with her forearm. 'I so wish I could do that.'

North shook her head. 'Don't waste your time. You're not me.'

'I'm not anyone.'

North didn't do sympathy. 'Don't be ridiculous. I play to my strengths. You should play to yours.'

Lockland sighed again. 'I could probably play to my weaknesses.'

'Exactly.'

About to feel sorry for herself, Jane paused. 'Oh.' She thought about it for a moment. This was a new idea to explore. She was the permanent underdog. No one ever had any expectations of her. She would always have the element of surprise. Which could be useful. She nodded at North.

'That's two lessons learned today, Lockland. Make use of them both.' She leaned over the still suffering lump on the carpet. 'Carry on, Trainee Parrish.'

She left.

'Eight years,' said a carpet-muffled voice.

'What?'

'Eight years. They say she'll be running this place in ten years and I reckon she'll be doing it in eight. Can you help me up, please?'

He rose painfully to his feet and looked at her.

'I suppose I should thank you.'

She automatically opened her mouth to tell him there was no need and then had second thoughts. 'Are you complaining?'

'Well, a little bit of me is.'

'Listen, if you'd got into it with that lot then you'd have suffered a lot more than just my knee.'

'There is no "just" about your knee, Lockland. Your knee is a force of nature all on its own. You haven't got any ice, have you?'

'Ice is only for grateful boys.'

'So, just to get things straight – figuratively speaking – you thought you'd save me by ruining my chances of fatherhood.'

'It could have been your face.'

'Oh. Yeah. So it could. Well done, Lockland. Good thinking.'

There was the sound of running footsteps and both of them looked up. Instinctively, Jane stepped in front of Luke, which seemed to cause him some amusement. Matthew was coming towards them looking angry.

'What happened to you? Who did this?'

Luke nodded at Jane. 'She did.'

Matthew slid his eyes sideways to Jane. 'Er . . .'

Luke put a hand on his shoulder for support. 'Do you have any ice on you?'

'I could get some, I expect.'

'Could you put it in a drink?'

Luke's room was a tip. It was very apparent he hadn't quite grasped that the housekeeping fairies no longer visited in the night.

Jane helped him on to his unmade bed and Matthew disappeared in search of alcohol for the patient.

'Drinking in our rooms is not allowed,' Jane called after him, in some alarm.

Luke closed his eyes. 'Good. Go and tell them I'm drinking in my room and invite them to chuck me out as soon as possible.'

She wet a flannel and passed it to him. 'Wipe your face.'

'Aren't you going to do it for me?'

'No. Who's Orduroy Tannhauser?'

He mumbled something.

'Sorry, I didn't catch that.'

Pain made him irritable. 'For God's sake, Jane, let it go.'

She shot him a look and got up to go.

'Sorry. Sorry. And I haven't thanked you for saving my life, even if it was at the expense of the next generation of Parrishes.'

She headed towards the door.

'Sorry. Again.' He sighed. 'No, I am.' He shifted painfully on the bed. 'I'm grateful, Jane. That could have been quite bad, so thank you.'

'You're welcome.'

'You're not asking about . . .'

'You don't want to tell me.'

'Yeah, well, it's not a pretty story.'

'Don't do that.'

'What?'

'Patronise me.'

'I wasn't,' he said, indignantly. And then thought about it. 'Was I?'

'It's not a pretty story so don't tell Jane. She might get upset.'

'Well, you must admit . . .'

'Oh, fire truck off, Parrish.'

She stormed out.

He lay back on his pillows. 'Wish she'd never thought of that.'

The next one in was Matthew with a very large glass and an ice pack.

Luke made good use of both. 'Thanks.'

Matthew nodded.

'God, do you ever speak?'

He shrugged. 'Does it matter? You never listen.' He left, shutting the door behind him.

Luke leaned back against his pillows, closed his mind against the pain and sipped his drink. The measure was a double – Matthew had been generous. He hoped he might fall asleep but the combination of throbbing and guilt kept him awake. He lay on his bed, alternately drinking and thinking.

An hour later, Ellis turned up, pale-faced and moving very slowly.

Luke tried to sit up. 'Should you be out of MedCen?'

'No.' He winced, pulled up a chair and sat carefully, grimacing in pain.

Luke grinned at him. 'Snap.'

'Oh? You've been shot, too?'

'Worse.'

'Yeah, I heard. Quick thinking on Lockland's part. A few hours' discomfort has saved you from a good seeing-to. You'll be all right again by this time tomorrow, which you wouldn't have been able to say if they'd had their way.'

'No.'

'You might want to get her something.'

'How do you mean?'

'A gift, perhaps. To show your appreciation. I don't suppose she's had many gifts in her life.'

Luke considered this. 'Good thought. I'll get my father's PA on it.'

Ellis sighed, wearily heaved himself to his feet and hobbled painfully to the door. 'I was wrong about you, Parrish. You're a bit of a lost cause, aren't you?'

Luke scowled angrily. 'For God's sake – now what have I done?'

'A teammate put herself at considerable risk for you and you thank her by getting your father's PA to buy her a gift. What do you think?'

He fumbled with crutch and door handle.

'Wait. Wait. Please.'

'What do you want, Parrish?'

'You once said I could come to you if I needed . . .'

'Help?'

'Advice.'

'All right.' He came back to the chair and, not without some effort, sat back down. 'What do you need advice on?'

'It's over a year ago now, but I don't know if you remember Orduroy Tannhauser.'

'I do, yes.'

'I was slightly involved.'

'Yes. I know.'

'In fact, it's the reason why . . .'

'You're here. Yes, I know.'

'It wasn't quite as bad as it appeared in the papers.'

Ellis remained silent.

Luke stared at his hands. The silence went on and on but this time, Ellis made no attempt to leave. The room was slowly darkening because Parrish had not set his room lights to come on automatically.

'We weren't best friends, but I knew him quite well.'

'The inquest said you played cards with him.'

'I wasn't the only one, but yes. He wasn't a bad player. If he'd just stuck to playing for fun . . . Sadly for him, he was

210

just good enough to know he was good, but not good enough to know he wasn't that good. If you understand that . . .'

'I do. Continue.'

'Well, I was with him that night. At the club. He'd been drinking. Not a huge amount but enough to impair his judgement. He was winning and losing equally to begin with but as the night progressed, he was just losing. Unfortunately, what he lacked in judgement, he made up for in enthusiasm. I could see how the evening was going to end.'

He looked up defensively. 'I did my best. One by one, I cut the others out of the game. It wasn't hard – they weren't that good, either. Finally, it was just him and me. He said, "One last hand, then?" and dealt before I could say anything. I sat looking at my really good hand. A full house. Aces and jacks. On any other occasion I'd have given my right arm for a hand like that. I didn't know what to do and while I was still thinking about it, he saw me with everything he had. It was all piled on the table in front of him and he just pushed it towards me. There was a big crowd around the table. His eyes were sparkling. He was enjoying being the centre of attention. He was excited.'

Luke shifted position, ignoring the throbbing.

'I didn't know what to do. I knew I could beat him but it would ruin him. I considered folding and letting him walk away but that wouldn't do him any good in the long run. He'd be back for more the next night, and he'd lose the lot – and more besides – because he'd never believe he couldn't win it all back again with the next hand. So I laid down my cards and watched his face as he realised he'd lost everything. He carried it off well but his eyes were . . . well, you can imagine.'

Ellis could imagine it very clearly. The bright lights winking

211

off jewellery and crystal glassware. The hum of excitement. The admiring crowd. And a young man very much out of his depth. He looked across at Parrish. Possibly two young men very much out of their depth.

'What did you do?'

'I picked up my winnings, shook hands and walked away. I wasn't going to keep any of it. He wasn't much more than a boy,' said the very young man talking in the dark. 'I don't take that sort of money off children. I thought I'd wait outside and give it all back to him but I couldn't find him anywhere. Then I thought perhaps that was too easy, and a sleepless night would do him good. Teach him a lesson. Give him time to see the error of his ways. So I took the water taxi home.'

He was silent a long time. 'I should have realised.'

'That he would shoot himself?'

Luke nodded.

Ellis said gently, 'Luke, you couldn't have done anything. It was already too late. From what I remember, while you were waiting for him at the front, he was blowing his brains out around the back.'

He said angrily, 'I should have known. I thought I was acting for the best.' He fumbled for the glass on the floor.

'Don't you think you've had enough?'

'You can never have enough.'

The glass was empty and with a sigh he let it fall again.

Ellis said, 'This was over a year ago now. What's the problem?'

'Orduroy had a mother. And, although I didn't know it at the time – a sister, as well. Someone had told me they weren't well off and I thought perhaps I could make things right . . . or something. I don't know.'

He stopped talking, staring at his past.

Ellis said helpfully, 'And now your income has dropped so dramatically you can't afford it and you feel bad about cutting them off.'

'Oh no. That's not it at all. Well, no, you're right, I can't afford it, but I can hardly stop now, can I? My personal circumstances are not important.'

Considerably surprised by this response, Ellis said, 'So what's the problem?'

'Well, these days I need to study my bank statements a little more carefully than in the good old days, and I've just discovered all the payments I've been making have been returned. Obviously, they'd worked out who was sending them.'

He heaved a sigh. 'So I've been thinking . . . I have the idea . . . that I should talk to them . . . but what if I make things worse . . . and then I think, what if they want to know, you know, what actually happened . . . and then I think, am I just being selfish and trying to offload my own guilt, because it *was* all my fault . . . and I've been going around in circles for some time now, trying to work out what to do for the best.'

Ellis was conscious of a feeling of astonishment and then, unexpectedly, deep satisfaction.

'Well,' he said slowly, 'why don't you let Mrs Tannhauser decide? And it might be best if you don't approach her directly. Is there an intermediary you could use to . . . test the water? You never know, she might welcome the chance to talk about Orduroy. And you can explain about the money and if she truly doesn't want it . . . well . . .'

He spread his hands and waited.

Luke stared at his feet for a while. 'Yes, there is someone.'

With a gleam of humour, he said, 'I'm afraid we're back to Ms Steel again. Although in this instance, I think she might be the very person. She hates me, so I can rely on her to present me in the worst possible light – so if Mrs Tannhauser does agree to see me, it'll be because she really wants to.'

'Well, there you go, then. A plan.' Ellis paused. 'If she does agree – for whatever reason – it won't be an easy interview.'

'No, it won't. But it shouldn't be, really, should it? Thank you.'

Ellis heaved himself painfully to his feet again. 'Let me know how it goes.'

Parrish nodded. 'Got to say, you look terrible. Do you need a hand getting back to MedCen?'

Ellis shook his head.

'They don't know you've gone, do they?'

Ellis shook his head.

'It's a chargeable offence – leaving without a doctor's permission. Would you like me to put in a good word for you at the hearing?'

'Would you like your testicles to benefit from an action replay?'

Parrish appeared to shrivel slightly. 'Not just at the moment.'

Ellis let himself out.

For a while, Luke lay looking up at the ceiling and then reached over and called up Ms Steel.

'Good evening, Ms Steel.'

She didn't waste time with pleasantries. 'What do you want?'

'I'm doing really badly, my life has gone right down the pan, I'm in considerable pain and I thought this news would brighten your day.'

'It certainly has, Mr Parrish. This is unexpectedly thoughtful of you.'

'And I wondered if you could do something for me.'

'Mr Parrish, you should be aware that I work for your father and not for you.'

'I'm perfectly well aware of that, Ms Steel. I've chosen you because you loathe and despise me.'

'And in full knowledge of my deep and abiding contempt for you, you want me to do what, exactly?'

He told her. It took quite a long time and afterwards there was an even longer silence.

'Ms Steel? Are you still there?'

'Yes.'

'Oh. I thought you might have forgotten to pay the phone bill or something and they'd cut you off.'

'You want *me* to do this for you?'

'Well, I don't expect you to do it personally. Bit below your pay grade, don't you think? I thought you'd despatch a minion.'

'No,' she said slowly. 'I'll do it myself. Just so I'm sure of my facts – exactly how much do you send her every month?'

He told her.

'Luke – Mr Parrish – that's nearly half of your current monthly income.'

'Well, it wasn't when I started.'

'But it is now.'

'Yes, but to use the popular phrase – I've started so I'll finish.'

There was a long pause. He could hear her tapping her pencil on the desk and suddenly lost his nerve. 'Sorry, Ms Steel – you must have a lot on. Forget it.'

215

'No – *I'm* sorry. Tapping is a bad habit of mine when I'm thinking. Yes, I will present your case and I'll do my best, but Luke . . .'

'I know,' he said, 'and if she doesn't want to know, then I'll just have to live with it. But thanks in advance for trying. Incidentally, I'm not advocating you keeping any secrets from the old man, but if you could avoid mentioning this unless actually asked, I'd be grateful.'

'You'd rather he didn't know?'

'Well, he does know about Orduroy, doesn't he? That's why I'm here. Under the yoke, so to speak.'

'I mean about your intentions.'

'Yes, but you know what he's like. He'll muscle in, take over, issue a barrage of instructions, and really, it's nothing to do with him, is it? It's my responsibility.'

There was another pause and then she said crisply, 'Very well, Luke, I'll be in touch,' and ended the call.

17

Everything healed. Eventually, Luke Parrish was able to assume an upright posture again. Jane's cuts and bruises mended. Matthew's hair regained some of its former exuberance. Their memories faded a little. There was no more brawling in the corridors but there was no point in taking chances so they stuck together as much as possible. Whether this strategy worked or whether people had lost interest in them was hard to say, but they were left in peace.

Rather to his surprise, Ms Steel was as good as her word and on his next free day, Luke changed out of his uniform and caught the Regent's Canal water taxi to Paddington where, obedient to Ms Steel's commands, he picked up the Hyperloop to the West Country.

Even without the statue of a small, marmalade-munching, catastrophe-laden bear, he'd always liked Paddington Station. Four times winner of the Best Kept Station Award and this year's front-runner for the prestigious La Voiture D'Or for its luxurious rolling stock, Paddington Station was the jewel in the Great Western Hyperloop crown.

In his pre-Time Police days – in what he liked to think of as his proper life – he hadn't had to think twice about taking the Hyperloop. These days his circumstances were vastly different, and he was surprised Ms Steel had booked him on this, rather than the overcrowded, dirty and frequently failing motorway system. Hyperloops – or trains, as they used to be known – were luxury transport – right from the moment smiling staff greeted you at the entrance to the station, miraculously whisked your luggage away out of sight and escorted you to the appropriate waiting room where they would supply top-quality refreshments.

Luke accepted a glass of wine and a small plate of smoked salmon sandwiches from another smiling attendant and sat back to admire the platform floral displays that had won Paddington yet another gold medal at the Chelsea Flower Show.

Two small robots chugged past, quietly bickering over which was to pick up a small and extremely rare piece of litter lying nearby. Attendants and porters proudly wearing the crimson and cream insignia of the Great Western happily escorted passengers to their allocated seats and handed them today's complimentary newspapers together with the beverage of their choice.

A personalised announcement informed Luke that lunch would be served between Reading and Swindon and that Great Western was proud to offer four courses – ravioli with langoustines or heritage beetroot, followed by suckling pig, roast pigeon or Cornish turbot, followed by crème brûlée or lemon tart.

The highlight of the menu, however, was the world-famous and enormously popular Great Western Cheeseboard – the result of a hard-fought international legal action preventing other, lesser cheeses being designated as Cheddar. To be followed by coffee and mints. All washed down with only borderline-legal

Great Western Cider, specially brewed to an ancient recipe by the farmers of Gloucestershire. Followed by a visit to A&E, presumably.

Yet another attendant murmured at Luke's elbow. Apparently, his train, the Sir Francis Drake, awaited his presence. There was a brief tussle over who was to carry his newspaper, which the smiling attendant won, and Luke was escorted to his train and seated as carefully as if he were made of the most fragile substance known to man.

On the opposite platform, resplendent in her Great Western livery, the Dame Agatha Christie panted gently, impatient to be on her way.

The seat moulded itself to his contours as he watched the giant clock's second-hand sweep dramatically to the hour. Doors slammed. Whistles sounded. Station staff windmilled their arms in gestures whose meaning could only be guessed at. At five seconds to go, the locomotive uttered the obligatory warning blast. People stepped back behind the safety line. And then, punctual to the second, the great engines rose to that familiar roar – and they were gone.

Mrs Tannhauser lived in a tiny house only half a mile from the station. The street was full of identical houses, all with lace curtains and faded paintwork and gleaming windows. Because poverty is acceptable when it's spotless. Cleanliness makes poverty respectable. Luke felt a spurt of guilty anger. What business had someone like Orduroy belonging to a gambling club frequented by people with ten times his annual income? And probably estates in Hertfordshire, as well?

Ms Steel had prepared the ground well. They were expecting

him. The door was opened by Orduroy's sister. Here were Orduroy's light amber eyes and dark skin, but while Orduroy's eyes had sparkled with light and excitement, those of his sister were flat and dead.

They looked at each other and for a long moment he thought she wasn't going to let him in after all. Then, wordlessly, she stepped aside. He carefully wiped his feet and entered.

The tiny house had long since been modernised. The walls had been knocked down to make one large room with access to a slightly overgrown garden at the rear. He wondered if it had been Orduroy who had cared for the garden. Or whether they just couldn't be bothered any longer. That nothing was worth the effort now Orduroy was gone.

Photographs of Orduroy were everywhere. Orduroy as a baby with his older sister sitting solemnly alongside him. Orduroy in a school uniform. Orduroy slightly older in a different school uniform. Orduroy in cricket whites. Orduroy graduating with that familiar ear-to-ear smile. Orduroy posing proudly outside the city office where he worked. Had worked.

Luke gritted his teeth and wondered why he was doing this.

Eventually, Orduroy's mother, an older, tinier version of Orduroy's sister, gestured to him to sit down. He perched himself nervously on the first chair that came to hand.

Still none of them spoke. The silence hung as heavy as the atmosphere in the room. With a flash of insight, he imagined long, long afternoons in this silent room waiting for a son who would never come again. The light of his mother's life had disappeared. And add to that the resentment of the daughter who was still here, but had to live with not being her brother. The only photographs of his sister were those she shared with

Orduroy. Luke wondered what job she'd had and whether she'd had to give it up to look after her mother. More lives than Orduroy's had ended that night.

He knew that Ms Steel had informed them of the purpose of his visit so he cleared his throat nervously and began.

'I wanted to talk to you. I wasn't sure what to do for the best. I expect you already know . . . It was me . . . I was with Orduroy that night. I was with him at the table. I tried . . . I did my best to protect him . . . I didn't want to embarrass him. Not in front of everyone. Please be clear, I could probably have stopped the game. But I didn't. He was so . . .'

It occurred to him they wouldn't want to hear about Orduroy's weaknesses. Now was not the time.

'I tried very hard not to . . . When I won, I wasn't going to keep the money. I was going to give it back. I waited outside for him but he never came.'

Because Orduroy was already dead. Dead among the wheelie bins, the empty crates and all the other rubbish around the back of the club. Waiting to be disposed of.

He fell silent. Still neither woman spoke.

'I don't know if he ever mentioned me – we were quite good friends . . .'

'A good friend would have had him out of a place like that in a heartbeat.'

The sister's voice was harsh. He realised he didn't know her name. He should have checked with Ms Steel first. He'd done it all wrong and if he wasn't careful, he would only make everything very much worse.

He drew breath. 'Yes, that is very true. I can't deny it. I should have. And if I could have thought of a way of doing it without a scene that would be embarrassing to everyone, then I would have.'

'Because that was more important?'

'It was important to Orduroy.'

She had nothing to say to that.

He pushed on.

'I thought, since I knew how valuable his contribution . . . how much you would miss . . .' He couldn't find the words and abandoned the sentence. 'I thought about returning the money he'd lost but that . . . I mean . . . so I arranged for a sum to be paid to you monthly. I didn't notice, at first, that it was being returned.'

'We didn't want it,' said the sister, harshly. 'We still don't.'

'But do you need it?' he said before he could stop himself, and she flushed with anger.

He tried again. 'Look, I'm sorry. If you are genuinely angered or offended by the offer, then there's no more to be said. I shall apologise and leave and you'll never hear from me again.'

'This is you buying us off, isn't it? To make you feel better about yourself.'

He opened his mouth to deny it, thought again and then nodded. 'Yes, to some extent. I was there. I was partly responsible. But if it hadn't been me, then it would have been someone else. There was no stopping him.'

No one denied it. Both mother and sister knew their Orduroy.

'So, perhaps you could tell me. What would you like me to do?'

Twenty minutes later he let himself out of the house, down the narrow path and out into the street again. The sun had disappeared and the air was full of a wet drizzle. He stood blindly for a moment or two and then, choosing a direction apparently at random, wandered the streets until he reached an ancient church with a stumpy tower, surrounded by a tiny churchyard. Leaving the path, he wandered aimlessly across the grass and around the headstones until he found himself a secluded spot under a very large cedar tree. Lowering himself slowly to the ground, he drew up his knees and put his hands over his face. He made no sound, but every now and then, a tear forced its way between his fingers.

Dusk was falling when he climbed stiffly to his feet and caught the Hyperloop back to Paddington. The urge to be alone hadn't left him and he chose to walk back through the steadily pouring rain – which took him some considerable time. He amused himself by counting the number of Time Police-sponsored electronic billboards he encountered along the way. The ones encouraging people to grass up their family, friends and neighbours for the public good and monetary gain.

Eventually, he crossed Barricade Bridge and wearily made his way along the embankment to the building he realised, with a shock, he now thought of as home. Ahead of him, Time Police HQ, the former Battersea Power Station, was silhouetted black and menacing against the darkening sky. A fitting home for a black and menacing organisation, he thought.

Originally built during the mid-20th century, Battersea Power Station comprised two halves – Battersea A and Battersea B. The building had been decommissioned some fifty years later and remained empty for some time, slowly falling to pieces.

Such a riverside site was far too valuable to waste, however, and was massively developed early in the 21st century,

223

providing luxury accommodation, shops and entertainment centres, all of which were virtually bombed out of existence during the Civil Uprisings. The original structure, the power station itself, together with the former Chelsea Bridge – now Barricade Bridge – had formed the centre of the resistance and was the first to declare victory over the government forces.

Again, it had lain derelict for a very long time. The government, possibly wanting to avoid it achieving monument status but lacking the nerve to demolish it, had left it to decay until finally, just in time to prevent its complete collapse, the Time Police had moved in.

No attempt had been made to soften its stark and uncompromising exterior, and to this day it stood four square to the River Thames, reminding the world that time travel was still an offence punishable by death. If you were lucky.

Floodlighting the building had not made it any less sinister and it glowered out over the river. A major London landmark. Occasionally, and for reasons never afterwards explained to Commander Hay's satisfaction, someone would attach a giant inflated pig to the dirigible tethering post.

The rooftop helipad was empty and likely to remain so. Commander Hay was known to dislike flying and the helicopter was used mostly by R&T, although how the sudden appearance of a black helicopter at a recruitment drive was supposed to encourage enlistment was a mystery to most. Popular opinion had it that Major Callen just liked flying in it.

The garden sloped right down to the river. This had been one of Commander Hay's attempts to show the softer side of the Time Police, because flowers are, apparently, reassuring. The general public was encouraged to bring the kids, eat their sandwiches, grass up a family member or two and then take themselves off home, conscious of a job well done and a nice day out.

The two high-speed pursuit launches bobbed gently at their moorings. Flying might not be her favourite pastime, but it was well known Commander Hay had no objections at all to zipping dramatically up and down the Thames whenever the situation demanded.

Battersea A housed the working areas and Battersea B was mainly staff accommodation. Senior staff lived on the upper floors; dogs and lesser ranks on the ground floor. The windows stared balefully out over London. London tried not to blink.

It was, he reflected, a blank, brutal, brick structure. If ever a building reflected the true nature of its occupants and the job they did – this was it. He wondered whether it had been allocated to the Time Police or whether they had appropriated it for themselves. The subject had probably been touched upon during one of their training sessions – History of the Time Police – and he'd missed it. His mind had almost certainly been wandering in the direction of the blonde from Logistics – to be followed shortly afterwards by the rest of him.

Illegally entering through the front doors – as a trainee he was only entitled to use a side entrance – he made his way through the almost empty atrium. Bored officers watched him go. One actually made a movement towards him, recognised him and decided he wasn't worth the effort. Which pretty much summed up his life, he thought.

He pulled out his ID and was waved through. His footsteps echoed in the vast space. The moving staircases were silent and motionless, the walkways empty of people. Even the electronic boards listing what the world persisted in referring to as Time Crimes were switched off. He walked past the pool, the indoor trees and the spectacular planting.

Passing out of the public area, he skirted the interview rooms, the presentation area, the Records Department with its vast storage banks, past the secure area housing the Time Map, through R&T and took the lift to the second floor.

Going straight to the bar, he ordered a large drink he couldn't really afford, found a seat as far away from everyone as possible and slowly, but with great deliberation, drank his drink.

When he'd finished, he took himself off to MedCen and asked to see Ellis. The medtec peered doubtfully at him, no doubt clocking the smell of alcohol.

'It's all right,' called a voice, and he was ushered into one of the convalescent rooms. North was sitting in the visitor's chair and a number of open files littered the bed.

North took one look and stood up. 'I'll organise us a coffee.' She left the room. Luke made no attempt to take her chair.

Ellis looked at him. 'All right?'

Luke sighed heavily. 'I think so, yes. His sister is going to put the money away for a rainy day.'

'Honour satisfied on both sides, then?'

Luke nodded.

'Get some sleep, Parrish.'

'Goodnight, sir.'

North stood in the doorway, a cup of steaming coffee in each hand. She watched him walk away.

'Did he finally call you sir?'

18

Two days later and Luke was striding down the corridors, looking for the other members of his team. He'd searched the general library, the technical library, and was now heading for the Time Map. Access to the Map itself was forbidden to non-geeks but he knew Matthew frequently spent time on the observation ring, studying the Map, and if hc found him there, then the two of them could look for Jane.

As it happened, he found them both on the observation ring, watching the Time Map slowly evolve before their eyes.

In a world full of utilitarian greige, the Time Map was a sight to behold. They'd been introduced to it and its functions during their training. Luke knew that Matthew rarely missed an opportunity to come and worship, and now it seemed he'd contaminated Lockland as well. Although, even he had to admit, it was a spectacular sight.

Three storeys high – and more – this colossal representation of Time itself was a giant sphere, incorporating two axes. The horizontal axis denoted space and the vertical axis time. Where the two intersected – at the same level as the observation ring and almost directly in front of their eyes – was the ever-changing now. It was widely accepted that those who roared up and down the timeline on an almost non-stop basis found it beneficial to visit the Map Room, to spend an hour or so re-acquainting themselves with their position in Time and space.

This is me. This is where I am now. This is where I stand in the scheme of all things.

Set into the walls, floors and ceiling, over a thousand computer-driven streamers beamed their mosaics of information into one giant sphere of brilliant silver filigree. Thousands and thousands of tiny glowing silver points connected in a vast network of fine, shimmering lines. Scattered throughout, tiny blue, green and purple dots of light denoted every jump of which the Time Police were aware. Superimposed over everything, larger red dots indicated major historical events. Not that anyone was much interested in those – their primary function was to act as points of reference when navigating the Map. Each red dot was joined to others – and not just those in close proximity but sometimes as far away as the other side of the sphere, because, as anyone from St Mary's will tell you – whether you want them to or not – nothing happens in isolation. Everything is connected to everything else.

He blinked for a moment to accustom his eyes to the gloom and realised they weren't alone. Several mechs were standing around the ring. Whether or not they were there in a technical capacity or, like Matthew, were just worshipping, was hard to tell. Silver light dappled their upturned faces.

Few people ever spoke in the presence of the Map. It generated a pulsing hum, but respect and awe kept most people quiet. Except Luke Parrish. Spotting Jane and Matthew on the far side, he strolled over.

'Good Lord, Matthew. I'm surprised you're not down there with the Map Master poking away at this monster's innards.'

228

'Banned.'

They stared at him. 'What?'

'I'm banned.'

'What did you do?'

He sighed. 'I broke it.'

'What? What did you break?'

'The Map.'

'You broke this colossal, glowing, humming, rotating, and I'll say it again – colossal – thing?'

Matthew nodded.

'How? How could you break . . . that?'

Matthew pointed. 'See that bit over there?'

Luke squinted. 'The 16th century and its immediate surroundings? Yeah.'

'It kind of . . . fell off.'

'Did it bounce?' enquired Jane, before she could stop herself.

'Of course not,' said Luke. 'It's the blood-soaked 16th century, Jane. Trust me, I did history at Uni. It would have been more of a squelch.'

'I like history, too,' said Jane.

Matthew nodded agreement.

'You're from St Mary's,' said Luke. 'You have to like history. Were they very cross?'

'Who?'

Luke sighed. 'The Time Police.'

'About?'

'About the Map. When you broke it.'

Matthew nodded. 'Oh yeah.'

'When was this?'

'A few years ago.'

'Wow – they can really hold a grudge in the Time Police, can't they? Hang on – I've seen you down there among the geeks, geeking away.'

'If I get permission from the Map Master. And if I'm escorted. And they like me to keep my hands in my pockets at all times. Did you want something?'

Luke abruptly remembered why he was looking for them. 'Yes – something to tell you.'

They followed him into the general library, further down the corridor. Herding them to a corner table, he whispered, 'Have you heard?'

Jane shook her head. 'Heard what?'

'Team 8.'

Matthew tapped the table, opening up a data stack to play with and not really listening. 'What about Team 8?' he said, vaguely.

'They're just back from some God-forsaken dump in the 14th century. Someone reported a time-slip. They went to check it out.'

Unable to stop herself, Jane picked up one of the books left on the table and inspected the cover. 'And?'

'A tiny village up in the mountains somewhere in Albania.'

They nodded. 'Yes?'

Luke looked around and lowered his voice even further. 'They're all dead.'

They stared at him. 'Who's all dead?'

'All of them.'

Jane stared at him in shock. *'Team 8 are dead?'*

Around them, heads began to lift.

'Shh. No.' He drew in his chair more closely. 'The illegals are all dead.'

Matthew shut down his data stack, saying, 'The time-slip got them? That's serious. Did we manage to shut it down?'

Luke lowered his voice even further. 'No – Team 8 killed them.'

There was a short pause. Intent as they were, none of them noticed heads turning their way. It is a well-known fact that whispering attracts attention. The best way to keep a secret is to buttonhole someone and scream the words into their face. They can't wait to get away. Their ears cease to work and thirty seconds later they've forgotten every word you said.

Jane said carefully, 'Are you telling us that Team 8 . . . ?' She stopped, seemingly unable to find the words.

'How many?' asked Matthew.

'The illegals? About eleven people, I think.'

Jane was watching his face. 'That's not what you're talking about, is it?'

He shook his head. 'And a couple of the villagers as well. Those that couldn't get away fast enough.'

'How many is a couple?'

He leaned across the table. 'Most of them.'

'Jesus,' said Matthew, faintly, sitting back.

Jane had turned as white as the pages of the books in front of her. 'But why? I thought . . . I mean . . .'

The words, 'I thought we didn't do that sort of thing any more,' hovered unspoken over the table. Her mind filled with images. A few tiny houses, their thatch thick with snow. The smoke from untended fires. A pile of bodies, dark on the ground. Silence, where once there had been the cheerful sounds of people. Emptiness where once there had been life. Blood in the snow . . . Dead people . . . Dead parents . . .

An officer from the next table spoke up. 'No point in cutting down the tree if you don't grub out the roots.'

It was Anders.

They turned to look at him. 'What does that even mean?' asked Luke.

'You don't leave witnesses.'

'No witnesses to what? The time-slip? Or Team 8 taking out a whole village to cover their tracks?'

'It's the 14th century,' said another officer, packing his gear away. 'People died all over the place.'

'Especially,' said Luke, unable to help himself, 'when there are the actions of an overzealous Team 8 to conceal.'

The phrase *Silence in the Library* took on a whole new meaning.

Seemingly unaware, Luke turned back to Matthew and Jane. 'Hay's doing her nut. She's got them all in her office. The team's being disbanded, apparently. Callen's in there with them now, trying to calm her down before she goes 14th century all over *them*.'

Someone out of sight made a rude noise.

'But why?' said Jane, still uncomprehending. 'Why would they do that? Team 8, I mean.'

'To send out a message to other illegals, stupid,' said Anders again. 'People think we're going soft.'

His tone implied that at least three of them were sitting in this library.

Luke rounded on him. 'Arresting them would have been sufficient.'

Anders slammed his scratchpad on the table. 'Sometimes you have to make a point. People get hurt. It happens.'

'But they killed civilians,' cried Jane. 'What *was* the point?'

'Yeah,' said Matthew. 'It was stupid because now we'll never know.'

Anders rounded on him. Behind him, Socko, Hansen and Rossi began to climb to their feet. 'Never know what?'

Here we go again, thought Wimpy Jane, wearily.

'Oh, come on,' said Luke. 'Use what little brains you have left. A 14th-century village in Albania is hardly the illegal time travel capital of the world, is it? There's got to be more to it. Was the time-slip naturally occurring or manufactured? And if the latter, then who funded it? Who supplied them? We'll never know now, will we? What a wasted opportunity.' His voice began to rise. 'You see – that's what happens when you send out a bunch of barely sentient, moronic . . .'

The librarian appeared. 'That's enough. Get out, the lot of you. Take your fight somewhere else.'

'We're not fighting,' said Jane.

'Look,' said another officer, not making a move. 'What does it matter anyway? They're all dead.'

'The minions are,' cried Luke in exasperation. 'What about the bosses? The money men? The people who matter? Nothing to stop them regrouping somewhere else and doing it all again. Jesus, you people are so bloody stupid sometimes.'

'It's another success,' shouted Anders. 'OK?'

'It's another lost opportunity,' Luke shouted back, 'and you're all too stupid to see it.'

All over the library, people pushed back their chairs and climbed to their feet. And they did it very slowly, which, somehow, is a hundred times worse.

The librarian was backing away.

Wait for me, cried Wimpy Jane.

And then the door opened and Officer North entered. Everyone immediately remembered an important appointment elsewhere.

She watched them go. 'Not you three,' she said to Team 236, who were trying to shuffle past her. 'Sit down.'

They sat. She stared at them and then said, 'I'm not going to ask, but I am going to give you some good advice. Pick your battles. Starting a fight in an enclosed space where you will be outnumbered at least three to one is not the action of intelligent officers.' She stared at Luke. 'Or even one who is going to live long enough to enjoy his lunch. Have I made my point?'

They nodded.

'Your feelings are shared by more people in this building than you are aware. Including many at a higher level than you three will ever achieve. Leave them to sort it out.'

They nodded again.

'Right,' she said briskly. 'An assignment.' She paused and then said, 'You will want to take notes.'

'Where's Ellis?' asked Luke, looking round.

'*Major* Ellis is still in the convalescent ward and won't be returning to duty for at least another week. Until then, you've got me.'

The silence was more eloquent than if he'd groaned loudly and shouted, 'Oh no, anyone but you.'

'I understand and sympathise with your pain, Parrish. Shall I alleviate it by drafting you into Lt Grint's team?'

'That's very kind, but I'm fine, thank you. Ma'am.'

'Then we'll get started.'

She waited.

234

They stared at her.

She stared back. 'You will want to take notes. Why am I repeating myself?'

Matthew and Luke scrabbled for their scratchpads. Jane pulled out her trusty notebook.

North cleared her throat. 'Now. 1837. South Australia has been declared a free settlement. Work has started on the capital city, Adelaide. You will find yourselves just outside where Adelaide will one day be, on the site of a small – a very small – settlement, not far from the River Torrens.'

She tapped away at her scratchpad. 'I can flash all relevant information on flora, fauna, weather and population directly to the pod. Or to your scratchpads if you prefer.'

'Scratchpads,' said Luke, quickly.

'Still working on your relationship with the AI, Parrish?'

'The bloody thing hates me.'

'It is a remarkably intelligent unit, yes.'

'Um . . .' said Jane, blushing slightly. 'You said, "you".'

'I'm sorry?'

'You said, "*You* will find yourselves", not *we'll* . . . Does this mean you're not coming with us?'

'No.'

'You *are* coming with us?'

'No. It means I'm not going with you. This will be your first solo jump. Do *not* screw it up.'

Perceiving Lockland to be near speechless with astonishment and Matthew just as speechless as usual, Parrish took on the responsibility for information gathering.

'So what's this all about then?'

North continued. 'According to information laid – it's not

clear by whom at this moment and another team is on that –
someone has taken a rabbit . . . *to Australia.*'

It might be fair to say the response to this dramatic announcement was underwhelming. Before Parrish could become fluent
in sarcasm, Lockland interceded.

'I don't understand. Why is this a problem?'

'It is a *huge* problem, Lockland. A potential ecological disaster. Australia is the last place on earth without rabbits. Our
entire planet is infested with them. They're everywhere. These
days they're even living in Antarctica. Australia is the last
country in the world to be rabbit-free. Australians are hugely
proud of this status and will go to enormous lengths to keep
it that way and today, so will you. Just to complicate matters
further – the rabbit was raised in a lab and, as part of an environmental experiment, is immune to super myxomatosis.'

'What does that mean?'

'It means it's immune to the normal chemicals used to keep
down rabbit numbers. And, as if that's not bad enough . . .'

'Yes?'

'It's pregnant.'

'Ah,' said Matthew, enlightened. 'So presumably all its offspring will be immune, too.'

'And their offspring and theirs after them. So – to sum-
marise the point of this mission – *do not come back without
that rabbit.*'

'Why would someone do that?' enquired Luke.

'Do what?'

'Attempt to bugger up an entire ecosystem with a rabbit.'

North shrugged and began to gather her briefing notes. 'Presumably because they can.' Her tone left them in no doubt

as to her opinion of people who did things just because they could. 'Don't just stand there. Drop everything, get yourselves to 1837 and sort it out.'

'Do we go now?' asked Jane, slightly aghast.

'Ten minutes ago would have been better.'

'But . . .'

Luke laughed at Jane's consternation.

'Lockland, it's not as if you had anything on. Your evening plans invariably involve washing your hair and going to bed with a good book.'

'Is that some sort of metaphor?'

'No, it's a way of life. Your way of life.'

'Next time I find you about to be on the receiving end of a good kicking I'll join in.'

'I thought you already had.' He turned to North. 'So we're supposed to find one rabbit?'

On her way to the door, she paused impatiently. 'Yes.'

'In Australia?'

'Yes. Why are you still here? Coordinates and everything you need have been flashed to your scratchpads. Go now and don't come back without the rabbit. Or possibly, given the way you're wasting time . . . *rabbits.*'

'How will we recognise it?'

'It's the only one in Australia.'

'Have you seen the size of . . .?'

'Parrish, just get your arse into a pod and out of my sight. Now.'

'All right. Which one of us in charge?'

She shrugged. 'Sort it out for yourselves.'

Parrish turned to Farrell. 'Do you want this one?'

He shook his head. 'Absolutely not.'

'Jane?'

'No.'

'Well, someone's got to be team leader.'

Silence.

'Why is it always me?'

More silence.

He said hopefully, 'Can we go armed?'

North briefly closed her eyes. 'Against a rabbit?'

'Vicious little buggers. And you yourself said this one was a super rabbit.'

'Explain to me why you're still here and not in 1837, Parrish.'

'I am endeavouring to equip my team appropriately for the forthcoming assignment. Ma'am.'

'You can take a net.'

'Electrified?'

'Against a pregnant rabbit? For God's sake, Parrish, what sort of a monster are you?' She turned to the other two. 'Get him out of my sight before I put you all on a charge.'

Twenty minutes later, she was reporting to Major Ellis.

'They've gone, sir. I saw them off myself.'

'I gather you volunteered them for this one.'

'I'm trying to get them out of the building as often as possible. Until memories of the scene in the library have faded. Or Parrish learns to keep his mouth shut. Or the earth is engulfed by the sun. Or Farrell gets a proper haircut. Whichever comes first.'

'We've never actually been at war with Australia, have we?'

'I don't believe so, sir. Why do you ask?'

'No reason.'

*　　*　　*

238

Their landing was successful. It was the nearest they'd ever got to a team effort. Jane had sat at the console and calculated the coordinates, Matthew laid them in and initiated the jump and Luke had watched them. Apparently, it was called supervising.

'We're exactly where we should be,' said Jane, consulting the read-outs in front of them.

'Which is?'

'Australia.' She stared at the screen. 'I've never been to Australia.'

'Haven't you?' said Luke, getting to his feet in a leisurely manner. 'I've been here several times. Surfing usually.'

Matthew surveyed the vast, surfless landscape. 'That should come in useful.'

Jane began to shut down the pod. Matthew rolled up the net and stuffed it into his backpack.

Parrish flicked from camera to camera. 'Well, I can't see it.'

Jane looked up. 'What – Australia?'

'Don't you start.'

'Can we go?' said Matthew. 'It's probably had about ten babies while you've been faffing around.' He shouldered his pack, Jane opened the door and they exited the pod.

Once outside, they paused to take stock and get their bearings.

It was a beautiful day. A brilliant sun shone from a cloudless sky. Early morning, decided Jane to herself, looking about her. Hot, and certain to become even hotter.

Green, silver and blue were the colours she saw around her. Blue sky, green grass and silvery blue-green foliage. Low bushes grew everywhere, interspersed with groves of tall, graceful trees. The air smelled faintly of dust and menthol.

239

'Roofs,' said Jane, pointing. 'Over there. Behind those trees.'

'We'll try over in that direction, then,' said Luke, consulting his scratchpad.

'Why? Won't it avoid human contact?'

'It was brought up in a lab. It will look to humans for food.'

'Oh. Yes. Good thought.'

Luke was staring at his scratchpad again. 'Tread carefully, everyone. I've just brought up a list of the most dangerous animals on the planet and nearly all of them live here.'

Jane stared nervously about her. 'What, right here?'

'In this country, yes.'

'Continent,' said Matthew.

'Shut up.'

'Such as?' said Jane. 'What sort of dangerous creatures should we be looking out for?'

'Jellyfish.'

Matthew ostentatiously looked about him.

'Sharks.'

'Both well-known rabbit predators,' said Matthew to Jane. 'Our lives are in peril. We must take great care.'

'Crocodiles. Funnel spiders. Eastern brown snakes.'

Matthew sighed. 'Are you going to go on all day?'

'Just saying.'

'Well, don't. Jane – which way?'

'This way, I think,' she said, and they set off. Cautiously and in single file.

'Right, team,' said Parrish, crisply. 'Remember, it's a tame rabbit. Born and bred in a lab, so it'll probably just lollop up to the nearest person and demand lettuce with menaces.'

'Or, alternatively,' said Matthew, 'it could be sixty miles

away and accelerating and we'll never find it and it'll give birth and Australia will be overrun by rabbits by next Thursday.'

'I hardly think so,' said Luke, gesturing around. 'Have you seen the size of this place? And the size of one rabbit? It would take millions and millions of years to overrun a country this big with rabbits.'

'Continent,' said Matthew.

'What?'

'Australia is a continent.'

'Well, there you are, then. Even better. *Billions* of years.'

Jane was scribbling in her notebook. 'A female rabbit can produce up to a thousand offspring in her lifetime. If half of those are female and they produce a thousand offspring, and half of those are female . . .'

'Yes, all right. I've got it.'

'And they produce a thousand offspring, then in five years' time you've got . . .'

She paused, entangled in the number of noughts on her page.

'A lot of rabbits,' finished Luke. 'Shall we get on with it before any of that actually happens?'

'Actually, I don't think it will be that tame,' said Matthew slowly, reading from his scratchpad.

'Why?'

'Well, according to this, some nutter with a thing for bunnies wanted to breed a rabbit immune to myxomatosis, which apparently he has done, but a rather unwanted side effect is unusual aggression.'

Jane sighed. 'Oh great, a rampant rabbit.'

Parrish sniggered.

She turned to him in puzzlement. 'What? What did I say?'

'Rampant rabbit. That's very good.'

Jane stared at him.

He sighed. 'You don't know what a rampant rabbit is, do you?'

'Not a bad-tempered bunny?' she said, uncertainly.

Matthew snorted.

'Bloody hell,' said Parrish. 'It laughs. Don't tell me you know what a rampant rabbit is.'

Matthew nodded. 'It's one of those.'

A large – a very large – white rabbit lolloped past.

'If it starts babbling on about paws and whiskers and being late, then I'm out of here,' said Parrish.

Jane was aghast. 'Did you see that? It's the size of a *table*.'

'Don't be such a wuss.' He pushed past her for a better look. 'Bloody hell. That's a very . . . solid-looking rabbit.'

'It's a very pregnant rabbit. Quick – after it.'

They jogged along the track and around the bend.

Ahead of them lay a small village, incomplete and raw-looking in the sunshine.

Half-built wooden cottages – 'Slab huts,' said Matthew, consulting his scratchpad again – stood either side of what would possibly, one day, be the main street. In contrast to the canvas-roofed, unfinished houses, the long garden plots behind them were well established. Which made sense. Food first, shelter later. Vines, vegetables and fruit provided welcome patches of shady green in hot sunshine. The gardens stretched back to some reasonable-looking pasture land on which grazed a few cattle and some sheep. Behind the pasture land and bordered by willows, a creek glinted in the sunlight.

At the end of the street, a small group of men swarmed over

a large stone and timber building. They could hear the sound of hammering and a voice raised in song.

'This is the church,' said Jane.

'Or school,' said Luke.

'Or both,' said Matthew.

They could see some women walking in the street or talking together in small groups, but most were in their gardens, hoeing or digging or doing something unidentified but probably horti-cultural.

'Peaceful,' said Jane.

Luke indicated the vegetable plots. 'A bit of a bugger if it's somewhere in among that lot, alternately chomping and giving birth.'

Each plot was enclosed by post and rail fencing that certainly wouldn't be any sort of barrier to a hungry rabbit. Everything was very neat, very tidy, very peaceful and completely rabbit-free.

They stood in a eucalyptus grove and peered cautiously around them.

'I can't see it anywhere,' said Jane, anxiously. 'Can you?'

Luke shook his head. 'No. I can't see how we'll ever find it in all this. And it might not even still be in this area. The bloody thing might be on its way to carving itself an under-ground empire, right this minute.'

A yelping dog raced past, tail well and truly tucked between its legs.

'A bit like you the other day,' said Matthew to Luke.

'Shut up. Did anyone see where it came from?'

'Yes,' said Jane. 'It came out of that barn over there.'

'OK. Let's check it out.'

They pulled back under the trees, and, staying under cover for as long as possible, made their way to a large wooden building. The door stood open and they peered cautiously inside. The sun streamed through tiny gaps in the roof and dust floated gently in the sunlight. The rich smell of earth mingled with the even richer smells of animals. As outside, everything was very neat and standing tidily in its place. It appeared to be empty, but as Luke said, rabbits were cunning.

'Let's use our brains for once,' said Jane. 'Close the door so nothing can get out.'

'If it's still in here,' said Matthew, staring around at the hard, earth floor and the harnesses hanging from the walls. Clean and well-maintained agricultural implements of all kinds hung or leaned around them.

'It could be anywhere in here,' said Luke. 'Probably gorging itself on the remains of that dog's little friend. Matthew, you stay by the door. Jane, you check over there.'

'Should we ask permission to be in here?' said Jane, doubtfully.

'No. We grab the rabbit and go and no one ever knows we've been here.'

'Like with Henry Plimpton,' said Matthew.

Jane turned to say something. There was a nasty sound and she fell to the floor.

'Jane?'

They ran over. She was stretched out on the ground. A wooden rake lay nearby.

'What happened? Did the rabbit get her?'

'No,' said Matthew. 'I did something similar once. When I was a kid. She stood on the rake and the handle flew up and knocked her out. It's bloody painful.'

'And bloody stupid.'

Jane stirred. 'I heard that.'

'Let's get her outside into the fresh air.'

They lifted her to her feet and sat her outside in the shade of a eucalyptus tree.

'Jane? Can you hear me?'

She blinked. 'Stop shouting at me. What happened?'

'You banged your head,' said Luke, unusually tactful. 'You weren't out cold but you might want to take things slowly for a moment.'

She peered around groggily. 'I've never seen a rabbit up close . . .'

'The world is full of things you haven't seen up close, Lockland. Now is not the time to start listing them.'

'Do they lollop along?'

'They do, yes.'

'On their big back legs?'

'They do.'

'We're going to need a bigger net.' She pointed past them.

They turned to look at the rusty red shape disappearing behind some bushes.

Luke sighed. 'Sweetie – that's a kangaroo.'

Jane blinked and shook her head woozily. 'I've never seen a kangaroo either. And don't call me sweetie.'

Luke shook his head. 'Mean and nasty.'

Matthew nodded. 'They kick as well.'

'I wasn't talking about the kangaroo. How are you feeling?'

'Fine. Just a bit wobbly.'

'Are you all right if we leave you here? Follow on when you can see straight.'

'OK.'

'Stay in the shade.'

'OK.'

'You've got water?'

'Yes. Go. I'll guard the barn.'

They left Jane guarding the barn and went.

As Luke said afterwards – it wasn't their finest hour.

Actually, locating one single rabbit in the vast continent of Australia turned out to be considerably easier than they expected. Luke and Matthew rounded a corner and there it was, happily nibbling something at the side of the track.

Without a word spoken, they moved apart, the net stretched between them.

'When I say now,' breathed Luke.

They approached very slowly and cautiously. Barely an inch at a time.

'Now.'

The net flew through the air and settled over the rabbit. Who promptly ran off. With the net. Luke lost his balance and fell heavily.

'Oh f . . .'

'Fire truck?' said Matthew, helpfully.

Luke sat up and breathed heavily. 'So – to recap. We've lost the rabbit. But that doesn't matter because we've lost the net. Jane is barely in this world but that doesn't matter because that's normal for her. You're being your usual unhelpful self and, as always, I'm the one holding things together.'

'If you mean presiding over imminent catastrophe – yes.'

Luke rubbed his elbow. 'We need to catch it before it kills someone.'

'I think you're exaggerating.'

As if arranged by a deity with a sense of humour, somewhere, from a small house off to their right, came a scream of surprise and the sound of breaking crockery.

'Or perhaps not.'

Luke climbed to his feet. 'It's eating someone. Come on.'

They peered cautiously around a corner.

A small slab hut stood some twenty yards away. In the open doorway, a young woman wearing a sun-faded blouse, a long, full skirt and a sun bonnet was holding a sweeping brush in a defensive manner.

'Shoo. Shoo.'

'I can't see it,' whispered Matthew, peering over Luke's shoulder.

'Leave this to me.'

He strolled forwards. 'Good morning, madam. I don't suppose you've seen our rabbit?'

She looked up angrily. 'Yours, was it? Then you can pay me for the dish it knocked out of my hands.'

'I shall be delighted to do so just as soon as we have apprehended the miscreant.'

She stared at him suspiciously. 'You making a joke?'

'I can assure you I am not.'

'Who are you?'

'Police, madam.'

'I don't think they've been formed yet,' whispered Matthew.

Luke rounded on him. 'What? Why not?'

They were given no time to investigate this unforgiveable lapse on the part of Australia.

'Are you them thieving tinkers back again?'

'Er . . .' said Luke.

She raised her broom threateningly. It would seem the broken dish had not put her in a good mood. They backed away and out of sight.

'Let's try down here,' said Luke. 'The undergrowth's so thorny it'll probably stick to the path.'

They set off at a trot and the first thing they saw was a small child, probably belonging to the house they had just left. The child was struggling to support a net-entangled and very large, fat, white rabbit. So large and fat that it was possible there was more rabbit than child. It hung heavily in her arms, its legs dangling.

Matthew nudged Luke. 'Go and get it.'

'Not likely. Suppose it bites me. They're poisonous, you know.'

'Rabbits aren't poisonous.'

'I meant the kid.'

'Just get it, will you? Haven't you ever heard the expression *taking candy from a baby*?'

Somewhat nervously, Luke approached the child, who had obviously been well coached in the 19th-century equivalent of Stranger Danger.

It opened its mouth and screamed. And screamed. And screamed.

Luke halted. 'Um, it's all right, little . . . um . . .' He stared at the child, looking for clues as to gender.

'Don't cry, little . . . um . . .' He reached out a tentative hand.

The child moved to DEFCON 2.

Luke staggered backwards, clutching his hand. 'It bit me,' he said in disbelief. 'The bloody kid bit me.'

The rabbit leaped to the ground. The child screamed again. Ear-splittingly.

'Sod the rabbit,' said Matthew, grabbing his arm. 'Run. Before they do us for child molesting.'

They ran, crashing through the undergrowth. Spiky bushes tore at their clothing. They could hear distant shouts and the sounds of people running towards them. The child continued to scream.

As Luke said later, there was no time to think about crocodiles or funnel spiders or jellyfish or brown snakes or sharks or even rabbits. The immediate and present danger was half a dozen settlers on the trail of a couple of rabbit-snatching child molesters.

Jane's voice sounded in his ear. 'I'm at the pod. You need to get back here.'

'We're on our way back now. Before Australia disappears under a furry onslaught of rabbits.'

'I think you might be slightly exaggerating.'

'We'll never be able to come back to Oz again,' he panted. 'Everyone hates us.'

'Does seem to be a common theme,' said Matthew, at his elbow.

Ten minutes later and by a circuitous route, they were back at the pod. The sounds of pursuit had faded.

Jane was sitting outside on a log, enjoying the dappled sunshine and sporting the beginnings of a spectacular black eye. 'What did you do? I could hear the screaming from here.'

'Don't ask.'

Luke threw himself on to the log beside her. 'We need a complete rethink, people. The locals are in an uproar. The rabbit's buggered off. No one's yet been bitten by something toxic or savaged by a koala but it's only a matter of time.'

'Or peed on by a possum,' said Jane.

'What?'

'Possums,' said Jane. 'They pee in self-defence.'

'I have an uncle who does that,' said Matthew.

Luke covered his eyes. 'What sort of country is this?'

'Continent.'

Luke had had enough. *'Shut up.'*

'I think it's time we took you home,' said Matthew. 'You're overtired.'

'You heard North. We can't go back without the rabbit.'

'Oh,' said Jane, casually. 'I've got the rabbit.'

'What? . . . You . . . What?'

'I found her all tangled up in your net. Which had caught on a stick. I picked her up and brought her back to the pod.'

'It's in there now?'

'Yes.'

'Why didn't you say so?' He stood up.

'Careful – don't let it out again,' warned Matthew.

'It's fine, I put her in my backpack,' said Jane.

Entering cautiously, they found Jane's backpack standing in the corner. A large white head protruded therefrom. The rabbit twitched her whiskers at them in a friendly fashion.

'Isn't she sweet?' said Jane.

They stared at the rabbit. The rabbit stared placidly back again.

'Actually,' said Matthew, 'I don't want to rush anyone, but

we really should get her back before she gives birth in here. Trust me – that would cause no end of complications.'

'What will happen to her?' asked Jane, squinting at the console. Matthew gently elbowed her out of the way and began to lay in the return coordinates.

There was a bit of a silence and then Luke said, 'Well, I expect they'll put her down.'

She was horrified. 'What? Why?'

'Easier and quicker for everyone.'

Jane's face was tragic. 'We can't take her back to her death.'

'Well, we can't leave it here. And we can't drop it off just anywhere, can we? It's myxomatosis-proof. It's like uranium or an old fridge – you have to dispose of it responsibly.'

'There's that zoo,' said Matthew, slowly.

'What zoo?'

'The petting zoo in Battersea Park. It's ideal. It's just next door. I used to go there all the time. We could even visit her occasionally.'

'Matthew – that's brilliant.'

Luke stared at them both. 'Lockland, are you concussed?'

'Probably. Doesn't stop it being a good idea.'

'And how do you propose we do this?'

'It'll be easy,' said Matthew. 'It's not like we're taking one out. We're putting one in.'

'And what do we tell North?'

'You're team leader. You'll think of something.'

Luke sunk his head in his hands. 'Oh, God.'

Five minutes later, they were looking at Battersea Park Zoo.

252

'Not many people about today,' said Jane, squinting at the screen and rubbing her eyes.

'What about children?' said Luke. 'Because I've gone off them in a big way. I'm not going out there if there are children everywhere.'

'Well, there are,' said Matthew, 'but they all appear to have their handlers with them. Let's go.'

The rabbit seemed quite happy to be conveyed from A to B in Jane's backpack and Matthew produced a small woolly hat he had found in one of the lockers. 'Perfect.'

Luke stared aghast. 'I am *not* being seen in public with you wearing that hat.'

'It's not for me.'

'Well, I'm not wearing it.'

'It's for the rabbit.'

He flattened her ears and placed it gently on her head, pulling it down over her eyes. 'There you are – she looks just like a baby in a baby carrier.'

Luke stared at him. 'What the hell do babies look like where you come from, mate, because this one's got whiskers.'

'Can we go?' said Jane, plaintively. 'Because I just want to go and lie down in a darkened room.'

'You're not the only one,' muttered Luke. 'Give me the backpack. Bloody hell – this thing weighs a ton.'

They set off across the park.

'This is rather nice,' said Jane, looking around. 'We should come here more often.'

'If they don't arrest us,' said Luke, 'and we have to spend the rest of our lives in prison avoiding the showers.'

Consulting a convenient 'You Are Here' screen, they headed

for the stables which were, apparently, home to a large number of donkeys, tiny ponies, Patagonian chickens and guinea pigs, as well as rabbits.

'Well, that was worryingly easy,' said Luke, staring at the mixed wildlife in front of them. 'It's not like us to have things go so well.'

They stared at the enclosure with the high, wire fence. A number of rabbits hopped happily.

'Oh good, some of them are white,' said Jane. 'She won't stand out. Quick, drop her over the fence.'

Luke gently lifted the rabbit out and pulled off the woolly hat. The rabbit gazed placidly about her. 'I can't. The fence is too high. I can't reach over.'

'What?'

'Well, obviously an enclosure designed to stop people taking rabbits out is going to stop them putting them in, isn't it?'

They stared, defeated.

'We could just throw her over and run away,' muttered Luke.

Jane stared at him. 'You can't throw a pregnant rabbit over a fence, for God's sake. The drop will kill her.'

Luke kicked the fence. 'Fire truck.'

'Very mature,' said Matthew. 'And there's a keeper coming.'

'Someone think of something. Quick.'

'Stop panicking, Jane.'

'Too late.'

'I've had an idea,' said Matthew. 'Luke, quick – put her down. Gently.'

Luke placed the rabbit carefully on the ground. She stood still for a moment, nose twitching, hopped a few paces and then stopped again.

'Oh, look,' shouted Matthew, pointing. 'Help. Someone help.'

'What?' muttered Luke. 'What are you doing?'

The keeper altered course. 'What's the problem, sir?'

Matthew gestured. 'I think one of your rabbits has escaped.'

The keeper bent casually and scooped her up. 'Now then, Mrs Rabbit, where do you think you're off to?'

Rabbit and assistant disappeared into the wooden stable. Minutes later, a door at the back of the enclosure opened and a massively fat white rabbit hopped out and headed for the food.

'See,' said Matthew to Luke. 'It was that easy.'

Luke told him to fire truck off.

They watched for a while. Luke shook his head. 'Can't believe we got away with that.'

'Can we go home now?' said Jane, plaintively. 'My head hurts.'

Back at TPHQ, they exited the pod to find North waiting for them.

She looked around in what Luke considered an unnecessarily exaggerated manner. 'Where's the rabbit?'

'Dead,' intoned Jane sepulchrally. 'Dead and gone. Sad. So sad. Tragic, even.'

Luke nudged her into silence and said hastily, 'The rabbit went in someone's pot. We found the bones on a compost heap and the pelt hanging up somewhere. Outside a barn.'

North sighed. 'That's a shame. I'd arranged for it to find a home with the zoo next door. Never mind. Thank you, everyone. Carry on.'

20

They met together afterwards to compare reports.

'Luke, you seriously headed your report *Rampant Rabbit*?'

'Yeah. Didn't you?'

She turned to Matthew. 'What was yours titled?'

He grinned. '*Rabid Rodent Ravages Rural Rustics*. Yours?'

'Report on Assignment 221/412/236/3,' she said primly.

Luke shook his head. 'Remember, Jane, no one likes a goody two shoes. Come and have a drink and I can show you where you're going wrong.' He looked at Matthew. 'What about you? Fancy a drink?'

After a moment's surprise, Matthew nodded and the three of them wandered along to the bar.

Given the Time Police love affair with utilitarianism, it was surprisingly welcoming. The colour scheme was uninspired, but the chairs grouped around low tables all matched and were comfortable. And well used. The Time Police were a twenty-four-hour organisation, therefore it was always drinking time for one shift or another. The bar was quite full that evening because of a savage rainstorm happening outside. No one was going out there without a boat.

'Right, I'll get these in,' said Luke. 'Matthew, you give me a hand and Jane, you can find a table.'

They stared at him.

He sighed. 'OK – you get the drinks and I'll find the table. Mine's a pint.'

He wandered off to a small table in the corner, arriving microseconds before one of the clean-up teams who had obviously marked it out as their own. They glowered. He beamed. Matthew and Jane arrived with the drinks, thus confirming ownership and the clean-up team retired, muttering and defeated.

Jane sighed. More friends made.

'What does it matter?' said Luke, taking his pint. 'Everyone hates us anyway. We can waste our time trying to persuade people to like us and failing miserably, or we can enjoy ourselves by living down to people's expectations and confirming their worst fears. Think how happy that will make them. In fact, I firmly believe it's our duty to make our senior officers' lives as happy as we possibly can. Cheers.'

They drank.

'A novel approach to gaining acceptance in our place of employment,' said Jane.

Matthew nodded. 'My mum always says something similar.'

'Yes,' said Luke, 'but your mum's from St Mary's and they're even weirder than you.'

Matthew opened his mouth, found himself unable to disagree and nodded.

'Have you been back again recently?' asked Jane.

He grinned suddenly. 'Not since I got my hair cut there.'

Luke put down his drink. 'You what?'

'I go back to get my hair cut. R&D do it.'

'You're kidding me,' said Luke.

'No, it's true,' said Jane. 'I went with him.'

'What was it like? St Mary's, I mean – not his haircut. The less said about Matthew's hair the better.'

'It was very nice,' said Jane loyally. 'There was a chicken and lots of water and that man nearly drowned and people shouted and they made me drink tea, but it was very nice all the same. And Matthew had his hair cut.'

'With a hand-axe, presumably,' said Luke, unconsciously patting his own immaculately presented but only very border-line regulation hairstyle.

'Ignore him. I think it looks very nice,' said Jane to Matthew.

'And it must really get on their nerves here,' said Luke.

Matthew grinned. 'Yeah. So much more subtle than getting yourself put on report twice a week.'

'Perhaps, but not so much fun.'

Matthew sipped his drink. 'Did your dad really sell you to the Time Police?'

Jane, who would never have dared ask such a question, glanced from one to the other, anxiously.

'Well, not as such,' said Luke, casually. 'He handed them a huge sum of money and I was the accompanying free gift. I've been told to stop telling people I was trafficked.'

The silence had a bitter quality about it and Jane thought it best to move things on.

'You?' she said to Matthew. 'How did you come to join?'

'Partly brought up here. Want to work on the Time Map.'

More silence. They waited but that was obviously it.

'You?' said Luke, turning to Jane.

She sighed. 'I broke my grandmother's seagull.'

Parrish and Farrell eyed each other sideways.

'OK, you win,' said Parrish, breaking the silence. 'Breaking granny's seagull is officially the best reason ever for joining the Time Police. My round, I think.'

He returned with the drinks. 'Right, orange juice for Jane. Beer for me. And a cider for junior.' He appeared to be struck by a thought. 'Are you even old enough to drink?'

'No idea,' said Matthew, sipping his cider.

'You don't know how old you are?'

'No one knows how old I am. Very useful, sometimes.'

There was a silence and then Luke said, 'Are you going to tell us?'

Matthew sighed and then said, reluctantly, 'If you want to hear.'

Jane nodded. 'I do.'

'And me,' said Luke.

'All right. Long story short. Stolen from St Mary's at six months. Trafficked around 19th-century London . . .' He grinned at Parrish. 'See, you're not the only one. Trafficked around 19th-century London. Finished up as a climbing boy. You know – chimneys. Not much to eat. They keep you small. Knocked about a bit. Rescued by my dad. It was a joint St Mary's/Time Police effort. Returned to my proper time. Brought up here and at St Mary's. Lots of food – as much as I can eat – but I'm still small and scrawny. Always will be, they tell me.'

He subsided, apparently exhausted by the effort.

Jane and Luke stared at him. He looked down at the table. The silence seemed to last a long time.

'Matthew,' said Jane, softly. 'That's awful.'

'Who stole you?' demanded Luke.

He shrugged. 'A bloke.'

'Why?'

'He didn't like my mum. He killed her best friend and snatched me.'

He stopped again.

'And . . .' Luke prompted, softly.

'And sold me. Several times, actually. Like that famous man who kept selling London Bridge to foreigners.'

'And that's how you became a climbing boy?'

'Yeah. Oh, it was all done properly. I was apprenticed. Apparently, there were papers signed and money changed hands.'

'Wasn't that a good thing? You being a proper apprentice, I mean?'

'Not really. If you run away – for whatever reason – you're breaking the law.'

He stopped again.

'I'm sorry,' said Jane. 'Is it difficult for you to talk about?'

'Not really. It's just that you're the first people I've ever told. Everyone else has always known about it before I arrived, so I've never had to talk about it.'

'It must have been pretty shit,' said Luke.

Matthew stared across the room, a kaleidoscope of memories flickering before him. Of standing barefoot and up to his ankles in dirty snow, soaking wet and shivering as the blows rained down upon him. Of the kicks that left him limping for weeks. Of the shouting and cursing. Of clenched fists. Of nursing his broken arm and trying not to cry because crying never helped.

Jane kicked Luke under the table and to lighten the moment, offered to get another round in.

When she returned, Luke distributed the drinks. She was just sitting down again when he asked Matthew what had happened to the bloke who had snatched him.

Matthew twiddled his beer mat for a long time, eventually saying, 'It was . . . I can't . . .'

He buried his face in his cider.

Luke opened his mouth to question him further, caught Jane's eye and changed what he'd been going to say. 'And that's why you don't talk much?'

Matthew carefully placed his cider on the beer mat. 'A bit. Plus, sometimes I'm not always sure what to say to people. What's appropriate. You both absorbed this sort of thing from your cradle. It's instinctive for you. Not for me. Besides, I couldn't really speak properly until my dad got me back. No one ever spoke to me so I never learned. Couldn't read or write, either. Lots of catching up to do.'

Jane and Luke eyed each other, each aware of standing on the brink of something that could sweep them all away.

'In that world, people could explode into violence at a single word. Sometimes not even that. I . . . I don't like angry people. It's not . . . it's not fear – well, it is . . . it's just . . . something shuts down inside me . . . and I can't . . . well, you know . . .'

'Yes, I do know,' said Jane. 'I don't like angry people, either.'

They both looked at Luke. 'Not a problem for me,' he said, cheerfully. 'I'm usually the one making them angry. You two can stand behind me, if you like.'

Matthew forced a smile and then said brightly, 'You'll be relieved to hear I've stopped hiding under the bed.'

'Well, good for you,' said Luke, secretly rather appalled.

Jane said hesitantly, 'Was it very bad?'

'No . . . no . . . Not always. Some days the sun shone. Or

there was bread. But Old Ma Scrope broke my arm once and I still had to work and it bloody hurt, I can tell you, and . . .' He pulled himself up. 'It's easier for everyone if I don't talk about it, but mostly . . . yeah . . . it was shit.'

He seemed to withdraw back into himself.

'Can I ask a question?' said Jane.

'Just don't put your hand up,' said Luke.

'Does it bother you, being back in London?' she said. 'You know, because you were here as a child?'

Matthew nodded. 'Grit Lane – where I lived – isn't that far from here. On the other side of the river, but not far.'

'It still exists?'

'Yeah. I went back once. It's all flats and a trendy wine bar now but if I stand very still and listen . . . I can hear the echoes.' He stared at his drink.

'And then your dad found you.'

'Yeah – with the Time Police.'

'Then what?'

'I had a bit of schooling here – because the bloke who took me was still around – and then there was a bloody awful row between St Mary's and the Time Police. Don't ask me about what because I never found out, and I went back to St Mary's.' He grinned. 'A great place to grow up, trust me. Then I came back here.'

There was more silence, then Jane said, 'Didn't you want to live with your parents?'

'I see them a lot.'

'When you have your hair cut.'

'Yeah.' He seemed uneasy.

Luke pounced. 'What aren't you telling us?'

262

It was an effort, but he grinned. 'Many things.'

Luke moved his drink out of the way, leaned across the table, fixed Matthew with a penetrating stare and said, compellingly, 'Tell us the most important thing you don't want us to know.'

Matthew stared at him in bafflement. 'Did you actually *do* the interrogation module?'

'Course I did. I thought it lacked subtlety – didn't you?'

Matthew shook his head. 'You don't need to be subtle when you have the truth cuff.'

Luke grinned. 'Do I need to go and get it?'

Matthew sighed and played with his glass. 'There's some-body at St Mary's.'

'Aha.' Luke sat back, satisfied. Jane continued to look puz-zled. He sighed. 'Girlfriend, Jane.'

'Oh.' It was a lowering thought to know that even Matthew had a girlfriend. And Luke had his blonde in Logistics while she had . . . She looked up and saw Luke watching her. She flashed him a small smile and he lifted his glass. 'Thanks for the drink.'

She nodded. 'You're welcome.'

He turned back to Matthew. 'So tell us about this girlfriend.'

'Well . . .' He looked around although no one was within earshot and the room was noisy anyway. 'She and her brother are on the list.'

Jane was puzzled. 'What list?'

'Our list.'

They gaped at him. *'You're having a relationship with a wanted illegal?'*

'Shh! No. Of course not.'

'Well, thank God for that.'

'It's not a relationship. Yet.'

Luke was back to interrogation mode again. 'But you'd like it to be?'

'Mm.'

'With a wanted illegal?'

Matthew grinned into his glass. 'Yeah.'

Luke sat back. 'Well, I don't know. What with you and your illicit yearnings and the Seagull Smasher of Team 236 sitting next to me . . . You two are a hell of a lot more interesting than I gave you credit for.'

'Shame we can't say the same of you,' said Jane tartly and they grinned at each other.

No one saw North, watching from the doorway.

She reported back to Ellis, sitting with his leg up and still convalescing in MedCen.

'It's a miracle. They're eating and drinking together. We'll make a team of them yet, sir.'

He sighed. 'It may be too late. Read this.'

'What's this?'

'New orders.'

She scanned his scratchpad. 'A new team member?'

'Well, we are one down.'

'It's a bit late for a fourth, sir, surely.'

'She's an experienced officer.'

Something in his voice made her look up. 'Who is it?'

He took a breath, doing his best to keep his voice light and neutral. 'Smith.'

'Sarah Smith?'

He nodded, saying nothing. She knew he wouldn't voice a criticism.

She protested. 'But the three of them are just beginning to gel.'

'Yes. This is really going to upset the applecart. Although to be fair, this time last week they didn't even have an applecart.'

'True, sir, but surely it's unusual to introduce a new team member so late in the programme.'

He shrugged. 'I'm stuck in here and you're only temporary. Having a senior member will keep them out of Grint's clutches. They wouldn't do well in his team; Parrish would be in hospital by the end of the week.'

'Smith's a long-standing officer,' North said bluntly. 'She'll have seniority over them.'

'Something they'll have to work out for themselves.'

She sighed. 'Well, it's a shame. I was becoming quite fond of the three of them.'

He laughed. 'Like pets.'

'Exactly. Reading their reports has given me a great deal of entertainment over these last weeks, and their attempts to capture and then find a home for that rabbit was one of the funniest things I've seen in ages.'

'They do have a style all of their own, don't they?'

'When does this happen?'

'Effective immediately. I'm to return to light duties at the end of next week and you . . .' He paused.

'Yes, sir?'

'Having Smith sets you free. You've got your wish, Celia. You're off to the Hunter Division. End of this month. Congratulations.'

'Oh.' There was a short pause before she said, 'Thank you.'

The pause was not missed by Major Ellis. 'You must be pleased, surely. It's what you wanted.'

'Yes. Yes, I am. I'm very pleased. Just a little concerned. Did I do something wrong?'

'Not that I've heard.'

'Did *they* do something wrong?'

'Again, not that I've heard.'

'Then why now?'

'Perhaps they've decided not to tie up a good officer.' He eyed her. 'That would be you.'

She said nothing.

'Anyway, I'm glad you're here. I wanted to take the opportunity to say thank you for serving on my team, no matter how briefly.'

'My pleasure, sir. Although . . .'

'Although what?'

'I'm not sure . . .'

'About what? Come on, Celia. Speak up.'

She appeared to make up her mind. 'Nothing, sir. It's just . . . well, as I said, they were just beginning to gel. And I know none of them are Time Police material, but . . . well, we have plenty of conventional officers already and I rather thought theirs was an interesting way of going about things. Now, of course, a fourth member will change that dynamic completely.'

'True, but for the better, one can only hope.'

'They could hardly get much worse.'

There was a slightly awkward pause and then he said cheerfully, 'And you'll soon be off to Hunter Division. You'll be a member of the elite. You'll get the best assignments. You can choose your own people. Autonomy – if you want it.'

'Did you have anything to do with that, sir?'

'I wrote the usual recommendation, yes.'

'Thank you, sir. And if Commander Hay confirms, of course.'

'Oh, she will. She always keeps her word. Congratulations.' He cocked his head. 'That was always part of the plan, wasn't it?'

'Plan?'

'Your career path? You've ripped through the ranks and now becoming a Hunter is the next step. You told me between ten and twelve years.'

She said absently, 'Between ten and twelve years until what?'

'Ten years until you're running this place.'

She laughed. 'I'm flattered, sir, but you overestimate my abilities.'

'But not your ambition?'

'Well . . .'

'That was why you left St Mary's, wasn't it?'

She smiled.

'Well, I'm glad you made the jump. So to speak.'

'I never congratulated *you* on your promotion, sir.'

'Yes. Well.' He looked around and lowered his voice. 'Sometimes I'm not sure I'll be around to enjoy it for very long.'

'No, that's what I was thinking.'

He blinked. 'Were you?'

'I'm not an idiot, sir. I can see the way things are going. The conflict between the old ways and the new. And if anything were to happen to Hay . . .'

'We're living in worrying times, Celia.'

'As you say, sir. And those three –' she nodded her head in the direction she assumed Team 236 to be at that moment – 'might be the first pebbles of a larger landslide.'

'A good landslide?'

'Possibly. New ways of looking at things. New ways of doing things. Better ways of doing things, sir.'

'With luck, the end of the old days could be in sight.'

'Not if certain people can prevent it, sir.'

'All things must evolve or die, North. The Time Police were formed to combat a dreadful threat. That threat has changed but such power as we possess is not given up lightly.'

'I agree, sir. Powers were created for us. But if we do not hold them, who will?'

He regarded her with interest. 'A very good point, Officer North.'

There was an awkward pause.

'I preferred it when you called me Celia. Sir.'

21

Jane got dressed the next morning with an unaccustomed feeling of anticipation and a little excitement. She wasn't sure why and then remembered the night before. They'd sat in the bar and talked until late into the night. They'd bought several more rounds between them – the last one only possible after frantic pocket scarching to reach the required amount of money. Somehow paying in pennies made everything hilarious. Being broke was fun.

Once the conversational barrier had been breached, there was a great deal to discuss. Mikey, Luke's father, St Mary's, Jane's grandmother. Several drinks down the line there had been a lot of laughing. They hadn't been rowdy but they'd attracted some looks. At some point, it had been agreed they'd ditch the name Team 236 and go with Team Weird. Luke was to have official team stationery printed. Matthew had volunteered to design the official team tie. She couldn't, at that exact moment, remember what her own contribution was to be. Therc was a vague memory of an official song. A lot of words rhyme with weird and it would appear she had written a large number of them on the back of her hand.

Someone banged on her door and she opened it to find Matthew and Luke grinning at her.

'Breakfast?' said Luke. She nodded, suddenly very much looking forward to the day ahead and pulled her door closed behind her.

Serving themselves, they took their laden trays into the dining room. It was crowded. They looked around for empty seats.

'Not sure we'll all be able to sit together,' said Jane.

'Follow me,' said Luke, setting off across the room.

He found a few spare seats at the end of a long table, saying, 'Morning,' cheerfully to a bunch of scowling officers as he dumped his tray.

Winking at Jane, he said in a low voice, 'Sit down. Bet you a tenner they'll push off in a couple of minutes.'

He was right.

'I was right,' he announced with some satisfaction. 'I thought the social stigma of being seen publicly with us would overcome their need for a second cup of coffee. They'll actually be reporting for duty on time this morning. And all thanks to us.'

Jane was slathering marmalade on her toast. 'Anyone know what they've got for us today?'

'I can't wait to see what they come up with next,' said Luke, pouring everyone coffee. 'Although I fear it's going to be tough for them to top the rabbit.'

'Good morning,' said North, appearing at their table. Behind her stood a tall, dark woman with full, red lips and large, blue eyes.

Luke sat up straight immediately.

North was speaking. 'As you know, this team has been a man down since its inception. It hasn't been a problem so far, but as your missions become more complex, it might be. This is Sarah Smith, an experienced officer, who will be joining you. Effective immediately.' She paused and then said, 'I'll leave you all to become acquainted.'

She walked away.

Both sides stared at each other for a moment and then Luke stood and pulled out a chair for her.

Smith flashed him a brilliant smile, and sat down.

Jane had no idea why, but a cold feeling was creeping around her heart.

'Hello, everyone,' said Smith. Jane wondered if her voice was naturally husky or whether she was just going down with a bad cold. For some reason, the hairs on the back of her neck began to lift.

'I'm Smith and I'll be the fourth member of your team from now on.' She laughed throatily. 'Makes me sound like a waitress, doesn't it? Anyway, we've not come across each other before – I've been away on one of Major Callen's recruitment drives and only got back last week. I've been reading your reports and Major Ellis has done an excellent job bringing you to this point.'

No mention of North, thought Jane. And who is she to pass judgement on a senior officer?

'Now I know late assimilation can be a little difficult, but I don't want you to worry about me. I'm very easy to get along with.' She was looking at Luke as she said it and then those blue eyes slithered to Matthew, who stared solidly back again.

'Officer North has scheduled us a get-to-know-each-other session this morning.' She slid her eyes to Luke again. 'I'm sure we'll all have many questions for each other. Briefing Room 2.'

271

She hasn't even looked at me, thought Jane.

Another dazzling smile. 'So, finish your breakfast – no need for haste.' She looked at her watch with the air of one already in charge. 'I'll meet you there in, say, twenty minutes.'

Luke watched her walk away. 'Like jelly in a sack,' he said, dreamily.

Jane stood up abruptly. 'I'll see you there.'

She did, arriving exactly on time, only to find the other two must have turned up some considerable time before her because the get-to-know-each-other session was already well under way.

Before she could sit down, however, Smith was speaking. 'Jane, dear, I understand you were injured on your last assignment and you don't yet look fully recovered. Why don't you take the rest of the day off? You need to make a full recovery. Report tomorrow when you're feeling a little more yourself.'

I am myself, she thought. This is me. She took a deep breath and felt the familiar hot flush start to spread across her face. 'Who put you in charge?'

Smith's bright smile never faltered for one instant. 'The Time Police, Jane. I have seniority. Did they not explain the way these things work when you were doing your basic training?' She paused significantly. 'It was only a couple of weeks ago, surely?'

Jane's flush had become very nearly incandescent. Any moment now she would burst into flames.

Luke apparently noticed none of this. He smiled at her. 'Yeah – good idea, Jane. Makes sense to get your head down so you're all ready to go tomorrow.'

She felt as if he'd publicly slapped her.

It was very important that no one – no one at all – had even the slightest inkling of the hurt coursing through her. Pride came to her rescue. She nodded and suppressed the unfamiliar but completely justified urge to punch everyone in the room. Her happy glow had disappeared, leaving plenty of room for the familiar sense of not belonging to come barrelling back and towing a shedload of humiliation behind it.

She blinked hard to dispel the pricking tears of disappointment. You don't cry in public. Not if you're in the Time Police. In fact, you don't cry at all. Crying was a sign of weakness and weakness could be exploited.

Looking back over her shoulder, she could see the three of them were already sitting around the table, their heads close. As she walked away, she heard a shout of laughter. Luke was moving scratchpads and pens around to demonstrate something or other and almost certainly being cruelly amusing at someone else's expense, she thought. Probably mine.

As she closed the door behind her, Smith was talking, making short emphatic gestures to emphasise the points she was making and Matthew was busy typing on his scratchpad. She wondered if they'd even noticed she had gone.

She trailed slowly down the corridor and eventually found her way back to her own room, where she sat on her bed, fired up her scratchpad and did a little digging on the Time Police site.

Sarah Mary Smith. Born in Scotland. Thirty-four years old. Considerably older than the rest of us, she thought. Probably why she thinks she's in charge.

She skimmed through Smith's list of qualifications – which were not that impressive – followed by her list of postings and promotions.

Sarah Smith had joined the Time Police just over seven years ago. Jane was slightly surprised to see she came highly recommended from the civilian police. So highly recommended, in fact, that it was a surprise they'd been able to bring themselves to part with her. Interestingly, since joining the Time Police she'd had very little front-line experience. After her gruntwork she'd started in Records and risen fairly quickly to become assistant to the Head of Records. From there, she'd applied for and got the post of Assistant Deputy Head of Admin. A post, Jane suspected, that wasn't anything like as grand as its title. From there she'd moved to Major Callen's department – Recruitment and Training, where she'd become PA to the Deputy Head of Training and finally, PA to Major Callen himself, which was where she'd been until last week. She was the equivalent of Charlie Farenden but, Jane was willing to bet, not nearly as well respected and nowhere near as good at her job.

And that was it. Unlike nearly everyone else in the Time Police, she'd never applied to become a Hunter. Apart from her own gruntwork, she'd never been part of a team or got her boots on the ground, as far as Jane could see. And here she was today, heading up a team of trainees. It just didn't make sense.

She shut down her scratchpad and spent an hour of her unexpected day off in her room, tidying and cleaning. She loved her room. Time Police accommodation was not luxurious, even for senior officers, but Jane still loved it. Her very own space. A room where she could close the door on the world and be alone.

Yes, it was very basic, containing only a bed with a small desk-cum-dressing table at the foot, and a window with an uninspiring view, but that was OK because she rarely had time to look out of it anyway. The opposite wall held a built-in wardrobe, some shelves for a few personal possessions and her books. Time Police wages are not overgenerous but for Jane there was always enough for books.

Her shelf contained a few books on art and history; the big, colourful book of Renaissance prints she loved to leaf through in the evenings; a couple of thrillers; an old copy of *Jane Eyre* found in an equally old bookshop; and right on the end, a really battered guidebook to London because she was sure, one day, she would have the time to explore.

Occasionally she would wonder what her grandmother had done with the books she had left behind. Sold or burned them, probably. One or two of them had been school prizes – old friends who had shared her lonely life. She felt a pang of regret at abandoning them to their fate.

To the right of the bookshelf a sliding door concealed a wash-basin and a small shelf for toiletries. Everything was painted in soothing Time Police beige. As opposed to the stimulating Time Police beige in the corridors, she assumed.

She was well placed, too – not too far from the bathrooms, but not close enough to be disturbed by those who had had a lively evening and tended to confuse their doors in the middle of the night.

She had been commanded to rest in her room. Defiance still burned brightly.

'I'm going out,' she told herself.

Wimpy Jane wasn't happy. 'You were instructed to rest in your room.'

'Yes, but not by anyone important.'

She changed and slung her bag over her shoulder and

slammed the door behind her. Sadly, there was no one around to witness this impressive display of self-assertion.

She set off to visit the National Gallery. The virtual gallery was featuring a Botticelli display and she spent a soothing afternoon walking around the life-sized, 3D representations of *The Adoration of the Kings* and *The Birth of Venus*, actually becoming part of the paintings, seeing them from unfamiliar angles and taking the time to admire tiny, previously unseen details. She finished her afternoon with coffee and cake in their café, deliberately taking her time. Because sometimes a rebellion begins with quite small steps.

It was dark when she got back. Wondering if anyone had missed her, she tapped on their doors on her way to dinner. There was no response from either of them. She peeked into Luke's room. By the looks of things, either he hadn't been in for some time, or a small tornado had popped by, played by itself for half an hour and then pushed off again.

She ate alone again that evening. So much for the newly fledged Team Weird. That hadn't lasted long, had it?

Fortunately – or otherwise – Smith's arrival coincided with a rare quiet spell. Temporally speaking, the world was being exceptionally well behaved. It did happen occasionally, they said. Hardly anyone was being assigned and those teams that did go out were the most senior because rank hath its privileges. Boredom set in. Their days offered only long sessions in the gym, weapons training and simulations. Jane conscientiously put in the time, alternating with study periods in the library. Keeping busy was good. Looking as if she had a purpose was even better. Apparently not caring what the other members of her team were up to was best of all. Oblivious to North's watching eyes, she pounded away in the gym, ran endless circuits, caught up on her reading and told herself she didn't need anything from anyone.

Emerging, sweaty and wobbly-legged from a particularly vigorous session, she encountered Smith in the corridor.

'Ah, Jane, dear, there you are. I have something for you.'

As usual, Smith was immaculately turned out. Jane was very conscious of her sweaty face, straggly hair and pit stains.

'Yes,' continued Smith, 'I've brought some magazines for you. I thought we could look through them together and perhaps choose you a new hairstyle. It'll be fun. I mean, your plait is fine, please don't get me wrong. I loved mine when I wore my hair that way three years ago, but I think it would suit you so much better to wear it short.'

She thrust a pile of women's magazines at Jane.

Lacking the social courage to club her to death with them, Jane took them automatically, realised her tactical error, and opened her mouth to say she didn't want them but thank you very much anyway, but it was too late. Smith was already swinging her way down the corridor, calling a greeting to someone she knew and stepping into the lift.

Jane found herself alone and clutching half a dozen glossy magazines. Her first instinct was to hurl them into an incineration chute – there was one just over there – but that might be considered impolite. This might be a genuine offer to bond. How hurt Smith would be to find her offer of friendship so rudely rejected. So she took them back to her room and shoved them under the bed. She showered, did her hair in the defiant plait she was now determined to wear until the end of time and went for another solitary lunch.

The following days didn't get any better.

Jane found it hard to believe a situation could go so downhill so quickly. She was conscious of the oddest sensation that, try as she might, she could never quite catch up. That every moment, her team was getting further and further away from her. That they were becoming the team they should have been, only she was no longer a part of it.

Far from all of them eating together, it seemed that no matter how early she arrived in the dining room, the three of them were always just leaving the table.

On several occasions, the briefing start times that flashed to her scratchpad turned out to be incorrect, and the other three would be there before her, all sitting together. She would quietly slot herself in behind them, hoping no one had noticed. What made things so much worse was Smith's supposed sympathy.

'Never mind, Jane. We all oversleep occasionally and you do look tired. I tried to cover for you and I don't think anyone noticed you were late. I'll let you have copies of my notes if you like.'

Jane started to say, 'But you sent me the wrong—' when the briefing officer looked over and said, 'Something to say, Lockland?'

Everyone turned to look at her. She felt her face burn. Would she ever grow out of that? She shook her head at the officer and pretended to be busy with her scratchpad.

Needless to say, the notes never turned up.

To keep them all occupied over this period of inactivity, the Time Police ran series after series of simulations. Various hair-raising scenarios were encountered and dealt with more or less successfully.

'Right,' said a slightly stunned Senior Instructor Talbot at the debrief following one of their more . . . exciting . . . sessions. Assuming the expression of false enthusiasm so necessary to training officers everywhere, he said, 'Does anyone have any suggestions as to how things could have gone slightly better?'

Jane, who'd made comprehensive notes in her book, swallowed hard and spoke up. 'Actually, we should . . .'

'We shouldn't have dispersed all our forces in one go,' said Smith, whom Jane suspected of reading her notes over her shoulder. She tried to keep on talking but Smith's cool contralto swept straight over the top of her. 'It left us vulnerable. We should have posted a second, smaller force on higher ground.'

The instructor nodded. 'Good point, Smith. Well done,' and the debrief continued with Jane red-faced and unsure what had just happened.

After that, it didn't take her long to realise that any points she raised were either talked over or talked down. In team situations, it was Smith everyone looked to. Jane was thanked politely for any contribution she cared to make and then had to watch that contribution being quietly ignored. After a while she stopped contributing. No one noticed.

The worst part was accidentally discovering there had been a team night out the previous evening. Except they couldn't call it a team night out because one member of the team hadn't even known about it, let alone been invited. The first she knew was when Matthew and Luke came in late for breakfast the next morning. The two of them shambled over to her table where they sat, white and fragile, in pale-faced silence, sipping black coffee.

She nodded. They nodded back. Neither of them was eating

anything. Not even Matthew, whose capacity for food was reckoned to be limitless.

'Big night, last night,' muttered Luke, followed by a silence as everyone present realised she hadn't been included.

'We looked for you,' said Matthew, defensively. 'You weren't in your room.'

'I was working,' she said briefly, which had the double benefit of making her look good and showing them both she didn't care.

'It was a good night,' said Luke. 'First we went to . . .'

'Sorry,' she said, getting up and cutting him short. 'Things to do this morning.'

Walking off and leaving them was a hollow victory. Without meaning to, she had distanced herself even further. Lacking guile herself, she was unable to deal with it in others. It never occurred to her that, to all intents and purposes, it wasn't Smith easing her out of the team. She was easing herself out.

She found a quiet place in which to stand and think for a while, at the end of which she tracked down North's whereabouts and set off, passing the time by considering how to phrase her questions without making herself sound wetter than the Atlantic Ocean.

North was in her quarters and Jane dithered for ages, passing and re-passing the door at least twice. Fortunately, not all the corridors had cameras and she could only hope no one was watching her extremely suspicious behaviour. On the third pass, she surprised herself by knocking, hoping all the while that North would, by now, be elsewhere.

North opened the door. Before she could stop herself, Jane

blurted, 'Why Smith?' which wasn't what she'd meant to say at all.

North folded her arms. 'You're a man down. Teams consist of four.'

'But why Smith?'

'No idea. I'm afraid I'm not privy to the thoughts of senior managers.' Her tone implied that was because those thoughts weren't worth her effort. 'It's always been felt your team was weak – numerically speaking. Smith is an experienced officer who will remedy that deficiency.'

'But she has no team experience.'

There was a long pause. 'Come in.'

North's quarters were just like North herself. Immaculate. Perfectly in order. Well presented. She did not ask Jane to sit down. Nor did she give Jane a chance to speak. 'I don't know Smith at all. Our paths have never crossed. I know some people don't like her. Women usually. Men don't seem to have a problem.'

She paused for Jane to become aware of her unspoken opinion of men and their judgement, but refrained from mentioning she knew several department heads had refused to take Smith before she had finally found herself a home in Recruitment and Training. Now, North suspected Smith had outstayed her welcome there, as well, and had volunteered for Team 236 before she was asked to leave. There had always been rumours about Smith and the methods she used to get what she wanted, but what she could possibly want with this team was, even to North, a mystery.

She said nothing of this to Lockland.

'I don't know what to tell you, Lockland. Parrish and

281

Farrell are a pair of idiots but they will come to their senses. They all do sooner or later. My advice is to step back, keep your distance and let events take their course.' She stopped and then said quietly, 'This situation has the potential for a great deal of damage, Lockland. Don't let that damage be done to you.'

Jane went away not much comforted and no wiser about her future actions. Should she sit quietly and wait for her teammates to come to their senses? Or hang around waiting to pick up the pieces? Or push off at the first opportunity and leave the pair of them to deal with the inevitable consequences of their own stupidity? Because there would be stupidity and there would be inevitable consequences, she was convinced of it. But why? Smith was obviously aiming for the top – she wasn't going to waste her time on the likes of such small fry as Parrish and Farrell. They weren't her type at all. They had no power. No influence. They couldn't further her career.

Luke Parrish is the only offspring of one of the richest men on the planet.

The thought came out of nowhere. And Matthew Farrell's ability to read and manipulate the Time Map had been causing comment for some time. Weird but gifted was the general verdict. Something else to think about. Was Smith ingratiating herself with Luke to further her personal ambitions? Or with Matthew to further her professional ambitions? Either way, Plain Jane obviously had nothing to offer and could, therefore, be discarded without a qualm.

Plain Jane with a brain, she thought defiantly, and lacking anything else to do, went off for an early lunch.

*   *   *

Over the next few days, Luke became even more full of himself, and under Smith's flattery and encouragement, even Matthew occasionally uttered enough sentences to be considered a short paragraph. By this time the three of them were a tight unit and Jane was definitely on the outside. She hardly knew who she despised most. Sarah Smith for being such a manipulative bitch, the two of them for being such hormonally manipulated idiots, or herself for caring either way.

During quiet sessions in the library, she frequently considered putting in for a transfer. Major Callen had expressed an interest. Perhaps he would take her before she'd completed her gruntwork. It seemed unlikely. She was barely halfway through and every day they weren't allocated an assignment added to the time she still had to serve. If the six-month training period passed and they weren't considered to have enough experience the period could be extended. Which was not something she wanted to think about.

'Just hang in there,' said Wimpy Jane, choosing the soft option. 'It's not usually this quiet. We'll get an assignment soon and then that's another one ticked off.'

'Oh yeah?' said the new Brave Jane. 'Would you really trust Smith to watch your back if things got rough?'

Wimpy Jane couldn't really find anything to say about that because even when Team Weird had been at their most disconnected, she had, at some level, always known she could trust them with her life. Could she say the same now that Smith had joined them?

'Why not box clever over this,' continued Wimpy Jane. 'If you put in for a transfer now, it's certain Smith would support it and you might, just might, get out of your gruntwork early.'

'And then what?' scoffed Brave Jane.

'Then you build yourself a nice little career in Admin or Records. You forget all this ridiculous jumping around and frightening yourself to death. You'll never have to stand in a dark place again. No more mud and ghosts and homicidal rabbits.'

Brave Jane wasn't happy. 'But I was beginning to enjoy it. I was achieving something. Something important. I . . .'

'Well, there's not going to be any more of that, is there? Not with Smith around. Apply for the nice, quiet job you always wanted. I bet you get it. Do it today.'

But she didn't. Perpetually on the verge of applying for a transfer she might be, but something told her that if she gave up now, she'd forever be in a dark place that had nothing to do with the absence of light.

And then, one day, it seemed the matter might have been taken out of her hands.

She was on her way to her room when that familiar voice drifted down the corridor.

'Jane, dear.'

Jane pinned on a smile and turned around.

'I thought you might like to see this. They're looking for a junior clerk in Records. My old department. Although not my old job, obviously. Not a *junior clerk*.' She tinkled a laugh that turned Jane's teeth furry. 'Anyway, have a look. If you're interested, I'll put in a good word for you. I still have friends there.'

She handed Jane a job sheet and passed on.

Jane decided immediately that wild horses couldn't induce her to put in for a transfer. Ever. The job sheet did go down the incineration chute. She watched the light turn red and wondered why she'd done that. Hadn't a nice safe job somewhere quiet always been her goal? Was it possible that if Smith hadn't been involved, she might seriously have considered it? Had she just cut off her nose to spite her face? Was it possible she might have been out of this awful situation by the end of the week?

'And out of the team, too,' said Brave Jane, stamping back down the corridor. 'This is *my* team. I won't be pushed out. If I do leave, it'll be my decision – not hers.'

Two days later, after the morning briefing, she looked up and Smith was there. Right in front of her. And she wasn't happy.

'Jane, you haven't followed up on that post in Records. The one we were talking about.'

The one you were talking about, thought Jane. I don't remember being part of the conversation at all. 'Mm,' she said. 'Well, there's no rush, is there. And at the moment, I prefer to stay with the team.'

Smith's eyes flashed and Jane knew that from this moment, the gloves were off.

'Really? You prefer to remain with the team? Well, that's a bit of a surprise, isn't it? I called in several favours on your behalf, you know. Obviously, I'm the newbie, so perhaps it's not for me to say, but I don't think I'd describe you as part of this team and I'm certain the other two wouldn't either. I don't think anyone would. You don't speak to us. You don't eat with us. You don't sit with us. Aren't we good enough for you?'

She stormed out of the briefing room before Jane could reply.

Shaken, Jane turned to find Luke standing behind her.

'For heaven's sake, Jane. What is the matter with you?'

'Nothing. Excuse me, please.' She attempted to get past him.

'Where are you going?'

'I have work to do.'

'What work? No one's going anywhere. Nothing's happening anywhere. What could you possibly find to do? Look, if this is about our going out without you the other night, then I'm sorry. We really did look for you to see if you wanted to come, too. We just couldn't find you.'

'I was working and then I was in my room.'

He blinked. 'Are you sure? Sarah said . . .'

'Of course I was in my room. Washing my hair. Or reading a book. As you have so frequently pointed out – I am always in my room.'

'Why are you shouting at me? How is your lack of social life my fault?' He turned to Matthew. 'Why is she shouting at me?'

'Leave her alone,' said Matthew. 'Not all women find you irresistible. Jane is only one of many.'

'No one asked you,' said Luke, conveniently forgetting that actually, he had. 'Jane, listen to me – I'm not sure what's wrong with you at the moment but something obviously is. Sarah's very concerned about you and so am I.'

This was too much. 'What do you mean – *Sarah's very concerned about me*?'

'Well, you don't speak – you're even worse than him, these days.' He nodded at Matthew. 'You don't join in. In fact, Sarah thinks you're avoiding us half the time. She says . . .'

'I'm not interested in what Sarah thinks or what Sarah says. Why are you listening to her? She hasn't had her boots on the ground any more often than we have. She's just a clerk. And – and you won't have noticed because you're thinking with your genitals – but your precious Sarah is also a bit of a bitch.'

Matthew gave a crack of laughter.

She wheeled on him. 'And you're no better. She's certainly taking the pair of you for the mugs you are.'

After that none of them were speaking to each other.

They attended subsequent briefings in silence. They worked in the gym in silence. They ate apart. Except for Luke and Smith, now seemingly inseparable, laughing inordinately at each other's jokes while Matthew watched expressionlessly from a distance and Jane went to great lengths to ensure she never watched at all.

And then, one evening, Smith was waiting for her outside her room.

'Lockland, I don't know what you said to Luke and Matthew the other day, but I can't allow you to continue disrupting my team like this. I'm going to request the major removes you. I feel bad about it but I've given you every opportunity and you just haven't responded in any way. I'm sorry, Lockland, but I think you've had your last assignment with this team. In fact, given your less than stellar performance, I suspect they'll let you go altogether. You'll be offered the opportunity to resign, I expect, although, after the damage you've done to my team, I think that would be more than generous.'

And off she went, leaving Jane reeling and without words. Somehow, she let herself into her room. Too stunned even to call for the lights, she sat on her bed and stared out of the window at the unconcerned darkness outside.

Wimpy Jane was all set for a good cry.

'No time for that,' said Brave Jane, sternly. 'Time Police officers don't cry.'

Getting to her feet, she called for the lights and stared at herself in the mirror. Major Ellis was far too senior to concern himself with such trivia, but she considered approaching North again. Except she could imagine the impatient contempt on her face at Jane's failure to deal with her own problems. Or worse, she too might see Jane as the problem. Perhaps everyone thought she was the problem and not Smith. In typical Jane fashion, she dithered all evening, finding excuses for doing nothing.

In the end the decision was made for her. North stopped her on the way to breakfast the next morning. 'What's going on with your team these days, Lockland?'

Jane hesitated. North didn't do self-pitying whining and her natural instinct was to say nothing.

North tilted her head to one side. 'Parrish making a fool of himself over Smith, is he?'

'He's not the only one,' Jane said bitterly.

'Farrell as well? You do surprise me. Well, what are you going to do about it?'

'I'm not going to have the opportunity to do anything about it,' she said, resentfully. 'Smith's recommended I be let go. She's going to have me dismissed.'

To her surprise, North laughed. 'She can try but Major Ellis will never let that happen.'

'But Major Ellis isn't here, is he?'

North shook her head. 'Just hang in there, Lockland. She'll overreach herself soon enough. She always does. You didn't hear this from me, but she's generally known as a bit of a one-week wonder. Ask Truman. Or Talbot. Or any of the others she's used and then tossed aside. By my reckoning, Parrish is due his any day now. And however it ends, Parrish and Farrell will need you to come back to.'

'Oh yes,' she said, even more bitterly. 'Good old Jane. Weathering the humiliations so she can stick around to pick up the pieces afterwards.'

North shook her head. 'Someone has to. It's the price you pay for being more intelligent than those around you. And I'm sorry, Lockland, but I suspect you'll always be the one paying it.'

Cold comfort there. And then, without any warning, matters came to a head.

22

Jane had booked herself a study carrel for that afternoon, intending to open a large number of books as camouflage – a book fort – and then to think very carefully about what to do next.

'You should get a move on,' said Wimpy Jane. 'Put in your notice while you still have a choice.'

'Jump before I'm pushed, you mean?'

'Go with dignity is what I meant.'

'Or I could wait and see what happens. North said Ellis would never allow it to happen. She said not to be too hasty.'

'Any excuse for not doing anything.'

'I'm biding my time,' said Brave Jane with dignity and not even she believed that.

Having no particular reason to hurry, she took her time getting to her study carrel, choosing to stroll around the walkway overlooking the atrium. She leaned on the railing, looking down over the landscaped indoor garden below.

Directly below her, visitors crossed and re-crossed the giant space, being directed to the appropriate departments by members of the Time Police specially selected for their social skills. The ones who could smile and talk at the same time and were definitely known not to eat children.

To her right, the waterfall cascaded spectacularly down into the ornamental pool. Enormous koi carp cruised smoothly, waiting for people to topple in. Rumour had it they could pull down a fully armoured officer and were the first line of Time Police defence.

'Hey,' said a familiar voice behind her. 'I don't seem to have seen you for ages.'

Luke Parrish was grinning down at her. As if nothing was wrong, she thought angrily. As if they hadn't spent the last few days alternately sniping at or ignoring each other.

Looking him in the eye, she said, 'I sat behind you at the briefing this morning.'

'Oh. Well, you never say anything, so I'm never sure whether you're there or not.'

'I'm there,' she said tartly. 'I'm always there. Only you're so tied up with your precious Sarah these days you never notice.'

She paused. This might be her last chance. What did she have to lose?

'Luke, just stop a moment and listen to me. She's playing you. She's out for what she can get. She was foisted on to us because no one else would have her. I think Callen just wanted her out of his department and so we were lumbered with her.'

'Oh, come on, Jane. She's not like that. You're just jealous because you wanted to be the only girl on the team.'

'Well, that's not going to happen. She's recommended my dismissal.'

He was genuinely surprised. 'Why would she do that?'

She stepped back from him. 'It's your money she's after.'

He shook his head. 'I don't have any. Everyone knows that.'

'Not now, perhaps. But one day . . . One day you'll look up

291

and realise you can't get away from her even if you wanted to. And believe me, Luke, one day you will very badly want to get away from Sarah Smith.'

And with that excellent exit line, she turned on her heel and stalked off. Which would, she realised three paces later, have been a great deal more effective if she hadn't stalked off in completely the wrong direction. This walkway led only to one of the smaller libraries, miles of Records storage, the two presentation rooms beyond and then back to the main concourse.

To return back the way she'd come would have been too embarrassing for words so she ducked into the library. Which also turned out to be a mistake because, on closer inspection, she appeared to be in the technical library, a cheerless, gloomy little room – as befitted the subject, she thought. There were no windows and no natural light. Closely packed shelves housed, among other things, all the current volumes of that monumental and still growing work, *Temporal Dynamics*.

She seized a book at random and found herself a quiet table. Not difficult. In a technical library all the tables tend to be quiet. Indeed, the only other occupant was their depressed instructor, Talbot, for some reason poring over a technical journal on the other side of the room.

She opened her own book and stared, unseeing, at various diagrams, graphs and pie charts, all surrounded by impenetrable, un-understandable and closely printed text. She sat quietly, slowly turning the pages until she considered enough time had elapsed for Luke to get clear. Standing up, she re-shelved the volume, smiled weakly at the disbelieving librarian and followed the instructor out of the door.

The first thing she realised was that she hadn't left anything like enough time for Luke to get clear. He was still here in the corridor. And he wasn't alone.

He wasn't happy either. Out of sight around the corner he might be, but she could very clearly hear their voices, and he and Smith were having a major row.

Whatever the original topic of conversation had been, Luke cut ruthlessly across it.

'Never mind all that now,' he said, dismissing whatever Smith had begun to say. 'What's all this I hear about Jane?'

'Jane? What about her?'

'That you've recommended her dismissal. On what grounds? I warn you – Ellis is very unlikely to back you on this. He rates Jane quite highly. As do Matthew and I.'

Concealed around the corner, Jane glowed. It didn't last long.

'Jane? Why are we still talking about Jane? I have such exciting news and . . .'

'We were talking about Jane because it's important. I don't know what you've been saying to her, but she was part of the team long before – well, a few weeks before you turned up and . . .'

Smith's voice was beginning to lose its syrup. 'Can you please stop banging on about Jane? I've something much more important to talk about.'

Luke said something incomprehensible.

'I only told Ellis he needs to drop her because she's dragging the team down. She doesn't do anything – she doesn't contribute anything – she barely even speaks. Trust me, Luke, you'd be far better off without her because . . .'

Luke said something. His deeper voice made his words more difficult to distinguish.

Smith swept on. 'No, of course I'm not advocating throwing her out on to the street – although I don't know why. I tried to find her a nice clerical job – something simple in Records, where she'd be much happier – and she just threw it back in my face. But I need to . . .'

Luke rumbled again. More angrily this time.

'Yes, and him, too. He's only putting in the hours until he can get to the Time Map, but he could easily wait out his time in IT. Major Callen would have a word with Hay if I asked him to. Neither of them will be a problem.'

Luke started to speak and she cut across him.

'So we can be together, of course. Because . . .'

A door slammed somewhere behind her and Jane missed his response but there was no missing Smith's.

'For God's sake, can we stop talking about bloody Jane Lockland. She's not important. Look, this is difficult – I hadn't wanted to tell you like this but, well, you should know – I think I'm pregnant.'

It would appear the universe had finally found a way to silence Luke Parrish.

Smith was continuing. 'Don't look so stunned, Luke. This is wonderful news. It's what we always wanted. You can take your place in your dad's organisation . . .'

He said something.

Her voice hardened. 'Yes, well, you'll have to, Luke, because everyone knows they don't take married officers in the Time Police and you're going to have to provide for me somehow.'

Jane tried to inch a little closer.

'Don't look like that. You didn't think you could treat me in the same way as that blonde slag from Logistics, did you?

That I'd sit around and wait for whatever time and attention you thought you could spare? That once you'd got what you wanted, you'd just sail on to your next victim? I'll tell you now, Luke Parrish, you'll see me right. In fact, you'll see me more than right. You'll keep me for the rest of my life.'

Now Jane could hear him. 'I don't think so.'

'Oh, I think you will.'

'Wrong again, Smith. You know, your staff work is really shoddy. No wonder no one ever wants you on their team. Have you never heard the word "research"? Did you never think to read up on a person before trying to blackmail him?'

She laughed. 'You don't weasel your way out of this situation.'

His voice was very calm. Very quiet. Very level. Very controlled. By now Jane knew him well enough to know how furiously angry he was. 'There is no situation, Sarah. You're not pregnant by me.'

'I think you'll find there's a very serious situation, Luke. And much though you may deny it, you've put yourself about to such an extent while you've been here that no one's ever going to believe a word you say. You can deny it until you're blue in the face but . . .'

'I intend to. Listen, Sarah – I'm not stupid. And my dad's definitely not stupid. He sent his legal people round when I was about fifteen. Because they said this sort of situation would arise. That there would always be some girl greedy enough and stupid enough to think she could blackmail me into keeping her for the rest of her life. Their words, not mine, but, for once, I listened to what they had to say, and I won't get any girl pregnant until both she and I are ready.'

'But I'm pregnant *now*, Luke.'

'For God's sake, Smith, have you thought this through at all? Contraception is compulsory in the Time Police. Are you seriously going to tell people you deliberately contravened the regulations so you could get pregnant?'

'But I did it for you.'

'I don't think so.'

'You begged me.'

'I did no such thing.'

'Oh yes, you did, Luke. You begged me. You pleaded with me. You're so desperate to get out of the Time Police that you deliberately got me pregnant so you'd have to marry me. The Time Police won't take married officers so we'd both be discharged. Which was what you wanted.'

'Are you telling me – all this . . . you and me . . . the last few weeks . . . ?'

'Well, yes, Luke. I really thought you would have worked it out by now.'

'Worked what out?'

'We both get what we want this way. You're out of the Time Police and I'm set up for life.'

'I am not marrying you.'

'Well, it won't be forever, Luke. In fact, I doubt it'll last longer than six months. You're very shallow, you know. And immature. And selfish. And full of shit. And, sadly for you, you're up against the one person in the world who's even more shallow and selfish than you are. Who'd have thought?'

'I'm not paying you a penny.'

'Oh, you will, Luke, you will. Your father will see to that. He dumped you in the Time Police to escape more scandal and here you are – barely three months later – with a pregnant colleague. A pregnant colleague you're determined to abandon. And your reputation counts against you. Since you've been here there's been that nurse . . . that Records clerk . . . that blonde in Logistics – really, Luke, you don't do yourself any favours, do you?'

'Smith – be clear. I shall fight you every inch of the way. Your own reputation is hardly spotless, is it?'

'Luke. Give in gracefully. This will happen.'

'I don't think so.'

'Well, I do.' Jane shivered at the malignancy in Smith's voice. 'I'll tell the world you raped me. You'll be the entitled rich boy who thinks he can have anything or anyone he wants. I imagine your father will have something to say to you about that.'

His voice was cold with contempt. 'I think it's far more likely the world will say you raped me.'

There was a moment's silence. Jane just had time to wonder if Smith had actually stormed off when the sound of a slap rang out, echoing along the corridor. By the sound of it she'd really given him one. Then a silence, lasting so long that Jane wondered if he was actually still conscious. Then he appeared round the corner, white with rage and with a huge red mark down one side of his face, striding so swiftly and so furiously along the corridor that he failed to see Jane at all. She tried to step back into the library but her fumbling hand failed to find the door handle behind her. His shoulder knocked against hers, sending her sprawling back against the door, and a moment later he was gone. Around the corner and out of sight.

Jane slowly straightened up, rubbed her shoulder and stared

down the corridor. Everything was very quiet. No Sarah Smith had come striding after him, seeking retribution. Nor were there any sounds of distress. No sounds at all, in fact. Was she still there? Rigid with rage, perhaps. Or was she too upset to move? She might even have been taken ill.

Jane wavered in a familiar welter of social embarrassment. What should she do? Tactfully walk away and do nothing? Go and offer Smith some assistance? But how could she do that without revealing she'd heard every word? No, she should go and see if she could help her. It was the right thing to do. Eventually, after a number of false starts, she straightened her shoulders and – walking very slowly, prepared to turn back at any moment – she turned the corner.

And really, really wished she hadn't.

Sarah Smith lay on her back in a pool of dark, wet, shining blood. And it wasn't just on the floor. A great gush had sprayed all the way up the wall and across the ceiling – a constellation of blood – shockingly scarlet against the Time Police beige.

Jane's first reaction was one of disbelief. There was blood everywhere. How could one person hold so much? Her training dictated she should move calmly forwards and deal with the situation, but all her stupid brain could do was run and re-run the famous quotation: 'Who would have thought the old man to have had so much blood in him?'

And then came the guilt. Was it possible that Smith had been bleeding to death all the time that she, Jane, had been standing around the corner, too embarrassed to move?

Slowly, on legs that felt too weak to hold her and trailing her hand along the wall for support, Jane moved towards the body. Smith's eyes were open. For a moment Jane grabbed at the thought she might still be alive after all. She licked suddenly dry lips and forced herself to look properly at the body. The hope died. Someone had cut Smith's throat.

Kneeling carefully on a blood-free patch of carpet, she struggled to put aside the shock and recall her first-aid training. First – she should check for signs of life. Her fingers felt rubbery as she picked up Smith's hand and fumbled for a pulse, but there was nothing. No movement of the chest. She stared at those glassy, lifeless eyes. Sarah Smith was definitely dead.

She swallowed down the impulse to throw up. Not here. Not now. Closing her eyes, she took two or three deep breaths to try and clear her head.

She should get help. She looked around for a corridor com and found the weapon instead. A blood-stained knife lay on the floor a little distance away where, presumably, it had been dropped or thrown down. Her heart, up to this moment pounding so hard as almost to break through her chest, suddenly ground to a complete stop. For a moment, her head swam. And then she thought – how typical of Luke. He'd left his knife at the scene of the crime. There was his number on the handle – 2044.

She could see it all so clearly. Luke and Smith had had a furious row. She'd slapped him. And then he'd stormed past Jane in a rage. Or so she'd thought at the time. Suppose it hadn't been rage? Suppose it had been fear? He'd killed Smith, brutally, bloodily, and then had been so desperate to get away he hadn't even seen her standing there? Questions rattled around her brain but one thought stood out from the crowd: Sarah Smith had had her throat cut and here was Luke's knife at the scene.

There had once been a series of brilliant detective books

299

written long ago by a woman named Agatha Christie. Jane had read them all, one after the other, during her last year at school. Each was a difficult and complex murder mystery, and only after a great deal of questioning and deduction was the murderer successfully unmasked at the end.

Jane looked at the bloody body lying on the floor. This was not a difficult and complex murder mystery and there was no need to wait until the last page to identify this particular murderer.

She looked at the knife again. Unbelievably, barely seconds had passed since Luke had stormed past her. No one, other than Jane herself, could have known Luke had ever been here.

There was an incineration chute not ten feet away. She could destroy the knife, whisk herself away and there would be nothing to link Luke with this.

No – she couldn't do that. That would be so wrong. Luke had killed Sarah Smith. She should report it.

Something inside her said, 'But it's Luke.'

'That doesn't change anything.'

'It's Luke.'

'You're being stupid.'

'It's Luke.'

'I notice you're not saying he didn't do it. Even you don't believe that, do you?'

There was no answer to that.

There was the corridor com over there. Next to the incineration chute.

Stiffly, she rose to her feet, bent and picked up the knife. She was still convinced she should report this. Because it was the right thing to do. She saw her hand reach out to the com unit. She *was* going to report it. Because that was the correct thing to do. She watched her hand reach out to open the com.

She hit the other control. The incineration chute opened. She reached inside to place the knife in the receptacle provided and a hand came over her shoulder and roughly grasped her wrist. A voice said, 'Oh, no, you don't, missie.'

In her shock she let go of the knife which clattered into the receptacle. The lid came down automatically and the red light came on.

Someone swore horribly. Another voice was shouting, 'Shut down all the incineration chutes on the walkway level.'

He was gripping her wrist so hard it hurt. There were voices all around. People shouting. The medics turned up. People shouted at each other not to stand in the blood. She was jostled in the crush but never once did they let go of her.

And then security turned up.

And everyone was looking at her.

Because everyone thought she'd killed Sarah Smith.

23

Jane had no idea what to do. What to say. What could she say? People were bombarding her with questions. She couldn't focus on any one person. Voices came and went. Except for the one in her head, repeating, 'What have you done? What have you done?' over and over again.

If they failed to find the knife in the garbage incinerator, then she would be their prime suspect. If they did find the knife, then Luke would be implicated and she would be found guilty of destroying evidence. Which she was. Whatever she said could only make things worse. She desperately needed time to stop and think.

They'd touched on basic interrogation techniques during her training. More specialised instruction would be given to those who made security their career choice after their gruntwork. She knew from the sessions she had attended that she wouldn't be granted the luxury of time. There would be no time to consider her strategy. No time to pull herself together. No time to get her story straight in her head. No time to think about what she could and couldn't say. No time to take a breath and face the situation calmly. They would deliberately hustle her. They would move her from room to room with no explanation. A number of interrogators would work on her. Sometimes together – sometimes alone. They would never stop. They would hammer away at her. Hour after hour. There would be no rest. No respite. There would be no food. No water. Toilet breaks only after she'd humiliatingly wet herself in desperation. They'd caught her at the scene of a murder with the body of an officer at her feet and the murder weapon in her hand. They'd caught her disposing of the weapon. They would keep on at her as her story floundered and she contradicted herself in exhaustion and eventually confessed to anything just so they would leave her alone.

Her instinct was to say nothing. Not a word. Although how long would she be allowed to get away with that? The Time Police did not recognise the right to remain silent.

She was marched through the building. Every corridor was lined with a sea of faces. She suddenly realised she didn't have a single friend in this place. Or even the whole world. There was no one alive who would care what became of her. No one to protest on her behalf. She was willing to bet that in a month's time, no one would even remember she'd passed this way.

They took her downstairs to the detention area. She closed her eyes, expecting the worst.

To her surprise, the initial questioning was quite mild. The Time Police were very good at this sort of thing. And they knew her. They knew her weaknesses. They would try the gentle approach first.

A female security officer sat opposite her, inviting her to give her side of the story.

'There must be some explanation, Jane,' she kept saying. 'We know it wasn't you, Jane. Tell me what happened so I can help. I want to help you, Jane.'

Standard procedure. Use the suspect's name in every sentence. She'd never been sure whether it was an attempt to strike up a relationship or drive the prisoner screamingly insane.

For what seemed like hour after hour, the tiny room was filled with sympathetic people who only wanted to help. Jane continued to say nothing.

Without warning – almost in mid-sentence – the security officer left the room. They left her alone for an hour. No one came near her. She sat as still as she could, knowing they would be watching her every move. Looking for signs of fear, or distress, or guilt. Something that would give them a way in.

Without warning, the door slammed back against the wall. Here was an officer she'd never seen before. He didn't bother to sit down, informing her harshly that if she didn't immediately give a statement or explain her actions then her next interrogator would be nowhere near as pleasant as the last one. He slammed back out and once again, she was alone.

And terrified. And shaking with cold and shock. And still completely silent. The effort of staying quiet gave her something on which to focus. She remembered reading an article once which said every person has all the strength they need to survive buried inside themselves. They have only to dig deep and find it. And then use it. She tried to use the long periods of solitude to disappear down herself. To find herself somewhere safe and quiet and far away from the nightmare she could hardly believe was happening to her.

No one said anything to her about the knife. Hadn't they found it? Or was it a trick? Were they waiting for her to ask about it? And what of Luke? If he had any sense, he'd have caught the next airship out and be in France by now. Once they discovered he was missing . . . then she could speak. But at the moment, the safest thing to do was to say nothing.

The next stage began. There were no more sympathetic young women trying to help. Now there were two men and they never stopped. On and on, bombarding her with questions. Their voices were harsh and loud. Whenever she tried to close her eyes and lose herself, they slapped the table, jerking her back to the moment. There was no chance of ignoring them. She wondered how much time had passed. Only a very tiny fraction of the eternity she seemed to have been in here, she was certain. She was exhausted and very, very thirsty.

As if they could read her mind, they banged out of the room and the female officer was back.

'You must be thirsty, Jane.'

She recognised they'd gone back to using her first name so she could see how friendly and helpful they wanted to be. She could have a drink if she asked for one. That's all she had to do.

'Just ask for a drink, Jane, and we'll bring you one. What would you like? Something long and cold? How about a fruit juice? With lots of ice? Won't take a moment; we've got bottles full in the fridge. What flavour would you like? Just tell me, Jane.'

She knew the moment she spoke she was lost. Say one word and the next is easier. And then the next. Until she'd told them everything. Saying nothing made it easier for her and harder for them. It's much more difficult to deal with someone who never says anything at all.

The worry was that they would use drugs. She knew they were considering it. They were discussing it in front of her. How they would do it. The things they could make her do

305

while under the influence. She knew they were just trying to frighten her, but it was working.

The two loud men were back. The men who never stopped talking. She tried to close her mind but they never stopped. One after the other with never a break. Sometimes both together and the clatter of words jangled around her aching head.

She tried to think what could be happening outside this room. Was Luke just calmly carrying on with his day? He'd murdered a woman and by great good luck, someone else had been arrested. All he had to do was hold his nerve, and as long as they never found the knife, he would almost certainly get away with it. And the longer she remained silent, the easier it would be for him. The Time Police were right. She should speak up. Speak out. Now. Because if she left it any longer, they'd think she was just accusing Luke to save herself. They were still talking at her. Her head ached. She wanted to lay her forehead on the cool, cool table, close her eyes and retreat from all this. Just for a moment. Just to have a moment to stop and think.

The door opened and suddenly Luke was standing there, sandwiched between two enormous security guards. A wave of hot relief washed over her. He'd confessed. She was light-headed at the thought. She was safe. He'd admitted what he'd done and she would be free.

The two shouting officers got up and left the room. The door closed behind them, leaving Luke and Jane on their own.

They looked at each other. Luke's face was completely blank. And then she realised the truth. They'd let him in because they thought she would talk to him.

They were alone together but neither made the mistake of thinking their faces weren't on half a dozen screens and being carefully scrutinised by a large number of security people. There would be hidden cameras all over this room. Not for one single second would they be unwatched.

He put his forearms on the table and leaned forwards. 'Jane – silence is not an option for the Time Police. They'll hurt you badly if you don't speak. Please – tell them exactly what happened and plead extenuating circumstances. It wasn't your fault. You've recently had a concussion. You didn't know what you were doing. Ellis will speak up for you. And North. You have to confess, Jane. Please. Make it easy on yourself.'

All hope drained away, taking her courage with it. He hadn't come to save her at all. He'd come to save himself. Contempt and disgust rose within her. Along with good, healthy rage. She was sickened to think Luke was going along with this when he knew very well she was innocent. She tried to express her disgust through her expression. She'd always known he was self-absorbed and selfish but surely even he could see the burning-hot contempt in her face.

She'd had enough of him – of the Time Police – of everyone. She folded her arms and silently vowed she'd see them all dead at her feet before she said a single word.

Whoever was watching obviously came to the same conclusion because the door opened and with a jerk of his head, the officer indicated Luke should leave.

They told her there was to be a formal hearing and waited for her to ask when.

She said nothing, concentrating on the texture of the table in front of her to try and shut out their voices.

Apparently, they hadn't completely abandoned the softly, softly approach, because the female officer was back again,

307

gently explaining she'd been appointed her escort. '"Prisoner's Friend", as it used to be called, Jane.'

Her nametag said Varma. She was brisk and matter-of-fact, but not unfriendly. Jane hardened her heart.

'Right, Jane, I'm here to represent you. It's not strictly necessary at this stage – it's not a court martial – it's simply a hearing to try to establish what happened. My defence – our defence – is that you are too shocked to speak at the moment. Playing to your strengths there,' she added with unexpected humour.

She looked at Jane for a moment and then said quietly, 'Your situation might not be as desperate as you think. Whether by accident or design, the murder of Sarah Smith took place in a blind spot. No cameras. So no clues there. Furthermore, when they took your clothes for analysis, they found no blood on them other than a small patch on your right knee – presumably where you knelt and a slight smear on your cuff where you felt for her pulse. My argument – and it's a strong one – is that given the amount of blood sprayed up the walls and across the ceiling, the murderer would be covered in the stuff.'

Unless he stood behind her, thought Jane, closing her eyes against a sudden picture of Luke, his hand entangled in Smith's thick, glossy black hair, pulling back her head . . . exposing her throat . . .

'Unless he stood behind her, of course,' said Varma. And waited.

This echo of her thoughts brought Jane up short. This officer – for all her designation of Prisoner's Friend – was not. She was simply here to ignite a flicker of trust in Jane and then exploit it.

There was a short silence as Jane bit back the words she had been about to utter. Was there a very faint flash of disappointment in Varma's eyes?

'Of course,' she continued, 'you're such a shorty that if you had been standing behind her, you probably wouldn't have been able to reach, anyway, so we should be able to kick that argument into touch quite easily.'

She paused again, then sat back in her chair. 'Jane, I have to warn you – if you continue to . . . experience difficulties . . . in communicating, then the hearing will arrange a medical examination to ascertain whether there is any physical reason why you cannot speak. If there is not, then I'm afraid, Jane, you will be subject to the full extent of . . . well, you can guess. Jane, I say this with all concern. They will hurt you very badly –' this repetition of Luke's phrase convinced Jane that Luke had been sent in to make her speak – 'and, sooner or later, you will tell them everything they want to know. Everyone does in the end. Jane, you are refusing to cooperate. Refusing to speak. It is very possible that after a full interrogation you will be *unable* to speak. Ever again. The irony of that would appeal to some of my colleagues. I beg of you – think very carefully before proceeding with this refusal to cooperate.'

Silence fell in the little room.

Why am I doing this? thought Jane. Why don't I just say what I saw? Which is nothing. And all I heard was two people having an argument and you get that all the time here. I didn't actually see anything. Why am I putting myself through this for that worthless piece of . . . ?

She closed her eyes and saw Luke's face, filled with concern and sincerity, urging her to confess to the murder he himself had committed.

Well, he could just fire truck off. Today was the day young Mr Parrish would finally be forced to face up to the consequences of his actions.

A soft voice asked, 'Are you ready to talk to me now, Jane?'

Opening her eyes, she looked at Varma sitting opposite, let her breath out in a long sigh . . . and nodded.

24

Varma was far too experienced an officer to let her satisfaction show. Yes, the wimp Lockland had held out for longer than anyone had expected. Varma herself had lost a considerable amount of money in the sweepstake, but she'd get most of that back in side bets because she was the officer who'd induced Lockland to speak. From here it was only a short step to a full confession. She'd be receiving her commendation in an hour. Another one to go up on the wall.

She set up her scratchpad to record, pushed it out of Lockland's line of sight and smiled invitingly.

Jane took a deep breath . . .

And the emergency siren went off.

Varma leaped to her feet. 'Shit.'

Because this wasn't the fire alarm. This eldritch, shrieking, teeth-on-edge screech signified a radiation warning. Somewhere in this building a massive radiation leak was building. There had been – or was about to be – a serious incident. One of the pods was about to blow.

It was an occupational hazard. A risk they'd lived with for so long that many of them believed it would never happen. Yes, it was well known that a pod had been blown up once at

St Mary's, but they were morons there and the only surprise was that it didn't happen every day. That explosion had almost completely demolished the structure in which the pod had been standing. The damage caused had been extensive and widespread and that had been in an underpopulated rural area. Here, the potential for catastrophe was massive. Because this was central London. And most of the Pod Bay stretched far under the Thames.

There was an established procedure. Drills were held monthly. The procedure was rigorous and unchangeable. You had thirty seconds to exit the building by whatever means seemed good at the time. After that, the blast doors would come down on every floor and all chances of escape would be lost. After thirty seconds, people were no longer important. Damage control was the main aim. The blast doors would come down – for all the good they would do – and anyone still in the building would soon find themselves buried underneath most of it. Which was the easy way to go.

Because there might not be an explosion. If the pod simply sat there, haemorrhaging radiation, then any survivors would spend their last few seconds hammering uselessly on the blast doors demanding to be let out and then, within a horrifyingly short time, succumb to weakness and fainting. Their gums would bleed and soon – very soon – their teeth would fall out. And their hair. Their skin would start to blister, split and then slough off completely. They would be consumed by raging fevers, bloody and involuntary diarrhoea, and massive vomiting. At that point it was generally reckoned that death wouldn't seem so bad after all.

Jane barely had time to jump out of her skin at the noise

before the door crashed open and two radiation-suited figures burst in, shouting, 'Get out. Get out. Immediate evacuation. Get out now.'

Varma headed for the door. Her scratchpad fell, unheeded, to the floor.

'Lead the way,' shouted the one on the right. 'You know the designated exits?'

'I do. Follow me.'

The corridors were choked with people trying to get to the lifts. The detention area was underground – along with the Pod Bay. They were at ground zero. The furthest point from safety.

The same thought was in everyone else's minds. There wasn't panic – they were the Time Police, after all, and they remembered their drills. Marshals and evacuation officers held doors open and ushered people in the right direction. Everyone moved at a fast trot, conscious of the seconds ticking away.

Each of Jane's arms was tightly held by the evacuation officers. There was no chance of escape. They followed Varma down the corridor at a running walk.

'This way,' she shouted. 'Exit C3.'

She turned right.

Jane was shoved left.

She tried to protest. Neither officer took any notice. She tried to struggle. They simply moved faster. Over everything – the shouting, the running footsteps, the screaming siren – she could hear the countdown.

Eighteen. Seventeen.

They crashed through a set of double doors, flattening themselves against the wall as five or six mechs from the Pod Bay raced past them going in the other direction.

Jane tried to shout for help and someone shoved a gloved hand over her mouth. She tried again to break free and they dealt with this by shoving her against the wall and leaning on her. She could barely breathe.

The stampede passed.

Thirteen. Twelve.

She was yanked off the wall. They ran her into a huge space. She was in the Pod Bay. Why? Were they going to leave her here to die of radiation sickness? Or to be blown apart in the explosion? A nasty and potentially embarrassing problem resolved the easy way. She wondered if Smith's body would be similarly disposed of. Both of them killed in the same unfortunate accident. No one would ever know. Problem solved.

She tried to resist but they were stronger than she was. Everyone is stronger than me, she thought, struggling wildly.

With a thunderous boom that made the whole building jump, the blast doors slammed shut. She could hear similar booming noises all around the building. All the doors were being locked. No one could get out. Everyone in the building was already dead. It just hadn't happened yet.

No one could get in, either. They'd brought her here to die. Did she care?

They slowed to a walk and halted outside a pod. The two officers pushed back their protective hoods and stood for a moment, chests heaving.

'Hate these bloody suits,' said Luke.

Matthew nodded, sweat running down his face.

She stared at them. What was happening?

'Jane, you need to go,' shouted Matthew over the sound of the klaxon. 'Now. Before they find out.'

She stood rooted to the spot. Find out what? She looked wildly around, hardly able to believe what they'd done. 'You've rigged a pod to blow? How could you do that? What were you thinking?'

Matthew shook his head. His hair was flattened against his head and dark with sweat. His golden eyes shone bright with excitement. 'No, stupid. I rigged the computer to find a fault and sound the alarm and they're going to work it out any minute now. If they haven't already.' He was pulling off his anti-radiation gear. Bundling it up, he tossed it into the pod.

'Jane, get in the pod.' Luke tried to push her through the door.

'But . . .'

'Just get in the bloody pod. Quickly. Before the doors come back up.' He turned to Matthew. 'Mate . . . are you going to be all right?'

Matthew nodded firmly. 'Absolutely fine.'

Jane seized Luke's arm. 'What are you going to do?'

He dragged out his sonic. 'Shoot him.'

Matthew braced himself. 'You need to get a move on. Try not to hit anything vital.'

They looked at each other.

'Don't just stand there,' shouted Matthew. 'Shoot me.'

Luke hesitated. 'Shit, Matthew.'

'For fire truck's sake – you have to make it look good. Shoot me.'

Luke raised his sonic. 'It's on maximum. Won't be pleasant.'

'Do it.'

With a deafening squeal of metal, slowly, ponderously, the doors began to rise.

Matthew said quietly, 'Luke – they're here. You have to do it.'

Luke pointed his sonic. 'I'm sorry, Matthew.' He fired.

Matthew dropped to the floor, convulsing violently.

Jane started towards him. 'Matthew . . . !' She turned to Luke, panic rising in her chest. 'He's going to need immediate treatment or he might die.'

'And he'll get it. Come on.'

She could hear shouts as officers tried to wriggle under the slowly rising doors. They weren't shooting. No one would risk hitting the pods.

Luke threw her bodily into the pod. She hit the wall and fell to the floor, banging her head on the console on the way down. Dimly, a hundred miles away, a voice shouted, 'Pod – emergency evacuation.'

The floor lurched beneath her.

The world went black. She felt vomit in the back of her throat.

At which point she gave up.

25

The pod touched down with a substantial thump although at least half the occupants were past caring. Inside, there was silence for a very, very long time.

Eventually, Luke said cautiously, 'Are you still alive?'

She opened first one eye and then the other.

He heaved a sigh of relief. 'I was worried I'd killed you.'

'You threw me into the wall.'

'I had to get you on board quickly. That was not the moment for you to be standing chatting to Matthew.'

Memories came back. 'You shot him.'

'Only very reluctantly.'

'For God's sake, Luke, how many more people are you going to kill today?'

'I told you – Matthew will be fine.'

The reference to his murder of Sarah Smith apparently passed him by. She wondered if he'd actually forgotten it.

She tried to sit up. 'We need to get away from this pod. It won't take long for them to find it and they could be here at any moment.'

'No huge rush.'

'Yes, there is, Luke.' She stopped and thought about his words. 'Why isn't there any huge rush?'

'Because we're only one of many pods here at the moment.'

'Where's here?'

He grinned. 'Rome, 14th March 44BC,' and waited to see if the date would mean anything to her.

It did not.

'Luke, they'll be after us already. We should go.'

He shook his head. Irritatingly calm. 'We have a little time. Yes, they will have worked out that it was the alarm that was faulty and not a pod, but regulations will still require them to run full diagnostics on all the pods before they can be used again. At the same time, they're going to be busy doing the PR thing – opening the doors, reassuring the public, the authorities and so on. They might even have to submit to some sort of inspection. It'll be a while before they can get around to us.'

She frowned. 'And when they do . . . Luke, they're not going to be happy.'

'They're never happy.'

'They'll track us here, eventually. They could be on their way right now.'

He turned from the console with that smug *I'm Luke Parrish and I'm amazing* look that made her want to slap him. And then, having slapped him, really get stuck in and do him some seriously enjoyable damage. She was already wanted for one murder. Two would make very little difference.

He was smirking. 'They're not going to have any spare people for a while.'

'Luke, it's not when they leave – it's when they arrive. You know that.'

318

'They don't have to arrive. They're already here.'

Just as her heart rate was beginning to slow, everything kicked up again. 'What?'

'I'll tell you in a moment. Just let me concentrate on shutting this down.'

He busied himself at the console, shutting everything down.

She looked around. 'What about Matthew? What will happen to him?'

'Well, I very much hope he'll receive tip-top medical treatment and be as right as rain in no time.'

'You had the setting on maximum,' she said accusingly, still struggling with the Parrish world view that he'd actually made things better.

'It had to look good. For his own protection. It was his idea.'

She was not reassured. 'They'll know he was involved, surely.'

'They'll suspect him, obviously, but there's no proof. It's well known that he and I don't really get on. Why would he help me? And he was disguised in a radiation suit. No one saw his face. The suit's disappeared –' he nodded at the heap in the corner – 'and best of all, he's stretched out on the Pod Bay floor, deeply unconscious.'

'But won't they wonder what was he doing in the Pod Bay in the first place?'

'They'll discover a technical manual and a couple of technical scratchpads and everyone will think he was just in there having a bit of a tinker.'

'Without permission?'

'Well, the poor sod never got the chance, did he? The alarms went off and then I shot him.'

She put her head in her hands. 'Oh God, Luke.'

'He'll be fine. Tough little bugger.'

'For God's sake, how many more people are you going to murder today?'

'Hey – a touch more gratitude if you don't mind.'

'Gratitude?' She was nearly speechless with fury. 'You think *I* should be grateful to *you* . . . ?'

The events of the day rose up and overwhelmed her. There were no words to describe what he'd done . . . or the way he'd done it . . . She seized Matthew's hazmat helmet and hurled it at him. It bounced off his head.

'Ow. Bloody hell, Lockland.'

'You stupid . . .' Still the words wouldn't come. Somehow, she heaved herself to her feet, snatching up whatever she could find and throwing it at him. He dodged as best he could but she was a good shot and the pod wasn't large. There wasn't really anywhere to hide.

'Jane, pack it in, will you? Ouch.' He batted aside the helmet which she'd retrieved from the floor and slung at him again. 'Calm down, will you? Jane . . . *Jane*.'

Ducking under what he later described as a hail of potentially fatal missiles and Jane maintained was merely a light rain of small, non-lethal objects, he eventually reached her, bore her to the floor and pinned her wrists over her head.

'Bloody pack it in, will you? Stop it. Stop it now.'

Eventually she ceased struggling but glared at him so he would know the cease-fire was only temporary. 'I haven't done anything wrong and you fire-trucking know it.'

'Well, I have.'

She nodded, saying more quietly, 'Yes, I know you have, Luke, but I'll never tell, I promise.'

He rolled off her. 'I don't think you'll have to. Everyone must know by now.'

'They'll all come looking for you, won't they?'

'Well, in my saner moments I rather think you may be overestimating my importance slightly. One team. Possibly two. No more.'

'Luke, you need to stop kidding yourself. They'll send everyone they can lay their hands on.'

He sat up and smoothed down his hair. 'Whatever for?'

She could hardly believe him. The rage began to boil again. Even now he wouldn't admit what he'd done. *'Because you killed Sarah Smith.'*

There was a long silence. A very long silence. Long enough for her to realise she was here, alone, and with a murderer. Dark shadows gathered around her.

His next words shattered them into tiny pieces.

'No, I didn't. What are you talking about?' He sounded so genuinely indignant that she very nearly believed him.

'Luke, you don't have to pretend with me. I saw you.'

He stared at her. She remembered the door was locked and he was only feet away. She really could have handled this better. And then realised she didn't really care. Whatever a tether was, she had come to the end of hers. If she could just get him to face up to the reality of his situation, then at least she would have achieved something in her life.

'Jane, what are you talking about?'

'I saw you.'

'Saw me what?'

'Kill Sarah Smith.'

'No, you didn't. You can't have.' And there it was again. Bewilderment and indignation.

'I did. You pushed past me. I don't think you saw me but I was there.'

'Oh – was that you? Sorry – I didn't notice.'

'Of course you didn't. Why would you? You'd just killed Sarah Smith.'

She finally had the satisfaction of knowing she'd rendered him speechless.

'What? . . . I . . . What? How could you think . . . ? Why would I kill Sarah Smith?'

She was unable to read his face but he sounded completely flabbergasted. Not angry. Or dangerous. Just – flabbergasted.

'You had a row, Luke. I heard you shouting at her.'

'The whole building probably heard me shouting at her. She was springing one of the neatest little traps I've ever seen. I could have been in real trouble there.'

She blinked. 'You were in real trouble there. She was about to eat you alive.'

'Jane, have a little faith, will you?'

'She was *pregnant*, Luke.'

He shrugged. 'Jane, if she *was* pregnant – and I'm not convinced – it was nothing to do with me.'

Jane stared at him. At that moment she had never disliked him more. The spoiled rich boy dodging his responsibilities with a casual disinterest that nearly took her breath away.

'Luke . . .'

He heaved an enormous sigh. 'Jane, please. Why is it always so easy for you to believe the worst of me? According to you,

I'm the sort of person who would murder his pregnant girlfriend to evade his responsibilities.'

'I didn't say that.'

'Yes, Jane, you kind of did. Look, my old man's a bastard, but he's not stupid. He knew this sort of thing would happen to me at some point in my life, so when I was about fifteen, we had "the chat". Well, not him, personally – he sent someone else, obviously, and they had "the chat", but "the chat" was definitely had. And after "the chat" came "the treatment".'

She stared at him. 'The treatment?'

He shook his head. 'Seriously Jane, I can't believe you don't know this. You nip into the clinic – a quick local anaesthetic – a tiny snip – and back out again in time to get down the pub and watch the footie that evening. No inadvertent Parrishes to clutter up the landscape.'

'But . . . that's awful.'

'No, it's not. One day – apparently – I'll meet the girl of my dreams – although I have to say that after today I'm in no great rush – there's a bit of unsnipping – and away I go, throwing out potential Parrishes in all directions. Although as I say it, I realise that could have been better put.'

'Luke, you could have told her that.'

'Yes, you're right. I could have. I probably should have. But to be fair, she was hardly playing by gentlemen's rules herself, was she?'

It had to be said. 'She might not have died if you had told her. If you hadn't stormed off – if you'd stayed with her . . .'

He nodded, not looking at her. 'That might be true, and I would have told her, probably tomorrow, but if you were listening, then you'll realise we'd both reached the stage where

323

sensible conversation was no longer possible. She threatened me. I insulted her. She landed me a slap that nearly took my head off and that was my cue to get as far away as possible and as quickly as possible. I pushed her off me and legged it. Straight into you, apparently.' He seemed to realise for the first time. 'What were you doing there, anyway?'

'Coming out of the library.'

He regarded her with total disbelief. '*You* were in the technical library?'

She bristled defiantly. 'Yes.'

'What on earth were you doing there?'

'Trying to avoid you.'

'So you hid in the library . . .'

'I wasn't hiding,' she said, inaccurately.

'So you heard everything and when I'd gone, you walked around the corner . . .'

He stopped, staring at her in exactly the same way that she'd stared at him.

'I'm so stupid – it's only just occurred to me. Jane, did you . . . ?'

Fighting hard to keep her voice steady, she said, 'I didn't kill her. I swear it. I honestly thought *you'd* killed her.'

'So you said and we'll be having a lot more words about that later on.'

'It wasn't me,' she said, beginning to panic, because if Luke didn't believe her then no one would. 'Why would you think it was me?'

'Well, you hated her. She was trying to get rid of you and you were caught at the scene of the crime, disposing of the murder weapon.'

Jane shook her head, vigorously. 'I walked around the corner and she was already dead. There was blood everywhere.' She closed her eyes and relived the scene. The blood spray up the walls. The pool of glistening red.

Luke was speaking. 'Well, it wasn't all over me. Did you see any blood on me? I would have been covered in it.'

'No, but your knife was on the ground beside her.'

'It can't have been. I've got it here with me now. Look.' He pulled it from his utility belt and flicked it open with a *snick*. The little sound was very loud in the silence and suddenly, he was holding an open blade. Looking from it to her and back again. Her heart lurched. She was alone with him and he was holding a knife.

And then, finally, common sense kicked in. If he was holding his knife here . . . now . . . then whose knife had she dropped down the incineration chute? 'Where did you get that knife?'

She could see he was beginning to be angry. 'It was issued to me on my first day. Remember? Same as you. There's my number. See?'

He held it up. She could see his number stamped on the handle. 2144.

She put her hand over her mouth. 'Oh.'

'Is that all you've got to say? "Oh"?'

'I got your number wrong.'

'What?'

'I thought you were 2044.'

'So you thought the knife was mine?'

'I thought you'd dropped it when . . .'

'. . . and that was why you were caught chucking it down

the chute, and you never said anything because you thought I'd done it. You let them think – Jane, you *idiot*.'

She gaped at him, speechless with anger – at both of them, because she was obviously as stupid as he was. And full of indignation at his ingratitude. And confusion – because if he hadn't and she hadn't – then who *had* killed Smith? Relief was there as well, but unable to elbow its way past all the other churning emotions. Relief would get its chance later.

Luke hadn't finished being angry. 'I thought it was *your* knife you'd chucked down the chute.'

She shook her head. 'Who is 2044?'

'Dunno. And you destroyed it . . .' He tailed off. 'I can't believe this, Jane. If you'd left well alone – if you'd raised the alarm – if you hadn't touched the knife . . . She was still alive and well when I left her. There was no blood on me. My fingerprints wouldn't have been on that knife. Nor yours. There was nothing to implicate either of us and – ouch, that hurt. Why are you attacking your rescuer? *Again*.'

She was so furious the words would barely come.

'*I covered for you. I tried to conceal a crime for you and you called me an idiot.*'

'Well, you are.' He paused. 'That's a very good point. Why did you cover for me?'

'I genuinely have no idea. I don't know what I was thinking. I tell you now, the next time I find a body with your knife alongside it, I shall shout, "Here it is. Luke Parrish did it," and throw a huge party on the day they execute you.'

'You know three people in the entire world, Lockland. How is that a huge party?'

326

'I know Matthew and Ellis. And North. And you. That's at least four.'

'Well, I'm not going to be there, am I, you dozy bint? You'll have had me arrested and I'll be on my way to the gallows.'

'Firing squad.'

'What?'

'Firing squad. We're in the Time Police. They'll shoot you.'

He flung his arms wide in exasperation. 'I can't believe I risked my career and my life to save you.'

'Well, there's a coincidence. I was just thinking exactly the same thing.'

They glared at each other and then, as the realisation hit both of them, she said quietly, 'Well, we're both in trouble now, aren't we?'

He shrugged. 'We were in trouble before. We've just dug ourselves in a little deeper, that's all. It's obviously a gift we both share. I thought you'd done it. You thought I'd done it. There's not much to choose between us, is there?'

Silence fell. They both stared at the floor and then she said, 'Why is everyone already here?'

He blinked and refocused. 'Sorry?'

'You said everyone was already here.'

He made a visible effort to pull himself together. 'Seriously, Jane? I gave you the date and it meant nothing to you? I thought you liked history.'

'14th March 44BC?'

'Tomorrow, Jane. The Ides of March?'

'Oh.'

The old, smug Parrish was back.

'That's how brilliant I've been. Because this is a major event

327

in time and everyone will turn up for this. Everyone. There'll be St Mary's – homing in like blowflies on a dead sheep, muddying the waters, getting in the way and initiating all sorts of crises. Then there'll be all the amateurs in their homemade pods, come for a good look. Rounding them up will take the Time Police some considerable time. There'll be any number of weird pods here so that'll keep the clean-up teams busy. With any luck we'll be lost in the crowd. At least until we can get ourselves sorted out.'

'But our personal trackers . . . ?'

'Yeah. There'll be signatures all over the place. Time Police, St Mary's . . .'

'And us.'

He lay back and put his hands behind his head and yes, managed that smug Parrish look again. 'Yep.'

'So they'll still be able to track *us*.'

He sighed, sat up and began to rummage in his pack. 'I really need to sit you down and explain how thoroughly Matthew and I planned this. Did you think we just threw all this together at the last moment? What did you think we were doing while you were under interrogation? Did you think we'd just wandered off for lunch and forgotten you?' He flourished a small device. 'Neutraliser.'

'Where did you get that?'

He smirked again. 'Blonde.'

'The one in Logistics?'

'That's the one. And you thought I was wasting my time there.'

'I'm not even going to ask what you had to do to get this.'

'Just as well because I am never going to tell you. Give me your arm.'

She sat quietly while he dealt with their trackers and then leaned back with her eyes closed.

He poked her. 'Don't go to sleep.'

She sighed. 'I've had a bit of a rough day, you know.'

'And you're not the only one. I rescued the princess and she tried to beat me to death.'

'Sorry.'

'So I should bloody think.'

They both sat in silence until she said, 'We can't stay in here, though, Luke. We need a secondary site. Another base. Somewhere safe, away from this pod. Because they will find it. Eventually. We need to find somewhere to live and . . .' She tailed away. 'Had you planned to stay here?'

'Well, Matthew and I picked today because there would be a huge number of pods here. And for the next couple of days, as well. We could, if you like, pursue that strategy across other major historical events. We can work our way from here to Waterloo, to Marathon, Cortez's arrival, Elizabeth's coronation or Victoria's funeral – anywhere you're likely to find large numbers of pods and historians and even larger numbers of Time Police there to keep them in order.'

He paused. 'Or, we can walk away from the pod and settle somewhere. Here would be good. Once the civil disturbances are over with and Octavian sorts himself out, this is a bit of a Golden Age for Rome. We could lie low, wait until everything settles down again and build a life.'

She fiddled with the visor on Matthew's helmet. 'You keep saying "we". Does this mean . . . ?' She stopped.

'Well, while they may only have suspicions about Matthew, I'm pretty certain they will have correctly credited me with being the brains and main perpetrator of your escape, so yes, it's "we", Jane. Unless you don't want to, of course, in which case I'll leave you to it.'

And here came the familiar stab of panic. To be on the run was bad enough. To be on the run and alone . . . She shook her head.

He heaved a sigh of relief. 'Thank God. I didn't want to go all wimpy on you, but I really didn't fancy trying to do this by myself.'

She threw him a quick glance. 'Me neither.'

'OK then – it's you and me against the massed ranks of the Time Police. Shouldn't be a problem.'

'You're very good at that, aren't you?'

'At what?' he said, vaguely.

'Steadying people. Getting them through sticky situations. Like with me in that tomb.'

'Am I?'

'I think you'd have done quite well in the Time Police.'

He grinned. 'Well, we'll never know now, will we? Let's just hope we're equally as good at avoiding them.'

She nodded. 'We could send the pod away. To distract them.'

'We could. I did consider it. How do you feel about that?'

'I'm not sure. Once it's gone . . . It's our lifeline.'

'It is, isn't it?'

'Do we have to decide now?'

'No – thanks to events tomorrow, we have a few days' grace to think about things.'

She sighed. 'Yes. But we will still need to find ourselves a secondary base.'

'Can you walk?'

'Of course. And I can probably run, too.'

'You may have to.'

'Where exactly are we?'

'I told you. Rome.'

'It's a big place. Whereabouts in Rome?'

He pulled out his scratchpad. 'Trans Tiberim. Quite close to the Field of Mars. Which is where it's all going to kick off tomorrow.'

'We'll be going in the opposite direction, surely.'

'And miss all the fun? Don't you want to see?'

'Actually,' said Jane, surprising herself as much as Luke, 'I'd love to see, but surely common sense dictates we should be as far away as possible.'

'Yes, it does,' said Luke. 'But if we were burdened with common sense then neither of us would be here in the first place, would we? It's a bit late for common sense now, Jane. Don't you want to catch a glimpse of the great man himself? No need to be squeamish. There won't be anything to see. It all happens inside and you're only a woman so they won't let you in anyway. Or, you know, there's the alternative, where we could sit around here all day, listening for approaching footsteps and imagining the worst.'

She glared at him in exasperation. 'Has anyone ever said no to you?'

'Oh God, all the time. That brunette in IT. The other brunette in IT. The tall one who works in Reception. The one in the library who wears her hair in that funny ponytail. The redhead in . . .'

'Yes, all right,' she said, realising they could be there all day. 'But not the blonde in Logistics.'

'Definitely not the blonde in Logistics,' he said with a fond smile.

'You're disgusting.'

'Yes,' he said mournfully. 'Yes, I am.'

'I don't even want to share a pod with you.'

'If we go outside and explore, then you won't have to.'

'Do you always get your own way?'

'Yes. You've admitted it, Jane, you want to see as well. And we're safer in a crowd than we are here, trapped in a pod. Imagine if someone knocked on the door this very moment. What would you do?'

'Give you up in exchange for a lighter sentence.'

He grinned the complacent Parrish grin. 'No, you wouldn't.'

'If we go outside, will it stop you talking?'

'Let's see, shall we?'

26

Ten minutes later they were cautiously exploring their immediate surroundings.

'This was someone's garden once,' said Jane. 'Look, there's an old fountain over there.'

'Not for a long time, though,' said Luke, surveying the tangled greenery all around them. 'And these buildings look deserted.'

They were standing in a secluded courtyard garden surrounded on all sides by four- or five-storey buildings. Like the garden, the buildings were also showing signs of neglect. Most of the windows were boarded up, except for a few cases where the shutters either hung forlornly or had fallen off altogether. The rendering was stained and marked with damp patches.

They stared around them, ready to flee back inside the pod at a moment's notice, but there were no signs of human activity. Birds sang around them and a small black cat slunk behind a bush with something in its mouth. There were no voices, no sounds of pots and pans, no smells of cooking, just a deep silence.

'Well,' said Luke. 'This isn't too bad.'

'No, it's not, is it?'

'Typical Roman design,' said Luke. 'Big posh house on the ground floor benefitting from the pretty garden and fountain. Cheap apartments above – possibly rented out, possibly for less affluent members of the family. Whoever they were, there's no one here now.'

They wandered around, getting the lie of the land. This had once been a very pretty garden. Not large, but well planted, and now considerably overgrown. Paths had been laid out once upon a time, shaded by vines now bursting with spring growth. A fountain stood in one corner, minus its traditional nymph, its basin filled with recent rainwater.

They walked around the outside, wending their way around the pillars supporting the covered area that bordered the garden. Empty niches showed where statues had once stood. Jane suspected they'd either been removed for safekeeping or stolen.

They tried all the doors and windows but the house was tightly boarded up – there was no chance of an entrance. Whoever had left – and for whatever reason they had left – their property had been well secured in their absence.

At the far end of the garden, however, opposite the house itself, they found a loose shutter over one window. Peering through, they could see a corridor.

'Not a part of the house, I think,' said Luke. 'Let's see, shall we?'

He pulled the shutter aside. 'We can push it back into place and no one will ever know.'

The corridor doglegged out of sight. The floor was of ordinary stone but Jane could see a faded lion painted on one wall. Shabby and water-damaged plaster was flaking away in the damp. The floor was covered in twigs and dirt. Only rats and birds lived there now. And died there too, judging by the occasional tiny skeleton. Jane thought of the cat.

'It's perfect,' she said, determined to be positive. 'Temporarily, anyway.'

Luke was horrified – which, given the normal state of his living quarters, was a trifle hypocritical. 'Live here?'

'No,' said Jane. 'We hide the pod somewhere far away from here and live in the garden. This is our way in and out.'

Luke hadn't finished being horrified. 'Live in the garden?'

'Why not? It's spring. The weather's warming up nicely. Shouldn't be a problem. And I strongly suspect that by the time winter comes around, we'll be dead anyway.'

'Let's hope so,' said Luke, cheerfully. 'Because I'm not living in a garden forever.'

Jane said nothing. The chances of them being offered the opportunity of living anywhere for any length of time were non-existent. She was convinced that by this time tomorrow they would have been recaptured. But Luke had risked himself for her. As had Matthew. The least she could do was put a brave face on things.

Similar thoughts were running through Luke's mind. He could only begin to imagine the cold fury with which the Time Police would hunt them down. His own estimate of their survival time was slightly less than Jane's, but having orchestrated her escape, he felt he owed it to her to put a brave face on things.

'Come on. Let's see where it goes.'

They climbed through the window and into the corridor, turning sharp left to see an old wooden door ahead of them. Luke pushed but nothing budged.

'Try pulling,' said Jane.

He scowled at her and pulled. The door opened reluctantly, scraping a path through dust, broken twigs and dirt.

'No one's been here for a while,' said Luke.

They squeezed through and found themselves above street level.

'Split level,' announced Luke. 'Now we're on the first floor.'

And they were. They were standing on a narrow balcony with a broken wooden railing. At the far end, a framework of rickety steps led down to the street.

'This is brilliant,' said Luke. 'Look, there's a way down. Someone had an outside entrance. We can come and go through this door and no one will associate it with the garden behind.'

Privately, Jane doubted that. She was certain the locals were perfectly well aware of this entrance and would have long since rifled the house and garden for anything valuable. After all, even the statues in the garden had gone, leaving only empty plinths. But it was better than she'd hoped for. And infinitely better than what had been happening to her only a few hours before.

So she nodded, smiled and said, 'Yes, it's perfect.'

They spent the rest of the day making themselves comfortable.

All Time Police pods are kept in a constant state of readiness. This one – their escape pod, as Luke insisted on describing it – was fully stocked, containing food for ten days and, for some reason, an enormous number of bed sheets, all neatly folded in the corner.

Jane held one up and raised her eyebrows.

'To wear,' said Luke. 'Obviously. You can't march around in

grey sweats all day long. They'll probably stone you as a loose woman or an enemy of the state or something. And I need to get out of these trousers before someone thinks I'm a Gaul.'

'Is that bad?'

'Yeah – Caesar and the Gauls. That always ends well. Can you sew?'

'I can thread a needle,' she said, uncertainly.

'You can't sew?'

'You can?'

'Actually, I went to a very progressive school. Girls were taught to strip an engine and boys learned to embroider. If we ever get out of this, I really must write and thank them. In my best handwriting, obviously.' He looked around. 'Right, reviewing our resources, we have matches, torches, water purification tablets – there's a well over in the corner of the garden – rations and the wherewithal to clothe ourselves.' He glanced at Jane's face. 'Could be worse.'

She made haste to nod. 'Yes, it could. A lot worse.' She stood in the doorway looking around the garden, at the new leaves slowly unfurling and the fresh green shoots everywhere. 'This isn't such a bad spot.'

'No, and if no one comes to claim it – and by the looks of it, no one's been here for years – perhaps we could dig a small patch and grow something.'

'And we could keep rabbits,' said Jane, recent rabbit-based events still fresh in her mind. 'For food, I mean.'

Luke regarded her sardonically. 'Yeah – you're going to wring their necks, are you?'

'No – you'll do that. Perhaps we could have chickens, as well.'

'Why not? And a guard dog – there are plenty of mongrels around. They can't all have rabies.'

'And there's already a cat to keep the rats down.'

'Well, there you are. We're going to be absolutely fine.'

She nodded. 'We're going to be better than fine – we're going to be great.'

27

Despite their brave words, they slept in the pod that night, going inside as soon as darkness fell. As Luke said, they'd had a tiring day breaking innumerable rules and regulations, and he needed his beauty sleep. Which might have been true, but neither of them slept. The pod had been powered down and they both lay awake, staring into the darkness.

Eventually, Jane said, 'Luke, if you didn't kill Sarah Smith and I didn't kill Sarah Smith, then who did?'

'Well, rumour has it she's pissed off any number of people over the years, so take your pick.'

'OK – don't take this the wrong way, or think I'm ungrateful, but what would happen if we gave ourselves up and explained?'

'I've been thinking about that.'

'And?'

'And it's a good idea, but . . .' He tailed away.

'But only if whoever killed Smith – and someone did, unless it's the most determined case of suicide ever – isn't in a position to issue a shoot-on-sight order.'

'Why would anyone do that?'

'Luke, someone killed her. Cut her throat in a moment of passion. Perhaps they overheard your conversation . . . heard her plans for your future, and was so overcome with jealousy that they killed her on the spot, dropped or flung down the knife and fled. In panic. They might not even have planned to kill her. It might just have been a spur of the moment thing and they were probably expecting to be arrested at any moment but I interfered. And then you and Matthew interfered some more. Which means that whoever killed her is getting away with it – thanks to us. When – if – they do catch up with us, I wouldn't be in the slightest bit surprised if we weren't both "shot while trying to escape" and then whoever did it is safe forever.'

He was silent for a while and then said, 'All right, if we're going to enter the realms of pure fantasy, here's something else to think about. Is it possible that Smith's murder was only a part of something else?'

'In what way?'

'Well, you're arguing that it's personal. That she was killed by, let's say, an ex-boyfriend. In which case, it could have been anyone. The whole building is probably littered with Smith's ex-lovers.'

Heroically, she refrained from making any comments.

'Or,' he continued, slowly, 'it was professional.'

'You mean – like a . . . a hit?'

'No, I mean a professional reason. Smith's death could be part of something larger.'

'I'm sorry, I don't understand.'

'A larger scheme within the Time Police. We all know what's going on, don't we? Hay's trying to modernise and reform and the old guard – the Albayans – are resisting her at every turn. Suppose they've gone on the attack. Think about it, Jane. A member of Ellis's team is murdered. Who's the main suspect?

Well, it's you, actually, but that's not a problem for them. Yes, perhaps it should have been me, but you're just as acceptable. Because what do we both have in common?'

She thought for a moment. 'Ellis's team. We're all members of Ellis's team.'

'Yes, it's not reflecting well on Ellis so far, is it? One of his team has been murdered and the other two are on the run. I bet you people are probably already saying, "What the hell's been going on there? What's Ellis been playing at?"'

She sat up. 'Matthew! What about Matthew? Will he be all right?'

'Half of me thinks he's in MedCen and is therefore perfectly safe, and the other half is wondering how easy it would be for him to die quietly of his injuries.'

'Should we go back, do you think?'

'Ellis is there. And North.'

'But why?' she said, puzzled. 'Why do this to Ellis? Our team?'

'Well, not to toot our own trumpet – we weren't as bad as people thought.'

'That's it? All this because we weren't as bad as people thought we'd be?'

'Jane, people thought we'd be useless and we weren't. We got Henry Plimpton and destroyed his machine. You stuck it out in Tutankhamun's tomb. Matthew stringed those illegals and dealt with Ellis's wound. Might even have saved his life. We got the rabbit, Jane, and saved Australia – which has been very slow to show its gratitude – but we can rise above that. The point is – we weren't doing too badly. And what's really pissing everyone off is that we're doing things our way. People don't like it.'

She shook her head in the dark. 'It's still hardly grounds for murder.'

'No, you're right about that. I suspect there's more going on than we know. You know – wheels within wheels.'

'Luke, we should go back. We should tell people.'

'You mean inadvertently tell the person who set all this up that we're on to them?'

Jane lay back down again, thinking hard. 'How about this? And believe me, I'll be delighted to hear I'm over-imagining things. Ellis was shot in the Valley of the Kings. Could that have been deliberate?'

'All right – I'll challenge that. Being shot is a bit of an occupational hazard. People shoot at us all the time. It's a badge of honour.'

'No one else was hurt.'

'Yes, they were.'

She shook her head. 'Rossi fell over his own feet and everything else was just minor scrapes and bruises. Only Ellis was shot.'

'You mean the illegals deliberately targeted him? Do you remember how dark it was that night? Visors were down, hiding people's faces. They couldn't possibly have picked him out among everyone else.'

She said slowly, 'I'm not thinking of illegals.'

'You mean . . . one of us could have shot him?'

She made no response. The pair of them lay in the dark, thinking.

Eventually, Luke said, 'Ellis is one of Hay's key people. He's popular. He's good at his job. He's moving up the career ladder. He could easily be her successor one day. It would look too suspicious if something happened to Hay, he took her place and then something happened to him. But if you did it the other way round . . . got rid of Ellis first . . . then you could pick off Hay at your leisure. Regardless, though – even if it's not true, officers shooting each other, stealing pods and setting off radiation alerts is not going to do Hay's reputation any good at all.' He sighed. 'We may have done their work for them.'

Jane was still thinking. 'Suppose someone wanted to discredit him. That's why we got the crap assignments. But as you said, we weren't as bad as people thought, so they tried to break us up instead. People would say Ellis couldn't hold a team together. Is that why they offered me a job with Callen? I did wonder about that.'

She waited for him to tell her that of course they'd wanted her for her own qualities, remembered it was Luke Parrish, sighed and abandoned the wait.

Luke was rushing on. 'And Smith was drafted in to cause trouble. Because that's what she does – only she didn't stick to the plan. She saw an opportunity for herself. She couldn't resist my charm, my good looks, my . . .'

'Money . . .' Jane supplied.

'And she made it personal, and perhaps whoever it was couldn't control her any longer, so they killed her.'

'Or it was just a jealous ex.'

'Or it was just a jealous ex.'

'Either way, the scandal might finish Ellis. Weaken him and you weaken Hay.'

'And now,' said Luke, 'we've done a better job of undermining Ellis and Hay than anyone could possibly have managed. A member of his team – either me or you, it's not important

– murdered a fellow officer and the other members of his team broke her out of gaol, stole a pod, triggered a radiation alert . . . bloody hell – we're real criminals, aren't we?'

Jane shivered. 'We are now.'

28

Neither of them got much sleep after that and eventually they gave it up. Jane assembled their breakfast while Luke sat cross-legged in the open doorway, manufacturing what he swore would be the very latest thing in Roman fashion.

They were ready to go as the sun rose. As was, apparently, the rest of Rome. The sun had barely risen and already they could hear the street noises drifting over the rooftops. According to Luke, every Roman must be out on the streets yelling at every other Roman out on the streets.

They turned to the AI for guidance.

'Pod – give details of this area.'

Obediently, the AI responded in its pleasant, female voice. 'The fourteenth district of Rome, Trans Tiberim, is situated on the west bank of Rome. The name means "beyond the Tiber" and . . .'

'Speed up, please.'

'Originally this area belonged to the Etruscans, who . . .'

'Never mind that – what's happening now?'

'This area is commercial and comprises many markets, trading in . . .'

'Skip all that.'

'The area is cosmopolitan with many vibrant . . .'

'I'm not buying a bloody house here. Get on with it.'

'A large community of sailors . . .'

'Bugger the sailors.'

'I do not have details for that type of establishment.'

Jane could only be grateful that long years with her grand-mother had taught her facial control.

The AI tried again. 'Jews and Syrians . . .'

'Bugger the Jews and Syrians, too.'

'Under the Emperor Augustus . . .'

'Do you actually have anything relevant? Anything at all?'

'The current climate is predominantly . . .'

'If I want to know the bloody weather, I'll look outside.'

Silence.

'Is that it?'

More silence.

'I think you've upset it,' said Jane.

'*I've* upset *it*? I pull off the most daring rescue in the entire history of daring rescues, and this witless, fire-trucking lump . . .'

'No one else has any difficulties with it. You don't ask nicely.'

'Jane, it's a machine.'

'Actually, it's an AI.'

'It's an AI that's going to find itself at the bottom of the river any moment now.'

The AI responded. 'Estimated river depth at this location . . .'

'Right – that's it. It's just taking the piss now. I don't care if an entire battalion of Time Police are outside the door at this very moment . . .'

346

'Proximities show no immediate activity.'

'I'm going to disembowel this thing.'

'Current records show you do not currently possess the required expertise to . . .'

'SHUT UP.'

Jane judged it time to stage an intervention. 'Pod – thank you.'

'You're welcome.'

She turned to Luke, still breathing heavily. 'Shall we go?' They stepped out of the pod and looked over the damp, misty garden. The smell of earth and wet leaves was very strong. Everything in their little garden was quiet and still.

Luke turned to Jane. 'Not too late to go back to bed.'

She shook her head. 'We should take a look around. Suss out our surroundings. Look for escape routes and useful hidey-holes.'

'Good thinking.'

Neither of them mentioned this might be the last opportunity they would ever have to wander as they pleased. If things went really badly – if someone really had issued a shoot-on-sight notice – then this time tomorrow they could both be dead.

'Well,' said Luke, offering her his arm. 'Shall we go?'

She adjusted her clothing. Luke had made her a long tunic by stitching a sheet together, cutting neat holes for her head and arms, and hacking the surplus off at ankle length. Jane had ditched the jogging bottoms so kindly provided by the security people but she couldn't be persuaded to take off her sweatshirt. She had pulled her tunic on over it and tied it firmly in place with a wide sash. She had then draped another sheet over her head, acting as part cloak, part stole, and there she was. As muffled as any proper Roman man would expect his woman to be.

Luke, on the other hand, enthusiastically embracing the double standards of the time, was rather racily showing a lot of leg with a knee-length tunic made in the same way as Jane's. He had no cloak. Cloaks, like helmets, were for wimps, apparently.

Crossing the garden, still wet with dew where the shadows lay, they reached the little corridor and made their way to the balcony. Luke cast a swift glance up and down the narrow alleyway. No one was in sight but he was prepared to bet any number of eyes were watching them. Not that it would do them any good. The pod was camouflaged and no one could get in, anyway. Unless they were Time Police, of course. He wrenched away the small wooden gate blocking the way to the steps. Jane winced.

'If it's any consolation,' he said, 'I don't think I'm the first person to do that.'

'I'm worried because now people can get in.'

'I'll wedge it when we come back. And the door.'

They slipped down the steps and stepped out into the alleyway. Picking their way around puddles of dubious-looking fluids, they headed for the street at the end and looked around.

So this was Rome. The Eternal City. It wasn't what Jane had expected at all. There were no gleaming white buildings. No statues to Jupiter or Romulus. No marble. No massive pillars.

'I think,' she said, looking about her, 'that Julius Caesar lives here somewhere.'

'Well, that settles it,' declared Luke. 'He's a neighbour. It's our duty to check things out.'

'You sound just like St Mary's.'

'That's a little unkind, Jane.'

They were standing in a narrow street made even narrower by the tall buildings on either side. Jane guessed the sun rarely shone here. There were paving stones beneath their feet but they were rough and uneven, and in some cases, missing altogether. Slimy rubbish had been trodden into the cracks.

The building opposite them seemed almost to lean over the street. Built of bricks and timber, its decorative cladding had mostly peeled away. There were few windows, even above street level.

At street level, the buildings were open and, squinting into the dark interiors, she could make out what seemed to be a series of small shops, each opening directly on to the street.

There was a wine shop, judging by the number of amphorae being stacked against the wall outside. And she could smell fresh bread, so there must be a bakery somewhere very close. Another shopkeeper seemed to be laying out baskets of olives on a wooden bench. They all shouted to each other. It would seem amphora man was trespassing on olive man's frontage. This was obviously an old battle though. Amphora man removed the offending stock with a grin and a rude gesture. Olive man responded in kind and they carried on with their day.

A street pedlar wandered past with a tray full of pastries. Customers happily accepted them from his filthy tray and even filthier fingers. A street barrow was setting up nearby, piled high with lettuces. A small boy continually sprinkled them with water to keep them fresh. On the corner, an old man slowly unfolded his stool and made himself comfortable alongside a small table stacked high with what looked like wax tablets. A public scribe, all ready for the day's work ahead.

Their scratchpad, hazy on historical details, had downloaded a rough map from the AI.

'We'll find the River Tiber,' said Luke, 'which is not far away.'

'How far is not far away?'

'Even we won't be able to miss it. Crossing the bridge will take us to the Field of Mars, which is where we want to be. We should be able to follow the crowds until we get to the Theatre of Pompey itself. What could possibly go wrong?'

Jane looked down at herself. 'We could be stoned by the fashion police.'

'Well, take your sweatshirt off, numpty.'

'I don't like to. This tunic feels . . . precarious. Suppose I have to run.'

'Good point. Although I don't think Roman women did a lot of running. Come on – let's go and have an adventure.'

'Yes, because we haven't had enough of those already, have we?'

He grinned at her but said nothing. He didn't have to. This was likely to be the last adventure they ever had. But – it was a lovely day and here was a chance to see ancient Rome and one of the defining moments of its history.

Still she hung back. Stepping out into the street implied crossing some sort of Rubicon. An apt metaphor, she rather thought. 'Is this wise, do you think?'

'I do,' he said firmly. 'It's better to be lost in a crowd than be picked out in a wilderness. If you get my meaning.'

'Does anyone ever get your meaning?'

He sighed. 'I am a lone voice in the Deserts of Incomprehension. Ready?'

'Yes.' She smiled up at him.

'Don't do that, Jane, it makes me nervous.'

'Sorry.' She scowled ferociously at him.

'Much better. Let's go.'

And off they set.

'It'll be interesting to see how far we get before trouble envelops us, don't you think?' said Luke chattily as they negotiated a street barrow half in and half out of a doorway.

Early it might be, but everyone was already up and shouting at the tops of their voices to celebrate that fact. From all sides they were bombarded with opportunities to purchase something they hadn't known they needed.

Their narrow street opened into one wide enough to have its own pavements, although these had been mostly commandeered by the ubiquitous street barrows – tiny enough to escape the ban on wheeled traffic but large enough to cause major obstructions – selling even more fresh lettuce, some risky fish, and some not yet fly-covered meat. The smell of leather and glue drifted from a narrow doorway. A cobbler, Jane guessed. A few doors down various mounds of green stuff and bowls of unidentifiable brightly coloured powders were piled high on the pavement. No one seemed to notice them slowly being covered with the dust of passing traffic. The air was flooded with the sharp, sweet smell of herbs and spices. From somewhere unseen came the musical rhythm of a hammer on metal.

Most corners seemed to be occupied by fast-food restaurants offering breakfast to those setting off to work. There was a small shouting crowd around each one. Most customers ate standing up and the eating places were doing a roaring trade.

Luke stopped and studied one thoughtfully. 'Here's an idea.

We could bring fried chicken to the Ancient World. What do you think? I'm convinced it would go down a storm. Don't know what we'd do for chips, though. Do you have any suggestions?'

Jane recognised he was doing his best to distract her.

'Yes, actually, I do. We jump to the New World to pick up some potatoes, bring them back here, plant them in our garden and become potato magnates. You'll ring chickens' necks and I'll chip potatoes. We'd be rich by the end of the week.'

He stopped. 'Do you know, that's not a bad idea.'

'Seriously?'

'Yeah, why not?'

She stared at him in disbelief. '*You'll* wring chickens' necks?'

'No, no, we'll get someone in to do that. What shall we call ourselves?'

'JFC.'

'Sounds like a football club and why JFC?'

'I thought of it.'

'I think you'll find it was my idea. LFC.'

'That *is* a football club.'

By now they had emerged into a main street.

They stood for a while. The streets were of much better quality here. The paving stones were rounded and shiny with more traffic and the buildings themselves grander and much cleaner. And much more colourful. Gazing about her, Jane realised that holos and films had misled her. Rome was not white. Well – it was, but the decorative details on each building were picked out in vivid colour. Statues were painted in a myriad of unrealistic hues. The cold, gleaming white marble of later ages did not exist here.

352

'Wow,' said Luke, which seemed to sum it all up.

The further they walked towards the river, the better the neighbourhood. There were occasional clumps of pine trees or other greenery for shade. And definitely much less shouting. Luke surveyed the crowded street. 'What time do you think he'll arrive at the Senate?'

'No idea. I think we should get there early and try to get a good place. You do know we won't get to see the actual deed, don't you?'

'Not sure I want to.'

Jane remembered Smith. And the blood. 'They won't let women in, anyway, but we'll certainly be able to see what happens afterwards. If we can elbow our way through all the historians who will be cluttering up the place.'

Luke stopped abruptly, apparently lost in thought.

'Luke?'

'Jane . . . I've had a thought . . . Do you think this is a good idea?'

'Is what a good idea?'

'We go to St Mary's and ask for sanctuary.'

'I don't think sanctuary's legal any longer.'

'No, think about it. I bet St Mary's would take us in, only if to wind up Commander Hay.'

'Luke – I'm a murderer and you're a traitor. Even St Mary's wouldn't touch us.'

He opened his mouth to argue, but fortunately, at that moment, they reached the Tiber which distracted him. 'Well, your fears about missing the river were slightly unfounded, Jane. It's a bit big, isn't it?'

It was indeed a bit big. In front of them, a wide, muddy,

smelly river, still swollen from the winter rains, stretched away in both directions. Jane couldn't help thinking that, corked or not, Pontius Whateverhisnamewas would have sunk like a stone.

Both banks were packed with towering buildings with small boats moored alongside, all loading and unloading bundles, sacks, crates and barrels into the warehouses behind them. There were even cages of animals. Men shouted and gesticulated. Carts were loaded and driven off to other warehouses, waiting for night to fall. More carts took their place and the whole procedure began again. Jane found it very easy to believe they were standing at the centre of the city that was the centre of the world. All roads – and rivers – led to Rome.

'It never stops, does it?' she said, gazing about her in wonder.

'The AI says nearly a million people lived in Rome at this time so no, I don't suppose it ever does.'

They crossed the bridge. 'Pons Aemilius,' said Jane, consulting Luke's scratchpad which was showing a helpful map.

'Let's have a look.' Luke took it from her, enlarged the map and looked about them. 'Hey, up there on the Palatine is the Hut of Romulus. The founder of Rome. It's been there for hundreds of years. We should definitely check that out. Especially since the scratchpad says it'll burn down in a couple of years' time. What do you think?'

'Absolutely,' said Jane, with enthusiasm. And then, 'Wouldn't it be nice if we were just ordinary tourists, without a care in the world?'

'What, Temporal Tourism, you mean?'

'Oh no. That's illegal.'

'Jane, you're wanted for murder. I'm probably wanted for treason. Temporal Tourism hardly registers on our criminal

354

scale, does it? So that's settled then. Tomorrow we'll go and have a look at the Hut of Romulus.' He turned his scratchpad around, trying to orient himself. 'Which way now?'

'This way,' said Jane and they turned left.

'To return to the sanctuary thing, Jane, I don't mean actual hanging on to the altar style of sanctuary, but we could ask them to take us in. We could say we're friends of Matthew.'

'Luke . . .'

He finished the sentence she had barely started. 'Yes, I know – it would probably start some sort of international incident.'

She considered this, head on one side. 'Actually, that might be the best way to approach them. It's not as if they're any strangers to international incidents. Don't trip over that rope.'

He dodged around a coil of rope. 'What do you think? Shall we give it a go? It's not as if we have anything to lose.'

'All right. If we get the opportunity. They might not be here.'

'And miss one of the most important events in history? St Mary's? Come on.'

'OK. I think possibly, in the first instance, I should make the initial approach. After all, I'm not the one who shot Matthew.'

'I don't think we should bring that up. Not initially, anyway. Wow – look at this.'

Rome was all around them. They stood for a moment, absorbing the sights, sounds and smells of Rome going about its daily business, completely unaware of the violent, history-changing events about to occur. The Field of Mars lay ahead of them, already dazzling in the morning sunshine.

'We're looking for the Theatre of Pompey,' said Jane, blinking against the brightness. 'It's a big building. The first stone theatre in Rome. Look for a curved wall.'

'Good God,' said Luke, surveying the tangle of buildings ahead of them. Buildings everywhere were surrounded in wooden scaffolding. Whether they were going up or coming down was unclear. Sweating men with bundles of long wooden poles shouldered their way roughly through the throng and everywhere was the sound of chisels on stone.

'Don't they have town planning here?' he continued, staring around. 'I thought Roman cities were all built on a neat grid pattern. Important buildings at the centre and so on.'

'I don't think that applied to Rome,' said Jane. 'It's already very old. I think they just built wherever the fancy took them, knocking down anything in their way, no matter how much people objected.'

'A bit like town planning today,' said Luke. 'Do you think there will be a big crowd to watch Caesar arrive at the Senate?'

'Well, no one knows what's going to happen, do they? It's just a normal day for most people. Luke, I'm still not convinced this is a good idea.'

'If we're going to contact St Mary's, then this is the only place to be. I just hope we can find them.'

Jane remembered her afternoon in R&D. 'Just head towards the shouting. They'll be at the centre of it. Or possibly the cause.'

They picked their way around the streets. Since crossing the river to the Field of Mars, the buildings had become bigger and more widely spaced – many of them standing in their own grounds. And much, much grander. Now there was more white marble about, dazzling in the bright sunshine. Friezes picked out in red, blue and gold adorned many of the larger buildings. There were statues on the roofs, vivid with colour against the blue sky, and even more of them at street level. And temples everywhere. All shapes and sizes. The smell of incense hung heavily in the air. Street barrows still existed, to service passing trade, presumably, but this area was much less commercial than the one they had just left. The streets were cleaner and better paved and the noise levels slightly lower. There were still the small groves of pine trees, brilliant green with their new spring growth, but these were furnished with stone benches, offering welcome rest and shade to pedestrians. Water sellers stood nearby with their big jars and wooden cups.

'There,' said Jane, pointing to the huge, white, curving wall ahead of them, bouncing the bright sunshine back into their eyes. The Theatre of Pompey stood four storeys high with arched porticos on the first three floors and small square windows on the upper floor. The whole building was topped with tall wooden poles – whether to support canvas awnings to shade the audience or whether they were flag poles, they didn't know. The new building was dazzlingly white, contrasting with pillars of red marble. The effect was eye-wateringly spectacular.

Luke consulted his scratchpad. 'That's it. The Theatre of Pompey.'

She shaded her eyes and tilted her head back. 'It's huge.'

'It is, isn't it? Let's see if we can find a way in. Keep your eyes peeled for anyone who looks as if they might be St Mary's.'

'Well, at least our lot will be easy to spot.'

'Yes, avoid the sinister black cloaks at all costs.'

They picked their way carefully around the building. The fast-food sellers were everywhere, bawling their wares from behind their trays. Enticing smells wafted through the air, although, as Jane said, in the way of fast food everywhere, it wouldn't taste anything like as good as it smelled, and for heaven's sake, Luke, you've already had breakfast.

The Theatre was massive. They worked their way past the actual theatre at the front of the building, craning their necks to take in the Temple of Venus, and turned right. 'Because we're at the wrong end,' said Jane. 'We need to be at the other end. The Senate meets in the Curia, round the back.'

A long, long colonnade lay to their right, approached by three shallow steps that ran the whole length of the building. The colonnade was supported by the same red marble pillars. Blood red. Which, as Luke said, was quite appropriate when you thought about it. Behind the colonnade, however, were only solid walls, decorated with painted pastoral scenes and the occasional lion bringing down a gazelle.

'There must be some way in,' said Luke in exasperation. 'There's a huge garden on the other side and they can't all troop through the theatre to get access to that. Let's keep going.'

They trudged along. The morning grew warmer. Luke grumbled at the lack of shade.

Turning right again at the end of the colonnade, they finally found themselves at the back of the theatre. A structure, probably quite small by Roman standards but still grand by everyone else's, was built into the back wall.

'This is it,' said Luke, consulting his scratchpad. 'The Curia.'

The crowds here were considerably denser and predominantly male. Many of them were clutching scrolls or a wax tablet. To petition the Senators as they arrived, possibly. Others might simply be hanging around for a glimpse of the rich and famous.

They couldn't just stand in the street being buffeted by what felt like all of Rome. Besides, they would be too exposed. They needed somewhere quiet to await events.

'Over there,' said Jane, pointing across the road. Four small and somehow much more homely buildings provided welcome shade. There were steps and pillars and even a handy statue to lurk behind.

Jane studied it carefully. 'I'm trying to make out who it is.'

Luke subjected it to ruthless artistic scrutiny. 'Some bald bloke with a scroll and a big nose. Which describes ninety per cent of Roman men. Could be anyone.'

The crowd around them was mostly masculine but there were some women about. Roman men divided women into two types. Those you'd want your son to marry and those you wouldn't. These were definitely the second type. Jane was interested to see they wore make-up on their faces and some had dyed their hair blonde – presumably in an attempt to attract those who'd served abroad and fancied a bit of foreign bar-barian. She pulled her sheet further up over her head to cover her own light hair.

Standing in the shade and half concealed by the bald bloke with the scroll and the big nose, they waited. The sun climbed higher in the cloudless sky. One of them waited patiently and the other slightly less so. Luke shifted his position again and enquired how much longer.

Jane sighed in exasperation. 'Listen – we're alive. We're safe. We have water and a couple of snack packs. No one is shooting at us. Be grateful.'

They were, however, in the right place. On the other side of the street, men were beginning to arrive. Important men, wearing voluminous togas with a purple stripe. Some were on foot; others were carried in wooden chairs. A few of them went straight inside but most gathered on the steps, conferring with each other. Many held scrolls or had slaves to carry them. They stood in groups of two or three, heads together, nodding importantly.

'Why don't they go in, I wonder?' said Luke. 'Get in out of the sun.'

'They're politicians,' said Jane, scornfully. 'How will people know how important they are if they don't hang around looking important in front of the people.'

'Such cynicism in one so young.'

'Any idea who's who?'

'Well, I don't think the great man has arrived yet. I'm certain he'll be among the last to arrive, but thinking back to my Shakespeare, there should be Cassius and Brutus and . . .' He tailed away, entangled in the mists of schoolday memories.

'And Cicero? And Mark Antony?'

'I don't know. I can't remember.'

'Well,' said a voice behind them. 'Why don't you ask an historian?'

Jane had not been so wildly and unrealistically optimistic as to envisage them both carving out a life for themselves as Rome's first purveyors of fried chicken and chips in a world that had, so far, encountered neither, but she'd never thought they'd be recaptured quite so quickly.

Two hours, she thought. If that. Just two fire-trucking hours.

She turned very slowly. In front of her stood a tall man dressed in white. His elegantly embroidered tunic bore a golden key design around the neck and he was wearing a toga with a wide purple stripe, so he was obviously a man of some importance. But, she thought, even without him speaking in English, she would have known he was not a Roman. His light hair was longer and far less disciplined than that of the men around him, most of whom sported really sharp hairstyles. She wondered if he was part of the Hunter Division. The ones tasked with the difficult jobs. If so, he was really, really good. He'd tracked them down almost before breakfast.

She stepped forwards before Luke could do anything stupid. 'It was me,' she said firmly. 'I did it.'

'Good heavens,' said the man mildly. 'Did you, indeed?'

'No, she didn't,' said Luke, grasping her sheet and pulling

her behind him. 'Ignore her. She's got concussion. It makes her confess to things she hasn't done. Neither of us did it.'

'Well, I'm very glad to hear that.'

'But I did,' said Jane, shouldering her way forwards again. 'Although I only hid the evidence because I thought he'd done it and now it turns out that he didn't. Do it, I mean.'

The man seemed puzzled. 'And you know this how?'

'He told me so.'

'Ah,' said the man. 'Well, then. That definitely settles it.'

He turned to go.

'You're not Time Police, are you?' said Jane, more for confirmation than information. He wasn't like any officer she'd ever seen. Not to make a big thing of it, but he was much too nice.

'Good heavens, no. And let me give you a word of advice: this place will be crawling with them. If it isn't already. It's a big day today and I appreciate you want to see what's going to happen here, but you need to be a little more discreet.' He frowned at their apparel. 'Much more discreet. As the more cultured among my colleagues would say, "You stand out like tits on a bull."'

Enlightenment dawned.

'You're St Mary's.'

'I am indeed. And you are . . . ?'

'In trouble,' said Jane.

'Friends of Matthew,' said Luke, quickly.

There was a long pause as the man looked from one to the other. '*You're* Time Police?'

Jane flushed at the incredulity in his tone.

'Yes,' she said defensively.

'To be fair,' said Luke, fairly. '*Ex*-Time Police.'

'*Not* a couple of enthusiastic amateurs who've just turned up today to see what happens?'

They shook their heads.

'And you're on the run?'

They nodded.

'From the Time Police?'

'Our former employers, yes.'

'I have to ask – what did you do?'

'Well,' said Luke, 'in the interests of complete disclosure – shut up, Jane, I'll explain this because you'll only dig yourself in deeper with every word – Jane's accused of murdering Sarah Smith, attempting to destroy evidence that she thought pointed to my guilt and refusing to cooperate with the subsequent enquiry. I'm accused of breaking her out of Time Police custody by triggering a radiation alert, stealing a pod and various other bits of kit, making an illegal jump in said stolen pod – with a known felon – oh, and I was late for the briefing last Thursday so I'm on report again.' He paused and then said, 'And I shot a fellow officer, too.'

'Good God,' said the man, faintly. 'Well, you two have been busy little beavers, haven't you?' A thought obviously occurred to him and he stared at them. 'So who did kill this Smith person?'

'Don't know,' said Luke. 'We had to leave in a hurry.'

'I can imagine. Which fellow officer *did* you shoot?'

Luke swallowed and squared his shoulders. 'Matthew Farrell.'

The man shifted his weight and suddenly he wasn't smiling any longer. 'Is he dead?'

'No. In my own defence . . .'

'Yes,' said the stranger silkily. 'Do, by all means, attempt to defend yourself.'

Luke swallowed again. 'It was his own idea. He helped me break Jane out of the Detention Centre and I shot him to cover up his part in rigging the computer to sound the radiation alarm.'

'What radiation alarm?'

'The one we set off so I could get Jane out.'

'You triggered a radiation alert? In central London?'

Luke shuffled. 'We may have done.'

'And then you shot Matthew Farrell.'

'It was his idea. And I did it as gently as I could.'

The man sighed. 'You're about to wish I *was* the Time Police.' He tapped his ear. 'Max? Where are you? . . . Can you get yourself down here? . . . Yes, just opposite the entrance to the Curia. On the steps of the round temple . . . No, I haven't yet discovered if it's the Temple of Hercules . . . Yes, I daresay, but something's come up that you might find a little more important. You're going to want to hear this, so shift yourself.'

He turned back to them, smiled encouragingly and said, 'You two are so dead.'

Jane had no doubt of that.

'In that case,' said Luke, backing away, 'I think we'll just . . .'

'What's happening?' said a female voice behind him. 'Is he here already? He didn't come past us. Who are you?'

Luke froze. Jane froze. A little pocket of silence enveloped them all. Around them, the people of Rome pushed and shouted and generally got on with things, while here, in this little niche built for the statue of the bald bloke with the scroll and the big nose, for Luke and Jane, the world ground to a halt.

'Yes,' said the man. 'That's a very good point. Who *are* you?'

'We're saying nothing,' said Luke stoutly. 'Nothing at all.'

'Jane,' said Jane.

Luke spread his arms in exasperation. 'Oh great – now you start talking to people. You couldn't have done that this time yesterday?'

Jane's lip quivered. She blinked furiously. Her eyes swam with tears and one rolled pathetically down her cheek. Luke was lost in admiration of her tactics. 'Now look what you've done,' he said accusingly to the tall man. 'You've made her cry.' He put his arm around her. 'There, there, Jane. Let me take you away from all this.'

'I didn't know the Time Police could cry,' said the man, making no move to let them get past. He looked over their shoulders. 'Did you know the Time Police could cry?'

A number of voices behind them assured him that no, they did not.

'Time for introductions, I think,' said the man. 'Turn around now.'

Feeling they had very little choice, they turned. And stared.

Three people stood before them. Two women and one man. Both women were quite richly dressed in long, flowing garments that fell elegantly to the ground and were not bedsheets. The shorter and older of the two – the one who also bore a disconcerting resemblance to Matthew Farrell – was festooned in additional layers of fabric as befitted her marital status. She wore a woollen stolla over her blue tunic, and was smothered in that infallible emblem of the respectable Roman matron, an all-encompassing palla. This draped over her left shoulder, around the back, under her right arm and then across the front of her body to be carried over her left arm. A particularly useless garment, thought Jane, specifically designed to restrict women's movements without actually going so far as to tie their legs together. From the expression on her face, being enveloped in massive amounts of fabric had not brought out the gentler side of Matthew's mother's nature.

The other, younger woman wore a simple green tunic. Her blue palla was prettily embroidered in silver thread.

Jane looked down at her impromptu bedsheets and suddenly felt woefully underdressed.

Behind them stood a short man in a plain tunic and heavy-duty boots, who was dividing his attention between the scene in front of him and what was going on around them.

Luke was staring at the older woman. 'He's got your eyes,' he said, eventually.

'Oh, so that's what I did with them.' She looked him up and down, visibly unimpressed. 'Which one are you – Luke or Jane?'

The tall man spoke. 'Behave yourself, Max.'

She let her eyes linger on Luke in a manner that did not bode well for his future wellbeing and turned to Jane.

'So you're Jane.'

Jane agreed that she was indeed Jane.

'Matthew's friend. He speaks very highly of you.'

'Matthew?'

'No – Leon.'

'I'm Matthew's friend, too,' said Luke quickly, possibly with an idea of making up lost ground.

The tall man interceded. 'Luke, Jane, my name is Peterson and this is Dr Maxwell and Miss Van Owen, formerly of the Time Police, whom you may remember.'

366

'We haven't been members of the Time Police for very long,' said Jane. 'Strictly speaking, we're still under training.'

'I think we'd all gathered that,' he said, gently.

The short man with unfashionably spiky hair, who had never taken his eyes off the area around them, coughed ostentatiously.

'Oh, yes. And this is our eunuch.'

The eunuch grinned. 'Markham. Security. Parasite-free. Would you like to see my certificate?'

Wordlessly, they shook their heads.

Maxwell stared at them but addressed Peterson. 'So what are they doing here? Dressed like that?'

'Well, Max, and I want you to remain very calm . . .'

'Yes?'

'They're on the run.'

She stared again at Luke and Jane. From the expression on her face, it was very obvious that, as fugitives, they did not rate that highly. 'Why?'

'Well, Max, and I want you to remain very calm . . .'

'You said that already.'

'Yes, but I felt the point needed reinforcing. They've shot Matthew.'

No one moved. Not even a muscle. Jane heard Luke swallow. She would have done the same but suddenly, her mouth was horribly dry.

'Is Matthew still alive?' asked Matthew's mum in a tone of voice which left them in no doubt as to what the correct answer to that question should be.

'Yes, yes,' said Luke quickly. 'He'll be fine. I was very careful.'

Her eyes seemed to bore into his skull. 'He will recover?'

'Yes, yes. He's receiving medical care and he's in no danger. I promise you.'

'The little bugger's been up to no good, Max,' said Peterson. 'Don't kill them now or we'll never hear the full story.'

'You're right,' she said. 'First things first.' She eyed them in a manner neither Luke nor Jane found reassuring, then looked up at Peterson. 'Caesar first, then these two.'

He nodded. 'Agreed.'

She and Peterson turned back to the street. The eunuch smiled sunnily at Luke and Jane and obediently, they shuffled back into their niche alongside the bald bloke with the scroll and the big nose.

'No Time Police that I can see,' said Peterson. He surveyed the milling crowds. 'How many of this lot are from future St Mary's, do you think?'

'Them,' said Maxwell, pointing at a group of three men and one woman standing to the left of the Curia.

'How can you possibly tell?' said Luke, baffled.

'Hair,' said Peterson, stroking his.

'Clothes,' said Miss Van Owen, stroking hers.

'Female security officer,' said Markham, not making any move at all.

'Really?' said Luke, squinting in the sun.

'Can't you see the bulge?'

'I thought that was her . . .'

'No – that's her weapon.'

'It's a big one, then.'

'I would have thought,' said Peterson to Luke, 'that referring to a lady's bulges would be unacceptable in your more enlightened times.'

Luke nodded ruefully. 'Oh, it is, believe me.'

'And them,' said Van Owen, nodding at two men standing just in front of them. One of them turned and looked them up and down for a moment. Professional nods were exchanged. 'Morning.'

In the distance, they could hear sudden cheering.

'Shit,' said Peterson. 'He's on his way. Places, everyone.'

'Too late,' said Maxwell. 'Too many people. We're better off staying here.'

'It's a bit more exposed than I'm happy with,' said Markham, glancing around.

'Hide behind me, then,' said Peterson and Markham made a rude noise.

Luke tweaked Jane's sleeve and jerked his head. They should quietly creep away now, while everyone's attention was elsewhere.

'Don't even think about it,' said the eunuch, suddenly behind them.

'He's here,' said Van Owen, craning her neck. 'Recorders, everyone.'

Their sudden focus was extraordinary, thought Jane. At once their whole attention was on the scene before them and nothing else. Neither God-hurled thunderbolts, nor nine different types of plague, nor even a herd of mammoths would have distracted them from what was happening in front of them. Well, all right, maybe the mammoths.

First to arrive was a group of citizens, chanting slogans – in Latin, obviously – and stamping their feet in rhythm. Behind them came a wooden carrying-chair with its carvings all picked out in gold and purple. It was a substantial affair and the bearers were sweating heavily. The chair's purple curtains were pulled well back to give everyone a good view of the occupant.

'Typical Caesar,' said Peterson softly, palming his recorder. 'He's not going to miss an opportunity to ingratiate himself with the crowd.'

'He doesn't need to,' said Van Owen. 'They love him already.'

And they did. A cheering mob surrounded Caesar's chair, jostling it good-naturedly.

Van Owen groaned. 'Poor sod. Do you remember, Max, when we were here before? How sick I was?'

'He doesn't look much better,' said Maxwell. She frowned. 'Is it me or does he look a bit yellow?'

'And older,' said Peterson. 'And it's only a few months since he last saw us. He's aged a bit, hasn't he?'

'Less hair, more nose,' said Markham, summing up the deteriorating health of the most powerful man in the world at this moment. 'He hasn't brought the girlfriend then?'

'Queen of Egypt she might be, but she's still not allowed in,' said Maxwell. 'Tim, are you all set to follow them inside?'

'I'm ready to try.'

'I still wish you were taking Markham.'

'They might let me in on my own – they'll never let me in if I'm accompanied by Piltdown Man here.'

'Is everyone getting this?' enquired Maxwell, ignoring Piltdown Man's indignant squawk.

The ensuing silence answered that question.

'Well, at least we know *today's* assassination attempt will be successful,' said Markham, chattily. In answer to Jane's puzzled look, he said, 'We had an earlier assignment. Some years ago for us but only a few months for him. To check out

370

Caesar and Cleopatra. Someone had a go at them with a bowl of asps. We had to leave town quite quickly. There were herds of stampeding bullocks and Sonic Screams and all sorts. For some reason, everyone blamed us.'

'Can't think why,' said Peterson, not taking his eyes from the scene in front of the Curia. Caesar was alighting from his chair and straightening his robes.

'He really doesn't look well,' said Maxwell, 'and I think it's more than just motion sickness.'

The shouting and cheering increased.

Jane, both excited and terrified, looked at the rapt faces around her. In less than ten minutes, this man, the man before them, the man whose state of health they were so dispassionately discussing, would be dead. The course of history would be irrevocably changed. And she was here – right on the very spot. For a moment, all her troubles rolled away and she could understand, very clearly, their all-consuming concentration. Their needle-sharp focus. This was what St Mary's were all about. This was what they did. And she was right alongside them as they were doing it.

30

Back at Time Police HQ, the alarms had been silenced, the authorities dealt with and control regained. Commander Hay was addressing a fragile-looking Major Ellis, whose premature attempt to leave MedCen to find out what was going on had propelled him straight back into bed.

'I'm really not feeling very well,' he said faintly, in a vain attempt to stem the seemingly never-ending flow of words.

'So, Major, just to sum up your team's actions today.'

A feeble attempt to deny any knowledge of his team's actions today died halfway through the first sentence.

'One member of *your* team is, at the moment, guilty of tampering with the scene of a crime, destroying evidence and possibly murdering a fellow officer. A second member of *your* team has stolen a pod to facilitate the escape of the first member of *your* team. A third member of *your* team, presumably feeling left out of the exciting events occurring around him, has initiated a radiation alert, leading to a major evacuation of the entire area and mass panic among our unfortunate neighbours. This team member would now, at this very moment, be answering a series of questions designed to establish *how* he rigged the computer and *how* he gained unauthorised access to a pod to facilitate the escape of the first two members of *your* team, only he can't because he has – as a member of *your* team – been shot. *By the first two members of your team.*'

She paused, possibly for breath but more probably to let her last words sink home, and Major Ellis took full advantage.

'I think, ma'am, you might be allowing current opinions relating to my team to colour your judgement slightly.'

'Am I? Speaking as the person who's spent the last hour explaining and apologising to the Home Secretary and sundry other politicians – who, incidentally, are still refusing to leave the safety of their fallout shelter – the Lord Mayor, the Metropolitan Police, the Queen, the media and God knows who else – *am I really*?'

She paused for more breath and Major Ellis seized his opportunity.

'Ma'am, with respect, in any other situation and with anyone other than Parrish, you'd be lauding his initiative to the skies. His improv abilities are obviously first-rate. Look at his planning and his execution. Look at his leadership skills. He's loyal to his team, which, I don't have to remind you, is a highly esteemed Time Police quality. It was Parrish who got Lockland through Tutankhamun's tomb, and thanks to him, the Lockland that came out wasn't the same Lockland who went in. Because he held her together. Yes, I know he's unconventional, but if you look at his results rather than his means of achieving them, I think you'll agree he has the makings of a fine officer.'

'Unfortunately, today, he has left me in a position where I'm required to scrutinise his means of achievement very closely indeed.'

She addressed the medtec calmly going about his business

in the happy knowledge none of this was anything to do with him. 'Where is Farrell now?'

'Recovery room, ma'am.'

'What's he doing there?'

'Er . . . recovering, ma'am.'

'Is he conscious yet?'

'Not really, ma'am.'

'You will advise me the second he can string two coherent words together.'

'Yes, ma'am.' He fled.

With a final glare calculated to sear Major Ellis to his own sheets, she left the room. As the door closed behind her, Major Ellis slowly and carefully swung his legs out of bed, at the same time reaching for his com.

'North? Come and give me a hand, will you?'

Ten minutes later, they were in the recovery room where Matthew Farrell, his hair even more vertically disarranged than ever, was staring vaguely around him.

Ellis sat heavily at the foot of his bed. 'Matthew.'

'Oh . . . hello. Uncle Sir.'

'Matthew, where did they go?'

'Mm?'

'Matthew, this is important. Where did they go?'

'Who?'

'Parrish and Lockland. Where did they go? Where did the pod take them?'

'Pod?'

Ellis took a deep breath but North forestalled him. 'One moment, please, sir.'

Sitting on other people's beds was for lesser people, but

she stationed herself at the foot of the bed where he could see her easily.

'Matthew, Jane forgot her notebook. You know how upset she gets if she doesn't have it with her. Can you tell me where she is so I can take it to her?'

His heavy eyes peered out from under his thick thatch of allegedly styled hair and it seemed to her that suddenly, they were nowhere near as hazy as before. His next words proved it. Holding out his hand, he said, 'I'll take it to her.'

'Excellent idea,' said Ellis before North could say a word. 'Let's get you dressed, shall we.'

Another ten minutes later and they were lugging an uncoordinated trainee in the direction of the Pod Bay. He could walk – he just needed steering. Ellis, however, still required some support.

'Right,' said North, effortlessly allocating responsibilities. 'You walk, sir. I'll hold you up. You steer Farrell. Farrell, you help hold up Major Ellis. Off we go.'

And off they went.

'So – just to recap,' said North as they made their uncoordinated way along a corridor. 'We've broken the final member of our team out of MedCen and we're about to appropriate a pod and make an unauthorised jump.'

Ellis nodded. 'Yes, got it in one.'

'That's all the team in trouble, then.'

'Pretty much, yes.' He stopped. Farrell stopped. North stopped.

'You don't have to do this, Celia. At the moment, you're the only one of us not guilty of something horrible. Perhaps you should step back from this. It's not what you're accustomed to.'

She stared at him, haughtily. Peasants down the ages were familiar with that stare. 'You do *know* I'm from St Mary's, don't you?'

'Well, yes, but . . .'

'That I'm Maxwell-trained.'

'Well, yes, but . . .'

'That I once left Herodotus himself bloody, battered and suffering from tray trauma, for no better reason than he had slightly annoyed me?'

'That I did not know. Tell me more.'

'Gladly, sir. You can buy me a drink while I do it. Here's the lift. Can you get the door?'

Emerging into the Pod Bay, the first people they saw were Lt Grint and Trainee Anders, apparently waiting for them. Armed, armoured, black-cloaked and waiting to go.

There was still the very faintest chance they could bluff things out.

'Good afternoon, Lieutenant. Can I help you?'

'I think it's the other way round, sir. Commander Hay instructed me to wait for you here. I'm to assist you in your efforts to recapture the members of your team. Sir. She said you wouldn't be long.'

Ellis sighed. 'I should have guessed.'

'Sorry, sir?'

'Nothing.'

'I gather we're going after the fugitives, sir.'

North, accepting the inevitable, took control. 'Thank you, Lieutenant, your assistance is greatly appreciated. Perhaps Trainee Anders could take this young man off our hands. He's very heavy.' Anders stepped up. 'Could you take him into the pod, please. Thank you. Yes, just put him down there. If everyone can just give me a moment, I'm sure we'll soon have the information we need.'

Five minutes later, she emerged from the pod.

'You've got it?' enquired Ellis.

She nodded. 'Rather brilliant, actually.' She ignored Grint's disbelieving snort. 'Rome, 44BC. Assassination of Julius Caesar,' she added in the face of Grint's incomprehension.

Ellis nodded. 'Clever – hide the pod among a multitude of signatures. Still a bit of a gamble, though. Half the Time Police will be there already.'

'Good,' said Grint. 'Plenty of reinforcement – should we need them. Right then, Anders – let's go.'

He moved towards the pod.

'And us,' said Ellis, placing himself meaningfully in Grint's path.

The pause was only very slight.

'Of course, sir,' said Grint. 'Let's go and get them.'

'And bring them back safely,' said Ellis, not moving.

'Of course, sir,' said Grint, fingering his weapon. 'And that.'

31

Several thousand and a bit years ago, the subjects of all this Time Police consternation were still in the street outside the Curia. The crush of people had rendered the street impassable and Luke and Jane were currently standing at the top of the temple steps, surrounded by a vast and excited throng. Caesar's fan club appeared to consist of most of Rome.

The entrance to the Curia and the gardens beyond were almost directly opposite where they were standing. Through the pillars, Jane could catch a fleeting glimpse of tall Cyprus trees and a splashing fountain. The gardens looked green, lush and inviting. A direct contrast to this airless and dusty street in which they were being jostled by excited people with many, many personal hygiene issues.

Having adjusted his purple robes to his satisfaction, Caesar slowly mounted the steps, still at the centre of a group of white-clad men.

Jane turned to Peterson. 'With all those people around him, how will they ever get close enough to stab him?'

'All those people around him have a dagger concealed on their person,' said Peterson grimly. 'I'm probably the only one who's going in unarmed. Max, if I'm going to try to attach myself at the back, I should go soon.'

'Agreed,' she said, without turning around. 'Wait until they're disappearing inside and then trot across the road and pretend to be a latecomer. You'll need to keep your distance once you're inside. Do *not* get caught up in what's going on. Remember – record and document only.'

He nodded innocently. 'Of course.' He ignored the disbelieving snorts from his colleagues.

Half a dozen slaves were following on behind the main party, burdened with scrolls and tablets. Several more were carrying their masters' togas, to be donned once they were inside, presumably. Jane wondered whether they'd come on foot and wanted to keep them clean until the last moment.

'They dust them with chalk,' she said, suddenly remembering from her school days. 'To make them look whiter.'

'They do indeed,' said Van Owen. 'Especially if they're running for public office. They call it a Toga Candida – from which we get the word candidate. Well done.'

Caesar had paused at the top of the steps, his head bent, apparently listening intently to the man talking urgently to him and attempting to press a scroll on him. Caesar took it absently, his eyes moving ceaselessly, assessing and observing the crowd.

'No bodyguard,' whispered Peterson.

'No,' said Max. 'He's famously putting his trust in the Roman people.'

'Hmm,' said Markham. 'I wonder how that worked out for him.'

'He's got legions outside the city, though, gearing up for the Parthian campaign.'

Jane thought how nice it was to be with people who actually knew what was going on.

She watched the man addressing Caesar speak urgently again, his face as close as a lover's. Caesar nodded politely. Again, the man gestured to the scroll. Whatever the contents were, they were obviously important.

'I wonder,' said Max, thoughtfully.

'Wonder what?' said Peterson.

'There was always a story that Caesar was warned beforehand. By lots of people, including his wife. That someone actually handed him a list of the conspirators and that he was distracted and never looked at it.'

Caesar, obviously not giving the man his full attention, nodded politely and turned to face the crowd, acknowledging them and their cheers. The shouts of acclaim redoubled.

And then, in one of those tiny moments that can change the course of History, a gap opened up in the mass of people standing around him. Jane, still unable to take her eyes off the scene, watched Caesar automatically unroll the scroll and glance casually across the road. His gaze alighted on Peterson, moved on and then snapped back again. As in all the best romances, their eyes met. Suddenly, the scroll was forgotten.

'Shit,' said Peterson, out of the corner of his mouth. 'Max, I think he's recognised us. Me, anyway.'

She spoke without moving her lips. 'Doesn't help that we're wearing the same clothes as last time.'

'And he's famed for his memory,' said Van Owen, stealthily stuffing her recorder in a hidden pocket.

'Now you tell me.'

Caesar's eyes darted from Peterson to Van Owen. Then on

380

to Max. Then to Markham. There was no doubt he remembered them. That he recognised the peculiar people who, only a few months previously, had been involved with the asp incident in his own home.

'Obviously not forgotten or forgiven,' said Markham, trying to usher them all down the steps and through the crowd.

Caesar drew himself up to full height, clutched his toga with his left hand and pointed dramatically with the other. The scroll dropped unheeded to the ground and bounced slowly down the steps. Out of history.

Caesar the orator, Caesar the general, had no difficulty making himself heard above the clamour around them. 'Seize them.'

Markham was pushing them all down the steps by sheer brute force. 'Move. All of you. Shift.'

Luke, being shoved along with the rest of them, became aware of dissent in the ranks.

'Dammit, Markham, we're going to miss the assassination.'

'Just move.'

'But that's why we're here.'

Markham turned to Luke. 'Help me get my team out of here, will you?'

'How?'

'They're historians. Sometimes you have to jump-start them. Just push.'

What saved them was that although Caesar, dramatically outlined against the white building behind him, was shouting for them to be seized, he had no personal bodyguards with him, so no one was quite sure who should be seized and who should be doing the seizing. People were looking around them for some sort of tangible threat – the Parthians, or maybe the

Celts again – some sort of barbarian invaders, anyway – and while they were doing so, the St Mary's contingent were quietly melting away. Although not without a great deal of complaint.

'We're going to miss it.'

'Fine, you stay here, then. The bloke is going to be very messily dead in five minutes. Want to guess who'll get the blame?'

'Good point.'

One of the two men in front of them turned, saying quietly and in English, 'Trouble?'

Markham nodded. 'Yep.'

'Go. We've got this.'

'Thanks.'

'Good luck.'

Like it or not, Luke and Jane were hustled along with St Mary's.

'But . . .' said Jane. 'We're not . . .'

No one was listening. The trick is not to run headlong. Running always attracts attention. As swiftly as they could, they made their way down the temple steps. The two men moved smoothly into the space opened up. The crowd milled around, but the two men must have been foreigners, confused by what was going on around them, and were completely failing to get out of the way when ordered to do so. Worse, their inability to understand what was going on was directly responsible for allowing the strangers to get away.

Caesar, surrendering to the exhortations of those around him, smiled brightly, and with one last wave, took a friend's arm and strode into the Curia. At that point he had less than a minute to live.

St Mary's, never once looking back, and shepherding Luke and Jane whether they wanted to be or not, strode briskly down two or three streets and then, at Markham's instruction, down an alleyway and out of sight. A narrow space between the backs of two buildings provided a handy shelter for them to pause and discuss what to do next. Squeezing themselves together, they became unpleasantly aware that providing a venue for workplace conferences was not its usual function.

'Sticky,' said Van Owen, lifting a sandal.

'Yuk,' said Max, peering at something dubious on the wall. 'Right. Regroup, everyone. How far back to our pod?'

'From here? Some considerable distance,' said Markham. 'We're parked in the Aventine.'

'Where exactly are we now?'

'Well,' said Peterson, hoisting his toga out of something unpleasant, 'if we orient ourselves to the north . . .'

'Hang on, hang on,' said Luke, 'I think you'll find the Time Police have got this,' and pulled out his scratchpad. Stabbing at it for a few seconds, he said, 'We're four hundred and seventeen yards from the Pontus Aemilius. We cross the bridge, travel two hundred and seventy-five yards south-west, turn left, then another one hundred and fifty yards north-west. We turn west, proceed for around thirty feet, climb six wooden steps on our left, pass through the broken door, along the passageway, out the window, through the garden and back to our pod located in the north-west corner opposite the well.'

There was a sudden silence.

'Takes all the fun out of it, somehow,' muttered Markham.

* * *

383

Whatever amateurish appearance they might present to the world, St Mary's possessed a smooth escape procedure almost certainly born of long practice.

Peterson walked ahead in his purple-striped toga, jaw jutting regally and pushing his way through the crowds. People actually fell back and made way for him. He was followed by Luke, Van Owen and Jane, all keeping close together and their eyes modestly downwards. They were followed by Max, who appeared to be indulging in a *sotto voce* monologue concerning the overzealous nature of some security officers not a million miles away. Followed by Markham himself, carefully watching their backs and ignoring everything said to him.

Luke was not surprised to see that no one appeared to be taking any notice of them in any way. They crossed the Tiber safely and once on the other side of the bridge, he said cheerfully, 'How far do you think we'll get before ... ?' and as he spoke, from across the river and over the rooftops there came a great shout. One shout but many voices, reverberating from wall to wall, echoing across busy streets. Not of triumph or victory but a cry of despair – of grief – of a sudden and dreadful loss.

Around them, all street life stopped. People lifted their heads and looked fearfully at their neighbours. A gradual silence fell. Across from where they were standing, a small boy, crying for a treat denied, hiccuped into silence, his dark eyes big and frightened above tear-stained cheeks. Many stood like statues, frozen in mid-movement. As if the city had paused to draw breath before a mighty storm broke.

'I don't like the look of this,' said Markham, quietly. 'We might want to pick up the pace a little, guys.'

Then came the screaming, street by street, square by square, spreading outwards like ripples across the still surface of a pond, and the spell was broken. Somewhere out of sight, a woman called her children back inside. Dogs slunk into alleyways, their instincts telling them to get off the streets. A shutter clattered as a shop owner pulled it across his precious goods. Then another. And another. Other shopkeepers were heaving their merchandise inside as fast as they could go. Doors slammed. The streets were emptying. Rome knew the beginnings of trouble when she saw it. In the strange silence, Luke could hear the whispers. The Latin equivalent of 'What the hell is happening', presumably.

And then, faintly at first but growing ever louder, the sounds of a panic. The crash of carts overturning. Smashing pottery. Shouts of alarm. Of fear. Of grief. And anger. The unbelievable news had hit the streets. The people's champion, Caesar, was dead. Shockingly, bloodily dead. Assassinated by members of their own Senate. He sprawled now, ripped and blood-soaked at the foot of the giant statue of his old rival, Gnaeus Pompeius Magnus – Pompey the Great.

Markham looked around, saying, 'We really need to be off the streets.'

Luke pushed his way to the front. 'Our pod's not far now. Follow me.'

Now there were very few women or children on the streets. Men were emerging from doorways and alleys, grim-faced, tightening their belts and armed with cudgels, long knives, anything they could find. The news was spreading faster than a forest fire.

Certainly faster than they could force their way through the

385

crowds, thought Jane. They couldn't run. They couldn't do anything that would attract attention to themselves. Never mind the official guards – the citizens themselves would be looking for someone to blame. Caesar was their leader. Their darling. There would be no mercy for anyone they suspected and unfortunately, that suspicion would include foreigners, those against whom they had a personal grudge and anyone else they just didn't like the look of.

Peterson was wending his way briskly through the crowds, giving every impression of a man with an important appointment elsewhere. They did their best to follow in his wake but there were knots of men everywhere, blocking their path and growing ever larger. Time and again they were forced to detour out of their way and into another street.

There was the crash of a cart being overturned. A man's voice was briefly raised before being drowned out in angry shouts. Someone was whipping up the mob. Caesar was the people's favourite. Had been the people's favourite. The next step would be armed gangs of men roaming the streets looking for someone to blame.

Peterson paused, pulled off his toga because now was possibly not the best time to be posing as a member of the Senate, bundled it up any old how and tossed it into a doorway.

'Come here, Max.' He put his arm around her and Van Owen. Now he was just a concerned family man trying to get his family off the streets. Luke did the same with Jane and they fought their way along as best they could, compromising the need for speed with not seriously upsetting the volatile mob on the way. Jane could feel the sweat sticking her clothes to her back as the uncaring sun shone brilliantly on a dark day.

Eventually, they turned into what Jane now thought of as their own alleyway, which was still deserted. As Luke put it, why would anyone hang around in this damp and smelly place when it was all obviously happening somewhere else? Then it was just a case of up the wooden steps. Leaving Luke and Markham to secure and wedge the outer door behind them, Jane led them back into the garden and, finally, with a huge sigh of relief, to the safety of the pod. They were home. They were safe. One set of problems safely disposed of – on to the next.

The six of them sat around the open pod doorway because the afternoon was still fine and sunny.

Any optimistic thoughts Luke might have had concerning the possibility that recent events might, just might, have distracted Matthew's mother's thoughts from her son's shooting were immediately dispelled.

She smiled at him and he really wished she hadn't. 'So – it was you who shot Matthew, was it?'

'It was his idea,' said Luke, feebly.

'It was my fault,' said Jane.

'Really,' Max said to Luke. 'That's how you get through life? Either blaming other people or letting other people take the blame for you?'

This unexpectedly accurate assessment of Luke's life to this point reduced him to silence. Not that he would have been able to get a word in edgeways anyway.

'You shot Matthew. Why? Tell me. What's this all about? What did you do? Is he all right? Do I have to go back to TPHQ and sort you all out? Again? Answer me.'

Peterson put a gentle hand on her shoulder. 'Now, Max,

we've talked about this. You have to let the other person speak occasionally. Remember?'

'Of course I do. And if you were listening, you'd know I've just invited this . . . person . . . to attempt to justify his actions before I strangle him with his own colon.'

Luke, searching for even the slightest hint that she was joking, failed. Failed utterly.

'Well,' he began, confident she would interrupt him before he could get more than three words out, which would give him the time he needed to think of an acceptable story.

Silence settled around him like a damp blanket.

'Well,' he began again.

Another damp blanket enveloped him.

'Well . . . and I think it's important to remember that examining an event without context doesn't always give an accurate representation of the actual occurrence . . . and indeed can be more than a little misleading, causing some people to . . .'

Max shifted her weight slightly and for some reason he abandoned what he had been going to say. 'Yes, I'm afraid I did. Shoot him, I mean. Which was unfortunate. Although, and I think this is something which should be borne in mind by everyone . . . and by everyone, I mean . . .'

'You shot him. You shot Matthew. Your own teammate. Another member of the Time Police. And my son.'

'Actually, I think willing volunteer might be a more accurate description and . . .'

'*You shot Matthew.*'

'Only as part of a . . . a *greater* plan and if I could just take you back to my earlier remark concerning context . . .'

'*You shot my son.*'

'Yes . . . well, no . . . but actually . . . yes.'

'You . . .' Max appeared lost for words, which was in no way reassuring because he was almost certain that actions were about to speak louder anyway, and that most of these actions would be happening to him. He drew himself up.

'I am a member of the Time Police and . . .'

'Max, let him live.'

'*He shot Matthew.*'

'Max . . .'

'They've had him less than six months . . .'

'Max . . .'

'I said this would happen . . .'

'Max . . .'

She wheeled on Luke. 'Bloody arseholing, witless, moronic, clueless, half-witted, useless fu—'

Both Peterson and Van Owen made a grab for her. Luke's life flashed before his eyes. Especially the last twenty-four hours. Which seemed to be on a kind of loop.

And then a nearby bush said, 'Excuse me.'

There are worse things to be threatened by than a talking bush, but few more surprising. For a moment, no one moved and then the bush rustled and a tall Time Police officer emerged.

'Good afternoon. In the interests of no one being shot – no one *else* being shot, that is – may I suggest that everyone remain very calm and make no sudden moves.'

'I think that applies to you, as well,' said Markham, appearing behind him, stun gun drawn.

'And you, shorty,' said Anders as first he, then Grint, appeared behind him.

There was a pause. 'Is that it?' said Markham. 'Because I thought you buggers always travelled in fours.'

'Hello, Mum,' said a slurry voice.

'Everyone stand quite still,' commanded Grint and was very nearly knocked off his feet as Max, Jane, Peterson and Luke rushed to get to Matthew who was gently urged to sit down. Someone passed him some water.

'There,' said Luke, unwisely. 'As you can see. Completely unharmed.'

Max turned to glare at him.

Markham, ignoring Grint, shook his head slightly at Luke

and made a surprisingly understandable *I'd shut up if I were you* gesture.

Peterson, observing Major Ellis closely, said, 'I think you should sit down, too,' and helped him to an empty statue plinth.

Ellis subsided gratefully and looked around. 'Well, isn't this nice.'

Seeing that Jane was still too busy with Matthew to speak, Luke asked how they'd found them.

Ellis gestured at Matthew who was beaming vaguely at a nearby bush. 'I asked him. Well, no, I can't take all the credit – North got it out of him.'

'She's not here as well, is she?' asked Luke, glancing nervously about him.

'No. We thought it advisable to leave at least one person behind to do the explaining. She was . . . reluctant.'

Markham grinned. 'Did she have that look on her face?'

Ellis nodded. 'Oh yes.'

'Do I gather,' said Max, narrowing her eyes at Ellis, 'that you think you're here to tidy up a few loose ends?' She gestured at Luke and Jane.

'I've come to return members of my team to TPHQ, yes. Where they should be at this moment.'

'As Deputy Director of St Mary's, I'm afraid I can't allow that,' said Peterson.

'I'm afraid you don't have any choice. Sir.'

'This is a St Mary's assignment.'

'That's a Time Police pod you're sitting outside. These are Time Police personnel. And this – all of it – is a Time Police matter.'

Max, glaring at Ellis, said dangerously, 'I've seen the way

391

the Time Police tidy up loose ends. You're not having them. In fact, after recent events, I rather think your two belong to me.'

'Actually, Max, no, they don't. They belong to me and we all belong to the Time Police.'

'That's hardly something to boast about.'

Grint shifted his weapon meaningfully. 'We should arrest them all. Aiding and abetting.'

St Mary's clambered to its feet. The Time Police assumed an aggressive posture. Everyone stared at everyone else. Dramatic music rose to a crescendo. Any moment now the clock would strike and everyone would go down in a hail of gunfire.

Or not.

Casually, Markham moved between the two opposing forces. 'Hey, Matthew, nice to see you again. Here – have some more water.'

Someone let out their breath and there was a general feeling that some crisis had passed without bloodshed.

It was at this point that Jane felt the need to be alone. It had been quite a long and eventful day and she was almost certain it wasn't over yet. She stood up to go. 'Um . . . I'm just going outside for a moment.'

Markham grinned. 'Are you going to be some time?'

Maxwell narrowed her eyes. 'What for?'

Jane blushed scarlet. 'Um . . .'

'No bathroom facilities in the pod,' said Luke, taking pity on her.

Markham looked around. 'What – none?'

'No.'

'None at all?'

'Nope.'

'Not even a bucket?'

'No. Can we move on?'

'How do you pee?'

'Well,' said Luke, 'I can't speak for Jane, but I do things the normal way. Rumours that Time Police shit solid gold, are, of course, well founded.'

Peterson shook his head. 'Shouldn't the question be, "Where do you pee?"'

'Never mind that,' said Markham. 'How do you shower?'

Luke drew himself up into full Time Police mode. 'We are the Time Police. We go on missions – not holidays. Why would we shower?'

'I'm not surprised to hear any of this,' said Max.

'Fun though it is to wind up St Mary's,' said Luke, 'in the interests of accuracy, our missions don't usually last that long.'

'We know,' said Maxwell. 'Jump in . . . shoot everyone in sight . . . and jump straight back out again.'

Markham persisted. 'Do you wear nappies, perhaps?'

Luke recoiled. 'What? No! Can we abandon this topic of conversation, please? Jane, go and do your thing.'

Scarlet-faced, Jane fled down the path.

Luke leaned closer to Peterson, nodded his head towards Max and said in an undertone, 'Is that it? Has she finished, do you think?'

He shook his head. 'Not even a little bit. You have the life expectancy of a Defence Against the Dark Arts teacher in a Harry Potter novel.'

Luke twisted round to address his bleary-eyed colleague. 'Matthew, can you please tell your mother why I shot you?'

Matthew looked vaguely around. 'Oh, hi, Mum.'

She smiled at him. 'Hello again. Everything OK?'

'Absolutely fine.' He swayed a little. 'Just need to take a moment.'

'We all need to take a moment, I think,' said Ellis, trying not to fall off his plinth.

Peterson stared in concern. 'You all right?'

'No, but I'm in the Time Police and we're very brave about this sort of thing.'

'Just as well given the way you're all having a go at each other these days.'

Ellis sighed wearily. 'Max, how are you?'

She moved straight into the attack. 'Well, thank you. Slightly concerned you allowed my son to be shot.'

'He triggered a radiation alert in central London. He's lucky he was only shot once.'

'*Was* there a radiation leak?'

'No.'

'Shooting seems overly harsh in that case.'

'He was involved in a criminal act.'

'I was helping a friend,' slurred Matthew, painstakingly following the conversation.

Ellis turned to him in exasperation. 'Who was also involved in a criminal act.'

'Is this the same criminal act or a different one?' enquired Markham with great interest.

Ellis, familiar with St Mary's tactics, ignored this.

'Perhaps,' said Peterson, in his role of peacemaker, 'we could have the whole story from the beginning.'

Lt Grint pushed up his visor and Max was distracted again. 'Hey – it's Grint. Look, everyone – Grint the Grunt is here.'

'That's Lt Grint to you,' said Luke before he could stop himself, and waited to see who would kill him first.

Major Ellis made a valiant effort to gain control of the situation.

'Lt Grint, if you and Anders would be so good as to secure the perimeter. Thank you.'

For a long time, nothing happened. Grint stared at him. Markham's hand strayed casually towards his stun gun. And then, with a jerk of his head, Grint led Anders away and they vanished into the lengthening shadows.

Ellis sighed. 'I'll tell you what happened, Max, and you can see for yourself that no permanent harm has been done – not to Matthew, anyway – and then I can return my . . . team . . . to its proper home.'

Luke was sitting in the shadow of the pod and doing his best to render himself invisible. Peterson, sitting next to him, grinned. 'Not so brave now, are you?'

'I never expected to come face to face with his bloody mother,' he muttered. 'It's a bit like Grendel and his mum, isn't it?'

'It's exactly like Grendel and his mother,' said Peterson, straight-faced. 'Can I compliment you on your perspicacity and recommend you comment on this remarkable coincidence to Max as soon as possible. I am certain her subsequent actions will go a long way to resolving all your issues almost immediately. You may never have to worry about anything ever again.'

The sun was no longer overhead and long shadows were falling across the garden. The air was still warm and the sounds of a city in tumult were just a faint and far off murmur. Max leaned back against the pod wall and stretched her legs in front of her. 'Go on then. Let's hear it.'

Luke drew a breath. 'I had a row with the fourth member of the team – Smith.'

'What about?'

'Not important right now.'

'She said she was pregnant,' said Matthew, still running his words together. An occasional but welcome after-effect of being sonicked by the Time Police was an overwhelming compulsion to tell the truth. 'She said you'd told her to get pregnant so you could get out of the Time Police. You said . . .'

'Yes, thank you, but not important right now, Matthew. Anyway. We had a row. In a public place. Jane overheard. I stormed off. She discovered Smith had been murdered. She thought I'd done it. She wouldn't give me up. No matter what they said to her.' His voice faltered for a moment. 'And I thought she'd done it because she was caught trying to dispose of the evidence. So I planned to break her out.'

'*We* planned to break her out,' slurred Matthew with all the careful enunciation of the recently sonicked.

'We planned to break her out. Which we did.'

With the cold condemnation of Judge Jeffreys himself, Ellis, seated on his plinth, said accusingly, 'You set off a radiation alert.'

Luke shifted to face him. 'Well, no, actually, no, we didn't. The computer set off the alert. We just rigged the computer. There was no radiation.'

'Sadly, you failed to advise any of the panic-stricken inhabitants of central London of that fact.'

'Well, that would have rather spoiled the point, don't you think?'

'Can't you call it a drill?' said Max, helpfully. 'And congratulate everyone on their rapid response. That's what we always do.'

'The Time Police do not necessarily base their procedures on those of St Mary's.'

'Really? Do you know, I think we might have identified the root of all your problems?'

'Can we continue, please?' said Ellis, wearily. 'Parrish . . .'

'Yes. Right. We grabbed Jane when the alarm went off. Matthew had . . . enabled . . . our acquisition of a pod, and to avoid any blame coming his way . . .'

'You shot him,' said Max, returning to this uncomfortable fact faster than a politician scenting a photo op.

'Yes, but as I keep saying, he told me to.' He looked at Matthew. 'Didn't you?'

Matthew remained silent.

'Matthew, now is not the time to stop talking.'

Matthew nodded. 'It *was* my idea.'

'And a very good one,' said Luke. 'Flawlessly conceived and executed.'

Markham grinned. 'You might want to avoid using the word *executed*. Just saying.'

'And then Jane and I escaped. To here. Because there are loads of people here today and we thought we could hide among all the pod signatures.'

Markham shifted. 'And then?'

'Well, we hadn't actually got that far. But we had several options under consideration.'

'Such as?'

'Well, moving from one historical hotspot to another until everyone lost interest in us.'

397

'Never going to happen,' said Ellis, grimly.

'Or . . .' Luke stopped.

'Or?' prompted Ellis.

'Well, we rather thought we might offer ourselves to St Mary's.'

Max blinked. 'In what capacity?'

'Well . . . um . . . we were discussing claiming sanctuary.'

'Not legal any longer,' said Peterson. 'Besides, we don't have an altar.'

Markham disagreed. 'Yes, we do. In the chapel.'

'Well, yes, but it's a bit out of the way, isn't it? Not very practical. I'm thinking much too far from the kitchen.'

'Good point. And no toilet facilities.'

'Speaking of which,' said Van Owen, looking around. 'Jane's not back yet.'

'She's been gone a long time,' said Luke, standing up and looking around the garden. Of Jane there was no sign.

And at that moment, because, as Luke said afterwards, there hadn't been anything like enough drama in their life so far, a shot rang out.

33

It was cooler now, Jane noticed, now that the sun had dropped below the rooftops. Long shadows slanted across the garden. The air was damp. No birds were singing. It would be dark soon.

She picked her way along the overgrown path until she found a likely-looking bush – one with enough foliage on it to grant a small degree of privacy, anyway – and busied herself.

Emerging a few minutes later and in no rush to return to whatever was happening at the pod, she took a moment to stare around the garden and at the tall walls and blind windows surrounding it. There was no wind in this sheltered spot. Everything was completely still. She could easily imagine a Roman family spending the long summer evenings here, reclining on couches, sipping wine, talking, playing or listening to music. There would be the scent of flowers on the evening air. A pleasant, peaceful existence. Something she would probably never know. In fact, never mind pleasant and peaceful, if the Time Police had their way, there would almost certainly be no existence at all.

She could hear their voices over to her left, but there was no shouting yet. She should hasten back and support Luke in his probably vain attempt to avoid the wrath of Matthew's mother, but everything here was so very calm and quiet. There had been very little calm and quiet in her life over the last twenty-four hours and she rather felt the moment should be savoured.

Rainwater had collected in the fountain bowl. Later, it would reflect the stars. The water looked clean enough so she swilled her hands and splashed a little on her face. The air was turning chilly. It was warm enough during the day, but it was only March, after all, and the night would be chilly.

She stood quite still, listening to the rise and fall of voices at the other end of the garden and tried to give some serious thought as to what on earth was to become of her and Luke. Something told her St Mary's would not be taking them in. She and Luke should return to TPHQ and surrender themselves. Save everyone else a great deal of time and effort.

Sighing, she dragged her sleeve across her face to dry it, turned back to the pod and was immediately aware she was not alone. Something large moved in the shadows. Her heart leaped unpleasantly before she realised it was probably Grint or Anders, doing a security sweep. She put her hand to her chest, took a deep breath to calm herself, and from over to her right, frighteningly loud in the still evening air, came the sudden crack of a pistol shot.

She froze – part fear, part caution – and then remembered her training. Really, the Time Police had a procedure for everything. Take cover and, as far as practical, identify the source of the shot. She dropped to a crouch staring around her, trying to see in the uncertain light. Far away, at the other end of the garden, she could hear shouting. Someone was shouting for the medkit. Someone had been hurt.

She was about to run towards the pod to help when two men suddenly erupted through a bush, crashed into the wooden trellis supporting the vines and brought the whole lot down on top of themselves. Once carefully pruned ornamental shrubs were crushed beneath them as they fought for possession of something she couldn't see. And this was a proper fight. They were serious. She could hear them grunting and cursing as they rolled about in the undergrowth, breaking branches and snapping twigs beneath them. She could hear the impact of their blows. First one was on top, viciously punching and kicking, and then the other was doing the same. They were big men and there was a lot of power there.

She stared. Anders and Grint were fighting. Why would they be doing such a thing? One or both of them must be the source of the gunshot. She should do something.

'Over here. Help. Over here!' She grabbed a piece of wood from the shattered trellis and hurled herself on Grint – who had the misfortune to be on top at the time – beating him around the head and shoulders which probably didn't do him a lot of harm. The wood was old and rotten and disintegrated with every blow, although she might have given him a splinter.

Unexpectedly, they rolled in her direction and she couldn't get out of the way quickly enough. They knocked her legs out from underneath her and she fell heavily to the fortunately soft ground. The next moment they'd rolled on top of her and she was crushed under their combined weight. Abandoning the piece of wood, she struck out wildly. 'Get off me. Get off.'

Not surprisingly, no one took any notice. Something heavy and cold fell on her face and instinctively, she grabbed at it.

A gun. An old-fashioned pistol.

She barely had time to wonder before Luke and Markham appeared on the scene. She heard Markham shout for her to get clear, wondered how on earth she was supposed to do that with two of the biggest men in the Time Police sprawled across her and then lost control of her arms, her legs, her entire body, her thoughts – everything – as he fired his stun gun. Every muscle in her body contracted painfully for a very long second or so before relaxing to such an extent she was vaguely grateful she'd had the opportunity to water that bush a moment ago.

She was struggling to breathe. Time Police officers are noted for their substantialness and both Grint and Anders were very substantial. The pain was subsiding but she rather thought she'd opt out of events for a few minutes. Just lie here and look up at the darkening sky. A faint star had emerged. It was very pretty. Cold and remote . . .

Someone hauled two heavy weights off her. The cold night air returned and air rushed into her lungs. Markham rolled her into the recovery position and enquired whether she was all right.

'You . . . sh . . . sh . . .'

'Yeah – sorry. It seemed the easiest thing to do. You'll be all right in a minute.'

'What's that in her hand?' enquired a voice she recognised as Peterson's. 'Is that a gun? Did she just shoot Ellis?'

What? She tried to shake her head. Of course she hadn't shot Ellis. Wait – had Ellis been shot? Or was that in Egypt? What was going on?

Someone was prising the gun from her grasp. She heard Luke's voice. 'Jane – for God's sake. How many more times can one person be found with the murder weapon in her hand?

Most people go their entire lives without ever being accused of murder and here you are – twice in twenty-four hours. Here.'

He passed the gun to Markham, who made it safe and stowed it away in a discreet pocket.

Murder. He'd said murder. She felt drool run down her chin and closed her eyes in mortification.

'Jane – wake up. You can't go to sleep now.'

Chance would be a fine thing, she decided, but obediently opened her eyes. The world was a little blurry but many people seemed to be looking at her. She should say something.

'Fighting . . .' she managed. 'Shot. Tried to stop. Fell on me. Gun. Shot.'

She closed her eyes. There. She'd given them the salient points. They could work the rest out for themselves.

'Let's get her up,' said Markham. 'Give me a hand, Parrish. What's the position with Grint and Anders?'

As he spoke, Anders jack-knifed to his feet, reeled sideways for a moment, and then, regaining his balance, shoved Luke into Markham. They both went down. Jane heard the impact as they hit the ground. Then there were stumbling, staggering footsteps. She heard the window shutter scrape as he pulled it aside to climb through the window, and then silence.

Except for Markham, entangled with Luke Parrish and cursing. Loudly, richly and longly.

They disentangled themselves and helped Jane to her feet. She gazed blearily around, feeling that events were rather getting away from her.

'Well,' said Markham, cheerfully, 'I've never known an organisation like yours for having a pop at each other. Let's recap, shall we? Someone, probably not Jane or Luke, killed

403

this Smith person. Someone, probably not Jane because I can't see it myself, has shot Ellis. We do know, however, that I stunned Grint and Anders, and regretfully, Jane, who's not having the best day. And now Anders has had a go at you and pushed off. It's a miracle there are any of you left.'

Luke was staring after Anders. 'I can't believe he got up from that. He must be built like a brick shit—'

Markham interrupted, looking down at the stirring Grint, still on the ground and struggling to get up. 'Let's get this one back, shall we, and see if we can work out what's going on. You'll have to manage for yourself, Jane, while we drag the fallen tree here back to the pod.'

It took both Luke and Markham to lift the unfortunate Lt Grint. Jane staggered along behind on rubber legs and wondered what on earth had happened to her world.

34

Back at the pod, Major Ellis was lying half in, half out of the doorway. Max and Van Owen had found the medkit and were working frantically. Apart from Ellis, everyone seemed unharmed.

Markham and Luke dropped Grint with a crash and rolled him over.

'Here,' said Luke, pulling a couple of ties from Grint's belt, and despite his mumbled protests, they zipped him and rolled him out of the way.

'How's Ellis?' said Luke, anxiously. 'Will he live? You have to save him.'

'Dammit, man,' growled Max. 'I'm an historian not a doctor.'

Jane stood, wobbly-legged, her teeth chattering. What was happening? Peterson helped her sit down next to Matthew who appeared delighted to see her again. 'Jane. Hi.'

Ellis was still conscious, faint but furious. 'I do not believe it. What has the world got against me? That's twice I've been shot in under a month. Parrish – check the pod for damage.'

'No need,' said Max, calmly. 'The bullet's still safely in your shoulder.'

'That's a relief,' said Luke and received a life-ending look for his pains.

'I don't think you should take this too personally,' said Peterson to Ellis. 'We don't yet know who they were aiming at. It might not have been you at all.'

'How is that supposed to make me feel any better? Ow!'

'Sorry,' said Max.

'All right,' said Luke. 'If it makes you feel better, they were aiming at you. The whole thing is one massive plot to obliterate you from the face of the earth.'

'What are you doing?' demanded Van Owen who was still rummaging through a medkit. Luke had previously marked her down as one of the more restrained members of St Mary's, but her expression was in no way friendly. She ripped a package open with her teeth and passed Max a dressing.

'I'm trying to make him feel better.'

'Well, don't. You're not helping.'

Markham seated himself next to Jane and said quietly, 'Can you tell me what you saw?'

Jane wiped her chin again and tried to collect her memories and focus. 'Not sure. Very dark at that end of the garden. Heard the shot and then they fell through that old vine trellis thing on top of me. Didn't know they had a gun until it fell on my head. And then,' she said indignantly, because she felt she had a great deal to be indignant about, 'someone sonicked me.'

'That was me,' said Markham. 'And not sonicked. Just a good old-fashioned stun gun. You'll probably stop dribbling in a few minutes and be absolutely fine.'

Peterson patted her shoulder. 'You're looking a little bit under the weather, Jane. Shall we have some tea?'

'They don't do tea,' said Maxwell, not looking up. Van Owen passed her another bandage.

Peterson sighed and looked at Ellis. 'If being shot is going to be a regular part of your life, then you might want to consider introducing it. Right – let's make a bad day worse, shall we? Coffee for everyone?'

Luke kicked the zip-tied Grint a couple of times.

Markham said disapprovingly, 'That's rather disrespectful behaviour towards an officer.'

'What are they going to do about it? Execute me twice?'

Jane was beginning to feel better. She sat straighter and looked around.

'Well,' said Luke, 'I think we've established it wasn't Jane who shot Ellis, so that leaves Grint . . .'

'Lt Grint to you,' said Ellis weakly.

'Or Anders. And since Anders has disappeared, I think we can draw our own conclusions.'

'Lemme go,' said Grint, slowly regaining the power of speech.

Luke grinned. 'I don't think so.'

'Trying to stop him, you . . .' He stopped, apparently unable to find words suitable for the occasion.

'Who?' said Luke. 'Who were you trying to stop?'

'Anders,' he said, blearily. 'We split up. He . . . went left. I went right. Searching the garden. Saw him by that big bush.' He stopped, swallowed a couple of times and then said, 'Thought he was watching Lockland.'

'What?' said Jane, outraged, and suddenly realised she wasn't blushing. 'I think I want a word with him.'

'Saw him raise the gun,' continued Grint, wearily. 'I moved but too late. Got to him just after he fired. Tried to get his gun off him. Which I would have. 'Cept you stunned me. And he got away. Now let me go.'

'I don't want to tell anyone their business,' said Markham, chattily, 'but the same story could equally apply to the other one. What's his name? Anders?'

Jane rested her forearms on her knees and tried to think. Her brain felt slow and stodgy but there were fragments ... memories ... She turned to Matthew. 'Matthew, when you were in Egypt ... ?'

He appeared to wake up. 'What?'

'When you were in Egypt ... ?'

'Yeah?'

'Ellis was shot. With a pistol. We thought it was one of the illegals.'

He nodded.

'And the gun was never found?'

He nodded.

'Anders and Grint – where were they?'

'With me. No, wait. No. Grint disappeared somewhere. Then Anders. They both pushed off.' He peered at Grint.

Markham stirred Grint with his foot. 'Where did you go?'

Grint tried to lift his head and glare. 'None of your business, shorty.'

'Where did you go?'

Silence.

'Well,' said Markham eventually. 'I think you have your culprit.'

At ground level, Grint sighed and then said, very quietly and with enormous reluctance, 'I went for a slash.'

'There was about to be a massive firefight,' said Luke, in disbelief. 'Illegals everywhere, a trainee to keep an eye on, and you wandered off to pee?'

There was a long silence. 'I need to go more at night.'

'What?' said Peterson. 'Oh.'

'What?' said Jane, mystified.

'Men's problems.'

'Really? You have those?'

'Beyond count,' said Luke. 'It's not just male-pattern baldness and erectile dysfunction, you know. Or so they tell me.'

'That's enough,' said Ellis, in some sympathy for the unfortunate Grint. 'Roll him over and cut him free.'

'No,' said Max.

'I give the orders here, Max.'

'Not at the moment, you don't. You're out of the game. This is not a normal situation. Security takes over. Markham's Head of Security. He calls the shots.'

Markham eyed Grint thoughtfully.

'You could do as Jane does,' said Luke, helpfully. 'She asks them to promise not to escape and they do. Or rather – they don't.'

'Parrish,' said Ellis, wearily. 'Is there any power on earth that would shut you up?'

'You could tell me you're pregnant. Speaking from experience, that tends to render me speechless.'

'Well,' said Max, closing the medkit. 'Far be it from St Mary's to interfere in what is solely a Time Police shambles, but what are you going to do now? Anders has almost certainly gone straight back to TPHQ. I think we can all imagine the story he will be telling them. They'll send a team.'

'Nothing so girlie,' said Luke. 'They'll send a full force equipped with a shoot-on-sight order, that's what they'll do. They'll shoot the lot of us. Me, Jane and Matthew, for certain. Ellis probably, since he appears to be the target du jour, and probably St Mary's as well just because they can, and call it a good day's work.'

'Wow,' said Max. 'It's all go in the Time Police these days, isn't it? The way you lot are trying to knock each other off, it's a miracle there's anyone left.'

'You should leave, Max,' said Ellis. 'All of you. They could be here at any moment and I doubt they'll stop to ask questions.'

She shook her head. 'Come with us. We'll all go back to St Mary's and you can sort things out from there.'

Jane, who had been thinking, shook her head. 'With respect, ma'am – no.'

Heads turned to look at her.

'No,' she said again.

Max stood up. 'We'll take you three, then. You can come back after Ellis and Grint have cleared things up.'

Markham shook his head. 'Actually, Max, I'm with Jane. Ellis and Grint could be in as much trouble as the trainees are.'

'Well, we can't leave Matthew – or any of them – here to be sitting targets, and Ellis needs urgent medical attention.'

Jane shook her head. 'No. This has to be stopped and I have an idea.'

Five minutes later she was still being stubborn, meeting all arguments calmly and reasonably and in the sure and certain knowledge her life was so far out of control that nothing she said or did could make things any worse.

'Well, we can't go back to our own pod,' said Maxwell, cunningly. 'The streets are far too dangerous at the moment and there's bound to be a curfew in force, so it makes sense for us to come back with you.'

'No. I thank you for the offer, but if anything happens to us then St Mary's can perhaps—'

'Make things considerably worse,' interrupted Ellis. He closed his eyes against a spasm of pain. 'Lockland . . .'

'Sir, with respect, my recommendation – with which I'm sure Mr Markham will concur – is that St Mary's spends the night here. If my plan works, then no one from the Time Police will come and disturb them and they can safely return to their pod tomorrow.'

'And if your plan doesn't work and something does disturb them?'

'They're St Mary's and I'm sure they'll think of something. Luke, be so good as to help the major back into the pod. Matthew – can you walk?'

Luke opened his mouth to argue and she turned to him, saying quietly, 'Luke, we're in trouble here. We're all in trouble here. Ellis and Matthew are out of the game. Grint's an unknown quantity but probably hostile. You're the only one I trust. I need your support with this.'

He closed his mouth and nodded.

They helped Ellis into the pod and lowered him gently to a seat. He looked up at them. 'Max, can we leave you any weapons?'

'No, it's fine. They'll manage to outwit the Time Police without artificial aids, but thank you for the offer.'

'For God's sake, take care.'

'If we're successful then they won't need to. For them it will be just a peaceful night in a garden speculating on what they might have been and indulging in a great deal of mockery at Time Police expense.'

411

He sighed. 'You said "they" and "them". You're coming with us, aren't you?'

She was packing her gear. 'In my capacity as neutral observer, yes.'

'Or, if I'm very, very lucky, primary target.'

'I shall hide behind you.' She turned to her team. 'No arguments.'

'Wasn't going to,' said Markham. 'It's a good idea. The presence of a neutral third party might calm things down a little.' He turned to Jane. 'Walk with me, please.'

They stepped outside into the garden.

'You appear to be the brains of your team – let me give you this.' He passed her the cloth-wrapped gun. 'Here. I've made it safe.'

She took it reluctantly. 'Why?'

'Because while they thought they were being clever using a weapon that couldn't be tracked back to them – actually they weren't.'

'If you mean fingerprints,' said Jane, doubtfully, 'Anders was wearing gloves.'

'No, I don't mean fingerprints. Just trust Ellis. Keep this safe for him until you get back to TPHQ. He'll know what I'm talking about and he's a good officer.'

'Is he going to die?'

'He's under Max's tender care. He wouldn't dare.'

Jane stared at her feet. 'I don't want to die, either.'

'Well, mostly, no one does, but it's the one thing we all have in common, isn't it? It comes to us all in the end.'

Still staring at her feet, she nodded.

'Listen,' Markham said gently. 'I've been in trouble all my

412

life and expect to be in a great deal more. Especially now I work with a bunch of hooligans who can't even go to the bathroom without triggering an apocalypse. Can I give you some advice?'

'Please.'

'We all pass through the Door of Death.'

He paused. Jane waited but that seemed to be it.

'Well,' she said eventually, and wanting to be polite, 'that was very helpful. Thank you.'

'I hadn't finished. I just paused for effect.'

'Sorry.'

'Where was I?'

'Passing through the Door of Death.'

'Yes. Anyway. It's not the passing through, it's the approaching that's important.'

'Is it?'

'Yes. You have to decide. Do you tiptoe up to the door, tap gently and whisper a request for admittance, or do you stride up, give it a couple of kicks with your hobnails and demand to be let in before you have the bloody thing off its hinges?'

Jane considered this. 'But the end result is the same. You're dead. It doesn't make any difference.'

'Not after you're dead, it doesn't, but it makes a hell of a difference to your life.'

'Oh.' She thought again. 'Oh.'

'Precisely. Shall we go back?'

Back in the pod, another argument was raging.

'Max . . .' said Ellis.

She knelt beside him, saying very quietly, 'You can see the state of Matthew. He can't look after himself. You're not firing on all cylinders. Jane and Luke are inexperienced and I'm not

413

sure about Grint. Either I come with you or Matthew stays behind here, where he's safe.' She put her hand on his forearm. 'Don't make me embarrass him in front of his friends.'

Ellis hesitated and then sighed and nodded.

She got up and turned back to her team. 'See you soon, guys. Stay safe.'

Peterson grinned. 'I still think we'll be a bloody sight safer than you, Max. Look after Matthew.'

The pod door closed behind them. Markham, Peterson and Van Owen moved back out of range. A brief wind fluttered the leaves and then the pod was gone and they were alone in the garden.

Peterson turned to Van Owen. 'Was it like this when you were with the Time Police?'

'God, no. If I'd known it was going to be this exciting, I might have stayed.'

35

It was Jane who laid in the coordinates and initiated the jump, and it was only as they landed gently in the pod's allotted space that she realised she'd done it all without even the slightest qualm. There's nothing like imminent death to put things into perspective.

They enjoyed nearly one and a half seconds of peace and stillness before the alarms started up.

Again.

Luke sighed. 'I can hardly remember a time when my life was unaccompanied by shrieking sirens, flashing lights and big men with bigger guns.'

'Well,' said Jane. 'You stay safely inside then and I'll pop out there and make everything better for you.'

'Lockland,' said Ellis, who, despite sitting down, was looking paler than he should be.

'Don't worry, sir. I'm going to be fine.'

'I'm worried they'll shoot you as soon as you set foot outside.'

'Well, if that happens then we have Luke as first reserve.'

'They'll definitely shoot *him*.'

All heads turned to Matthew, who smiled amiably, if a little vaguely. 'And then there was one.'

Max folded her arms. 'If they shoot you then they'll have me to deal with, and before anyone makes the obvious remark, shooting *me* will bring Leon down on everyone's heads, and as the Time Police know, that never ends well.' She gestured to Jane. 'Have at it, kid.'

Jane turned towards the door. Luke stood in her path. He said, 'Jane . . .' and stopped.

Unable to meet his gaze, she stared at his sternum. 'Um . . . Luke . . . if . . . um . . . if things don't go well, please promise me you won't hang around trying to be heroic. Get yourself straight back to St Mary's.' She found a smile. 'Find yourself somewhere safe and do the fried chicken thing.'

Ellis raised his eyebrows and glanced at Max, who shrugged. 'No idea.'

'I will,' said Luke. 'And,' he added, generously, 'I'll call it JFC.'

'No – it's OK. LFC is fine. Or MFC if Matthew's with you.'

He grinned. 'It's like the alphabet, isn't it? JFC. LFC. MFC.'

'What happened to KFC?'

'That'll never catch on. Go on, Jane. Off you go now.'

Jane stood before the door and squared her meagre shoulders. 'Ready when you are.'

The door opened. She gave brief thanks they didn't have a ramp, squeezed through the gap as soon as it was wide enough for her to do so and stood very still with her hands on her head wearing her very best unthreatening expression.

Within seconds, she was surrounded by a half-ring of armed officers, all of them bristling with weapons and all of those weapons pointed at her. Beyond them, three teams stood in familiar formations, their officers conferring together. Beyond them, mechs clustered around three pods, prepping them for immediate use. She estimated between fifteen and twenty people all looking directly at her.

And the biggest of them all was Anders.

For a second, he stood motionless, as if frozen with surprise. And something else. Alarm. He – or possibly they – whoever *they* were – had not banked on this. They'd thought she would run. That they would all run. As far and as fast as possible. Fleeing the might of the Time Police while they could. Not for one moment had they thought she would return to the lion's den.

And then his eyes bulged. Pointing dramatically, he shouted, 'That's her. She killed Smith. And Ellis. Get her.'

He looked wildly round as if expecting a hail of supporting fire. If he was, he didn't get it. Not immediately.

The second person she recognised was Officer North. Whether she had been incorporated into a team or was there solely to give an insight, Jane never discovered, but present she was. Which meant that not everyone in the Pod Bay was out to kill her. It was extraordinary how heartening she found that thought.

They were all shouting at her. Everyone was shouting conflicting instructions. She was to get on the ground now. She was to stand still and not move. She was to put her hands in the air. All of it designed to terrify and disorient her and it was working very well. She was terrified and disoriented.

The air was electric with tension. She could feel it crackling around her. It would only take one shot – just one nervous finger on a trigger and they would all fire. Blaster, sonics, everything they had. She had a brief but very vivid picture of her body jerking and jumping as the charges impacted. Their combined firepower could blow her apart.

Remembering Ellis's instructions, she remained absolutely motionless.

'Just stand still, Lockland,' he had said. 'Don't get down on the floor. Don't make a single move that could be construed as hostile. They're not all out to get you. Most of them are just normal officers doing their job. Just stand still and wait. Let someone else make the next move.'

Obediently, she stood still and waited.

Gradually, just as Ellis had said they would, the shouts died away. The mechs had withdrawn. Not a good sign. Trouble was obviously expected.

Red-faced, Anders was urging them on. 'What are you waiting for? Shoot her. Quickly.'

He fumbled for his own weapon, still holstered on his hip, and the officer next to him knocked his hand away and relieved him of it.

Jane stood very, very still, barely able to believe she'd got this far. That she hadn't been shot out of hand. According to Ellis, this would be the most dangerous time of all. When they could only see her defiance but hadn't yet got around to wondering why.

'Commander Hay,' she said quietly.

'Get down on the ground.'

Two officers approached, guns stowed behind them, all ready to make her comply. Inside the pod, Luke left the screen and headed for the door, tripping over the recumbent Grint on the way.

Ellis made a protesting sound and tried to get up.

'No,' said Max, grasping Luke's arm. 'Leave her. She's doing very well.'

'You mean they haven't shot her yet.'

'Exactly. And the longer they don't shoot her, the less likely they are to shoot her. She's doing fine. Just let her get on with it.'

'This is why Ellis let you come, isn't it?'

'To stop you doing something daft. Yes.'

'Bit of a novel experience for you?'

'Yes, but quite enjoyable so far.'

Jane's voice recalled them to the screen. 'Commander Hay. I would like to see Commander Hay.'

One of them seized her arms, forced them roughly behind her back and tried to push her down on to her face.

'I would like to see Commander Hay, please.'

'Shut up. Down on the ground.'

'Commander Hay, please.'

'This isn't going to work,' said Luke, staring at the cameras. 'Sir . . .'

But Ellis had closed his eyes. Max felt for a pulse. 'We can't sit here forever. He needs medical attention.'

Back outside, Jane was still requesting Commander Hay.

'Shut up.' An officer balled his fist to punch her to the ground. She closed her eyes but stood her ground. Still with her eyes tightly shut, she said, 'I need to speak to Commander Hay.'

'Enough.'

Jane opened her eyes to find North standing between her and the two men. North was a respected officer. No one messed with North. 'Step back, please, gentlemen.'

'What are you waiting for?' shouted Anders from the back of the Pod Bay. 'Shoot her. She's a fucking murderer.'

419

Jane braced herself again.

Holding the officers' gaze, North opened her com. 'Captain Farenden. Good afternoon. Could you request Commander Hay's immediate presence in the Pod Bay, please. We have a situation. Yes. Immediately, please.'

She closed her com. 'The commander is on her way. I suggest we allow her to form her own assessment of this situation and then follow her instructions.'

'Good move,' said Luke, still watching from the pod. 'No one can really argue with that.'

And no one did. The silence in the Pod Bay was so complete that Jane was convinced she could hear the two officers' heavy breathing. Even Anders remained silent. The seconds ticked past and the wait seemed endless but, at last, the doors opened and Commander Hay entered, unarmed, closely followed by Captain Farenden, whose hand rested lightly on his weapon.

'What's going on here?'

Jane was certain Commander Hay knew exactly what was going on here, but asking the question and listening carefully to who said what would give everyone some much-needed time to calm down.

Anders rushed to explain. 'We found her.'

She was deliberately irritable. 'Who's "we", Anders? Report properly.'

He flushed again. 'Beg pardon, ma'am. Major Ellis, Lt Grint and I went to apprehend the fugitives. Their accomplice, Farrell, had told us where they were. We caught them in Ancient Rome. The major was talking to them. Lockland, who had separated herself from the main group, shot the major. She hid in the bushes and shot him. She attacked Lt Grint and then she

420

pointed her weapon at me so I made haste to return to TPHQ to request assistance.' He gestured at the teams lined up. 'We were about to depart.'

Commander Hay surveyed Jane. 'It would seem there is no longer a need. The culprit now stands before us.'

'There's the other one,' he said. 'Parrish.'

'Yes,' she said. 'Do explain Mr Parrish's role in all this, Mr Anders. I assume he's not here since it seems so very unlike him to remain quietly in the background.'

Back in the pod, Matthew snorted.

Anders was shouting. His face gleamed with sweat. Flecks of spittle flew from his mouth. 'I tell you, ma'am, she's a killer.'

'You have told me she has assaulted two of my officers. Where are they now? Have you abandoned them?'

His colour deepened even further. 'I would have stayed, but then she was shooting at everyone. Ma'am, she's out of control.'

Major Callen stepped up and put a hand on his shoulder. 'Yes, all right, son. Leave it to us. Commander, if this is true, then Lockland is indeed out of control. A shoot-on-sight order has been applied for.'

'But not yet signed.'

He bowed his head. 'As you say, Commander. Not yet signed.'

Jane felt herself grow cold all over. Luke had promised her he would remain faithfully in the pod until she herself told him it was safe to come out. Matthew was still weak and would be unable to prevent Luke doing anything stupid. Ellis was probably unconscious by now. Grint was still securely zipped. With his own zips. That left Maxwell – arguably the most erratic and catastrophic member of an organisation famed wherever it went for erratic and catastrophic behaviour. She really was on her own.

Commander Hay was speaking. 'A shoot-on-sight order. For *Lockland*?'

Anders was beside himself. 'Smith, Ellis, Grint – she's killed them all.'

'We don't know that.'

'We have Anders's testimony,' said Callen, quietly. 'A reliable officer who has never given any trouble. As opposed to Lockland and her team, all of whom have given plenty of trouble and are patently unsuitable Time Police material, as their behaviour has plainly shown.'

'I'm not clear, Major. What are you saying?'

'Their apprehension of Henry Plimpton was . . . unconventional, to say the least. In fact, I believe Plimpton has now been returned to the 20th century to continue whatever mischief he was planning. I think it's no coincidence that Major Ellis was wounded in the Valley of the Kings – an assignment at which Lockland and her team were present. I know that initially we assumed the perpetrator was an illegal, but Farrell was there. Right on the spot and unsupervised during the attack. And now, on his first assignment since his injury, Major Ellis tracks them down and is shot virtually on sight. Closely followed by the attack on Lt Grint. Commander, is there nothing these people won't do to protect themselves?'

'You raise a very valid point, Major. As you rightly say, some people will do anything to protect themselves. Let's see what this one will do, shall we? Lockland – report.'

Jane swallowed hard to get her voice working again.

'Ma'am. I did not murder Smith nor . . .'

'Never mind that. I want to hear how you were able to overcome two experienced officers and, apparently, shoot them both dead.'

'I didn't, ma'am.'

'Was it Parrish? Did he carry out the shootings?'

'No, ma'am.'

'Well, it couldn't have been Farrell because I saw the state of him after Parrish had shot him.'

'My point exactly, ma'am,' broke in Anders. 'Not only did they take out their own team leader but they shot a teammate as well. I think we can assume they'd have no difficulty mowing down anyone who stood in their way.'

'Trainee Anders, can I invite you to compare the relative sizes of Lockland here to . . . say . . . Officer Chigozie, standing next to her. Or the possibly late Lt Grint. Or even yourself. Are you really telling me that Lockland, who, as any number of you haven't hesitated to remind me, barely clears the height requirement, has apparently overcome two of my biggest and best officers?'

'She was armed, ma'am.'

'With what? A thermo-nuclear device?'

There was a pause, and then he reluctantly said, 'A pistol, ma'am.'

'And you know that how?'

'He was there, Commander,' reminded Major Callen.

'Ah, yes. Our Mr Anders had plenty of time to identify the weapon before running away.'

'I didn't run away,' he shouted. 'I returned to TPHQ for reinforcements.'

'The accepted procedure,' murmured Major Callen.

'Of course. Although you appear to have armed yourselves with enough reinforcements to invade a small country.'

Callen said quietly, 'Commander, I appreciate your point but in slightly over twenty-four hours, Lockland and Parrish collectively have murdered one officer, severely sonicked another, stolen a pod, triggered a radiation alert and probably shot and killed two more officers.'

'You know,' murmured Luke to Max as they stared at the screen, 'no matter how many times I hear it, it never sounds any better. And Jane's out there all on her own.'

'Just a little longer,' she said. Something complained from floor level. 'Sorry, Grint. I'd forgotten about you. Did I stand on you?'

'I want to see,' he said. 'Help me up.'

'Not bloody likely,' said Luke.

'I want to see.'

'Let's take a leaf out of Jane's book, shall we?' said Max, brightly. 'Clever girl, our Jane.' She bent down and addressed Lt Grint. 'Do you promise not to try to escape?'

He regarded her with utter disbelief. 'What?'

'Do you promise not to try to escape?'

'You have got to be kidding.'

'OK. Stay where you are, then.' She turned back to the screen.

'All right. All right.'

They heaved him to his feet, cut his ties and brushed him down.

'Just in time for the good part,' said Luke.

Jane, meanwhile, was reviewing the last few months of her

life and coming to the conclusion that wrecking her grand-mother's seagull had probably been the high spot if only she'd had the sense to realise it at the time. She stood silently while arguments raged around her, trying to keep alive her little flame of optimism but it's hard to be brave when what looks like every weapon in the world is being pointed at you by people just waiting for an excuse to use them. She wondered if closing her eyes would help.

'Enough,' said Commander Hay, raising her hand. 'We are all still waiting to hear what Trainee Lockland has to say. Lockland – report.'

'I didn't kill Smith.' She swallowed and blushed because this was the shameful bit. 'I found a knife by the body and I thought it was Parrish's so I tried to dispose of it. I didn't say anything because I thought it would give him time to get away.'

She waited in case anyone wanted to comment but there was only silence. And not a good silence, either.

'We . . . escaped . . . to Ancient Rome. The date of Caesar's assassination, because everyone would be there and we could hide our pod among the other signatures.'

'That was my idea,' muttered Luke to Max. 'I'm the one who deserves credit for that. She's not telling it properly. There should be more me in it.'

'Major Ellis, Lt Grint, Anders and Farrell tracked us down. They were persuading us to give ourselves up. I . . . I left for a moment.'

'What for?'

'To find a spot from which to ambush us,' shouted Anders.

'And Major Ellis let you go?' enquired Commander Hay. 'Alone?'

'Er . . . yes.' She could feel the blush starting.

'Why?'

'Er . . . toilet, ma'am.'

'You can't tell me an experienced officer let a suspect go off alone?'

'I don't think he regarded us as suspects, ma'am.'

Even Major Callen looked surprised. 'He was in it with you?'

Commander Hay intervened. 'Shall we let Lockland continue? Go on, Lockland.'

'I . . . um . . . emerged from the bushes and heard a shot. Quite close to me. Very close, actually. I looked and Grint . . .'

'That's Lt Grint,' said Grint, wearily.

Max grinned at him. 'You do know they can't hear you out there, don't you?'

'. . . and Anders were rolling around on the ground.'

'She's lying,' shouted Anders. 'She shot Ellis and then attacked Grint when he tried to stop her.'

Commander Hay rounded on him. 'One more word, Anders, and I'll have you removed.'

He was beside himself with rage. And fear, thought Jane.

'You'll have *me* removed? She's the criminal. Remove her.'

Heads were nodding, Jane noticed, but perhaps not as many as before.

'Go on, Lockland.'

'I . . . um . . . I picked up a piece of wood and started to hit them.'

'Which one?'

'Both of them.'

'Why?'

'I didn't know which one had fired the shot. It seemed the safest thing to do.'

'And?'

'They rolled into me and knocked me down.'

'Which of them had the gun?'

'Well, at that point, me.'

'How?'

'It fell on my head.'

'Which of them relinquished it?'

'I didn't see. It was dark.'

'And then?'

'Anders pulled himself free, and ran away.'

This was too much for Anders, who snatched a gun from an inattentive officer and raised it in Jane's direction. 'I did *not* run away.'

'Shit,' said Luke, heading for the door, but someone else had the situation well in hand.

36

Pods are complex machines, made up of many parts. Some of them quite small. These, in turn, as any mech will explain, often at tedious length, are held in place by even smaller parts, many of which, during maintenance sessions, will frequently roll across the floor into some alternate dimension, never to be seen again.

At some point, a more than normally frustrated mechanic had hit upon the brilliant idea of magnetising metal trays. Of varying sizes and shapes, these could be utilised in any area, and used to keep tiny screws and seemingly irrelevant pieces of metal from being lost or falling into the machinery where they could do disproportionate amounts of damage. There were any number of these trays stacked around the Pod Bay, some holding various bits and pieces for future use, but most empty. Useful pieces of kit, as anyone would testify. Multi-purpose, even.

Anders was a big man. A big, frightened man. A big, frightened man with a purpose, which was to silence Jane Lockland before she could say any more. What the consequences would be, he had no idea, but he was confident of protection from above. He was a Time Police officer doing his duty. He'd followed his instructions to the letter. Ellis was dead. Grint out of the game. Or soon to be. And, now, inexplicably, the scapegoat had returned to TPHQ.

He plunged through the crowd. Officers went down in all directions. Like skittles, thought Jane, rooted to the spot, staring at the fast approaching Anders. Over all the confusion, she could hear his blaster whining as it charged and then there was the most enormous metallic crash. As if someone had banged a huge gong in some sort of cosmic echo chamber, but much louder. With the sound turned up.

It didn't happen often, but right at this moment, Officer North was Not Happy. With an already badly dented metal tray in one hand, she brought her arm back for the return blow – a professional-tennis-coach-honed swing that caught Anders across the bridge of his nose again and nearly knocked him off his feet. Followed by her oft-practised backhand. And then her only marginally less lethal forehand. She was building up a nice rhythm. Forehand. Backhand. Forehand. Backhand. The Pod Bay reverberated with the results of years of dedicated practice.

'Help me up,' said Ellis faintly. 'I must see this.'

'So must I,' said Max, zooming in and turning up the volume.

Years at St Mary's had made North more tolerant of irregu-larities than her family and friends would ever have believed possible. Some things, however, still set her off very quickly. The modern expression is *trigger point*. And this was hers.

Knowing her team as she did, she was convinced Lockland had not shot Ellis. Nor Grint, of course. Which meant Anders was lying. Which meant he was the one who had shot Ellis. And Grint, of course. Anders's actions had resulted in irregular events. And being associated with irregular events was not good for her career. And no one messed with North's career.

429

'Wow,' said Max over the sounds of metal regularly contacting nasal bone. 'Remind me to write a thank-you note to the god of historians.'

'That's my girl,' said Ellis, fuzzily.

'What?'

'Nothing.'

One massive blow finally knocked Anders sideways and down he went.

'Like a redwood,' said Luke, happily.

'I had no idea you had so much fun here at TPHQ,' said Max. 'Sadly, he forgot to incriminate himself before he hit the floor.'

'No matter,' said Ellis, wearily. 'Gunshot residue.'

'What?'

He sighed. 'Well, as I suspect your Mr Markham is aware – with these older weapons, a simple chemical test applied to Anders's hands and gloves will prove that he pulled the trigger. The same test applied to Jane will prove she didn't. That's where they – whoever they are – have been too clever. They thought they'd use a weapon that couldn't be tracked back to them and forgot – or never knew in the first place – about the existence of gunshot residue. Although, of course, if no one restrains Officer North soon . . .'

'For fu. . . could someone tell me what the hell is going on?' demanded Grint, staring at his fallen colleague.

Max said quietly, 'Grint, even you must be aware of what's going on here. You're in the first stages of a coup.'

In so much as a six-foot-four, sixteen-stone man can look panicky, Grint looked panicky.

Ellis tried to sit up straighter. 'They – the Albayans, if you want to name them – are trying to get rid of Hay. Max is kindly calling it a coup but it's not. It's mutiny. Plain and simple mutiny. Not today, perhaps, but soon. Very soon.' He paused. 'For God's sake, Gordon, remember who you are.'

Back in the Pod Bay, matters were not progressing well for Anders. The fact he was stretched out on the floor had not in any way prevented Officer North from putting the boot – or rather, the tray – in.

'Someone really ought to intervene,' said Max. 'He's no good as a witness if he's dead.'

'Yeah,' said Luke.

No one moved.

North had stopped hitting Anders but only to give herself a moment to draw breath. 'Tell the truth, you lying piece of shit. You shot Major Ellis.'

Anders shook his head, blood flowing freely from a couple of nasty cuts across the bridge of his nose and above one eyebrow.

'No. I swear. She did it. She did them both.'

Major Callen turned to Hay. 'As I see it, it's just a case of he said, she said, Commander. Anders versus Lockland. One word against another. I think we should accept that, in the absence of any reliable third-party evidence, this will be a difficult matter to adjudicate.'

'Quick – that's my cue,' said Max. 'Out of the way, stumpy.'

Still bemused, Grint stepped aside.

Ellis said weakly, 'Max . . .'

'I know.'

'Let Hay handle this. There are other issues here.'

She said again, 'I know.'

'Don't mention the gunshot residue test.'

431

'I know. Let them incriminate themselves.' Max opened the door, stuck her head out and grinned. 'Cooee.'

As she said afterwards, their expressions were priceless. Those who didn't know her simply stood and stared. Those who did know her wore expressions ranging from politely neutral to outright horror.

Someone said, 'Who's that?'

She stood alongside Jane. 'Good evening. My name is Max. I'm from St Mary's and I'll be your neutral third-party evidence for the evening.' She grinned at them.

Commander Hay turned. 'Thank you, everyone. Major Callen, Trainee Anders and Officer North will remain. Everyone else is dismissed.'

Callen turned to her, saying in an urgent undertone, 'Commander?'

She held his gaze. 'I think it's wise not to wash our dirty laundry in public, don't you?'

'I don't understand your meaning, Commander.'

'Then you have nothing to fear, do you?'

Everyone remained very still until the last footsteps died away and the doors closed. Silence fell.

'Who else is in the pod, Dr Maxwell?'

'Major Ellis.'

North lifted her head. 'You brought the body back?'

Max was watching her. 'No, he's alive. There's a bullet in his shoulder that needs to come out, but he's alive.' She noted North's expression with some satisfaction. 'He's pretty pissed off, of course.'

'Does he know who shot him?'

She shook her head. 'The shot came out of the dark.'

'Do *you* know who shot him?'

'No.'

Callen interrupted. 'It's as I said, Commander. It's simply a case of one word against another. Except that one party is an exemplary officer and the other is already wanted for murder and a whole string of other crimes. It's hardly rocket science, is it?'

'On the face of it, Major, I agree. Except that it's so very hard to believe that Lockland here is the vicious thug everyone believes her to be.'

'Appearances can be deceptive, Commander.'

'You were deceived enough to offer her a job in your own team.'

He stiffened. 'I thought she had something, but obviously I was mistaken. Poor judgement on my part, Commander, I freely admit.'

Commander Hay was turning away. 'You're right. We have conflicting testimony and no way of discovering the truth for ourselves. Charlie, call up a detention team, will you? Tell them to bring a truth cuff. That should ensure we get to the bottom of this.'

Major Callen was outraged. 'Commander, I cannot advocate using the cuff on our own people. It's never been done before.'

'And this is why I had the Pod Bay cleared. We need to get to the truth of this matter. The whole truth. And the only way to do that is to use the cuff. Sadly, we've run out of witnesses.'

Back in the pod, Ellis looked at Grint and Grint looked at Ellis.

'I'm sorry, Gordon.'

Grint nodded. 'So am I.'

He opened the door and stepped out.

Luke watched the door close behind him. 'Tosser.'

Ellis rounded on him. 'Grint has given nearly all his life to the Time Police. Today he's been betrayed and attacked and he doesn't understand what's happening to the organisation he loves. In so much as it can, his heart is breaking, so shut up, Parrish.'

Luke shut up.

Aware of his colleagues' habit of shooting first and apologising to the widows and orphans later, Grint was careful to emerge very, very slowly, to stand alongside Jane and Max.

'They're all in it together,' shouted Anders, clambering unsteadily to his feet. North tightened her grip on her tray. He swayed and tried to wipe the blood off his face. 'We should deal with them now and then go back to Rome and take care of everyone else left on site.'

'Such as?'

'Parrish. He's not here. He must still be there. And anyone else there.'

'Shoot on sight?' said Commander Hay.

'We have no choice, Commander. We have to deal with this now.'

They're trying to eliminate the witnesses, thought Jane. I don't know what to do. They're going to kill us all. This isn't going to work. They'll shoot me. And Hay. And North. And then Luke will burst out of the pod and they'll kill him too, and then they'll go in and cut down Ellis because he's too weak to defend himself. And Matthew. And then they'll jump back to Ancient Rome and kill an entire St Mary's team, and then all hell will be let loose because St Mary's will retaliate, and

434

then they'll have the war everyone here so badly wants and full powers to deal with it and I can't think of any way to stop it.

Callen pushed his way forwards and put a hand on Anders's shoulder. 'Time to shut up, son. You're just making things worse for yourself.'

Anders stared at him, red-eyed with rage. Foam had collected in the corners of his mouth. '*I'm* making things worse? . . . She's the one . . . They said . . .'

Pulling out his knife, he lunged. Whether he was heading for Jane, Grint or Commander Hay was never clear. One moment he was looming over them, wild-eyed, his meaty face running with blood and sweat, and then the next, he was toppling slowly to the floor and Major Callen, white-faced, was lowering his gun.

Anders hit the floor. His knife tinkled to the ground beside him. North knelt over him and then looked up. 'He's dead. At that range . . . You deliberately killed him.'

For a long second, no one moved. No one spoke. And then Callen drew a long, deep breath.

'Everyone stand very still, please. I mean it. Let's not have any silly accidents. Everyone's hands where I can see them, please.'

Commander Hay said very quietly, 'What are you doing, Major?'

'We all know what this is about, Commander. There's more going on here than is immediately apparent.'

'Do we?'

'Well, I do and I'm certain you do, too. You cannot have been blind to certain . . . unrest.'

'Let's say I have been. What do you hope to achieve by this?'

'Well, that's the thing – I'm not really sure what's going on at the moment. No one is. No one knows who stands where. Or with whom. We are divided and it makes us weak. People we've worked with for years – where do their loyalties lie? We don't know. Well, I do. I know where I stand and at this precise moment there is only one single person in this bay that I trust, and that person is me. There are far too many people with something to hide for my peace of mind. But don't mind me, Commander. You carry on.'

She looked him up and down for a moment and then, deliberately, she turned her back on him. It was a calculated insult.

'Who shot Ellis, Grint?'

Grint nodded at the lifeless Anders. 'He did. A member of my own team. And Major Ellis says there's a test that will prove it.'

Hay contemplated Callen. 'Is this testimony reliable enough for you?'

Inside the pod, Parrish looked at Ellis. 'So what do we think? Callen – guilty or not guilty?'

Ellis shrugged. 'I honestly don't know. Has he just prevented a mutiny? Or has he silenced a possible witness? It's not for me to say and it's definitely above your pay grade. Help me up.'

Luke opened the door, shouting, 'We're coming out.' He helped Ellis out of the pod. 'He needs urgent medical help.'

Commander Hay sighed. 'Get the medics in here, Charlie. I'm not sure even we can handle any more deaths today.'

They must have been waiting outside the door because the medteam was there within seconds. A dark and depressed doctor stood with his hands on his hips, surveying the scene.

'Right, Major Ellis, sir. Let's get you back to MedCen right now. You should never have left.' His tone implied that if Ellis was stupid enough to discharge himself without authorisation then being shot was his own fault.

'Who's next? Yes, Farrell. You're one of mine as well. Off you go.'

He moved on down the line. 'Lt Grint. You're not looking too good, either. MedCen for you.'

He paused in front of Jane and looked her up and down. 'Well, why not you as well? I'm on a roll today. Join the queue.'

Finally, he pitched up in front of Luke. 'You look comparatively undamaged.' He turned to Commander Hay. 'You can have this one to play with, ma'am.'

Luke winced. 'Actually, I can feel a slight headache coming on.'

The doctor moved on to stand in front of Max. 'You again.'

She beamed. 'Hi.'

'You're not one of mine. I have no interest in you.'

He bent over Anders's body. 'Even I can't help this one. I'll send a clean-up team.' He turned to go. 'With your permission, Commander.' He disappeared after his prospective patients.

Commander Hay turned to go. 'Charlie, tell the doctor to feed them, water them and clean them up. With the exception of Major Ellis, I want every one of them in my office in one hour's time. You too, Major Callen.'

She walked out.

37

Half an hour later, Max was saying goodbye to a recovering Matthew.

'I suppose you know what you're doing.'

'I do, Mum, and it's important.'

'OK. Your choice. Just try to get to the end of the month alive. It's my birthday. Don't worry too much about my present – anything big and expensive will do – but your father's looking forward to seeing you.'

'I'll be there. Promise.'

She wandered outside to the medtec's station. The duty medtec asked if he could help her.

'Just waiting a few minutes for a friend, if you don't mind.'

He nodded and retired behind his desk.

Grint emerged slowly from the treatment room. Like a bewildered little boy on his first day at school, his world was upside down and he wasn't dealing with it very well.

Max said brightly, 'There you are.'

He looked up. 'What do *you* want?'

'I brought you a coffee.' She passed him a paper cup.

He glowered suspiciously. 'You spat in it.'

'And not just me.'

'Why?'

'No one likes you.'

He sighed, visibly making an effort. 'I mean, why would you bring me coffee?'

'An old enemy is the next best thing to an old friend and we go back a long way.'

He sat heavily on a bench and said reluctantly, 'Thanks.'

'Old enemies have a lot in common.'

He made no reply.

She seated herself beside him. 'Listen, feel free to ignore me if you want, it's up to you, but why don't you talk to Hay?'

He frowned. 'Why would you say that? The two of you can barely be in the same room as each other.'

'It's true that we agree over nothing, but that doesn't prevent her being a good commander. Talk to her, Grint. Get it all out into the open. Stop mooching around the corridors full of a vague discontent that even you yourself don't understand. Stop listening to rumours and gossip. Stop letting yourself be used in other people's schemes. Take charge of your own life. Go and speak to Hay.'

He looked down into his coffee. 'Like I'm going to take advice from St Mary's.'

She sighed. 'We're just like Rome and Carthage, aren't we?'

He stared, baffled. 'Who?'

'Rome and Carthage. St Mary's and the Time Police. Two superpowers battling for supremacy which can only be achieved if one of them is completely obliterated. The other will go on to achieve total domination and impose its own language and culture all across the known world.'

He considered this. 'They fought?'

She nodded. 'Yeah. They fought.'

'Who won?'

She sighed. 'The god of historians help me – I'm surrounded by Philistines.'

'Not Romans? Or Carthaginians?'

She stared at him suspiciously and he stared blandly back again. 'Grint, you old bugger, I do believe St Mary's is rubbing off on you.' She reached up and kissed his cheek.

He rubbed his cheek angrily. 'Stop that right now.'

She regarded him for a moment. 'Wait here.'

Returning with a pen and piece of paper, she wrote busily for a while. Grint watched her suspiciously.

She passed it over. 'There you are.'

'What's this?'

'I've written down every emotion known to man – or woman, rather. Just tick as appropriate and pass it to Commander Hay. That way you don't have to talk about your feelings.'

He ignored the paper.

'Go on – you know I won't leave until you do.' She rustled it under his nose.

Angrily, he snatched it off her and ran his eye down the list. Finally, and most reluctantly, he made a small mark and passed it back again.

She looked at it. 'Calm. You're very calm.'

He nodded.

'And that's it?'

'How many more should there be?'

'Well, I don't know. Five or six, perhaps.'

He was dumbfounded. *Five or six?* How can anyone

possibly experience five or six emotions all at the same time? I'm not a bloody girl, you know.'

'Angry,' she said, making a tick. 'Frustrated. Impatient.' She paused. 'Afraid.'

He lunged. 'Give me that.'

She held it out of reach. 'I'm doing you a favour. Now you don't have to say anything to Hay. Just hand her your list. She'll take it from there.'

She held it out to him.

He scowled. 'I'll throw it away as soon as you've gone.'

'No, you won't. Gordon, everyone has a moment in their lives when they have to make a choice. I've had mine. Years ago, I had to decide whether to let other people define my life or choose my own path. It wasn't easy – none of it was – but I made the difficult choice. Now it's your turn. Make the choice.'

He took the paper without looking at her, folded it very small and tucked it into a pocket.

The nurse looked up. 'Message from the Pod Bay. Your pod is ready, Dr Maxwell.'

Grint turned his head to look at Max. 'Next time I see you, I'll shoot you.'

'Grint, you couldn't hit a barn door if it stood three feet in front of you.' She clapped him on the shoulder. 'Good luck.'

The door swung shut behind her.

Back in Commander Hay's office, Captain Farenden was carrying out his instructions.

'Major Callen is here, ma'am.'

'Thank you, Charlie. Ask him to come in, please.'

'Do you want me to remain?'

'I think this is something we don't need a witness to.'

'I shall be just outside in my own office, ma'am.'

'Where you can usefully spend your time corralling Grint and the others. You have my permission to turn a hose on them if they become unruly.'

'With pleasure.' He stepped back. 'Major Callen to see you, ma'am.' He closed the door behind him.

'Come in, Major. Please sit down.'

'Thank you, Commander. I'd rather stand.'

'Then so shall I.'

They faced each other across her desk.

'Don't *ever* pull a gun on me again, Major.'

'Commander, it is very possible I saved your life. One wrong move today and there could have been a bloodbath. I don't know who would have survived but you wouldn't. Nor Farenden. Nor Ellis. And most importantly – from my point of view, anyway – I saved my own life. I doubt I would have survived the crossfire either and then where would we be? A radiation scare, closely followed by the unfortunate deaths of the commanding officer and her senior staff. Time Police firing on Time Police. What a gift to our enemies.'

'And you saved us from all that?'

'Well, modestly, of course – yes, I did.'

'I know you, Callen – you don't have an altruistic bone in your body.'

'That's very true. I disagree – sometimes quite vigorously – with your plans for our future, but that is part of my function. I am a member of your senior staff and it is my job to challenge you when appropriate. What I prefer, however, is that you and I maintain a strong and united front by arguing these things in

442

private, rather than lose autonomy and have future initiatives imposed on us by a remote third party. We wield enormous power, and I, like you, would not be at all happy about losing that to people who might not share our way of thinking.'

'You shot Anders.'

'Yes, I did.'

'Deliberately.'

'I'm sure he would have had plenty to tell us, but do you really want to know?'

'The names of his fellow conspirators? Yes, I rather think I might.'

'Trust me – today's events will have frightened the vast majority of them shitless. You'll have no more trouble from most of them. It's one thing for them to mutter among themselves in private but quite another to see fellow officers gunned down in front of them. Now Anders is safely dead, and as long as they behave themselves – and they will – no one need ever know where they would have stood today had the shit actually hit the fan.'

'And you, Major – where do you stand?'

'Right behind you, Commander.'

'Then I shall know where to find you in future.'

They regarded each other and then Callen said, 'Well, Commander – where do we go from here? What's the next move?'

She smiled slightly, saying, 'Actually, I was planning to promote you to head of the Hunter Division,' and stood back to watch the effect.

That she had astonished him was very obvious. 'But that's a prestige appointment. The Hunter Division takes only the cream. Why would you do that?'

'To rehabilitate you. There'll be no room for gossip once it's seen you have such a plum posting. It is my way of broadcasting my faith in you to the entire organisation.'

'Am I supposed to be grateful?'

'You can be anything you like. I ask only for your loyalty.'

His face was expressionless. 'As my commanding officer, you are entitled to nothing less.'

'Well, Major?'

'Are you waiting for me to thank you?'

'I am waiting for you either to accept or decline the position.'

'I accept, Commander.'

She nodded. 'You'll be aware it's a very hands-on post. You'll need to lead from the front, Major, so you're going to be out in the field for most of the time. It's a position where the slightest lack of commitment will be immediately apparent. Should I be concerned about any future lack of commitment?'

'No,' he said shortly. And then again more quietly, 'No.'

'Then, finally, we both know where we stand.'

'I know exactly where I stand, Commander. And you, as well, although I'm concerned you might not be looking in the right direction.'

'The appointment is effective immediately.'

'Then with your permission, Commander . . .'

He closed the door behind him.

Captain Farenden was back. 'I still can't agree that was a wise choice, ma'am.'

She sighed. 'I don't know, Charlie. I don't know whose side he's on. Other than his own, of course. There's never anything you can get hold of with him. Not until it's too late, anyway.'

'He pulled a gun, ma'am.'

'Yes, he did, but actually I thought he handled things rather well. Hardly anyone died. There was no deadly crossfire as two sides were forced, unwillingly, to confront each other. No one found themselves in a position from which they couldn't extricate themselves even if they wanted to – and he's right. After today I'm betting a lot of people *will* want to extricate themselves. And best of all – I wasn't forced to take action everyone might have regretted. So yes – it could have been a lot worse.'

'But, in effect, you've promoted him, ma'am.'

'I might be doing him an injustice. He might only be sitting on the fence, but I don't want to push him the wrong way. Treat an ally as an enemy and you soon have another enemy. Let's see what happens, shall we?'

'As you wish, ma'am.'

'Who's next?'

'Lt Grint.'

'Is everything set up?'

'It is. Loaded and ready.'

'Then send him in, please.'

Like Major Callen, Lt Grint preferred to stand. The phrase *a monument of misery* crossed the commander's mind.

Very carefully, she said, 'It wasn't you who shot at Major Ellis, was it?'

He shook his head.

'You see, I know that because I know you. I know all my officers. I know Lockland didn't kill Smith and I know you didn't try to kill Ellis or the others. You tried to prevent it, Lieutenant. Someone had a plan – to kill Ellis first because he was armed, and then take down Lockland, Parrish and everyone

445

else there. Thanks to you, it went badly wrong. A great many people owe you their lives.'

He said nothing.

She regarded him thoughtfully for a few seconds and then walked around her desk to join him, saying in quite a different tone of voice, 'Why didn't you come and talk to me, Gordon?'

He blinked.

'I think it's apparent to both of us that you've been unhappy here for quite some time. Why didn't you come and talk to me about it? We could, perhaps, have saved ourselves a great deal of trouble if you'd brought your misgivings to me instead of joining those who conspire in corridors and dark corners.'

Without looking at her, he nodded.

She said sadly, 'Am I so very unapproachable?'

Still without looking at her, he shook his head.

'So, come and sit down.'

Awkwardly, he sat. As he did so, he took something very small from his pocket and held it tightly in his hand.

'What's the problem, Gordon?'

As is often the case with inarticulates who have bottled everything up for far too long, a dam burst somewhere inside him. 'It's . . . everything. Everything is wrong. We don't do things like we used to. There's all these freaks and weirdos around the place. And . . . girls. And having to be nice to people. We're the fucking Time Police, for heaven's sake. We're not supposed to be nice. We're supposed to turn up, put the fear of God into people and push off again. Not hold their hands and listen to their problems. They'll have us in pink next.'

He swallowed, pulled himself up with a visible effort and

stared furiously out of her window at London going about its business for the day.

She gave him a moment to recover and then said, 'You were one of Colonel Albay's recruits, weren't you?'

He nodded.

'Gordon, Colonel Albay was the last of the old school. Most of us now recognise the need to change. We were formed for a purpose. That purpose is changing. We must change with it. We adapt to a changing situation. We do not adapt the situation to suit us.'

'But you're filling the place with women. There are people from St Mary's taking over and we – the rest of us – are just being shoved aside to make room for them. That North – she'll be running the place in ten years' time.'

'She's a very capable officer, certainly. Wouldn't you rather have her with you than against you?'

He took a deep breath and made another effort to calm down. 'Ma'am, it's just – there doesn't seem to be a place for us here any longer. After all the work we've put in.' His voice cracked. 'For some of us . . . it's our life. Or it was.'

She nodded. 'I understand your point of view, but you must be aware that the days of brute force are gone. We're not a blunt instrument any longer. The situation has evolved. And so must we.'

'Yes, but the threat's always out there and if we don't keep on top of it . . .'

'You're right, Gordon. You're absolutely right. But the threat has changed. It's not nation versus nation, any longer. It's devolved down to an individual level. Amateurs with their unstable pods, damaging the timeline everywhere they go. And now there's big business moving in. Yes, some time ago we took down Atticus Wolfe and that was good work, but word has got out somehow that safety protocols can be bypassed. What we face today are well-financed and well-organised criminal gangs whose technology is very nearly equal to ours. The threat has changed and so must we.'

'But what about respect?'

'I think possibly you are confusing respect with fear. Remember, Gordon, those who hold power rarely need to use it.'

He appeared bewildered.

She continued. 'These days, I want bright, modern officers who can think for themselves. Whose answer is not to shoot everyone on sight and set fire to what's left. There will be no more Team 8 situations. I want this organisation to be the still, calm centre in any storm. I want people to know that when an officer is attending an incident, it will be correctly resolved. By an officer who is impartial and fair. Whose authority is without question. Believe me, that's not anywhere near as easy as just shooting people. Could you do that?'

He said nothing.

'Come and look at this.'

She crossed to her briefing table and waved him to a seat. 'Computer, play presentation TP/MH/1/1/1c.'

She watched his face as he watched the screen. 'A complete re-organisation,' she said. 'A new Time Police to meet a new threat. You see, Gordon, the problem with organised crime is that it's considerably better organised than most national governments. And better funded, too. That is the even more difficult challenge we must meet today. I propose splitting us into two main divisions – Intelligence, which will cover IT, the Time Map and Records and Research – and Control, which will be divided into five teams.'

She sat back and waited for him to ask. He had to ask. If he didn't, then she'd failed. And if she failed with Grint then she'd failed with everyone. She too stared out of the window, and watched a stream of laden barges making their way down the Thames. They were riding low in the water and so must be on their way down to the Princess Mary Docks to unload their cargo.

'What five teams?'

She kept her voice casual. 'I'm sorry?'

'Control. What five areas?'

'Oh, yes. Five departments to meet the five main threats we face today. The first, despite all my best efforts, will, I am certain, be referred to as Hitler's Little Helpers. They'll be a specialist group, drawn mostly from people with a historical background. We both know there are any number of people around who think they can solve the world's problems by offing everyone with whom they disagree. Hitler's a perpetual favourite and I suspect most of their time will be spent just keeping him alive. Hence – Hitler's Little Helpers.'

He nodded.

'The second will be dealing with the threat from big business. There are powerful people out there, Gordon, convinced there must be a way to pillage the past and they just haven't found it yet. Or private treasure hunters. Think of the Tutankhamun job. There will be many more like that. And an offshoot of this is Temporal Tourism. You were there. You saw the damage done to the 16th century some years ago.'

She waited and he nodded again.

'Then there's the amateurs. Idiots who have flung together homemade time machines that trail lethal radiation wherever they go. Looking for a quick and easy profit. Lottery tickets, betting slips and so on. They won't all be as easily dealt with as the likes of Henry Plimpton. They think they'll nip ahead to next Saturday, note the numbers, jump back and pocket the money. Just a tiny jump, they say. Not doing anyone any harm. A victimless crime. Except when next Saturday comes around and they and their past self are there at the same time and suddenly they're both doing everyone a great deal of harm.

'And then there's the Hunter Division, of course. Everyone wants to be a Hunter. They're virtually autonomous.'

She waited, but he said nothing.

'And finally, the Religious Nutters team, who will target those seeking to prove or disprove the existence of their own or someone else's god. Anyone with even the tiniest scrap of imagination can see just how dangerous they could be.'

She waited again. 'Well, Lieutenant, which will it be?'

He stared at her in confusion. 'I'm sorry, I don't understand.'

'These units will be up and running in the new year. I shall be taking requests from October onwards. I'm offering you a head start on everyone else. Which unit would you like?'

'You're offering me a choice?'

'I am.'

'Even after . . . ?'

'The fault was partly mine, Lieutenant. I should have seen your frustration and I didn't. Do you want some time to think about it?'

'No,' he said slowly. 'No, I don't.'

She pulled her scratchpad towards her. 'In that case, in which unit would you like to serve?'

'Well, if it's all the same to you, I'd like the department dealing with the biggest threat – big business and organised crime. Ma'am.'

'I rather thought you might. I must remember to collect my winnings from Captain Farenden.'

He couldn't look at her. 'Will I . . . am I still . . . ?'

'A team leader? Yes, of course.'

He stared ferociously at his boots.

Commander Hay gave him a moment then rose to her feet and held out her hand. 'Congratulations, Lieutenant.'

He took it almost blindly. 'Thank you, ma'am.' He swallowed. 'Thank you.'

Captain Farenden was not happy. 'You're rewarding him, ma'am? One of his people tried to kill Major Ellis. It's only by good luck that he experienced a last-minute fit of conscience.'

'He was naïve and taken advantage of, Charlie. That'll never happen again. He'll see to that. I shall place some responsibility his way and cross my fingers that he blossoms.'

Captain Farenden blinked at the thought of a blossoming Grint.

'Right, who's next?'

'Team Two-Three-Six are waiting, ma'am.'

'All of them? They're all out of MedCen?'

'They are, ma'am.'

'And functioning?'

'That could depend on your definition of functioning,

ma'am, but they're definitely all here. In the physical sense of the word "here".'

'Let's have them in, then.'

He ushered them in. Instinctive discretion had kept him away from the Callen and Grint interviews, but instinctive curiosity kept him present for this one. He took his traditional seat in the corner and waited. Unlike Major Callen or Lt Grint, Team 236 was not asked to sit and the silence was not comfortable. Each of them stood quietly, awaiting dismissal from the service. If they were lucky. If they weren't . . .

I'll get a job in a supermarket, thought Jane. I'll make sure all my tins face the right way and take a quiet pride in my work.

I'll go and find Birgitte, thought Luke, and had no idea where that came from.

Matthew amused himself by imagining the hero's reception given by St Mary's to someone who had managed to get himself sacked from the Time Police. Always supposing the team managed to avoid a lengthy term of imprisonment, of course.

The silence lengthened. Commander Hay, becoming aware that her usual ploy of waiting for people to rush into rash, hasty, and above all, incriminating speech, wasn't working on this team, enquired coldly if they had anything to say for themselves.

Luke sought permission from his teammates with a look. 'Jane didn't kill Smith.'

'Well, of course she didn't,' said Hay, irritably. 'As the evidence from the recovered knife clearly showed. And if any of you had stayed around long enough for justice to take its course, then Jane's innocence would have become clear long before you embarked upon your trail of destruction.'

'So who did?'

Commander Hay turned her attention to Jane. 'Do you remember Senior Instructor Talbot?'

She frowned. 'He's one of our instructors. And he was in the Technical Library with me.'

Matthew turned to her. '*You* were in the Technical Library?'

'Yes,' she said, defensively.

'Why?'

'She was avoiding me,' said Luke.

'Understandable,' said Hay. 'May I continue?'

'Sorry.'

'Mr Talbot was your predecessor, Parrish.'

'Eh? Oh.'

'He did not take kindly to hearing Ms Smith's innovative plan for getting the pair of you discharged from the Time Police.'

'Oh. Has he confessed? What's he saying?'

'His confession was discovered. Along with his body.'

Luke swallowed. 'So you're saying . . . he's dead?'

'He is.'

He was very white. Jane could guess the thoughts in his head. First Orduroy Tannhauser, then Sarah Smith and now . . . She wanted to touch his shoulder – just so he would know he wasn't alone – but they were all still standing to attention.

'Are you saying they're both dead? Smith *and* Talbot? Because of me?'

'No. I think we can assume if it hadn't been you it would have been someone else. However, Mr Parrish . . .' She waited, eyebrow raised.

Luke swallowed again. 'Your point is taken, ma'am.'

'I was hoping it would be.'

Silence fell again. Captain Farenden sat very still.

'I will admit that, for this team, the last twenty-four hours have been more than a little traumatic. You may not wish to continue in this organisation. That would be understandable. You are still under training and so, theoretically, if any of you wish to leave the service, you may do so. By this time tomorrow, you could be free to pursue whatever alternative careers you choose for yourselves.'

'I'm not clear,' said Luke. 'I thought we were being thrown out – after a suitable period of hard labour, of course?'

'Is that an alternative you wish me to consider?'

'No,' said Jane and Matthew together.

'Do you require time to consider your decision?'

'No,' said Jane, Matthew and Luke together.

Her shoulders seemed to sag very slightly.

'Very well. Captain Farenden will draw up your discharge papers. You understand your uncompleted service means you will not be entitled to any of the bounties or pensions usually available. Nor, from this moment, are you entitled to have your funeral expenses paid. Please exercise extreme caution, therefore, until you are safely out of the building.'

She began to busy herself with files on her desk.

'Um,' said Jane.

She didn't look up. 'Yes, Lockland.'

'Actually, ma'am, I think I might like to stay. If I can.'

Beside her, Matthew nodded.

Commander Hay frowned heavily. 'Let me be clear about this. You have been offered an honourable discharge, which you have refused.'

'I want to complete my gruntwork,' said Jane.

'I see.' Hay looked at Matthew. 'And you?'

He nodded. 'The same.'

Unseen, Captain Farenden listened, frowned and then got up and left the room.

'And then?'

'Actually,' said Jane, 'I don't think any of us have thought that far ahead. Not least because we never expected to live long enough to complete our gruntwork.'

'Give it time,' said Hay, drily. 'And what about you, Parrish? Are you clamouring to complete your gruntwork too, or is this the opportunity you've been waiting for ever since you arrived here?'

Luke opened his mouth and at that moment, Captain Farenden came back into Hay's office.

'Ma'am, Mr Parrish is here.'

'Yes, I know.'

'No, ma'am. Mr Parrish senior is here and he wants to see you now.'

She looked at Luke and said slowly, 'Do we know why?'

Luke shook his head. 'Not a clue, ma'am.'

'Nothing new there, then. Ask him to wait, please, Charlie. I shan't be a moment.'

'Yes, ma'am.' He turned to leave the room, but obviously waiting was something that happened to other people because, without warning, Parrish senior was suddenly in the room.

He was a big man. As tall as Luke but much bulkier. Here, however, was the same hair, the same eyes. This was Luke as he would be in thirty years' time. Here also was the same air of being slightly better than everyone else, strengthened and enhanced by considerably more than thirty years' strong evidence that he was, in fact, a great deal better than everyone else. He was what Luke Parrish would be after thirty years of ensuring the world gave him everything he wanted whenever he wanted it.

Jane was looking from one to the other, making the inevitable comparisons – as was everyone in the room – and she could see Luke didn't like it. His old Parrish expression was back. Condescension mixed with light amusement. The one that made everyone he met want to kick him. He hadn't inherited it from his father, she realised. His father was the cause of it.

Commander Hay rose politely. 'Mr Parrish, good afternoon. I'm in the middle of a meeting at the moment . . .'

Giving people moments was not something that Mr Parrish senior did. He'd built a massive commercial empire by not giving people moments. In a voice accustomed to annihilating boardroom mutinies at birth, he said, 'I shan't take up too much of your time, Commander.'

Commander Hay hadn't fought in the Time Wars for nothing. 'No – you won't. Captain Farenden will show you where to wait.'

Raymond Parrish was not a fool. Unbending slightly, he smiled. 'I beg your pardon, Commander. I can see you're busy, but I think I can save you some time here. Luke – get your stuff.'

'Eh? Why?'

'Your time here is up.'

Luke's voice was light and amused but his eyes were suddenly wary. 'Actually, Dad, tiny mistake. I still have time to serve.'

Parrish senior shook his head. 'No, you don't. I've just discovered you've pulled yourself together and you're making an allowance to the Tannhausers. No need for you to do that. I'll speak to Ms Steel and have the payments transferred from your account to mine. And I'll bump it up a bit, so they won't have any redress in the future.'

'Actually, Dad . . .'

'Luke, you're cured.'

The sudden silence was absolute and then, in the voice with which Major Ellis and every other training officer in the Time Police was only too familiar, Luke said lightly, 'Sorry, sir. Not with you.'

'You've learned your lesson,' he said impatiently. 'Come to heel.'

'Come to heel?'

Parrish senior gestured around. 'This wasn't serious, boy. This was just to teach you a lesson. Which, I'm happy to say, thanks to me, you appear to have learned.'

'Dad . . .'

'You're on your way to Hong Kong, Luke. To take over the office there. Sally Yang's retiring. You're to take her place. Don't just stand there. I want us both in Paris by six o'clock. There are some useful people there I want you to meet. I don't suppose you have anything of value here, but if you do, then I recommend you get it now. We're leaving.'

There was another long pause. Commander Hay was watching Luke Parrish very carefully. Everyone was watching Luke Parrish very carefully. Jane remembered he hadn't actually said whether he intended to remain in the Time Police or not. Her heart contracted. His wish had come true. He was

457

leaving. Returning to his old life. But to lose him now . . . after all this . . . Just as he was beginning to . . .

Luke took a very deep breath. 'Actually, Dad, you're wrong. The things I have here are of great value to me and I won't leave them behind lightly. In fact, I won't leave them behind at all. I regret to disoblige you, sir, but I am *not* going to Hong Kong.'

'Don't argue with me, boy.'

'I'm afraid, Dad, that it is you who are arguing with me. To clarify the situation – I am a member of the Time Police and I still have time to serve.'

Parrish senior waved that aside. 'I bought you in – I can buy you back out again.'

Luke was very pale. 'I wonder, sir, when it will occur to you that I am not a commodity to be bought and sold at times and places advantageous to you.'

'I don't intend to argue with you, boy.'

'Excellent. I'm glad you have so easily grasped the point I was making.'

Raymond Parrish's voice was iced steel. 'The arrangements are made. You will come with me.'

'I will not.'

'You dare to defy me? You are my son.'

'Am I? When exactly did you remember that?'

'This is insolence. I will not stand for it. I placed you here so you would not continue to disappoint me and . . .'

'Tell me, sir – as my father – what's my favourite colour? Or here's a better one – do I like sprouts? That's an easy question. Just think back to our last Christmas dinner together. Oh wait – I don't think you can, because we've never had a Christmas dinner together, have we? Or a birthday. In fact, I don't think

458

you've ever been present at any of the key points of my life, have you?'

'Luke, I don't understand the point you're trying to make and I don't have time for this. I want you installed in the Hong Kong office by this time tomorrow so that I still have time to make the climate conference in Sydney.'

He turned to Commander Hay, whose face was even more expressionless than usual.

'Commander Hay, if you would be good enough to arrange my son's discharge papers, I'll sign them immediately.'

There was a long pause and then she said, 'Regretfully, I am unable to comply with your . . . demand.'

He rocked back on his heels and stared down at her. 'Ah, yes, of course. How remiss of me. How much, Commander?'

A chair creaked in the corner as Captain Farenden got to his feet.

Meeting his gaze, Commander Hay shook her head fractionally.

'An interesting question, Mr Parrish, but as I said, I'm unable to comply with your demand and I meant it. Unless he is being dishonourably discharged – which he certainly is not – only Trainee Parish himself can initiate his own discharge. Concerning the amount of money required, I regret to inform you that without his written request, even *you* will not have enough money to secure his discharge against his will.

'Conversely, if he *does* wish to leave us, then the answer is no money at all. Before you so propelled yourself into our meeting, Trainee Parrish was just about to favour us all with his decision regarding his future here. Parrish, I hesitate to put you on the spot like this, but if it helps your decision in any way, let

459

me assure you that whatever action you take will have my full and unqualified support, together with that of the organisation I command. *My full and unqualified support.*'

Wow, thought Jane. She really doesn't like you, Mr Parrish.

Luke was staring at Commander Hay, who sat calmly back in her chair, one eyebrow slightly raised – which, to be fair, was about the most expression she could manage.

'Blue,' she said. 'And no.'

Parrish senior snapped his gaze back to her. 'What?'

She ignored him, saying to Luke, 'Am I right, Trainee Parrish?'

He grinned the full Parrish grin. 'Spot on, ma'am.' He turned to his father. 'Did you kick out Sally Yang just to give me this post?'

'Ms Yang is retiring. On a very generous pension, I might add.'

'Dad, you can't do that. She's worked for Parrish Industries for years. She's been with you almost from the beginning and you've just chucked her on to the scrap heap to make room for me?'

'Ms Yang is about to enjoy a comfortable retirement which will enable her to pursue any future interests she may develop.'

'She has stood by you through any number of crashes, scandals, crises . . .'

'Ms Yang's past performance is not the issue here. I've spent enough time on this already, Luke. You will come with me.'

All eyes switched back to Luke, who was looking his haughtiest and most unpleasant. And, coincidentally, not unlike his father.

'Sorry, Dad. No can do. Busy evening ahead. I need to visit

Major Ellis and see how he's doing. I need to congratulate Officer North on her tray technique. And then I'm going to take Jane and Matthew out for a drink and a nice meal. On me, guys. So, sorry, Dad, as you can see – no time to go to Hong Kong.'

They stared at each other.

Parrish senior's voice was flat and dangerous. 'I see you continue to disappoint me.'

'Well, Dad, I suspect until you stop measuring me by your own standards then I will always do so. In fact, now I come to think of it – I'm rather proud to do so.'

'Luke – I am your father.'

There was a moment's silence and then every person in the room suddenly found something to look at that didn't include any of the other people in the room. Jane mentally scrutinised her wardrobe with regard to the forthcoming evening out. Matthew stared solidly ahead, turning his mind to solving a complex Time Map issue. Commander Hay regarded her empty desk with an expression of fierce concentration and Captain Farenden mentally reviewed the agenda for Friday's budget meeting.

It was Luke himself who broke the silence. Shrugging, he said, 'Well, that's as may be, sir, but I no longer regard myself as your son. You shoved me into the Time Police to suit your own ends and it's turned out to be exactly what I needed. Not what I wanted, but what I needed. And I quite like it here. So no. No, I'm not leaving. And no, I'm not going to Hong Kong. I'm staying here with people who know my favourite colour is blue and that I don't like sprouts.'

Parrish senior glanced at his watch. 'In that case, Luke, you may expect no further communication from me.'

461

The door slammed behind him. Captain Farenden followed him. 'I'll just make sure he can find his own way out, ma'am.'

'Thank you, Charlie.'

Commander Hay turned to Luke, who was looking rather white. 'Well, was I right?'

He pulled himself together. 'Good heavens, no, ma'am. Can't stand the colour blue and sprouts are the food of the gods.'

'Oh. Well. Never mind.' She smiled slightly. 'After such a public display of affection it looks as if we're stuck with each other for a while, Mr Parrish.'

'Looks that way, ma'am.'

'I suspect that, for one reason or another, we shall be seeing a great deal of each other in the future.'

He smiled that confident, cocky Parrish smile. 'If I am very lucky, ma'am.'

'Lockland, Farrell – get him out of here. Now.'

'Yes, ma'am.'

Epilogue

Jane stood in her room, examining herself in the mirror. A new day loomed before her. As a trainee Time Police officer. She studied her reflection for another moment and then, on a sudden impulse, unwound her plait.

Gathering her hair up in one hand, she pulled it up into a cheeky little ponytail and twisted a hairband around it. That was so much better than her previous style. She moved her head and her ponytail swung with her. And back the other way. Yes. This was a confident, cocky, *don't mess with me if you know what's good for you* ponytail. A Time Police ponytail. And if Matthew's hair got much longer, then he could have one, too. They could start a fashion. Although, to be fair, she really couldn't see it catching on with the crew-cutted Grint.

Stepping back, she studied herself again. Something still wasn't quite right. Frowning, she adjusted her belt to sit lower and more rakishly on her hips. The way real officers wore theirs. And that empty holster wasn't going to be empty for much longer. She stood up straight and pushed her shoulders back. A Time Police officer stared back at her.

This is what I am, she thought. This is what I do. I am an officer of the Time Police. I have duties and responsibilities

463

and the authority to carry them out. The Time Police is not somewhere to hide. It is somewhere to shine.

Luke and Matthew were waiting for her. They nodded a greeting and the three of them walked illegally three abreast down the corridor. For some reason, Luke was humming the theme song to *Rocky*.

They stood together, waiting for the lift to arrive. Two very new trainees approached and stood nervously nearby. Jane turned her head and regarded them coldly. Not a word was spoken and after only a very few seconds, they simply wilted away.

'Seven seconds,' said Luke. 'I think that puts you in the lead.'

The doors parted. Without breaking formation, they stepped inside and turned to face the doors.

'Because we're the Time Police,' said Luke.

'Because we're Team Weird,' said Matthew.

'Because we're utter bastards,' said Jane.

Luke donned an expensive pair of sunglasses and struck a pose.

The lift stopped.

'Right then, utter bastards,' he said. 'Let's see what they've got for us today, shall we?'

He strode forwards.

There was the sound of an impact and he reeled backwards, clutching his nose.

'Aaarrgggghh.'

'We usually wait for the doors to open first,' said Matthew.

THE END

Author's Note

The description of the damage to Tutankhamun's tomb was as accurate as I could make it. A number of golden rings, loosely knotted in a piece of linen, were found – presumably dropped during the thieves' hasty exit. When Howard Carter entered the tomb, there were actually the outlines of dusty footprints on a wooden chest where someone had stood on it, thousands of years before. And on opening the sarcophagus, there was evidence that the mummy had smouldered in its wrappings.

The character Sarah Smith was named after the winner of the CLIC Sargent auction – a wonderful charity which raises money to help young people with cancer. The auction was to name a character in my forthcoming book. The entry form included a short bio for the real Sarah Smith which made it very apparent she was a lovely person and I was quite concerned people would think she resembled the man-eating harpy prowling the pages of my book. Only the name, people – not the person herself.

All thanks to my editor, Frankie Edwards, and everyone else at Headline whose lives have taken a sudden downward turn since I arrived.

Thanks to everyone who had to live with me while I worked on this one – I know it wasn't easy.

Thanks to Phillip Dawson who told me about liquid string and so forth. All mistakes are his and nothing to do with me.

And thanks to my Chanel-bedecked agent, adrift on a sea of Prosecco and caviar, currently buying her third holiday home in the Bahamas, who promised me jam on my crust if I got this finished before April.

A Note on Recruitment

Following a government report highlighting the lack of diversity within the ranks of the Time Police, a major recruitment drive was mounted, focusing on the need to tempt more women into the organisation. Their first attempt was hugely popular but for all the wrong reasons.

First attempt

Question:	What's the difference between a male Time Police officer and a female Time Police Officer?
Answer:	About four inches

The advert was withdrawn after twenty-four hours when it became apparent that the reference to the difference in the minimum height requirement had been widely misunderstood.

Second attempt

Recruitment poster featuring a pretty blonde and bearing the following legend:

> She serves the Time Police

This advert was withdrawn after the inadvertent omission of the word 'in' was noticed and male recruitment had inexplicably increased by 300%.

At this point, the decision was taken to abandon attempts to emphasise the Time Police diversity initiative – to international disappointment – in favour of highlighting the many benefits offered instead.

Join the Time Police today

Travel the timeline . . . Legally!
Excitement and adventure.
Adequate pay rates.
Generous death in service benefits – we guarantee your loved ones will not suffer after you're gone.
Contracts for two, seven and, for the survivors, ten years.

For some reason, this failed to ignite any desire to serve in the Time Police and, eventually, someone just scribbled something on the back of an envelope.

Protecting the past to ensure your future.

Have you ever wished you could make a difference?
Fed up with the daily grind?
Do you hanker after something a little bit different?
Join the Time Police today.
